The Election

Omar Shahid Hamid

Published by Liberty Publishing
C-16, Sector 31-A, Mehran Town Extension,
Korangi Industrial Area, Karachi – Pakistan

This is a work of fiction. Names, characters, places and incidents are either the product of the author's imagination or are used fictitiously and any resemblance to any actual person, living or dead, events or locales is entirely coincidental. The opinions expressed in our published works are those of the author(s) and do not reflect the opinions of Liberty Publishing.

ISBN 978-627-7626-40-2

To my father, whom I think about every day even after twenty-seven years.

About the Author

Omar Shahid Hamid is an acclaimed Pakistani novelist who lives in Karachi. In addition to his writing career, he has served as a senior counter-terrorism police officer who, in between writing books, has survived several attempts on his life, investigated the international murder of a journalist in Kenya, and had his offices blown up by the Taliban.

His first novel, *The Prisoner*, was published in 2013 by Pan Macmillan India and proved to be a huge critical and commercial success. It has also been translated into French, German, and Urdu, and is being adapted for a screenplay. His second novel, *The Spinner's Tale* (2015, Pan Macmillan), won the Italy Reads Pakistan prize and the Karachi Literature Festival fiction prize and has also been translated into Italian and German. His third book *The Party Worker* (2017, Pan Macmillan) won the Karachi Literature Festival fiction prize, making Omar the only writer to have won in consecutive years. His fourth book, *The Fix* (2019, Pan Macmillan) explores the world of match-fixing in women's cricket. His fifth book, *Betrayal* (2021, Lighthouse Publishing) won the Karachi Adab Festival award in 2023. *The Election* is his sixth novel.

Table of Contents

Table of Contents

1.

THE

INTERVIEW

I LOVE AMERICA. Actually, no, I love the idea of America. I'm addicted to it. I have been since I first binged on late-night television while inhaling Cheetos from an industrial-sized bag that my parents bought for me and my sister from Costco. It was the summer of 2008, and I had arrived in America for the first time on a family vacation. The world economy was collapsing around us while American troops were dying trying to fight two unwinnable wars in Iraq and Afghanistan. Not that I gave a shit about such momentous events. Hell, I barely understood them. The only thing I cared about that summer, were the nightly monologues of Jon Stewart, David Letterman, Steven Colbert and Jimmy Kimmel. I lived for late-night TV. Its combination of humour, and celebration of success bewitched me. It enshrined the mantra in my head that truly anybody could make it in America. I hankered for that. From that moment on, I decided that I wanted to live here. My aim in life was to one day make it to one of those shows, to highlight my success in America. That was my American dream.

But let's back up a little. Let me introduce myself. My name is Waj. Short for Wajahat, but nobody calls me that anymore. The last person who called me Wajahat was my class Ten Physics teacher, who always added a mister in front of my first name, but would end up pronouncing it *Meester Waj-a-hat*. Like I said, just Waj is fine.

And this is the story of my American dream. Which started, funnily enough, as perhaps many American dreams have, in the deserts of Arabia. More specifically, the oil-soaked deserts of Saudi Arabia.

My dad worked as a financial advisor to several senior princes in the Kingdom. Growing up, the only bit of economics I understood was that as long as oil prices remained high, we were golden. At least that's what my mom would constantly tell my sister and me. When I was about 11, a couple of years before my life-changing summer, my parents decided that in the interests of my sister and I continuing to get a quality education, they would split the family up. While my dad stayed on in Riyadh earning his share of petro-dollars, mom would move back to Karachi with my sister Zara and me. That way we would be better prepared in our quest for the holy grail of all upwardly mobile middle class Pakistanis like ourselves: admission into a really top-notch foreign university.

The month-long trip that summer was an attempt by dad to make sure we all spent some quality time together as a family before Zara and I went off to college. Up till that point, I hadn't really bought into the whole spiel about needing to get into a good college. That was my sister's department. She was two years older than me, and from the age of six, she had gotten the notion in her head that she wanted to go to Harvard. What made it worse was both my parents acted as enablers, feeding Zara's crazy Ivy League junkie habit at every turn, getting her extra tuitions, changing schools, moving countries, hiring admissions consultants, whatever Zara thought she needed to get into Harvard. I continued to muddle through school, not really concerned at all about my future prospects or where I would end up. I mean, you have to have a particularly craven way of thinking if you're worrying about this stuff at age 13. But that trip to America changed my perspective.

Now before you start judging me as a fresh-off-the-boat desi from some rural backwater, let me stop you right there. We were as urbane and sophisticated a family as could be. I mean, we had grown up in Saudi and Karachi, we had taken holidays in London, Dubai,

Sri Lanka, the Far East, and even spent one winter break attempting to ski in Bulgaria (top tip: it's the same action as Switzerland, at a third of the cost). But America was something else altogether. The lights were brighter, the portions were bigger, the music was louder.

America felt like you were looking at life hopped up on Ecstasy. For a kid who had grown up in two places where progression always seemed to be linked to having connections, a useful bureaucrat uncle here, an indulgent princeling there, America's meritocracy, as seen on late-night TV, pulled at my heartstrings. It wasn't till much later that I discovered how flawed my hypothesis was, but that summer, I decided that I had to somehow dip my toes in this fast flowing river of fame and fortune.

From that point onwards, I worked much harder in school, with the goal of punching my ticket to America. The problem was, despite the petrodollars gushing into his bank account, dad could only afford to pay a portion of my tuition. After all, he had to bankroll two of us at the same time. That left me having to climb the steep and slippery slope of admission with financial aid. Zara of course managed much more easily than me. The mothership of Harvard did not call out to her, but Stanford did. After crying for a day over the fact that she would not, in fact, be sculling on the River Charles, she accepted her fate and embraced the sunny climes of California. She graduated a couple of years ahead of me and got a job at Google, much to the delight of my parents, who now insist on holding those stupid oversized *Googler* mugs every time she or I Facetime them.

I wasn't as bright as Zara, but I did manage to get into Iowa State on a scholarship. The fact that I was stuck in a conservative-as-fuck flyover state for four years, only enflamed my ambition to get out of there as soon as possible. When I graduated, there was only one place that I wanted to go: New York City. The media and entertainment headquarters of the world, and generally considered, especially by New Yorkers, to be the centre of the known universe.

My dad would have much preferred me to follow a career in banking or accounting, or even a law degree. A reliable, predictable, and very desi career. He wasn't quite sold on my formula of success through the media. Grudgingly, he covered the rent for a studio apartment for six months. Get a job in that time or come home, he said. He was fairly confident in his prediction of my failure.

Which is what brought me, on a wet Tuesday morning in April, to the steel and glass monstrosity that was the Diamond building, on the corner of 9th Ave and 57th. Or, as New York cabbies like to refer to it, Ron's Erection, due to its unmistakeably phallic shape and the fact that the owner and chief occupant was formerly the porn king of America. But I was at the end of my tether. Days away from my precious OPT visa expiring, I was desperate. I had tried everything. There was no job in the entertainment and media industry that I hadn't applied for. I had offered to work as an unpaid intern at CNN; I had stood in line for four hours in a blizzard to apply for a job as a junior writer on The Daily Show; I had temped for a month at Fox News, getting lattes for douchebags whose faces I couldn't stand on TV. Their politics didn't matter to me. I just needed to get a toe in the door. But I hadn't been able to get anything permanent. New York's media industry was just not interested in a Pakistani with a Communications degree and little else. My father's deadline had passed me by two months ago. He gave me a three-month stay of execution when I broke down and started crying on the phone. But he had been very clear that this was it. The end of the line. The spectre of a one-way plane ticket to Karachi in June, followed by mind-numbingly boring internships in firms owned by his friends, hung over me like a noose.

The Diamond Organisation was a last ditch attempt, a scrape at the bottom of the barrel. To call it a media organisation was a stretch. Ron Diamond had made his money in porn, first as an actor and then as a distributor. I would be telling you an egregious lie if I said I had never watched any of his movies. Though they were a little before my time, I had what is known as a 'vintage fetish'. But you would be hardpressed to find a red-blooded, heterosexual male who came of age in the 1980s and hadn't seen his movies. Back then, Ron Diamond had been a household name, the pornographic equivalent of Michael Jordan. This was perhaps, as he himself once hypothesized with me, the very reason for his meteoric success in his endeavours.

He had then spun those cumshot-tainted millions into a real estate empire in New York. And to further expand his 'brand', in the last five years, he had accentuated it by creating a hit reality TV show. And he had named this amalgam of porn, real estate and shitty TV, appropriately enough, Rock Hard Productions. My mother would have killed me if she found out I was applying to a porn production house, but I was a desperate man. If they had told me that my only chance of staying in America was to become an actor in one of Ron Diamond's movies, by this time I probably would have said yes even to that.

As I entered the Diamond Building that morning, the headquarters and nerve centre of the Rock Hard empire looked very much like something stuck in a time warp. The lobby of the building was pure '80s' bling, with a lot of fake gold leaf and mirrors everywhere. The 20th floor, where I was first dispatched to, looked exactly like what it was: a dodgy 1970's style porn distributor's office. Threadbare office furniture and ancient PCs were interspersed among old posters of Mr. Diamond's hit films, and boxes full of DVDs and VHS cassettes that seemed to have been there ever since those formats went extinct. A man dressed in suspenders and a bow tie, and still smoking indoors despite the city-wide ban, took my CV and went through the pretence of interviewing me. My heart sank. I could see, as he paid more attention to dunking his donut in his coffee than to my CV, that this was the end of the line. It wasn't even a matter of not having the money to make rent after another three weeks. My girlfriend had offered to let me move in with her. It was that I had run out of places to apply to in New York.

As I started seeing visions of myself sitting for accountancy exams in the heat of Karachi, a funny thing happened. The Bowtie put down his half-eaten donut and without any indication to me, left the room. He was gone for a half hour. I didn't know what to do. Was this a good thing, or had the old guy just decided to go for his morning crap in the middle of my interview, just because he didn't give a shit about me? Nobody else in the office had a clue. I was debating about actually getting up and leaving, when the Bowtie came back.

'You're wanted upstairs. You came to the wrong place.' He shoved a thumb towards the elevators, his cigarette still perched between his lips.

'Excuse me? But this is Rock Hard Productions, right?'

'We do the tits and ass stuff on Twenty. *Reality Losers* is on Forty-eight. And the boss is on Sixty-nine. Take the elevator to Sixty-nine. They're lookin' for a personal assistant for Mr. Diamond.'

Overjoyed at my sudden turn in fortunes, I was effusive in my thanks to the Bowtie, but he was having none of it.

'It ain't a promotion. It's the worst job in the organisation. They can't get anyone to fill it. Since your CV's useless, I might as well put you up for it. God knows I have no use for you here.'

With that less than resounding endorsement still ringing in my ears, I climbed into the elevator and pressed the button. The 69th floor was a stark contrast to the rest of the building. Modern, airy, with freshly cut flowers adorning every nook and cranny. As I stepped out of the elevator I was welcomed by an Amazonian goddess at the reception desk. In fact, the entire floor seemed to be populated solely by gorgeous, perfectly coiffed, six-foot tall blonde women.

'This way please. Mr. Diamond hates to be kept waiting.' The Amazon's fake smile momentarily frayed and her voice betrayed a hint of nervousness.

She led me to a boardroom where three people sat facing me, reality show style. In fact, the entire room looked like a set for one of Ron Diamond's TV shows. A massive portrait of him and another stunningly attractive woman, whom I assumed was one of his wives (I cursed myself for not having googled the New York tabloids so that I could know which one), hung on one wall. The other side was a video wall which seemed to be randomly jumping from Bloomberg Business to reruns of his shows. Another massive, almost presidential photo portrait of his hung on the wall behind where my three interlocutors sat. Under the photo, big, bold brass letters spelt out The Diamond Organisation.

Only one of my interviewers was instantly recognisable. It was the man himself, Ron Diamond. I had not expected for him to personally sit in on my interview, but there he was, dressed in his trademark blue suit and ketchup-and-mustard coloured tie. His golden hair was arranged in a mane, which made me wonder if this is what Lion-O from the Thundercats would have looked like had he ever reached middle age. I suppose you could say he was still handsome, in a 70's beach surfer type of way. Although it was evident that his body had slipped somewhat in the fitness department, a testament to a self-confessed addiction to fast food and fizzy drinks. It was also strange to see Ron Diamond without the thick blonde moustache that was his calling card in his heyday. He had carried it through his showbiz career, deep into his real estate days too. It was only when he turned to reality TV in the 21st century that the image consultants suggested it was too dated for Millennials.

On Mr. Diamond's right, was perhaps the ugliest man I had ever seen. Completely bald, with beady, deep set eyes, a hooked nose and wrinkled folds of skin under his chin that made him look like an especially predatory vulture. On the other side of Mr. Diamond was a much younger man, handsome, and dressed very expensively, in a way that suggested that he wanted to show the world that he had money to burn.

'So you're the kid, huh?' The words came in the form of a sneer from Mr. Diamond. He seemed to be holding a piece of paper that looked like the improbably padded CV I had handed the Bowtie. I had still not been asked to sit, so I stood awkwardly, feeling the rivulets of sweat forming in my armpits as three sets of eyes bored holes into my soul from across the table.

'Excuse me, sir?'

'You're the kid who's been breaking down the doors on Twenty for two weeks, begging them to put you on the list for this job.'

At this point, I was genuinely puzzled. Much later, as I grew to understand Mr. Diamond's stream-of-consciousness style of expostulation, I would learn to mask my shock or lack of understanding. In fact, I would become a champ at it. But this day, in my first ever meeting with him, I had not yet mastered that art, and so my confusion was plainly evident on my face. I was about to interrupt and correct him, two things that I later learnt were cardinal sins in Ron Diamond's world, to inform him that I had not, in fact been coming to Twenty for two weeks to beg for this job. And that my interest in the Diamond Organisation had only begun three days ago when the last of the legitimate media outlets to whom I had applied, sent me their rejections. Ok, perhaps I wasn't that much of an honest dipshit even back then, but I was about to point out that there had been some mistake, when a look from the bald, ugly guy on Ron Diamond's right stopped me dead in my tracks.

His name, I was later to learn, was Harvey Calzone, but everyone called him the Oracle. He looked like a cross between a mob hitman and a Transylvanian undertaker. Which may actually have been a fairly accurate description of what he did for Ron Diamond. He had the look of a man who could fuck you up if you crossed him, and so when he turned that icy glare on me and imperceptibly shook his head to signal me to stay quiet, you can be assured that I clammed up immediately.

'And this, this is your CV?' Mr. Diamond held up the paper as if he were about to declare it defence exhibit A and cross examine me on its contents.

'Uh, yes sir.'

'Well, if this is your CV, it's full of shit, and so are you. I haven't seen something this padded since my second wife decided to come out with her own brand of Wonderbras. Here, take a look Han, and see if you can smell the bullshit.'

He handed the CV to the handsome man on his left. Han rifled through the three pages of the CV with his immaculately manicured nails, and looked up at me and smiled. 'Dad, why don't we let Mr. Shak... Shaka...'

'Shakaib'.

'Mr. Shak-abe, take a seat.'

I was about to pull up the chair, when Mr. Diamond decided to literally keep me on my toes.

'No, I haven't decided whether I want to let him stay that long. So tell me Mr. Hotshot, which of those jobs that you've listed over three pages have you actually done?'

'All of them, sir. Uh, I mean, I haven't lied about anything. I have done all those jobs, it's just I may not have been in some of them for very long...'

'And what exactly, does a lifestyle management assistant do?' This time, the question came from the Oracle.

'He's the little asshole who gets the bigger assholes coffee. Isn't that right, Iowa State?'

Say what you will about Ron Diamond, the man is blunt.

'Yes, sir.'

'And why did you do that shitty job, Iowa State? I know Paulie Mcgrath at Fox News. He's got the shittiest toupe in the business. Jeez, what a cheapskate. I told him to go in for a transplant if he wanted to keep his ratings. He didn't listen to me and now he's in the toilet. As Fox anchors go, he's the king of the assholes.'

It was at that moment, in that gaudy, made-for-TV boardroom, that I had an epiphany. I decided to speak the truth. I don't know why I did it. Perhaps it was Ron Diamond's piercing gaze, that look he has that makes you think he knows something about you that you yourself may not know; or perhaps it was just my desperation.

'I did it because I wanted to get my foot in the door, sir. I... uh... I want a job in media. I was willing to do anything to get it. It's the only career I've ever wanted to do. Sir.'

'There we go. Now we're finally getting somewhere. Much

better, Iowa State. Now, where are you really from? Obviously not Iowa.'

'No, sir. I'm from Pakistan.'

The mention of Pakistan gave Han, the son, a look on his face that was somewhere between imagining the space-time continuum and suppressing a particularly loud fart. 'Pakistan? Is that near Dubai? Do you speak Arabic?'

'No you idiot, it's next to India.' It seemed strange to see Ron Diamond mouth exactly what I was thinking. 'I know a lot of people from Pakistan. Good textile industry. Cotton. Lots'a cotton. I gave the orders for my signature Diamond shirts to guys from there. Decent quality work. Better than those fucking Cambodians, right Harvey?'

Harvey sneered in a way that didn't make it clear whether he agreed with Ron's opinion on Cambodians, or whether he generally thought all foreigners were pricks.

'And you were at Iowa State on a scholarship, or was daddy paying the bills?'

'Scholarship, Mr. Diamond.'

'But your old man can't be thrilled that you're seeking a career in the media. Doesn't he want you to do something more stable?'

'He did, sir. He wanted me to become a banker or a lawyer.'

'Meh. Overrated professions. Bankers queue around the block to give blowjobs to people like me, and lawyers, well, Wall Street lawyers are just a fancy haircut and an expensive suit. I'll back Harvey any day over any of those pricks. Harvey would have eaten you for breakfast had you become a lawyer.'

Although I was a little shocked at Ron's profanities, I was to learn later that to him, 90% of the world were 'pricks'.

'So my Pakistanian friend, now that you've burned that bridge and struck out with all of the network pricks, what will you do if you don't land this job?'

I was too nervous to try and correct Ron's terminology for Pakistanis. 'I...don't know, sir.'

'You'll have to go home, won't you? You're on your OPT. You don't get a job here, you're gone. Bye Bye, Miss American Pie. Right?'

'Yes, sir.'

'Interesting. Suddenly, this interview became interesting.'

Ron began to stroke his chin, and I thought my heart would burst out of my chest. But he wasn't looking at me anymore. Rather, he was looking past me, at the video wall that had begun to replay a clip from a recent White House dinner that had gone viral. Suddenly all three of my interlocutors' attention was on the screen. Ron unmuted the volume and I could hear the voiceover from one of the late-night talk shows. I had an urge to turn around to sneak a peak, but I resisted it. Besides, I knew the clip by heart. I had seen it dozens of times, alone and with friends, and I had found it hilarious every single time. It was of a speech given at the dinner by the President, Lincoln King. The President had mocked Ron Diamond, who had been one of the invitees, making fun of his past, and of his political aspirations. On a recent episode of his reality show, Ron had made the comment to one of the contestants that he might think of running for President next year, because he was sure he could do a great job running the country. It was a passing comment, perhaps not dissimilar to the sort of thing many rich people might often have said in private. Had the President not retold the story in his speech, it would have probably gone unnoticed. Truth be told, the President's mentioning it had been a low blow. As my mother would have said, it was horrible manners to call someone to your house for dinner and then to mock them. But this was politics, and for the President, assailed as he was by his enemies in Congress and a falling approval rating, Ron Diamond represented an easy target. Someone to pick on haplessly, to collect cheap points with his liberal base, and since a couple of senior Republican pundits on Wolfson News had said it would be interesting to have Ron Diamond in the race, to tag his right-wing political opponents as sharing some of the ridiculous assertions of a figure who was on the fringes of pop culture. As the late-night show host airing the clip said in his punchline, how serious were you if you had the same views as a retired porn star who built buildings that looked like variations of his penis?

As the late show host delivered the line, I had to struggle to contain the smile that started forming across my face. I was sure that I had managed to hide it, but then Ron Diamond turned his eye on me. He must have caught something, because his face had darkened when he turned towards me.

'You've seen this?'

There was no point in lying. You needed to have been stuck on an Oceanographic exploration vessel off the coast of Antarctica to not have seen it. 'Yes, sir.'

'And what did you think?'

'Sir?'

'What did you think about it? You're the kind of demographic that watches these crappy shows. What did you think about what King did?'

I knew there was no coming back if I gave the wrong answer. The way Ron Diamond was staring at me, he would spot an insincere answer a mile away. 'Uh…he…was…he has been…suffering from low approval ratings. He took a cheap shot.'

'Hmm. And how would you respond, if you were me?'

'Respond, sir?'

'Yeah. Respond. How do I get back at him?'

'Well uh sir…I…I…I would run. For office.'

My answer came out so quickly and spontaneously that Han Diamond (I presumed at the time that Diamond was the actual family name), let out a contemptuous snort, that immediately led to a vicious glare from his father.

'What's the matter with you, you fucking moron? You think his idea is that laughable?'

'No, Dad, no…I was just…this guy obviously doesn't know a thing about politics…I mean, he isn't even an American for Christ's sake…'

'Shut the fuck up. Why do you think I should run, Iowa State?'

'Because it would prove all of your detractors wrong, sir. If you entered the field, the fact that the President singled you out, would automatically make you a serious candidate. He wouldn't have bullied you like that if he didn't think you were a threat.'

'Wait a minute. You think I got bullied? You think that snot-nosed little Harvard asshole bullied me?! I'm Ron fucking Diamond, I don't get bullied! And if you don't know that, then you don't belong in my organisation! Get the fuck outta here!'

Ron's sudden change of tone totally bamboozled me. I had thought, just thirty seconds ago, that I was doing all right. And now, his face turning beet red, he was pointing me towards the door. For a moment, I was frozen in my seat, not knowing where to go, slowly registering the disastrous implications of being thrown out of this, my last interview. I only snapped out of it when I saw two blazered security guards enter the room and walk towards me. For a millisecond, my eyes locked with Harvey's. His expression was guarded, but I thought I saw an ounce of sympathy in those beady eyes. He didn't say anything, but he tilted his head towards the exit, as if to ensure that Ron's message had gotten through to me. In a trance, I got up and, without saying another word, walked to the door with the security guards in tow.

I don't really recall the next six hours. I know I walked, a lot. I walked from midtown to Washington Heights, but I can't remember a minute of that journey. I was in a trance, as my mind came to terms with the final shattering of my dream. This was it. I was going to have to catch that Emirates flight back to Pakistan, to an existence designed by my father.

When my girlfriend found me, I had been sitting on the stoop of her apartment building for an hour, staring at the road. Sonia was Puerto Rican, the daughter of working-class parents, born and bred in the city, taking a step up the social ladder by having become the first college graduate in her family. She was now pursuing a Master's degree in Anthropology and Race Studies at Columbia, having decided to make a virtue of her humble origins by making them her academic project. We had met at a college party five months ago. I guess you could say I was a project to her as well. The anthropologist in her was intrigued by me, this non-practicing Pakistani Muslim who had spent four years in Hicksville, Iowa, and was jobless and without prospects in New York. At times I thought she viewed me with the same intellectual fascination as a lab researcher views a guinea pig who's grown an extra testicle.

For my part, she seemed amazing when I first met her. She was attractive, brilliant, extremely interested in me, and she had a great pair of tits. My level of amazement lasted for the first month. Since then, the relationship had felt like a drag. For someone like me, who has no interest whatsoever in the socio-political history of the Puerto Rican people, who sees a food cart as a simple food cart and not a tool of ethnic subjugation, it became boring very quickly. In truth, we had survived this long together partly out of politeness (I've never learned how to move on from women; In Iowa, I had met my white, stepped-out-of-Tennessee-for-the-first-time-in-her-life, college girlfriend during Freshman week and stayed with her till the end of junior year, when she dumped me so that she could enjoy her final year unencumbered); and partly due to the fact that when my paternal funds ran out and I had no more money for rent, Sonia offered to let me crash with her.

And so for another three months, I had continued to put up with interminable discussions on race, ethnic identity, and how different it was to be from a Barrio in the Bronx, to one in Brooklyn. But as I sat down in her living room for what would surely be one of the last times, I reflected on the fact that back in Pakistan, I would even miss those mind-numbing conversations.

Instead of being sympathetic to my predicament, Sonia came home and launched herself into a fresh discourse on the struggles of brown immigrants against the social construct of the United States. After an hour, it began to grate on me and so I took out my laptop and sent an email to my dad to inform him that I would be returning and that he could go ahead and purchase that one-way ticket he had been threatening me with all these months. I wanted to be away from Sonia's prattling, so I decided to take a walk around the block.

The air was cool outside, unusually so for April. I closed my eyes and breathed in the smells of this great city. The wafting aroma of bubbling mozzarella from the pizza joint round the corner, the gasoline fumes from the cabs parked out front, and the pungent smell of dog shit from the dumpster. God, how I had fallen in love with New York. The thought of never experiencing any of these sensations ever again was breaking my heart. Hell, I would probably even miss Sonia and her anthropology.

It was at this precise moment that my cell phone rang. The shrillness of the ringtone broke me out of my reverie. I stared at the unrecognised number on the screen for several seconds, and was about to let it go, but some sixth sense told me to answer it.

'Waj-a-hat Shak-abe?'

'Wajahat. Yes, this is him.'

'This is Harvey Calzone, from the Diamond Organisation. I was in your interview this morning. Mr. Diamond has decided to give you a second interview. He'll see you in his office at ten sharp, tomorrow. Don't be late.'

And with that, my mysterious caller hung up.

I couldn't believe it. I looked up my call history to confirm that the call hadn't been a figment of my imagination. I was about to redial the number, but held back at the last moment. The one thing I'd learned today was how capricious the Diamond Organisation was. One wrong word and you were screwed. So what if I called back to confirm, and they changed their mind about me? What if this Calzone guy decided that a stupid shmuck who couldn't follow simple instructions, wasn't worth a second interview? I couldn't afford another fuck up.

I couldn't sleep a wink that night. This was probably what condemned prisoners feel like when they get a last-minute reprieve from the gas chamber. I didn't even tell Sonia, for fear of jinxing it.

I left her place at dawn and by the time of my appointment, I had ingested 8 cups of coffee and circled the block around the Diamond building 36 times. The security guards, who had grown increasingly suspicious of a brown man staking out the landmark building, were more than a little relieved to watch me enter and give my name at the front desk.

This time I was immediately sent to the 69th floor. The Amazons smiled benevolently, not quite understanding how I had gotten back here after being virtually thrown out the day before. I was later to learn that my little feat made me a bit of a legend in Diamond Organisation circles. Like Lazarus, I had come back from the dead.

I was shown into the same boardroom, but this time, the cast of characters had increased. Now, sitting across from me, in addition to Ron, Han and Harvey Calzone, was a breathtakingly attractive woman. To say she looked like a supermodel, would be an understatement. I had seen plenty of supermodels who wouldn't hold a candle to her. She was a vision, a blonde goddess with perfectly arched eyebrows and ruby red lips that pouted just so, to give a suggestion of desire, dressed immaculately in a figure-hugging dark business suit and Louboutin heels that made her look smart and sexy all at once.

I was so bowled over by her that it took me a few seconds to recognise that she was the same girl whose portrait hung in this same boardroom. But the portrait had not done justice to her. In the flesh, she looked too young to be Ron's wife.

'This is my daughter, Krystal.' Ron was the first to speak, as if having read my mind. Or perhaps my ogling was too obvious. 'And my younger son, Luke.' I noticed a dishevelled youth sitting next to the goddess, scowling at me as if I had just made a pass at his sister.

Which I suppose I had, at least with my eyes. At the time, I thought this was why Luke looked like he hated me from the word go. Later, I was to discover that the nasty scowl was a permanent feature and Luke Diamond went through most of his life wearing it.

'I called the rest of my family together', he said by way of explanation, 'because I wanted them all to hear and evaluate what Iowa State here, said yesterday. Go on, Iowa State.'

'Uh, what sir?'

'What did you say yesterday? What did you tell me, your so-called opinion about me and the President?'

I was blank, like a deer caught in headlights. I was desperately trying to remember anything non-controversial that I may have said the day before. I did not want to get kicked out of here a second time. It was my last chance.

'He said he thought you should run for President.' It was Harvey Calzone who spoke up this time.

'Yeah, that's right. He thought I should run for President. I want to hear his explanation as to why he thinks so, or was it just some smart ass remark you made on the fly, Iowa State?'

This was it. The precipice. If I jumped here, there was no turning back and no guarantee of where I would land. I didn't have a choice. I took the plunge.

'Yes, sir, I do think you should run, Mr. Diamond. Ever since that clip of the President making fun of you first ran, it's become viral. Everyone has an opinion about you, good or bad. You've got name recognition because the President picked on you. For his opponents, you've become a symbol of resistance to him. His supporters are overconfident. They believe President King is untouchable because he's the first black President. But his term's coming to an end, sir. Someone is going to replace him. He's a pretty polarising figure in the country. If you ran, and ran seriously, you would become the immediate front runner. None of the Republicans, or Democrats for that matter, have the same name recognition as you. You would disabuse everyone who ever thought your suggestion to be a bad joke because you would become a serious contender in a heartbeat. Everybody who said anything about you after that clip, would have to eat their words. That's why I think you should do it. Because it would shut everybody up.'

For some reason, while Ron Diamond's eyes bored into

me, I looked at his children for their reaction. Han, after being reprimanded yesterday, was guarded, choosing to stare with great interest at the piece of paper lying in front of him; Krystal's ice-blue eyes looked at me intriguingly. It was Luke who couldn't resist saying something.

'Are you fucking stupid? Do you even know how American elections work?'

'I minored in Poli-Sci.'

'Yeah, well whoop de fucking do. And you think that makes you a fucking expert on Presidential elections? Dad, I can't believe you called this guy back. This logic is laughable. I mean, you, a serious presidential contender?'

He realised his mistake the instant the words tumbled out of his mouth. Even if he hadn't, Ron's stare would have frozen the blood in his veins.

'That's exactly why I called him back. Because Iowa State here, despite his various shortcomings, thinks out of the box. You, on the other hand, are such a moron you wouldn't know where the fucking box was.'

'Mr. Shakaib has a point, Dad.' The goddess spoke, in a surprisingly deep voice, but she pronounced my name perfectly the first time. 'The minute you announce, you'd go to the top of the list of contenders on name recognition alone. It doesn't even matter whether you win, or even whether you win the nomination. The branding and marketing opportunities alone are worth it. It makes good business sense, Dad.'

'Finally, a child of mine who has both my looks, and my brains.'

'Uh, yeah Dad, I'm totally with Krystal. You should do it, if you want to.' Sensing which way things were going, Han spurted out his answer, not wanting to be left behind.

'Are you guys all forgetting the not insignificant fact that Dad's a retired porn star, for fuck's sake! Nobody's going to vote for a porn star to become President!'

'JFK was having numerous affairs when he decided to run.

Nobody gave a damn. Everyone knew about Clinton's women from his time as Governor of Arkansas. It didn't matter. Even President King. He was an unsuccessful businessman, with several failed ventures and certainly nothing in his history to suggest he could be President. But once the momentum starts going your way, it doesn't matter where you came from or what you did.' I decided to speak up again, to push my idea, whether it was because I felt emboldened by the fact that it had raised considerable interest among my audience, or that Luke Diamond's scowl had just pissed me off, I couldn't tell you for sure. But I felt I was on a roll here.

I was rewarded with an admiring shrug from Ron Diamond. 'You seem to know your politics, Iowa. So tell me, if I did follow your advice, what would be my strategy here? What would I do first?'

If I ever get around to writing my political memoirs, I will look back on this moment and almost certainly write about how, without missing a beat, I revealed to Ron Diamond a nine-point plan to win the Presidency. I did not. I could barely keep up with the direction the conversation was going in.

'Well sir, if you were… serious… about this, you announce now. Before anyone else. And you announce a platform in total opposition to the President, so that anyone who's opposed to him automatically seeks you out. You position it as a mano a mano contest between you and him. Doesn't matter if he isn't running. If everyone sees it as a contest between you and the President, no one will pay attention to the other candidates. And you file your nominations in the early primary contests, Iowa and New Hampshire. Start campaigning there. The more traction you get there, the more serious your candidacy will become. And nobody will be laughing at you after that. In my opinion. Sir.'

Ron Diamond smiled. 'Pretty good, Iowa State. You're hired.'

2.

THE

CHOSEN ONE

IT'S A COLD, wet and windswept day, and Shai feels the early April chill as she steps off the train from Grand Central onto the small platform at Katona. She feels the cold despite having worn her most expensive Cuyana wrap winter coat and her knee-high Stuart Weitzman boots. The wind whips the drizzle into an almost horizontal trajectory, making it uncomfortable for commuters coming out of the station into the parking lot. The handful that do get off here huddle under caps and umbrellas and raise their hands to cover their eyes from the swirling spray. Shai doesn't. She loves the rain on her face. It cleanses her, makes her feel born again. This is a special day, a day she and the Senator have been waiting for. Nothing can spoil it.

Her Uber is already waiting at the kerb and pulls away as soon as she is seated, undertaking the short drive through winding back roads that bypass the estates of the rich and famous in this particularly prosperous corner of Connecticut. She remembers her first journey here, as a college sophomore. It was still the early days of satellite navigation, where all cab drivers did not automatically possess Google Earth on their mobile phones, and you still had to occasionally work with physical directions. Jessica's directions, scribbled down hurriedly on a piece of paper as she ran out of her dorm room at Yale, seemed surreal to her. *Turn off the I-95 at the Grist Mill Road. Then take a right at Martha Stewart's property, and go straight past the Ralph Lauren estate and keep driving straight for another ten minutes till you get to my house. If you hit Keith Richards' gate, you've gone too far.*

It wasn't as if she was some fresh-off-the-boat, daughter of a starving farmer in Haryana. Shai had a privileged upbringing herself, her parents standard bearers of the great brown meritocracy that emerged in America as a result of President Johnson's 1965 Immigration Act. Both had been immigrants from Pakistan, but met here. Both were scientists, her father a renowned Oceanographer and her mother a professor of psychology. They had brought up their youngest daughter, born and bred in this country, as a living symbol of their American dream. That you could come from anywhere in the world, but as long as you worked hard, you could avail yourself of the best institutions that this country had to offer. Didn't matter if your father had been a penniless leftist pamphlet publisher in Lahore, or your mother an illiterate washerwoman from a village in Vehari. Your daughter could still attend Yale and be selected as an intern for Senator Jessica May.

But this world, this little corner of privilege in America that Shai had entered that April day of her sophomore year, was something else altogether. Many undergrads became interns at the offices of their senators. But few senators had Jessica May's pedigree. Born into one of America's oldest and most hallowed families; they say (only partly in jest) that the 'May' in the 'Mayflower' came from them. In the four hundred years that they had spent in the New World, the Mays of Connecticut had produced one signatory to the Bill of Rights, one President, four Governors, numerous prominent cabinet members and an almost unbroken line of senators, going back to the founding of the Republic. In fact, the longest period in Connecticut's history when the state had not been represented by a May in the US Senate had been from when Jessica's father had taken oath as a well-meaning, but largely bumbling one-term President (remembered mainly for running the economy into the ground and choking violently on a piece of Halibut during a state dinner for the Japanese Prime Minister), to the time, a decade and a half later, that his daughter had finally reclaimed the family's mantle as the junior senator from the Nutmeg state.

Jessica May's personal CV was no less impressive. Miss Porter's School, Yale, and then a stint volunteering in the Peace Corps while daddy was in the White House. Law school at Harvard on her return, then the next ten years divided equally between working with non-profits, to burnish her humanitarian credentials, and big fat New York law firms, to burnish her wallet. Fell in love along the way, and married a venture capitalist. Joined the cabinet briefly as Education secretary, and resigned to mark her opposition to the President's habit of getting blow jobs from barely legal interns in the Oval Office, a move that catapulted her to the front of the class of prospective presidential hopefuls in the Democratic party. She had ridden that wave of popularity, capturing her family's Senate seat and becoming one of the most high-profile opponents of the Republican administration that took office after President Blowjob crashed and burned. That of itself should have made her the party's presumptive candidate in the next election cycle, until she was upended and swamped by the phenomenon of Lincoln King. She had declined his offer to join his cabinet after he became President, and had instead won herself a second term in the Senate.

It was in her second term that Shai had caught her eye. Jessica had wanted to recruit interns from her alma mater and Shai had stood out head and shoulders above everyone else.

Besides, there was an affinity that the Senator felt for the nineteen-year-old Shaiza Naqvi, the supremely intelligent, go-getting daughter of Pakistani immigrants who happened to be housed in her old residential college. Jessica had also spotted, beneath the veneer of brash confidence and all-knowing superiority that all Yalie sophomores cover themselves in, a vulnerability that she recognised from her own youth. That desire to be heard, to break out from the chains of the patriarchy, however gilded those chains may have been.

A bond formed between the women and Shai gradually moved from being Jessica May's bag carrying intern in her first summer, to her one indispensable aide. She had returned the following summer to the Senator's office, and by the start of her Senior year, was essentially commuting to her classes from Washington. Straight after college, she had been hired as the Senator's top political aide, a move that had raised plenty of eyebrows at Democratic National Committee headquarters, but none among the Senator's other staffers. They all knew that Shai had become Jessica's alter ego a long time ago. Her age, or lack of experience was irrelevant. She had plenty of experience in the only area that mattered: knowing how to handle Jessica.

And today is the culmination. Or rather, the beginning of the culmination of the dream that Shai and Jessica have dreamt together. So many late nights talking, sharing their hopes and aspirations, the older woman mentoring her young apprentice, planning this journey for years. Perhaps even more than Jessica, Shai has been preparing for this moment, training herself, networking within the Party, glad-handing constituents and donors, mastering the arcane election laws of fifty states, becoming even more indispensable than she already was. All done for the single-minded objective of being able to walk into the Oval Office on inauguration day, one step behind the first female President of the United States.

The Uber pulls into the gravel driveway of the old stone farmhouse. It's always been a bit frumpy and rural for Shai's tastes, but Jessica had insisted that Tim, her husband, buy this particular house. It fits the folksy image that she wants to give to voters. She even had a swing and a rocking chair placed on the porch, as if the only way she could be eligible to run for President was if her house resembled a Norman Rockwell painting. Shai's never understood that side of Jessica but like a good aide, she's never questioned it.

She walks past the main house where a Secret Service advance team is in the process of setting up a command post. Another thing Jessica insisted on and demanded from the President as a special request. Being assigned a Secret Service team this early lends gravitas to a campaign, and it shows that the President is behind me, she had said.

Shai walks towards a detached barn that Tim had converted into an office a few years ago. In contrast to the main house, which looks empty, the barn is buzzing with activity. Jessica's core team is already inside, although she herself is not. There's Maury, her pollster, a wiry New Yorker who, despite being one of the most successful political operatives in the country, still dresses like he just walked out of Yankee Stadium; Johnny Raines, her whizz kid political director, who walked out on a foreign service career to serve her in the Senate; and Mike Cochrane, the adult in the room, her old Chief of Staff from when Jessica ran the Education department more than a decade ago.

'Hey, the Princess is here! Finally! Did ya get us some food from the city? I love Jessica, but I can't stomach that lean, mean, vegan cuisine that the housekeeper serves up here. Come on, Princess, tell me you got me something!'

Shai raises her eyebrow in mock annoyance. All of these men are older than her, but she knows them all, in and out. And they know that, irrespective of their closeness to Jessica, Shai is the Senator's gatekeeper and alter ego. She puts down the shopping bag on the beaten-up old wooden bench that serves as a conference table.

'Careful Maury, call me Princess again and you'll have to stick to Alda's beancurd patties. Here, I went to Zaybar's and got bagels and lox, pastrami on rye, and a Reuben.' She tosses a wrapped bagel to Maury. 'So, what's the verdict?'

Mikey purses his lips as he picks up a sandwich. 'Where is she, Shai? She needs to be here for this.'

'She's flying up from Washington in the afternoon, and she expects us to have had this meeting already. She knows that she's running. She expects us to figure out all the obstacles that are going to show up between her and the White House and to figure out a way around them, by the time she walks through that door.'

'Obstacles? What obstacles? We got a clean run here. She's the chosen one. The party's standard bearer for the post-Lincoln King age. Have you seen her numbers? Sixty-two percent of registered Democrats likely to vote for her. Forty-nine percent of registered independents say they'll vote for her. It's a lock. And I don't just mean the nomination, I mean the general as well.'

'Come on, Maury. That kind of thinking will get us killed.' Johnny takes a french fry from the shopping bag. 'There's always something lurking behind the corner. Someone's bound to take a shit on us.'

'Ok smart guy, who? You tell me? This country is ready for a woman in the White House. And if that woman happens to be a May, that's an unbeatable combination.'

'The May name isn't what it used to be, Maury. The last great May was her grandfather. And he was a senator 70 years ago! Nobody remembers him, outside of academics and historians writing books about the fifties'. It's worse with her dad. The only thing that remains in the public consciousness about his presidency is Halibut-gate. Jack May, bless his soul, was a moron who stumbled in and out of the White House.'

'No one else is running, Johnny. It's eight months to the Iowa caucus and no other Democrat has declared. No one's even set up an exploratory committee. Everyone acknowledges it's her turn. Ok, so we got bushwhacked last time. No one expected Lincoln King to run. He was a nobody, a two-term congressman from LA. He was cool, he was hip, he was black, all the college kids backed him, and he ran to her left. He was the fucking LeBron James of politics. Nobody could have predicted that. But this isn't eight years ago. Back then, she was just Jack May's kid. Now, she's the senior senator from Connecticut, ranking member of the Senate Judiciary committee, a huge fundraiser for Democratic candidates across the country, a leading advocate for women, for unions and the LGBTQ community. Hell, we own the Party. I bet Shai's getting all sorts of calls from people begging to be first in line to endorse her. And the donors are lining up around the block, right Shai?'

'That is true. Twenty senators, the governors of New York, California and Illinois, the mayor of Boston, half the cabinet. They're all vying to be the first to endorse her candidacy. They all owe her. And as for donors, we have thirty million in pledged donations already, before declaring our candidacy. We expect to clear a hundred mil in the first month after announcing. A lot of people want to be on Jessica's right side when she wins.'

'If she wins, not when. What about the President? His is the biggest endorsement and the only one that matters.'

'Well, Mike, he hasn't said anything officially. Obviously, there was some bad blood from eight years ago. You were there. But Jessica's told him she's running. He intervened with the Secret Service to ensure she got early protection. And he's the one who leaned on the Vice President to commit to not running against her. That's a pretty strong endorsement, even if he hasn't said so explicitly.'

'Ok, what about the other side? Assuming we get the nomination, who can we expect to face in the general election, Johnny?'

'We have the usual gaggle of mid-western governors, a couple of senators, and that nutty congressman from Texas who wants to make gun ownership compulsory. But none of them have the charisma or the money. In my mind, there are only two serious candidates. It's going to come down to the General, or the Reverend. Between them, they're the yin and yang of the Republican party. The Reverend's got the support of the religious right, but the General has everybody else. Neocons, centrists, Wall Street. The General's also a war hero and he's straight out of central casting. Looks like he was born to be President. But he's going to have to slog it out in the primaries, because most of those contests favour the Reverend.'

'Jessica's concerned about the General. Her thinking is, it'll be a bloodbath, but he will prevail in the primaries over the Reverend, because no one, even in the bat shit crazy Republican party, is going to give the nomination to a guy who's basically a Christian Ayatollah. Jessica's worried about the General because he's got serious foreign policy experience. He's been the supreme NATO commander in Brussels, he commanded a division in Iraq, and he commanded ISAF in Afghanistan. She's largely been a domestic presence.

Even her senate committee placements all focus on domestic policy, not foreign affairs or defence. How do we overcome that?'

'Foreign policy experience never won anybody the White House. Trust me, Princess, I've been in this business a long time. If we get the General, we can take him. If we get the Ayatollah, we can definitely take him.'

'What about internals? What do we need to look out for, from her past?'

'There is the husband problem.'

'There's no husband problem.'

'Come on, Shai. There have been rumours of women over the years. And also, more recently, of some shady dealings with his business partner. We should probably do some internal research, just so we know what we're dealing with, if she does get hit with any of this stuff in the campaign.'

'Yeah, sorry Mike that's going to be a no. You know how private Jessica is. She's never going to speak about her marriage. Her instructions on this are unambiguous.'

'Shai, we can't go into an election campaign without having examined the vulnerabilities of our own candidate.'

'Jessica says there's nothing there. It's all bullshit rumours spread by the Republicans over the years. There will be no internal investigation.'

'We did this last time too, Shai.'

'Yeah Mike, and it wasn't a pleasant experience for her. Which is why she says this time round, she wants a totally positive campaign.'

'You go into a presidential campaign without having vetted your own guy, you're asking for trouble, no matter how long she's been a public figure for.'

'Ok Mike, you can tell her that. Then when she freezes you out, you can go back to working for whatever rinky dink consulting outfit you've been working for the past eight years, instead of becoming the White House Chief of Staff. Guys, Jessica wants me to make this clear to everyone. This is her campaign, and she is going to run it whichever way she likes. Get on board, or get out of town. Now she is going to be here in an hour. Do we think there is any major hurdle to her becoming the next President of the United States?'

The three men exchange looks, but remain silent. Finally, Mike speaks up. 'No. There are no hurdles.'

'Awesome. Jessica's going to go over the details with you herself, but the basic campaign structure she wants is for Mike to be the campaign manager, Johnny to handle the message, and Maury as chief pollster.'

'And what are you going to do?'

'Me? I'm going to be everywhere. Right next to her. Look guys, you know how she is. It's all about equilibrium with Jessica. She likes structure, and she likes positivity. We stick to those guidelines and this should be a cakewalk, like Maury says. Any bad news comes along, don't go to her. Come to me first.'

'Well, I don't know if this counts as bad news, but...'

'What is it, Johnny?'

'There's a strong rumour going around that Ron Diamond might run.'

'Who?'

'Ron Diamond. The porn star. The guy with all the buildings in New York, and the cheesy reality show. Jeez Shai, you must know Ron Diamond.'

'I'm sorry if I didn't spend the last few years watching a lot of porn, Johnny. Why is this even a thing? Is he running as a Democrat, or a Republican, or as the nominee of the Monster Raving Loony party?'

'Actually, no one knows his politics.'

'Why are you even flagging this?'

'He's got a lot of name recognition, from TV, and...well from porn. He could be a wild card in the campaign.'

'Please. A porn star? That's laughable. Let's stick to focusing on opponents who haven't exposed their penises in public to earn a pay cheque.'

3.

BRAINDRAIN, KALE AS A SUPER-FOOD, AND OTHER STORIES FROM FOREIGN LANDS

APRIL TURNS KARACHI into a sauna. Shakaib Qureshi wipes a river of sweat from his brow, soaking his sleeve, the last remaining dry part of his shirt. How he misses the arid Arabian desert heat. These evening walks were a pleasure there, even in the hottest summer months. The heat has never bothered Shakaib. It's the humidity of this city that really kills him.

As he turns into the cul-de-sac where his house is located, he sees the sun dipping into the Arabian Sea. Any minute now, the muezzins will fire up their loudspeakers and announce the evening prayer, allowing for the opening of the fast. The drivers, domestic servants and labourers of the surrounding houses have already laid out a *dastarkhan* on the roadside, pooling their various iftari items to put together an impressive feast. Many of them are already holding a glass of ruby red sherbet and a date in their hand, anticipating the muezzin's call.

Panting, Shakaib reaches his front gate and turns to look at the road behind him. It weaves out from the cul-de-sac and extends in a straight line, running parallel to the sea. After a couple of blocks, the houses thin out, and there are empty plots of land covered in *kikar* bushes, stretching as far as the eye can see. It's one of the city's newer cantons, the land freshly reclaimed from the sea and not yet fully populated. His own house can best be described as one of modest grandeur. It isn't one of the larger plots in the area but his front door opens into an internal courtyard bursting with a riot of colours. An array of seasonal flowers frames half the courtyard, while the other half is taken up by a small, man-made pond. The walls are decked with expensive hand-woven rugs, impressionist paintings, and a black cloth inscribed with the 99 names of God.

'You're late. You won't have time to shower before Iftari.' Umber, his wife, greets him at the door.

'I had to clock up my 10,000 steps for the day on this contraption Zara gave me.' He points to the FitBit strapped to his left wrist.

'Huh. Fat lot of good 10,000 steps is going to do if you keep eating a tub from Baskin Robbins every day.'

'Arre begum, take my wealth, take my health, take even yourself away from me, but for the love of God, please don't part me from my Jamoca Almond Fudge. Civilisation has finally come to this country with the arrival of Baskins. Do you remember when the first store opened in Riyadh? There was a line around the block, at midnight. When was that, '96? '97? We took the Prince, too, remember? Made him stand in a line for the first, and perhaps only time in his life.'

Just then, the muezzin finally calls out and the two of them sit down in an elegantly furnished dining room that looks out on to the courtyard. The table is laden with a simple meal, consisting of dates, a single plate of rice pulao and of course, a tub of ice cream from Baskin Robbins. Shakaib makes straight for the tub.

Umber looks upon him disapprovingly. 'Your daughter will not be happy when I tell her about this teenager lifestyle that you seem intent on pursuing. No dates, no water, no food, straight to ice cream! What is wrong with you Shakaib!'

'If my daughter has a problem with my eating habits, she should move back to Pakistan to correct them. I fast from daybreak to sunset for the glory of the Almighty, and Baskin Robbins is my reward. You can keep the dates.'

He sniggers as he takes his spoon and starts eating directly from the tub. Umber rolls her eyes and takes up the plate of pulao. 'By the way, speaking of your beloved Prince, he sent something for you. It's lying on the side table.'

The mention of the Prince's name animates Shakaib. He rises from his chair and picks up the ornate, sandalwood box with the royal crest engraved upon it. He opens the box, which contains dates, and smiles at the note, written by hand on the personal stationery of the Crown Prince.

'He still hasn't learnt how to spell. He's become the virtual ruler of the country, but he still can't differentiate between sole and soul.'

'Next time, tell him to send something expensive. Virtual ruler of the largest oil producing country in the world, and still just palms us off on dates. Hmpff.'

'For God's sake, Umber. What do you expect from him, Cartier bracelets? He's still a kid, with so many responsibilities thrust on him all of a sudden. It's good of him to even remember us. Besides, the Royal family were always generous to us. We have this lovely house, all of these things, because of their largesse.'

'They were hardly giving us charity Shakaib. You worked for them for thirty years. Pass me the dates. I hope they're at least Ajwas.'

Shakaib returns to his ice cream, digging into the tub with renewed relish, the melted cream running down the side of his mouth. 'You know, that kid, he used to love pistachio. I don't know anyone who likes pistachio flavoured ice cream.'

'The time he spent in our house was probably the only time in his life that he did normal things.'

'That's exactly why I would bring him over. I wanted him to learn that there was a world outside of the cocoon of the Royal Palace.'

'By the way, both Zara and Wajahat emailed. Zara wants us to start eating kale. She says it's a superfood, especially for people in our age group. And Wajahat got a job.'

'This daughter of mine, she's gone soft in the head living in Palo Alto. All this new-age stuff she's started pouting. Kale as a superfood. What rubbish! And where the hell am I supposed to get kale in Karachi, the local sabzi wallah?'

'Did you hear me? I said Wajahat said he got a job. In New York.'

Shakaib grimaces as he swallows another spoonful. 'Yes, I read his email. He's apparently working for that bizarre man.'

'It seems to be a good job. Wajahat says he'll be working directly under this Ron Diamond. That's good, isn't it? It'll give him plenty of networking opportunities, to try and find a better job.'

'I don't think Wajahat would want to avail of any of the 'networking' opportunities that arise out of being close to Mr. Ron Diamond.' Shakaib is pretty sure his wife wouldn't have heard of Ron Diamond, but he has. He recalls a memory, from his early days in Dammam; a group of friends, all men, all unmarried at the time, clandestinely watching pirated 'blue films', recorded from shaky camcorders on bulky VHS cassettes, surreptitiously smuggled into Saudi Arabia. They would always draw the curtains, even in the middle of the day, out of fear of the religious police. Once watched, the tape would be moved from one house to another, from one watcher to the next like some pornographic relay baton, to ensure that if the religious police did decide to track it, it wouldn't be easy to find. Ron Diamond was often the male lead on those VHS tapes. But Shakaib never expected his son to end up working for him.

'Look Shakaib, there's no point in looking so glum. You were the one who set the terms for the boy. You said if he could get a job, he could stay in New York. You thought he wouldn't be able to manage it, but he has. The boy strived and struggled, and he got what he wanted. Isn't that exactly what you wanted to teach him? If he wants to stay in America, what can we do? He says they're even giving him a place to stay, an apartment in one of this Mr. Diamond's buildings. That's delightful. He'll be living in Manhattan.'

'First of all, this job is hardly a career. He'll be a glorified personal attendant for this Diamond fellow. Secondly, my objection wasn't to his living in America, it was…'

'Of course it was. You didn't want him to stay on. And now he's confounded you, so you're acting like a sore loser. I don't understand, you don't have the same issues with Zara. You're quite happy for her to remain in Palo Alto for the rest of her life. You weren't shocked when she introduced us to that Chinese boyfriend of hers, you're not concerned about her getting married. All of your angst is reserved for Wajahat. Why?'

'It's not angst. Zara…well she's found herself. She couldn't ever do the things she's doing there, over here. And she can fend for herself. She's proved that. Wajahat is confused. Always has been. These silly dreams about getting into showbiz. I mean come on. He's got no direction…I guess I had always hoped he would grow out of these daft ideas and come back home. He's our son, he'll be the one who'll carry on the family name. I would have liked for him to be here, to be with us…I could have introduced him to people, important people, we could get him married to a girl from a good family…'

'Why Shakaib? Why the double standard? I also wanted these things, for both of my children, but I understood, when we made the decision to educate them abroad, that this was a sacrifice I would probably have to make. To lose my children, so that they could have the opportunity for a better life elsewhere. And you're hardly one to talk. You made the same choice yourself. You left your parents and family behind and worked in the Middle East for thirty years.'

'The Middle East is not America. It's next door to us. It doesn't change who you are. And I…I don't want to die alone. Every day, I go for my evening walk and I pass all these mansions, filled with people like us. The Lalanis, the Fazails, the Kheishghis. People who have lost their children to the West. Because the world we made here, the Pakistan that our generation made, was lousy. It is corrupt and venal and unequal. And our children don't want to come back to it. So we sit in these big houses, growing old alone. Do you remember last year, when old man Lalani died, there wasn't anyone from his family to carry the coffin. Because of his six sons, one was in Dallas, one in Toronto, one in London, one in Sydney, one in Hong Kong and one in Singapore. And none of them could make it back in time for the funeral. It was the drivers and the plumbers and the gravediggers who buried Lalani. How unfortunate can a man be, to have six sons, and not be able to get even one of them to bury him? We have become a nation of parent-orphans. I had thought… Wajahat wouldn't be able to hack it in America, and so he would come back and live with us. I would like to have a more intimate relationship with my grandchildren, than a weekly Zoom meeting. I would like my son to bury me when I die.'

'Come on, Shakaib. You're not dying anytime soon. Who knows, this whole thing with Ron Diamond might fall apart in a year or two, and maybe Wajahat will come back anyway. Maybe Zara will want to move back here, once she marries that Fu Manchu of hers.'

'Umber, for God's sake, that's racist. How can you… oh hello!'

The houseboy escorts a tall, balding, bearded man wearing a shalwar hitched above his ankles, into the dining room. The man looks extremely familiar, although Shakaib can't put his finger on where he has seen him before. The man senses Shakaib's confusion and smiles.

'Shakaib sahib, I don't think you've become that old, that you've started forgetting faces. It's me, Colonel Hamza, from the Pakistani embassy in Riyadh.'

'Hamza? What's happened to you? What's with the beard and the piety? My God, you look like you've aged fifty years!'

Hamza chuckles, a curiously effeminate sounding chuckle. 'Oh sir, I am just the same, just stopped dyeing my hair after I retired. Alhamdulilah, after Allah gave me the opportunity to serve in Saudia, these changes were only natural. I am surprised to see you haven't changed, despite so many more years in the Kingdom than me.'

Shakaib isn't quite sure what to make of that statement. 'Uh yes, well, you know me, it was always work, work, work. Never had the time to delve upon the spiritual. Uh, sorry, let me introduce you to my wife. Umber, Colonel Hamza used to be the military attache in the embassy in Riyadh. This was back in, when, the early 2000's?'

'That is correct sir. I was there from 2000 to 2005. Salaam, Bhabi.'

'Salaam, Bhai, please sit. I will bring some tea. Have you had iftari? Let me reheat the pulao for you. Unfortunately, my husband insists on only having Ice cream for Iftari, and by the looks of it, I don't know if he is willing to share his Baskin Robbins.'

The effeminate chuckle comes out again. 'No thank you, Bhabi, I have had my iftari. I see that Shakaib sahib's predilection for ice cream is still there. A cup of tea would be fine, thanks.'

As soon as his wife leaves the room, Shakaib turns to Hamza with a conspiratorial air. 'Tell me, you old rascal, what is all this? Weren't you the one who was having an affair with that Filipino secretary in Riyadh? Now you've got the whole holy man garb on?'

'The mistakes of an ill-advised youth, Shakaib sahib. I retired from the Army shortly after my return from the Kingdom. God was kind, I made money on some business ventures that came my way as a result of my time there. Alhamdulillah, I bought a farm house in Raiwind, I help out with the Tableeghi Jamaat there during their annual ijtimah. And recently, some friends introduced me to a remarkable young man. Well, he's not young, he's our age, but he has an amazing vitality about him. So I've been helping out with some of his new endeavours.'

'Who?'

'Javed Afridi.'

'The footballer? The one who's on this kick to reform politics? Didn't he lose every single seat he contested in the last election?'

The chuckle again, a little nervous this time. 'True, the party was not able to secure a National Assembly seat, although it did win six seats in the Punjab Assembly. But that was four years ago. The party was very disorganised back then. And of course, the performance of this present government has proved Javed Afridi correct in every way.'

'You're right about that. This lot are complete jokers. Can you believe the scandals that are coming out every day in the media? These people have no shame.'

'Exactly Shakaib sahib. Things have to change. I believe Javed Afridi is the change that we need.'

'Well, I'll probably need some more convincing, but if you believe it, good for you Hamza.'

'Tell me Shakaib sahib, when we were in Riyadh, in addition to your duties with the oil company, you served as a tutor for the current Crown Prince when he was a young boy, isn't it?'

'Yes. My wife and I were just talking about that earlier today.'

'What exactly did you tutor him in?'

'Well, I didn't have a specific subject. But his father, the King, who was at that time the Crown Prince, wanted the boy to get out of the bubble of the royal palace. He wanted him to understand how the world worked. He knew me because I used to give regular briefings at the Palace on the global oil situation, since that was part of my job. So he assigned me to the Prince. I would sit with the boy and teach him little things; for instance, how the oil industry worked, how international politics worked, something about how hard the lives of the expatriate workers in the Kingdom were. In short, anything that I thought would be useful for him to know whenever he became king. It was all very informal, of course.'

'Are you still in touch with him?'

'Off and on. An occasional message every few months. He sent us some lovely dates from the royal orchards. They just arrived today. Why, you want to squeeze him for some money for Javed Afridi? I don't think he's going to give a cent to some half-baked ex-footballer who thinks he's a messiah.'

'I…we…don't need his money. We've got our own money. Trust me Shakaib sahib, we are very well financed. Actually, I came here to ask you a favour. I would like you to be a guide, a tutor of sorts, for Javed Afridi, just as you were for the Crown Prince.'

'Hamza, how can I do that? The prince was a boy when I knew him. Afridi's a grown man. It makes no sense.'

'In many ways, he's still like a child. He's lived all his life in a bubble of celebrity and wealth that his footballing success created for him. He wants to bring change, but he doesn't really have a good understanding of how this country operates. He needs someone who will explain these concepts to him.'

'Hamza, do you know how daft that sounds? How can a man who professes that he wants to become the next Prime Minister, have no idea how this country operates? And you're actually supporting such an idiot?'

'Shakaib sahib, he has a vision. He just needs to learn the nitty gritty stuff. But he has a good heart, he is an excellent Muslim and a true patriot.'

'Weren't his escapades a regular feature in the gossip pages of the tabloids in England, when he was playing football there? Wasn't there a rumour that he had even had an affair with the Princess of Wales?'

'Arre Shakaib sahib, all old news. He had a reawakening several years ago. He's a totally different man now. Listen, I came here to ask you for a favour. Don't commit to anything, but just meet him. He's in town, doing some fundraising and meeting some of his local party candidates. He's staying close by, at the house of one of our major benefactors. Come with me and meet him. After that, if you feel that it's a waste of your time, you can walk away. But Shakaib sahib, you yourself just said this political system of ours is bankrupt. Don't you think you should at least listen to the one man who says he wants to change it all?'

* * *

The benefactor's house is indeed just a few streets away. But in terms of opulent luxury, it may as well be in a separate galaxy to Shakaib's cosy abode. It is a sprawling estate with an elongated driveway lined with gleaming SUVs, that leads to an imposing front door that resembles a castle portcullis. The building itself is half mock-Tudor, and half Arabian nights, clearly constructed by someone with a penchant for the bizarre and plenty of cash to indulge in their fantasies. A fully grown palm tree greets visitors in the foyer of the house. An attendant leads them to a massive drawing room, which looks out onto an Olympic-sized swimming pool. The room is brightly lit with gaudy chandeliers, and filled with gaudier furniture; gold sofas and silver-coloured tables, bought more for their hefty price tag rather than any innate sense of taste.

A group of men clusters at one end of the drawing room. They are a motley crew; a couple of long bearded religious types, in deep conversation with a man in a pin-striped suit who has the air of a banker; another banker-type, albeit dressed casually in slacks and a pink polo shirt, wearing a thin, gold Patek Phillipe that probably costs more than the six SUVs parked in the driveway; a famous TV news anchor, known for his somewhat right-wing views and vitriolic hatred of the present regime, looking considerably more haggard and overweight without makeup or flattering camera angles; and another man, younger, with a military bearing and haircut.

At the centre of this menagerie sits Javed Afridi. He is an impressive physical specimen, a head taller than everyone else in the room, his powerful forearms showing through the loose-fitting shalwar kameez that he wears. Shakaib remembers Afridi being ruggedly handsome in his football-playing days, and that handsomeness is still evident, despite the advances of age. The face is craggier, more weathered, and the hair, still shoulder length as in his youth, has streaks of grey.

He holds court like a medieval potentate, surrounded by fawning courtiers. At first, he doesn't deign to acknowledge their presence, even though he sees them walking in. Afridi continues to be ensconced in private conversation with the man with the military haircut, who bends low and whispers in his ear. One of the long beards, who is apparently the owner of the house, wordlessly ushers Hamza and Shakaib into two chairs a slight distance away from the durbar. An attendant brings them glasses of bright red sherbet and places a tray of Baklava in front of them.

After about ten minutes, Afridi finally acknowledges Hamza with nothing more than a half nod. As if by prior arrangement, he rises and walks out of the drawing room. The man with the military haircut signals them to follow. They walk through to a smaller study connected to the drawing room. The room has no windows, and the walls are lined with books from floor to ceiling. It takes Shakaib a moment to realise that the books lining the shelves seem to all be almanacs or encyclopaedias, as if the owner has bought a book collection wholesale to appear more learned. Javed Afridi is already seated behind a desk, now staring intently at Shakaib from across the table.

Shakaib has never felt so utterly unprepared for a meeting. For someone as meticulous as he is, this is purgatory. He curses Hamza silently for having ambushed him like this, and desperately tries to remember all that he knows about Javed Afridi. He's a Pathan, or maybe a Punjabi? Or perhaps a Pathan settled in Punjab. Well-to-do family, as Shakaib seems to recall. Went to school or university somewhere in England, and started playing football there. Became good enough to turn professional. This was back in the 80's. Played for several top clubs in the Premier League, won a few trophies. Played for Chelsea, didn't he? Manchester United too. Or was it Manchester City? Definitely one of the Manchesters. Also gained a reputation as a ladies' man. Bedded a number of top models and actresses of the time. Hence the rumours about the Princess of Wales. But Shakaib has never been an avid football fan, and this is the extent of his knowledge. He now regrets not having paid extra to get the sports channels package on his satellite dish connection all those years in Saudi.

It is Hamza who finally breaks the silence. 'Javed, this is Shakaib sahib. I told you about him. Shakaib sahib has enjoyed a very distinguished career. He was a chartered accountant…that's correct, isn't it, Shakaib sahib? Yes, a chartered accountant in the Middle East. Worked for Saudi Aramco for many years. We were in Riyadh together when I was posted at the embassy there.'

'In Riyadh, you served as an advisor to the Crown Prince. Before that, you were in Dammam, where you were in charge of international operations for Aramco, reporting directly to the

Oil minister. And before that, Abu Dhabi, where you advised the government, and before that, Amman and Muscat, where, again, you headed high-profile consulting projects that made you work very closely with the ruling families of those countries.' It's the Haircut who speaks, rather than Javed Afridi. Shakaib is a little astounded at the extent of information that this stranger has about him and starts to think that he may be working for an intelligence agency.

'Yes. When you spend thirty years in the Middle East, you tend to get around.'

There is another period of silence, and Shakaib is uncomfortably aware that Javed Afridi's eyes bore into him. Finally, he shrugs his head in the direction of the Haircut.

'This one and Hamza tell me you're the man I need to advise me on sensitive issues. Is that true?'

'I'm sorry, Mr. Afridi, I'm not sure what sort of advice you require, and how I can be of help.'

'Javed, Shakaib sahib is a bit sceptical about your prospects.' Hamza speaks up, somewhat apologetically. Afridi keeps staring straight at Shakaib, and then finally breaks into a grin.

'I don't blame you, Shakaib.' Afridi slips into a familiar tone, as if he has known Shakaib all his life. 'If you based it on my party's performance in the last election, I would probably share your lack of enthusiasm. But we weren't ready then, and this bloody government cheated their way to victory. They stole the election. We didn't realise the depths that they were willing to go, to stay in power. It was naïve of me, I admit.'

'I seem to recall that the international monitors from Norway said that they thought the election was pretty fair.'

'What do those bloody Norwegians know? Do you know how easy it is to fool them? Trust me, I've spent my life playing and working in the west, I know how soft in the head these goras are. Especially the bloody Europeans. I played for six different English and Spanish clubs, played in the UEFA Cup and Champions' League. They're all a bunch of idiots.'

'I…I couldn't possibly say…I mean, I'm not an expert on football, or Europeans…'

'No, no, I'm telling you. All idiots, easily manipulated.' Afridi suddenly eyes him suspiciously. 'Wait, you're not a supporter of these bastards, are you?' He turns and glares at Hamza, who seems to visibly shrink in his chair. Even the Haircut, normally so cool and reserved, betrays a look of abject panic. 'Who did you vote for, in the last election?'

'I didn't. I didn't vote. I was in Dubai at the time. I hadn't retired yet, I was doing a consulting project and resultantly, missed polling day. Just as I have every time. I vaguely remember voting once, back in 1977. I think I voted for Mr. Bhutto, but I can't possibly remember. I do think that the…present government…has made an absolute mess of things. We are one oil price hike away from total economic meltdown. The Saudis aren't going to keep giving us subsidised crude. They have their own problems and, when I last spoke with their top people, they openly admitted that they were getting a bit sick of repeatedly bailing us out.'

Hamza lets out an audible sigh of relief, as if impending economic Armageddon is the best news he's heard in a while. Afridi smiles, the first time he has done so, that Cheshire cat grin of his that was on so many magazine covers back in the day, and Shakaib begins to understand why so many attractive women were ready to throw their panties at this man.

'You see? You see Hamza? This is what I keep saying. This,' he points at Shakaib, 'This is the common man. He's the voter I'm looking for. He's never voted and, as an educated man, he understands the ruin that this fucking government has brought upon us. A man like this needs to be with us. This is exactly why I need you to join me, Shakaib. You know these things.'

'Uh, what things?'

'You know, like about oil price hikes and what the Saudis are thinking. This sort of inside knowledge. I mean, I know in general that the economic situation is bad, but even I couldn't imagine how dire things are, until you just articulated it so brilliantly, in a single, easy sentence. That's what I need.'

'Mr. Afridi, sir, this isn't difficult. This is basic economics. I'm sure you have dozens of advisors, far more qualified than me, to make these arguments for you.'

'My advisors are all a bunch of greedy bastards. I mean, you saw some of them out there. They're ok, I suppose, but they all have their own agendas. I need them to manage party affairs, so I keep them around but I need someone whom I can trust, who will tell it to me straight. Who can coach me about these things, advise me privately. After all, I'm going to be inheriting these problems soon enough and I need to be prepared when I become Prime Minister.' He gives a knowing look to the Haircut.

'The election is…still a while away. A lot can change in that period…'

'The election is not as far away as you think, Shakaib sahib.' It's the Haircut's turn to speak.

'Well, I mean the government still has about eighteen months to run in its term.'

'The government will not complete its term. Things are so bad, that we predict that it will be removed from office in a matter of months. And in the fresh election, Mr. Afridi's party will come to power. Inshallah.'

'Inshallah.' Both Hamza and Afridi chant the prayer in unison.

'Excuse me, I'm sorry sir, I don't know your name, even though you seem to know an awful lot about me. And I am sorry, Mr. Afridi, for being blunt, especially as you have been so kind as to meet me, but I just don't see it. How can you go from being a party with no parliamentary seats, to getting the 170-odd needed to form a government? I mean, if we had a presidential system, it would perhaps be different. I understand that your popularity is increasing, judging by the number of posters that I see around the city, and the number of TV anchors who now support you. If that is an accurate indicator of political success, then you're well on your way to it. But to become Prime Minister, you have to win a majority of seats in the Assembly, and that requires grass roots politics, the kind of dirty politics that the government and the opposition parties excel at. That's exactly how they beat you last time round. I just don't see it changing.'

'You know Shakaib, I like you. You're honest, and you have the guts to say uncomfortable things to my face. None of the people sitting outside this room have those guts. If you view things in a conventional way, you're right. But there is a hankering for change out there. People are sick of the same old lousy choices. Look, I'll be the first to admit that I'm not the smartest guy around. During my playing days, the tabloid press had given me a nickname: Dim Jim. Sometimes even the fans would chant it on the terraces. I didn't mind. I never said I was the smartest guy in the room. But what I could do, what I've always been good at, has been building a team around me. I get people who are smarter, more talented, and I play them around me. I feed off them and it makes us all a better team. It's this ability that helped me to win three FA cups, a Champion's League, and four championships with three different clubs. That's why I want you to be part of my team. You become my playmaker, create openings for me, and I'll be the striker who finishes off by scoring goals.'

'But…I've never been part of any political party. I don't know the first thing about politics.'

'You don't need to. I know all about politics. You just need to advise me on the things I don't know anything about, like foreign policy, international trade, oil markets. Come on Shakaib. Let's work together. Let's reclaim our country from these thieves and charlatans. Listen, do you have children?'

'Uh…yes. A girl and a boy.'

'Are you happy for them to live in the country the way it is now?'

'I…they don't live here. They live in America.'

'Because they felt they would have more opportunities there, right? And you felt the same way?'

'Yes.'

'If things continue the way they are, with the current lot of politicians, both in government and in the opposition, your children will never come back. Why would they? They've probably built their own lives. But if we build a better nation, a better Pakistan, a country that your children can be proud of, maybe one day one of them may want to return. Wouldn't you like that?'

Shakaib stares back into Afridi's intense gaze. He doesn't know much about this man, and almost all of what he does know is overwhelmingly negative. Most of what he has seen tonight hasn't impressed him either. Most. But one thing has. His sincerity. Without breaking his gaze, Shakaib lifts his hand and presents it to Javed Afridi.

'Ok, Mr. Afridi. I'm with you.'

4.
THE
ANNOUNCEMENT

'**SHIT THIS IS** bad. Suicide car bomb attack in Kabul. At least twenty dead.'

Amanda Spano looks up from her notes at her intern. They keep getting younger every year. This one looks virtually pre-pubescent. But she's leggy and blonde, with a figure that looks like it was poured into her pants. Just the type that the ghouls at HR love to hire, so they can get their rocks off. The girl's lucky she joined after the scandals. A year ago, the bastards on the 10th floor would have been hunting her in packs with their dicks in their hands.

Amanda Spano has never lived up to the Wolfson News Network stereotype. She isn't blonde, for one thing. And she's not from a deep red state like Texas or South Carolina, where most of Wolfson's employees hail from. She rests her 130-pound, South Boston, Italian-American frame on a 5'1 body. She's proud of the fact that her parents were working class. She isn't part of the trust fund crowd that populates Wolfson News so densely, who like to wrap themselves in the flag and pontificate about 'Middle America' while inhaling $150 Wagyu ribeyes in the commissary. She went to public high schools, worked her way through Boston College and then crawled and clawed her way through the trench warfare that is the modern media industry, to get to where she is now: The number one show on the number one conservative channel in America. If you're a Republican, as Amanda has been since she was 14, it doesn't get any better than this. She's always been proud of her ability to succeed as an outlier, not just at Wolfson News, but also within the Republican establishment. After all, how much more atypical can you be in the Republican party, than an Italian-American woman from Boston?

She realises that she's been staring at the intern without saying anything. 'Sorry, what?'

'Suicide bombing in Kabul. Twenty dead, round the corner from ISAF headquarters. Just came on the tickers. Jeez, these pictures are horrific.'

'Any Americans?' She turns to look at her producer, Gary Patton, sitting across the small conference table. The Pattons have been Virginia born and bred, going back to at least the Civil War. Gary speaks with an exaggerated southern drawl, as if compensating for the fact that he's lived in the northeast for most of his life. What Amanda loves about him is that he too is an outlier at Wolfson. He's a hard core newsman who's spent the last thirty years dissecting what housewives in Peoria want to tune in to. It's almost irrelevant to him whether you're Republican or Democrat, or whether the story is joyful or tragic. All he cares about is what lens the American people will view it through. Old man Wolfson abhors him and would have thrown him out years ago, if he weren't the best at what he does.

The intern, still new to the business, seems to be internalising the ghastly pictures of children's body parts splayed across an Afghan bazaar. It takes her a moment to respond to Gary's question, a delay that elicits a typical 'come the fuck on!' response from him.

'Uh, yeah. Three marines. It says they were part of some joint checkpoint, along with Afghan security forces.'

'Fuck me. That's going to kick off a shitstorm. That's going to be the lead on all the networks tonight. The Republican debate's fucked for sure. We coulda' buried the story if it weren't for the American casualties.'

'Why would we bury it? There were kids killed. It's so horrible… it's a huge story.'

'Come on Twinkie, I know you're new, but are you also fucking stupid? Am I going to have to teach you TV 101? That story that you're getting so teary-eyed about, isn't kids killed in the big, bad bomb blast in some fucking Kabul market. It's three body bags arriving at Dover Air Force base. American bodies in those bags. At a time when America wants to forget this shitty war. This October will be the twentieth anniversary of the invasion. You know what that means? It means you were doing Twinkie shits in your Twinkie diapers when we first went into Afghanistan. Americans don't fight twenty-year wars. That's something the English and the French and the Swedes did. In the 15th fucking century. And you know who gets tagged with this? Us. The Republicans. We started the fucking war.'

'I don't think you can call her a Twinkie anymore, Gary. HR will come looking for you.'

'Oh come on, Amanda, six months ago those assholes would've been fist bumping me. Besides, she knows I'm not trying to fuck her, I'm trying to teach her.'

'Why do you say the Republican debate's fucked? I admit, the war started during a Republican administration, but King's owned it for the past eight years. Each of the Republican candidates will say the usual bullshit lines about ensuring that the lives of American boys weren't for nought.'

'Regular Republicans can get away with that Amanda. The empty suit governors and senators can duck the issue. Congressman Crazy from Texas will get off on this, because he's always opposed the war. Hell, he believes we shouldn't even have a fucking State Department. But the two main contenders are gonna get tagged. The General was the biggest proponent of expanding US forces in Afghanistan when he was the commander there. He was the one who sold everyone on 'Hearts and Minds', and 'Standing shoulder to shoulder with Afghan troops.' This is what happens when you stand shoulder to shoulder. Your boys die with their boys. It's his chickenshit plan that they're still followin' out there.'

'And the Reverend's the one who has always called the struggle against the Taliban a crusade.'

'Exactly. First question of the debate: How's that crusade goin' for ya? Saved any souls yet? 'Cuz you've lost 5,000.'

'They could flip flop on the issue.'

'Come the fuck on! You can do it on abortion, or gay marriage, but you can't say you now oppose a war which you were the head cheerleader for, on the day that three American boys have been blown to bits. The Democrats are going to hit us hard on this.'

'Which brings us back to our current topic: The Jessica May interview. In light of this attack, the stakes have gone up. We've got to prep even harder for this piece. We've got to be able to take her down hard. Gary, you think she'll come after the General on Afghanistan?'

'Naw, she's light on foreign policy and she knows it, so she sticks to conventional positions. She can't do what King did eight years ago. She also doesn't have King's balls. He came out against Iraq at a time no one else had, and he rode it. Daddy's little Jessica would never take such a risk. Not when she's been waitin' eight long years for a second shot. She isn't going to do anything to mess that up. I bet you, if you asked her what flavour ice cream she liked, she'd hedge and say 'Well, Amanda, there are strong arguments to be made in favour of both chocolate and vanilla'.'

'You don't like her.'

'What I like or dislike doesn't matter. For the record, I think she's a very capable Senator, and if she stuck around in the Senate like her granddaddy did, she'd become one of the all-time great senators. But she doesn't have guts. And the American people like guts. That's why they're never going to vote for her as President.'

'Well, looks like you're right about the debate.' Amanda holds up her phone. 'Leonard just pinged me. He wants to talk strategies about deflecting attention from the Afghanistan situation away from the party. He's called me upstairs right now.'

'Good luck. And don't forget to wear your hockey pads. Old man Wolfson is gonna be pissed as hell.'

* * *

Old man Wolfson's suite occupies the top floor of the Wolfson News building in Foggy Bottom, and from that perch, he commands a staggering view of the Potomac and the Virginia countryside across the river. In his typically disruptive, counterintuitive manner, Leonard Wolfson deliberately chose to headquarter his news outlet in Washington, away from the traditional media powerhouses in New York. He's never had any interest in becoming part of the old boy's cabal of owners, senior executives and marquee male anchors who enjoy their decadent lunches at Jean Georges, their opulent Upper East Side penthouses overlooking Central Park, and their weekend homes in the Hamptons. He has always found them crass nouveau riches trying to overreach themselves. Wolfson News is in Washington because Leonard Wolfson believes in proximity to power. Real power.

In the last decade, Leonard Wolfson has transformed an old Wall Street fortune into a right-wing media juggernaut, overtaking even Fox News as the preferred home of the Right. He's been an outlier all his life. He's never owned a gun, doesn't really care about abortion and can't remember the last time he went to church. He hates shmoozing with the movers and shakers of the modern Republican party. He detests their 'Aw shucks' folksiness, their fake camaraderie when they court him and their insistence on calling him Lenny or Len. He only ever answers to Leonard. There is no political compartment, no pre-set profile, that he fits into. Fifty years ago, he would have been called a Rockefeller Republican, except for the fact that Leonard Wolfson had a visceral hatred of Nelson Rockefeller. The only thing that fires him up is his passionate and genuine hatred for the progressive/liberal left, a reaction no doubt, of having grown up as the scion of a New York banking dynasty that was hopelessly progressive and aimlessly liberal. He has thus spent most of his life using his immense fortune to destroy his family's social legacy.

Amanda Spano has always had an awkward relationship with Leonard Wolfson. On the one hand, she headlines his number one show and is responsible for millions of dollars of advertising revenue coming in. She is also, in Leonard Wolfson's perception, ideologically sound. On the other hand, as a self-confessed misogynist dinosaur, he has never been comfortable with her activism, her refusal to back down or indeed her being a woman. Last year, when the news leaked about several key executives at Wolfson News who had been involved in the systematic harassment and abuse of junior level female employees, it was Amanda who championed the cause of the young woman who had been the whistleblower. Amanda advocated the issue hard, calling out Wolfson's own executives on her show, and demanding internal accountability. Her pushiness had irritated Leonard Wolfson. Not because there was any suggestion that he too may have been a sexual predator. Indeed, most people, including Amanda find it difficult to imagine Leonard Wolfson ever thinking about sex or, even more markedly, deigning to talk to a junior employee. His snobbishness and his puritanism both vouchsafed for him. Nevertheless, he had been reluctant to take action against the perpetrators because like most men he initially didn't believe that such tawdry things had happened at his channel, and when it became incontrovertibly clear that they had, like most channel owners, Leonard Wolfson chose to believe that the whole situation was an ambush, set up by his competitors, to make Wolfson News fail. Amanda had resorted to calling him an ostrich for his ability to bury his head in the sand. She never said it to his face, but to enough people around the organisation for it to get back to Leonard. He hadn't liked that. He hadn't confronted her (because he hated confrontation in real life as much as he enjoyed it on air). But he had noticeably cooled towards her, especially after he was forced to fire his predatory executives.

In the year since the scandal, his previously regular meetings with her have been curtailed and although nothing is ever said overtly, Amanda keeps getting the distinct impression that she is on thin ice with him. She keeps getting forwarded emails from him via the president of the news division, in which every segment on each of her show is dissected and reviewed for its impact on the core viewing demographics. She's heard that Wolfson has an extensive and constant focus group program, that feeds him reactions to his shows in real time. The rumours are that the focus groups report in directly to him and based on their preferences, Leonard Wolfson instructs his executives accordingly. It's his way of staying in direct contact with 'real America', something he has never actually been a part of.

The elevators open onto a small, unexceptional lobby on the fifth floor, and Wolfson's executive assistant, an unsmiling, white haired woman who reminds Amanda of her high school librarian, receives her and leads her to the inner chamber that is Leonard Wolfson's office. In spite of the panoramic views, the shades are drawn down on the floor to ceiling windows. A bank of TV screens glows on the opposite wall, displaying not only Wolfson News' current broadcast but all the other networks as well as camera feeds from focus groups around the country. The audience in the groups can be seen, watching content from the channel and instantly responding to it.

'Amanda, how nice to see you again.' Wolfson says it without a trace of warmth, sitting behind his antique mahogany desk, dressed in an out of fashion double-breasted suit and a bright red bowtie.

'Leonard. A pleasure as always.'

'Please, it's Mr. Wolfson.'

Amanda bristles at his putdown, but masks her irritation behind a 400-watt smile. 'I hear you're going to interview Senator May.'

'Yes, I am. We're setting up for tomorrow. I was just discussing it with my team.'

'You've seen this Afghanistan thing.'

'If you're referring to the deaths of three servicemen in the high security red zone, yes I have. It's very tragic.'

'It's going to be a disaster for the party. Twenty years of this war, five hundred billion dollars, and suicide bombers are still going off like firecrackers in the heart of the capital. Something must be done to stop this. That's why this Jessica May interview is critical now. You've got to really give it to her, really put her in a jam.'

'Well, you know I prep hard for all of my interviews. You can rest assured that Senator May isn't going to get a free pass.'

'You don't understand. She's the Democratic frontrunner, we've got to find some dirt on her. You need to do more than just give her a bloody nose, you need to cause her some permanent damage. She's been in plenty of messy situations, hasn't she? She just looks corrupt.'

'Well, I'm not sure how you can look corrupt. Generally, Jessica May has had a pretty decent record in the Senate. We know she was also an enthusiastic supporter of the war, unlike the President, who opposed it from the beginning. So she's not exactly bold in her political choices. She tends to follow the herd. But she did of course take that principled stand when she resigned as Education Secretary over President Baird's sexual indiscretions.'

'Well, was it really a principled stand? I mean, everyone knew Andy Baird had a problem keeping it in his pants. I'm sure she knew. There were some rumours that she may have been complicit. I know some people who say it was that husband of hers who used to get women for Baird. They say that's why Baird made her Education Secretary.'

'OK … is there any proof of any of these wild rumours? Or have we just decided to become another BreitBart? I know we're right-wing media, but we are still a news organisation, right?'

'I hear she's got a girl. Some intern or aide, supposed to be her confidant. I hear she runs everything by her.'

'Yeah. Her name's Shaiza Naqvi. She's the gatekeeper. Smart kid, but a real pain in the ass. She insisted on negotiating everything about the interview, from lighting to camera angles.'

'Really? Interesting. And apparently, she's a Muslim. Why would a US senator have a Muslim aide? And one so powerful? I think this girl's background needs to be investigated. We need to find out whose agenda she's really pushing.'

'Would we be having this conversation if she were a blonde, blue-eyed Finn called Maria?'

'Need I remind you, Amanda, that it wasn't the Finns who crashed those planes into the Twin Towers.'

'That was twenty years ago. You can't demonise every Muslim out there...' As she speaks, her phone starts buzzing incessantly. Leonard Wolfson, who has been speaking to her while absently staring at his bank of TV screens, also seems distracted all of a sudden. 'Sorry, that's Gary. Something about Ron Diamond announcing for president?'

All the networks cut their regular programming to go to Diamond's press conference at his Manhattan headquarters. No one had planned to cover it live, but Ron Diamond knows how to put on a show, so within five minutes of his starting to speak, he is being beamed live into the homes of a 100 million Americans.

Amanda frantically scrolls down her message feed, a feeling of incredulity spreading through her with each read message. 'Ron Diamond says he's going to run for president as a Republican? Time to take America back... Lincoln King has made the country weak at home and abroad... allowed psychotic foreigners to rape and pillage our women and our society... they should all be locked up... America for real Americans only... lock up all the Muslims... what?!'

Her startled cry doesn't elicit any reaction from Leonard Wolfson, who is engrossed in a phone conversation while reviewing the live reactions of his focus groups to the Diamond speech. On one of the screens, from somewhere out in the midwest, a man in a baseball cap gets up from his chair and raises his fist to the screen, loudly shouting 'Hell yeah!' His spontaneous cry creates a chain reaction, with several other participants of that focus group getting up and breaking out into loud applause.

'Leonard... Mr. Wolfson... who are these people?'

Wolfson concludes his phone call with an amused look. 'I like to livestream our focus groups. There's a lot to learn from monitoring the spontaneous reactions of these people, as you can see.'

Amanda looks up at the bank of monitors, at least eight of which are now relaying live feeds from focus groups. 'How many of these are you running?'

'At any given time, we're recording in eight to ten different cities. It depends on the show or news item as well. I find the pure ratings figures to be a bit dry. Fine for advertising, but I like to get a feel of what real Americans like and dislike. That's the barometer of a successful broadcast. You'll be surprised at how many people love the idea of being paid $50 to watch TV for an hour.' Wolfson looks especially pleased with himself, like a proud scientist who has just figured out how to get a guinea pig to run a maze in a lab.

'Diamond's crazy. It's got to be a publicity stunt, right? I mean I didn't even know he was a Republican. Maybe he's trying to boost his ratings for the next season of Reality Losers.'

'King seemed to think he was important enough to make fun of.'

'The President made him the butt of one joke, at the Correspondent's dinner. From that, Diamond infers that he's a contender??'

'Well, whatever it is, he's got the attention of real America. Look at their reactions. This is politics as theatre. We need to give him blanket coverage. Stunt or not, we are going to give Ron Diamond a fighting shot at the title.'

'What? Why? He's clearly nuts.'

'It's going to boost our ratings with our base if his message is sincere. If, on the other hand, he is nuts, as you say, it's still great television. Ron Diamond will flame out in a couple of months, but we get to shape the ideological debate in the Republican party. And best of all, it gets us past this whole Afghanistan problem. Nobody's going to be interested in the Kabul bombing after that announcement, I can tell you that.'

'And what if he doesn't?'

'Doesn't what?'

'Flame out. What if the base thinks he's the real deal?'

'Don't be ridiculous Amanda. Ron Diamond is a flash in the pan. A useful distraction. But the conservative, church-going, bible-thumping, homosexual-hating Republican base is never going to fall in love with a *pornographer.*'

5.

THE

FAMILY

I KNOW MY background isn't like a regular politician's. I didn't go to a fancy prep school, I didn't go to Harvard or Yale (pronounce it Hahvad, just to sound sarcastically snooty like a Boston Brahmin). I haven't spent years in Congress padding my own nest. I had a risque career. I took risks with my life, in order to make it better for me and my children. I could have easily failed, I had no safety net. But I didn't. I worked my ass off and I succeeded. And I promise you, I will bring the same risk taking approach that has served me so well in my personal life, and I will try and make the lives of all the American people better. Together, we'll make America fantastic. (Wait for applause).

For the umpteenth time, I re-read the words I had written for Mr. Diamond. I had been reciting his announcement speech out loud to myself, again and again, as if I was learning it by rote for some bizarre elocution contest. I was so immersed in my recitation that I missed the first couple of knocks on the door. The third, significantly louder knock, shook me out of my reverie, and I opened the door of my new apartment to find Harvey Calzone at my doorstep.

'What the hell's wrong with you kid? You on drugs or something? If you are, I'll personally kick your ass right back on the street.'

'No. No sir, Mr. Calzone, I'm clean. I was just, uh, lost in my thoughts for a moment. Sorry sir, won't happen again.'

'It better not. Ron doesn't like space cadets. If you're going to be his PA, you've got to be sharp as shit.'

'Yes, sir.'

Harvey's face morphed into a half leery sneer, a look I would later learn was his expression of glee, and looked around the living room of my new apartment. It was small, even by New York standards. I suspect in the original building plans it may have been a janitor's closet, before Ron Diamond decided to squeeze an extra ounce of revenue from it by converting it into a Lilliputian studio. But when you had a view like mine, glimpsing at the edge of Central Park from the 50th floor of Ron's Erection, having to wash the dishes while sitting on the pot was a small price to pay.

The cramped space in the apartment had been further cramped by the fact that I hadn't yet finished unpacking. The detritus of my life in America for the past four and a half years was spread all over the place; a poster advertising the first comedy improv workshop I ever participated in; a super value pack of 100 condoms that I had, somewhat ambitiously, bought from a Walmart in Des Moines in my freshman year; coffee mugs from the various temp jobs I had been doing the last six months.

Harvey took in everything, probably trying to work out exactly how pathetic I was. But he didn't comment on anything. Instead, he absentmindedly picked up one of my CNN mugs. 'So you like the view, eh?'

It wasn't said as a question, more as a definitive instruction.

'Yes, sir. Thank you for letting me use this apartment.'

'I got nothin' to do with it. You can sleep in the Park, for all I care. But since you're gonna be Mr. Diamond's PA, he's got to be able to have access to you at all times. It was his idea to park you here. You need to thank him, not me. You're gonna get the opportunity tonight.

The Family's goin' out for dinner. Since you're his Guy, you're gonna tag along. Be at the penthouse at 6pm sharp. And wear some decent clothes for God's sake. You dress like a fuckin' hobo.' He lifted a couple of random shirts out of one of my boxes. Unfortunately for me, it was my outfit from when I used to work at the Donut King in

Ames, not necessarily a fair indicator of my sartorial sense.

'Yes, sir. I've got some dress shirts and a …'

'Mr. Diamond is very particular about his employees being smartly dressed. He doesn't like guys who dress like bums. Call the store downstairs in the lobby and get some proper clothes. Make sure the shirts and ties are from Mr. Diamond's collection. It pisses him off when his employees don't wear his brand.' He picked up another one of my shirts and suddenly grew animated. 'And whatever you do, never fucking wear Ralph Lauren in his presence. Got that?'

Harvey said this with a degree of violence in his voice that I would never have believed could be triggered by a Polo shirt. 'Uh, yes sir. What's wrong with Ralph Lauren sir?'

'He's a fucking prick.'

'I don't know him personally sir. I just bought one of his shirts. Once. At an outlet mall. It was seventy percent off.' I don't know why I felt the need to give Harvey this information, but I felt that my revealing that I had not paid sticker price for the shirt would somehow mitigate the fact that I owned it.

'Mr. Diamond absolutely hates that asshole. He had a condo in the building, once upon a time. His clothes used to sell more than Mr. Diamond's line in the store downstairs. Pissed off the Boss. He booted Ralph out of the building and forbade the store from selling any of his clothes. Lauren called Ron a jumped up jack off merchant in the tabloid press. So Ron had the store burn all of its remaining Ralph Lauren stock. Soon after, Ralphie boy started having some union troubles. Who's the jack off merchant now, eh?'

Harvey emitted a sound, which I later identified as his signature laugh, that was a mix between a Hyena screeching and a patient wheezing on a ventilator, which seemed to indicate that he had something to do with Ralph Lauren's union troubles.

'Uh, got it, sir. No Ralph Lauren in the future. I'll, uh, get rid of this one too.'

'When you go to the store, tell 'em who you are. They'll give you a discount. And show me your nails.'

'Sir?'

'Your nails. Mr. Diamond is also very particular about personal hygiene. Nails should be cut, hands should always be clean. Also, wear cologne when you're around Mr. Diamond. He can't stand even a whiff of BO. Ideally, get one of Krystal's signature scents, but you can get something cheaper too. I'm an Old Spice man myself.'

'Yes, sir.' As the man bizarrely examined my nails, an exercise I had not partaken in since the seventh grade, I couldn't resist broaching the question that had been bothering me since Mr. Diamond's announcement. 'Mr. Calzone, can I ask you something?'

Harvey turned his head to look at me with utter disgust. He wasn't much of a question answering type of guy. Another thing I learned later. He didn't say anything but his scowl relented just enough for me to dare to venture further.

'I wrote Mr. Diamond's announcement speech. He asked me to do it. I showed it to you, I showed it to him, both of you seemed to think it was balanced and decent. I thought he would use it. But he didn't. He went and said things that were never in my draft. All this stuff about locking up Muslims and culture wars. Why did he do that? Does he actually believe in all that?'

Harvey's leery sneer returned. 'How do you think it played out?'

'I mean, it got a lot of coverage, but incendiary comments like that always get coverage. He doesn't really believe in all that, does he? And if he does, what am I doing here? I mean, I'm an immigrant, and a Muslim to boot. It doesn't make sense.'

'Incendiary. That's your problem right there, kid. Using a five dollar word when you can say something in a much simpler way. Ron's lit a fire under everybody's ass. That's what he does. That's what this whole campaign is about. You got a problem with that, take it up with him. You're meetin' him for dinner. Ask him yourself.'

Harvey put down the CNN mug and turned to leave. Halfway out the door, he turned to me again. 'Oh and one more thing. The kids are gonna be there at dinner tonight. You may have guessed during your interviews that you ain't exactly a favourite of Han or Luke's.

And that situation hasn't gotten any better with you bein' appointed Mr. Diamond's PA, and given an apartment in the building. The boys hate you anyway and Krystal, well, she's always a hard one to read. They don't like outsiders encroaching on their turf. So watch your back.'

'But Mr. Calzone, I haven't encroached on anyone's turf, sir. I'm just an employee.'

'You're in the big game now kid. Ron didn't breed humans, he bred Rottweilers.'

* * *

Dinner was at Smith & Wollensky on the Upper East Side. I missed the departure from the Penthouse because I had to rush across Midtown to buy a Diamond Collection shirt and tie from Macy's. Apparently, sales for the formal collection were so poor that the in-house store had stopped stocking it. All they had was the Ron Diamond Hawaiian Tropic collection. I was informed by the sales assistant that the one with bananas that looked like penises was a particular best seller. I didn't think it would be appropriate for the dinner.

I debated over what would be considered the greater sin, being late for the departure or turning up on time wearing my Ralph Lauren shirt. I opted for being late. My lucky day, as Sonya decided this was the perfect time to harangue me about working for a 'pig' like Ron Diamond, and to announce that she was breaking up with me as I cabbed it to Macy's. That wasn't the bit I minded. What was a pain in the ass was, having had her hang up on me, gotten out of the cab and run an obstacle course through the store to select a shirt and tie in record time, the return call I got from Sonya as I tried to do the impossible of hailing a cab in rush hour. She was even more pissed that I hadn't disputed our break up, and worse, hadn't bothered to call her back after she hung up on me. She said, with great contempt, that I had the social graces of a South Bronx Puerto Rican, which, I took it, was just perhaps a half step above human excrement in her anthropological rankings.

There wasn't time to go back to the building, so I told the cabbie to take me straight to Smith & Wollensky. Meanwhile, I attempted new feats of acrobatics by trying to change into my new shirt and tie while staying on the line with Sonya, and giving directions to my fresh off the boat Ghanaian driver, all at the same time. For some unfathomable reason, despite all my transgressions that she had listed in such detail in the last half hour, Sonya still wanted us to stay together. As she said, almost pleadingly, if only I would apologise and see the error of my ways, and above all, quit my job, she would welcome me with open arms back to her apartment. I couldn't take the melodrama anymore, so I decided to end it once and for all, by saying the one thing that I knew there was no coming back from. Just as my cabbie pulled up in front of the restaurant, I told her she sounded just like a nouveau, jumped up Spic from Bushwick. And then I hung up on her for good.

I was late. The Diamond party had already been seated in a private dining room on the first floor of the restaurant and as I walked in, the bread basket had already been served. Two things saved me: my attire, particularly the Diamond Collection labels on my shirt and tie, which Ron looked at approvingly; and the fact that his younger son Luke turned up five seconds after me in a very obvious state of dishevelled inebriation.

Taking advantage of the deathly stare Ron gave to Luke, I mumbled my apology and found an empty seat next to Mrs. Diamond, or Erika, as she was known to everybody in the Diamond world. Erika was Ron's third wife, roughly six months younger than his daughter, a fact that I was later to learn grated on Krystal endlessly. She was a foreigner, German in fact, and had been a VJ on MTV Europe before Ron's roving eye fell upon her. Like Krystal, Erika too looked as if she had just walked off a fashion ramp. In fact, at closer observation Erika looked uncannily like a brunette version of Krystal, the same pouting ruby red lips and severely arched eyebrows, the same statuesque height and perfect, sculpted aquiline nose. I wondered if I was the first person to spot this weird resemblance, and if not, did anyone else find it creepy?

The table was set for eight people. At the head was of course Ron himself, with Erika opposite him and Krystal at his side. I couldn't take my eyes off her. I mean, Erika may have been hot, but Krystal was a goddess at another level, wearing a little black dress that showed off her toned, tanned legs to the maximum. I couldn't help but notice that the stranger sitting across from her, the only non-family member apart from me, couldn't take his eyes off those legs either. Then there was Han, rakishly handsome and looking like a walking, talking Abercrombie & Fitch commercial, and his girlfriend Abby, who was a weathergirl on a local channel. Poor girl never had a chance. Abby was, well, I guess you could say an attractive girl from some angles, but sandwiched between Krystal and Erika, she always came across looking frumpy, no matter how hard she tried. She would often attempt to make up for it by being the most vocal person on the table, expressing an opinion on everything under the sun, not realising that this pissed off Ron, who felt that he was the only one with the right to express an opinion on anything and everything.

I was surprised to see that Harvey wasn't there. I had expected that if I was invited, he would definitely be there. Instead, when he finally lifted his gaze from Krystal's legs, I recognised the stranger as an anchor from the Wolfson Network, whose face used to be plastered on one of the dartboards at the Fox News offices, right next to Wolf Blitzer's. The folks at Fox used to point to the dartboard as a sign of their impartiality. They hated Wolfson as much as they hated CNN. The anchor (I think his name was Phil something) had been placed on Ron's right, across the table from Krystal. It gave him the best view of her legs, and he seemed to have given up all pretence of pretending not to ogle her. She had obviously noticed, but totally ignored it. In fact, she seemed to have put on a full court charm offensive for him. She was oblivious to anyone else on the table and laughed coquettishly at every utterance that came from his lips. She certainly didn't bother to look in my direction.

This was unfortunate, because it meant that I got stuck sitting opposite the last, and saddest entrant in the room. Luke Diamond looked like a mess. Unlike his brother, he couldn't pull off the studied casual look. His turnout was more garbage dumpster chic. His shirt hung out from his trousers, his tie hung loosely from his neck and he smelled as if he had taken a bath in a tub of Smirnoff. Having been chastised by his father's icy stare, Luke sat down across from me and leered at me quizzically, a schoolboy contemplating new methods of inflicting torture on a lab rat.

'New experience for you isn't it?' The leery grin grew wider as the waiters handed out the menus.

'Yeah, I haven't been here before. Heard a lot about it, though. Everybody says Smith & Wollensky is a New York institution.'

'No, I mean eating with a fork and knife.' Luke rattled his fork and knife in his hands like a child who's been made to sit at the adults' table for the first time. I could actually smell the booze on him from across the table.

'Luke put those down. Dad, why couldn't we go to Daniel? The new menu is supposed to be amazing. The foie gras is to die for. We've been coming here since we were like, five years old. Can't we try something new for a change? This place is so 1980's. And it's hardly haute cuisine.' I didn't fail to notice that Krystal had intervened in a potentially ugly situation and diverted the conversation without missing a heartbeat.

'Haute cuisine is just a fancy word for overpriced, pansy food. Besides, why would I go to a French restaurant for a steak? You want a steak, you go to a steakhouse. Am I right, Phil? Besides, the chef at Daniel is a real prick. Listen to this, Phil. A few years ago, I gave him the opportunity of a lifetime, back when he was startin' up. I used to own a bunch of strip clubs in the city. Sorry, 'exotic gentlemen's clubs'. That's what they call them nowadays. Anyway, they were real classy joints, beautiful girls, *beeyootiful*. All models. And an upscale clientele, lotsa' investment bankers and lawyers. So I got this idea of opening a top-class restaurant inside the club. You come in, you have a good time seeing the girls, get a lapdance or two, and then you can eat a five-star meal at the same time. No Nachos and wings. Proper food, steaks, lobster, starched linen, a real fine dining experience. Genius, right? So I approached this guy, the guy who's the chef at Daniel now. Back then, he was a fucking nobody. I bring him to the club, get one of the girls to give him a free lap dance, and while she's shaking her ass on his crotch, I take out a cheque for fifty thousand, and slide it across to him. I tell him, I think you're a very talented guy, and I want you to cook over here. I want you to try and make this the first Michelin star strip club. I tell him, if you cash the cheque, I'll know I have a partner. And then I walk away, leaving him to enjoy the free fucking lap dance that I arranged for him. And what does the prick do? Sends me back my cheque in the mail the next day, with a note saying he doesn't think it's appropriate to combine the sex industry with the fine dining industry. Prick didn't even tip the dancer. Can you believe the kinds of jerks there are out there, Phil?'

Phil nodded silently, his mouth filled with a bread roll, his eyes bulging in a way that suggested that not only could he not believe that there were people who didn't tip exotic dancers after receiving lap dances, but he could barely believe what a man like Ron Diamond was doing in the Republican party.

'Well, you can't blame him can you Dad? The guy ended up as the chef at New York's best restaurant, and the Michelin star strip club idea never really took off. I mean how much money did you dump into that project?'

Luke's ill-timed intervention drew him withering looks from both Han and Krystal. Erika stared down at her menu with such an intensity that you would have thought she was reading the gospels. But nothing compared to the dead, reptilian stare that Ron Diamond gave his son. I can honestly say that I have never seen any father give such a look to a child.

'I still made a profit when I sold that place. Which is more than I can say for the money I dumped into your education.' The line was said without a hint of emotion. It seemed to frighten the living daylights out of Luke, who mumbled his order to the waiter who had appeared at his side.

'Don't bother to bring that to the table. Make a doggy bag. My son won't be staying for dinner. Iowa State, take Luke down and get him a cab. Make sure he gets home without getting into any further trouble.' The words were said with an unquestioned finality.

As I rose from my seat, Luke looked as if he had been slapped. After an awkward moment, he downed the glass of scotch that had just been placed in front of him, and walked unsteadily towards the exit. I followed him out onto the street, unsure of what to do next. Since Ron had told me to get him a cab, I raised my hand to hail one.

'Hey asshole, I don't need a fucking camel jockey to get me a cab. I'm Luke Diamond. All these cars, and all these goons driving them, belong to me.' He pointed to the fleet of SUVs in which the party had arrived.

'Hey man, sorry, I'm just trying to help.'

'Fuck you. Just because you're dad's new little bitch, doesn't mean you can tell me to do anything. I can get you fired and deported back to that shithole you call home in the blink of an eye, you fucking sand nigger!'

'Hey, fuck you.' My response seemed to shock not only Luke, but all of Ron's security guys who had started crowding around us. Most of all, I surprised myself. I still don't know why I reacted so strongly to being called a sand nigger. I mean, for someone who went to college in Iowa, it was hardly my first introduction to being racially abused. Nor am I a hot-headed person. But something about the way he said it, his tone of entitlement, that sneer that was permanently fixed on his face, riled me up.

It was unfortunate then, that just as I regained my composure, Luke, who had been stunned into silence by my response, lost his. He saw the smirks on the faces of the security guys, who were thoroughly enjoying this. He saw the physical difference between us, my six foot one inch frame towering above his scrawny, five four. And so he decided, in that instant, as a true disciple of Ho Chi Minh and Osama Bin Laden, to use asymmetric warfare against me. He grabbed the doggy bag that had just been handed to one of the security guys by the waiter, and flung a three-course meal at me. Like any good insurgent, he then made his getaway by immediately jumping into one of the SUVs and shouting at the driver to drive away, leaving me standing on the kerb, covered in a buffet of fat dripping lamb chops, mashed potatoes, creamed spinach, shrimp cocktail and some sort of pudding (its viscosity and colour indicated it was sticky toffee).

I was humiliated. There was no way to sugarcoat it. Not when you're standing on the sidewalk in midtown covered in sticky toffee pudding and fast congealing lamb fat. There was no way I could walk back into the restaurant. Not like this. But how could I get back to the Tower? No cabbie would take me in my condition. The security guys, while sympathetic to my plight, weren't going to allow me anywhere close to their pristine SUVs. Finally, a couple of them took pity on me and hailed down a cab, giving the driver an extra twenty to take me in my current state. I made the walk of shame through the lobby of the Tower, up to my apartment. As I stripped and stepped into the shower, I started to cry. I know I wasn't supposed to, according to some Cro-Magnon code of manly conduct. I should have been tougher than that. But the stark reality of the situation hit me. I was going to lose everything, just when I had got a toehold in the door. Obviously, the snotty little son of a bitch was going to get me fired. I cursed his name out loud. I'd be out on the street again, this time without even the option of going back to my ex-girlfriend. I cursed my own hubris for having called Sonia a Bushwick Spic, and for having bought the ridiculously expensive Diamond Collection shirt and tie, which now lay on the floor, ruined forever.

When I finally stopped weeping, I sat down on the one chair in the room, catatonically staring out of the window at the view that had so enthralled me when I first got here three days ago. At length, I started to hear a buzzing, and then a light knocking on my door. I could see my phone light up from within the wrecked pair of pants that lay abandoned on my bathroom/kitchen floor. I opened the door to find one of the security guys, asking me to come up to the penthouse. This was it. The last walk of a condemned man.

The penthouse was eerily quiet as I entered. The security man led me through a darkened corridor into a kitchen area, where Ron Diamond sat alone at a small breakfast table, his hair tousled, wearing nothing but a monogrammed dressing gown and eating from a KFC bargain bucket.

'You manage to get the shit out of your hair?' he pointed a chicken leg towards a chair. I sat down and nodded. He pushed the KFC bucket towards me.

'Mr. Diamond, am I fired? I'd rather you told me straight up so I can start packing my things, sir. I can't take the uncertainty anymore.'

He nudged the bucket further towards me. 'I don't imagine you got anything to eat tonight. The first thing I learned when I started working as an actor, when somebody offers you free food, take it because you never know where your next meal is comin' from.'

It was true. My stomach rumbled audibly at the sight and smell of the fried chicken. Hesitantly, I picked up a breast piece from the bucket. Ron picked up another leg for himself and dug into it with relish, ignoring my presence. When he had demolished it, he lunged for the fridge without really getting up and took out a couple of cans of Cherry Coke, tossing one to me. I have always hated Cherry Coke, it's always tasted like cough syrup to me, but I didn't think this was an appropriate moment to lodge an objection. I sipped it and winced, as if I had just ingested a particularly bitter cocktail.

'How did Krystal do? She was lookin' hot, wasn't she?'

'Sir?' I was a bit taken aback by the bizarre turn this conversation had taken.

'I wanted that cocksucker Phil to be drooling all over her. I wanted her to captivate him. I gave her specific instructions to do just that. I need Wolfson to be in my corner for this campaign. So, you think she succeeded?'

'Uh, sir, I…guess. He seemed to be staring at her throughout. Although I wasn't there very long.'

'No, you weren't. Because my idiot second son decided to show up drunk and threw a tantrum. And I asked you to handle it for me.'

'I'm sorry I messed up sir.'

'It's ok. Your first rodeo. You'll have to get better at it, though, if you want to stick around here.'

'Sir?'

'Still, you showed huge balls to tell Luke to fuck off. I like a man with big balls. Too bad he made you wear his dinner.' Ron chuckled at his little joke.

'So…you're not gonna fire me?'

'I don't know. I haven't decided. You're bright, but you haven't shown much game so far. I'm not gonna fire you today over Luke's behaviour, if that's what you're worried about. My son is a pretentious, entitled asshole. He thinks throwing a two-hundred dollar meal at someone makes him a man, somehow.' Ron sighed. 'Sometimes I look at him and honestly wonder if that's my sperm standing in front of me.'

'Thank you, sir.'

'That speech you wrote for me was dog shit, Iowa State. Harvey told me you were askin' why I didn't use it. That's the reason.'

'Sir, it was a balanced, reasoned introduction. There's so much negative stuff about you out there on social media, I wanted to write something that would give you gravitas.'

'Gravitas is dog shit. This nomination is going to be a down and dirty knife fight. Goin' with your speech would have been like entering this fight armed with a dildo made of cotton candy.'

'But sir, the stuff you said, that…that was dynamite. That was dangerous stuff. That's playing with fire.'

Ron downed his Cherry Coke and burped loudly. Then he took a TV remote and clicked on a small TV that was mounted on one side of the kitchen. As he flipped randomly through local and national channels, it was clear there was one common factor in all of them. All had wall-to-wall coverage of Ron Diamond, even a week after his announcement.

'Looks like I'm doin' alright, playin' with fire. The only candidate they're talkin' about, is me. Jessica May, the darling of the Democrats, made her announcement three days after me, and got about five minutes on CNN. The General is tellin' the Wolfson guys that if they don't put some coverage of him out there, Republican voters are going to forget what he looks like if this keeps up. The Reverend is traipsing through the Bible belt, goin' to three churches every Sunday, trying to fire up the base. It doesn't matter. I've got TV locked on me. And I'm just getting started.'

'But, are these…I mean…are these your actual views? Do you actually feel that way about Muslims?'

'You may be a smart guy, Iowa State, and those Poli Sci courses may have taught you all about who Kennedy was fucking and who Nixon was spying on, but you don't understand TV. TV is America's modern God. This country processes everything through the lens of their TV screens. Politics? Politics is a reality TV show. And I know reality TV. The only way somebody like me, an ex-porn star with two ex-wives, can get a seat at the table, is if I throw some elbows. Its working, isn't it? You were the one who said, I needed to get them to take me seriously. Well, they're doing that now, aren't they?'

I stared at the KFC bucket for a long moment. Then I finally grabbed another piece of chicken. 'Can I ask you a personal question, Mr Diamond?'

'Sure.'

'Why did you name your kids Luke and Han? It's ruined Star Wars for me forever.'

Ron burst out laughing. 'It seemed like a good idea at the time, when I was coked up and ass fucking their mother, back in 1978.'

'Why didn't you name Krystal Leia then?'

'She came later. In the late eighties. By that time, her mother was crazy over *Dynasty*. I think she was trying to convince Aaron Spelling to give her a role on the show. Dumb bitch actually thought she had a chance.'

'She was an actress?'

'That's what she called herself. She was an adult performer. She wanted to cover up her past, especially after the kids were born. She was desperate to become mainstream. But back then, mainstream America was never going to give a porn star the time of day. No, they only respect you when you start shitting money. That, and crazy ambition. America loves naked ambition. The more naked, the more outrageous, the better. That's why my campaign is gonna succeed. Because Americans see themselves in me. They can't relate to any of the other cocksuckers. Jessica May? She's probably never even wiped her own ass. Daddy got her a maid to do that. The General? He's so fucking plastic he might as well be a credit card. Lived all his life on army bases overseas. What the fuck does he know about the lives of real Americans? That fucking preacher? Normal folks, even god-fearing ones, can't ever possibly live up to his bullshit holier-than-thou ideals. Me on the other hand, I'm one of them. I came from them. Working class Polack from Chicago, pulled himself up by his own bootstraps and made a fortune, exactly what every American dreams about, unless you're a fucking socialist like Lincoln King. Nobody gives a fuck if I fucked pussy on screen to make my money. All that matters is that I made it. And now I have the ambition to run for President. America sees their hopes and dreams in me. You better up your game, Iowa State, because I'm gonna win.'

And there, sitting in that small kitchen, eating from a KFC bargain bucket, dressed in his bathrobe, for the first time I saw the political genius of Ron Diamond.

6.

SEX, DRUGS, ROCK 'N' ROLL
(AND A LITTLE BIT OF POLITICS)

ISLAMABAD'S NEW AIRPORT is unfamiliar to Shakaib. He was originally supposed to land in Karachi, but Hamza's panicked call last night forced him to change his itinerary from Doha. Shakaib isn't happy about it because he knows that he will personally have to pay the charges for last minute booking changes. He may have a fancy title proclaiming him to be the head of international finance for Javed Afridi's party, but he, above all, knows that doesn't mean a thing. There is no party structure, no accountants, no system of expense receipts. It's just him alone and the suitcase full of donor cheques that he has brought back with him from his travels.

The thought makes him smile, in spite of his irritation. The structure, the accountants, the expense receipts, will all come. In no small part thanks to his suitcase. For the past month, he has travelled around the world, looking to drum up enthusiasm for Javed Afridi among the Pakistani diaspora. He has not been disappointed. He has spent the past month sharing greasy chicken biryani with hardy, Pashtun labourers constructing the next Tom Wright masterpiece in Dubai, who will be forgotten just as soon as they put in place the last girder. He has spent evenings with London investment bankers and Hedge funders who have drained $1000 bottles of Mouton Rothschild-like tap water and pontificated on government corruption in the country, while in the same breath, asking if he had a connection with the current finance minister to push through some lucrative deal. He's attended gala dinners with uber wealthy doctors in Houston who spend more time involving themselves in local and international politics than they ever spend in their practices. Wherever he has gone, he has found a messianic devotion for Javed Afridi.

Pakistan's diaspora has always been famously divided in their political choices. When Shakaib lived in Saudi, the old joke was that you put 30 Pakistanis in a room and 15 of them would each form their own political party, and the other 15 would sell their support to the highest bidder. These divisions have seldom been ideological. Sometimes they have been based on a caste and biradari system that supposedly died out centuries ago but has unofficially continued to flourish not only in the cantons of Toba Tek Singh and Chakwal but also in the council estates of Glasgow and the suburbs of Sugarland even today. At other times these divisions have been exacerbated by a simpler desire to pull down their fellow compatriots. But more than anything, these political divisions have always been driven by self interest. Overseas Pakistanis, perhaps more than any other diaspora, have been strong adherents to the Jerry Maguire school of political thought. They demand that their political leaders show them the money, and they dump them as quickly as a footballer changes agents if those politicians fail in this endeavour.

But Javed Afridi, as Shakaib has learned, is viewed differently. His aura seems to transcend politics. Shakaib doesn't know why that is. Whether it's a hero worship driven by his footballing exploits in England and Spain in the 80's and 90's, which allowed Brummie factory workers and Barcelona taxi drivers to hold their heads high in societies that still viewed immigrants with a jaundiced eye, or whether it was the salacious stories of his sexual exploits with an impressive number of (overwhelmingly Caucasian) beauties that fuelled innumerable desi male fantasies of fucking white women, or indeed, something as simple as his good looks, that draw admiring gazes not only from a bevy of middle class matrons in Milan and Maryland, but also a number of strapping Pashtun youths in Doha and Dubai.

Whatever the reason, Javed Afridi has an almost mystical grip on these people. They see him as a saviour. A messiah in a starched shalwar kameez and Nike trainers. Shakaib has seen the evidence of this a dozen or more times on his travels. There were the construction workers in Dammam who, upon learning who he represented, conducted an impromptu whip around and presented him a colourful, neatly wrapped headcloth, borrowed from one of their own, brimming with five and ten Riyal notes; the owner of Bradford's most popular curry house, who opened his cash register and gave him a whole day's take as easily as if he were giving sweets to a child; and the New York City society hostess who swooned at Afridi's name and took a Warhol off her wall and handed it to him as a donation. When he began the trip, he had hoped, at best, to perhaps raise a hundred thousand dollars, with commitments and promises of perhaps another two hundred and fifty. He has returned with almost five million. And the Warhol.

As he exits the jetway, he is received by two men who by their deportment, appear to be some kind of government functionaries. At first, Shakaib is alarmed. He thinks they are there to relieve him of the cheques he is carrying in his suitcase, but one of them whispers in his ear that they have been sent by Hamza. They whisk him through passport control and past the luggage carousels in record time. In a lifetime of passing through airports, Shakaib has never gotten out so quickly. Even the baggage handlers seem to sense his importance, as his suitcase is the first one out.

Outside, he is taken to an ostentatiously large and shiny Toyota Landcruiser with blacked-out windows parked alone, right opposite the arrivals gate, in an area which is otherwise restricted for parking.

'Shakaib bhai, thank God you are here. But what took you so long?' Inside the SUV, Hamza greets him with a worried expression. On the front passenger seat sits the Haircut (whose name, Shakaib has subsequently learnt, is Taimur), wearing an equally worried expression.

'Hamza, I literally landed seven minutes ago. And can you people try and be a little less obvious? Why don't we just put a banner on the side of the car, saying 'Property of the Deep State?' Subtlety eludes you fellows, doesn't it?'

'Arre Shakaib bhai, subtlety can go lie in a ditch. We have a serious problem. Javed Afridi isn't coming down from the container.'

'I'm sorry, is this a metaphor for something? What do you mean?'

'You know he's on a container. At D Chowk? He's been there for two weeks.'

'Yes, I've been following that on the news. Why he's been on a container at D Chowk for two weeks is beyond me.'

'So, uh, we convinced him it would be a good idea to do this. We thought the government would order the police to beat up and disperse the protestors and when that went wrong, it would pressure the government into calling for early elections.'

'Why did you think that standing at D Chowk for two weeks would force the government to concede to early elections? Why would they beat up the protestors? Wouldn't it be easier for them to just come up with a traffic diversion and just let us sit there?'

'Uh, well yes, that's exactly what they ended up doing after the first two days. We had hoped it would be a kind of battleground where the government would be broken, but its' become more of a carnival type of thing. The bus conductors of Islamabad and Pindi call it the Afridi Circus. Local entrepreneurs have set up burger and chai stalls. People come for a picnic at night, have a cup of chai, listen to Afridi's daily speech, and then leave. Not quite what we wanted.'

'Who's imbecilic idea was this?'

The Haircut bristles at Shakaib's outburst. 'Well, I mean, to be fair, it was a tactically sound operation but strategically, our chances were hurt because the government didn't cooperate with us. But tactically, very solid. Very solid.'

'I'm sorry, did you expect them to cooperate with you in plotting their own downfall?'

The Haircut, chastened, turns around and stares out the windscreen.

'Shakaib bhai, now we have a bigger problem. Javed is extremely frustrated. He says he is going to take all his supporters and attack the parliament. He says he wants to do it like the French, storming the Basturd.'

'The Bastille.'

'Bastille? Oh yes, that makes far more sense. Although I could have sworn Javed called it the Basturd.'

'This is madness, Hamza. He can't storm the parliament.'

'Shakaib bhai, you need to tell him that. He doesn't listen to any of us. Blames us for the D Chowk plan. And, he's going into one of his…dark moods…'

'What dark mood?'

'Shakaib bhai you have to see it. Let us hurry, please. I'm worried he will give the order to storm the parliament before we get there.'

'Ok, but I'm not going there in this ridiculous thing. All the expats I met on my travels wanted my assurance on one thing: that Javed Afridi wasn't a front for you people. If we go to D Chowk in this monstrosity and the TV cameras get one picture, we'll never get our credibility back. Get a normal size car, for God's sake.'

Fifteen minutes later, the Landcruiser has been ditched for a far more modest Toyota Corolla. At Shakaib's insistence, the Haircut has also been dispatched with the SUV, leaving Hamza and him to drive alone to D Chowk.

'Hamza, what the hell is wrong with you? Why did *he* have to come to the airport?'

'Who? Taimur? But, he's always around.'

'That's my point. Why is he always around? Why are you giving him access to Javed all the time? This is supposed to be an independent political party, not a front for anybody else. Don't you understand, that's Javed Afridi's selling point. That he's not in anybody's pocket. Why would you allow an idiot like Taimur to be involved in any kind of decision making?'

'Shakaib bhai, this is the point you don't understand. I didn't give him access. He gives me access. Javed had been in contact with them before I joined. I was brought in because I had recently retired, and therefore could serve as a kind of day-to-day liaison without raising any alarms on the government side. And also because I could bring in good people like you to the party.'

'So what are you saying? That everything you told me is a lie? That Afridi is just some puppet?'

'No, no! Not at all. Of course, Afridi is real. He is a real leader. You have seen him. You agreed to work with him because you believe he is the right man, not because you thought he was connected. Trust me Shakaib bhai, we are not that good as to be able to fool someone as seasoned as you. Javed Afridi is the right future for this country and we didn't invent him. But when he started faltering after the last election, we stepped in to help him a little bit. Just to give him some direction. He needed to have people like you around him. Sensible people who understand the world. Unfortunately, he has a tendency to attract the wrong…sort of friends. And they tend to take him into these dark moods, where his functioning becomes a little…challenged.'

'What do you mean by the *wrong* sort of friends?'

Hamza hesitates before speaking. 'Shakaib bhai, Javed is lovely man, but he has a very colourful past. He has been rubbing the shoulders with all sorts of *kanjars* and *marasis* in his life. Some are international level *marasis*, like that Mick Joggers and that model Irina Shaikh. And some are domestic level *kanjars*. Like Turhan Agha.'

'It's Jagger, not Joggers, and I'm pretty sure it's not Irina Shaikh, because she's not from Chiniot. And who is Turhan Agha?'

'You know, the fellow who was the singer in that band, Mash n' Bangers. The one with all the patriotic hit songs. Remember *Soda Pop Pakistan?*'

'*Soda Pop Pakistan!* Of course! Now I remember. But the band broke up a few years ago, right?'

'Our misfortune. That his fellow *marasis* threw this *kanjar* out of the band, and he attached himself to Javed Afridi. He has styled himself as the official Voice of the party. I have no idea what that means, but he shows up to every jalsa and sings songs that he has written praising Javed Afridi. I suppose that makes him the official marasi of the Party. But Javed loves having him around. In the last two weeks he's been around a lot more, since he performs every night. And that's the problem. He's…influencing Javed in everything. He's the reason Javed is mad at us. He told Javed that we had betrayed him and misled him. And Javed has become…a bit paranoid.'

'Well, Turhan Agha wasn't wrong about this scheme of yours. It is stupid. Why would you send Javed Afridi down this dead end path? What had you promised him?'

'Nothing! Shakaib bhai, I swear, we didn't promise anything. We…I mean they…just felt that having this showdown at D Chowk would put some pressure on the government, and would trigger a sceniaro whereby elections would get called.'

'Scenario.'

'Hain?'

'It's scenario, not sceniaro.'

'Shakaib bhai here the future of the country is being ground into mud and you are correcting my English like a primary school teacher! Please, you've got to help get him off that container. He won't even allow me to enter, you'll have to go up there alone and get him out of his…dark mood.'

'What is this dark mood you keep talking about? Is he manic depressive?'

'No! God forbid! No mental issues. But he is sometimes under the influence of some…pharmaceuticals.'

'Drugs? What kind? What exactly are we dealing with here?'

'Turhan always brings some with him. I don't know which ones. Definitely cocaine is one of them…'

'You're telling me Javed Afridi is an addict?! And using more than one drug? What the hell have you gotten me into?'

'No, no. Not addict. Just…occasionally falls off the wagon. It's all that bloody bugger Turhan's fault! Javed is fine on his own.'

Shakaib Qureshi has never been to a political jalsa. He has seen some on TV, so he has some notion of what a Pakistani political protest should look like. He has visions of charged political workers shouting angry slogans, waving party flags like medieval lances, and nervous looking policemen standing behind barricades in anti-riot gear that makes them look a little like a desi version of the Teenage Mutant Ninja Turtles. But D Chowk is nothing like what Shakaib had imagined. It's a kind of Twilight zone, some alternative dimension of politics. Pop music blares from the speakers (He assumes the lyrics are Turhan Agha's creations) and the massive screens behind the stage flicker with images of Javed Afridi either addressing other jalsas, or scoring the winning goal in a Champion's League final. The jalsa area is only about half full, and people keep flitting in and out in a disinterested manner. There is no political tension at all. A group of youths smoke spliffs in front of a group of policemen who couldn't care less, and both groups openly ogle a group of college girls who are offering to paint their cheeks in the colours of the Party flag. Several young couples who can't afford to go to a restaurant for a date, sit on the police barricades sharing a simple meal of Bun kebab and chips, and surreptitiously try to hold hands. An entrepreneurial traffic warden, having taken money from a chai wallah, attempts to adjust his chai stall in the middle of the dozen who have already staked out their spots. A speaker on the stage appears to be doing little other than lip synching some of the lyrics and calling for the government to go home every time there is a lull in the music.

The famous container from which Javed Afridi has refused to come down, is actually a set of interlinked containers that were originally placed there for the simple purpose of providing a raised stage at D Chowk, but have evolved in the past two weeks into a kind of bunker complex that houses, under the stage, a secretariat, an eating and catering area, a green room for the gaggle of party stalwarts and celebrities who headline each evening's speeches, and a den, referred to as 'the Lair' by party flunkeys, reserved for Javed Afridi.

Admission to the Lair is extremely restricted, and it takes Shakaib several minutes, despite his exalted party title, to get access and that also only when one of the minders checks with Javed Afridi personally. Once inside, Shakaib understands immediately why access is so restricted. The Lair looks less like the mobile camp office of a politician, and more like a hotel suite in the immediate aftermath of a visit by a heavy metal band. Cans of beer and empty whiskey bottles litter the floor, along with discarded fast food wrappings. Hard rock ballads from the 1980's blare on the speakers, competing with the sound coming from the seventy-inch TV screen that takes up most of one corner of the room. The far end of the container is set up like an office, with a revolving chair and a large desk. Behind the chair is another door, partially ajar, through which the sounds of a woman orgasming loudly can barely be heard above the din produced by the TV and the speakers. On the other side of the room, two men sit on a half converted sofa bed, huddling so low around a coffee table that their noses virtually touch the glass. One of the men raises his head as Shakaib enters, a white powdery substance glistening on his sweaty upper lip. His long silver hair is tied in an untidy ponytail, which allows long strands of his locks to frame his lean face. He wears what can only be described as a gold-coloured band uniform three sizes too big for him, with the massive epaulets on his shoulder pads making his body look disproportionate to his face.

Although he doesn't recognise him, Shakaib knows that this can only be the infamous Turhan Agha.

The other man in the huddle also raises his head slowly, his nose caked with cocaine. Shakaib recognises him as a famous YouTuber whose channel has more followers than the population of Portugal, and whose Vlogs have famously pontificated on such theological conundrums as whether a girl who continues her education past middle school can be considered a whore, to the acceptable length of pubic hair for a man and woman on their wedding night.

As the YouTuber raises his head, Shakaib can see four neatly drawn lines of cocaine on the table, and two rolled thousand rupee notes placed alongside the lines. Both men stare at him expectantly but he remains quiet, not knowing how to address this situation. Just as Shakaib wonders how things could get any more bizarre, a woman emerges from the little door behind the office desk, clad only in her bra and panties. She stares at all three men for half a second with a degree of shock, which rapidly transforms into a kind of condescending haughtiness, as she traipses across the room to collect her Shalwar Kameez from the debris of bottles, cans and condom wrappers on the floor. Just as quickly, she disappears back in to the room she emerged from, which Shakaib realises is a small attached bathroom. A moment later, a relaxed-looking Javed Afridi walks out, wearing nothing but the briefest of briefs, his six-pack abs and oak-like thighs glistening with sweat and making him look like a Greek God who's just descended from Olympus.

Without deigning to put anything on, he slumps into the revolving chair and randomly takes a bite from a half-eaten burger lying on the desk. The woman re-emerges, now fully dressed with a dupatta demurely draped on her head, and without acknowledging any of them, walks straight out of the Lair. A minute later, Shakaib can see her live on the television, giving a speech from the stage above them and screaming at the immodesty and moral corruption of the present government. The caption on the screen proclaims her as the president of the party's young women's wing, which makes Shakaib wonder whether there are separate presidents for middle aged and geriatric women in the party.

At length, Javed Afridi finally focuses on him. 'When did you get back?'

'I just arrived. Came straight from the airport.'

'Did the bloody sheedas give you anything or were they cheap as always?'

'Sheedas?'

'That's what we used to call the expat desis when I was playing football. Always wanting something from me. Autographs, shirts, footballs, pictures. An appearance at someone's wedding, or some restaurant opening. It was so demeaning. And they never gave anything back to me. They're cheap bastards. I don't expect that they gave you much.'

'Actually, they gave me nothing. But they gave a lot to you. Five million dollars in cheques and pay orders. And an Andy Warhol original that alone could probably fund your next five election campaigns.'

Suddenly, he has Afridi's complete attention. 'For real?'

'I have the cheques in my suitcase. And the Warhol is being packed and shipped by the donor. A very nice, and very generous lady whose husband is a senior executive at JP Morgan. Both are expat desis and not at all cheap. They were both swooning over you and happily donated the painting to you. And not just them. Everywhere I went, rich or poor, the expats opened their hearts to you. They believe in you.'

Shakaib can see that it takes Afridi a minute to process this information. It has opened up vistas in his brain that he had never quite considered before. 'Well, of course, I always said expats were the salt of the Earth. Irritating at times, but they are the real Pakistanis. The ones who can recognise the injustices that the ruling elites are committing on the people of this country. I knew I was right to send you. You've been able to articulate my message to the overseas Pakistanis like no one in my party has before.'

'When can we use the money?' The discussion seems to have piqued the interest of Turhan Agha, who puts down his rolled thousand rupee note and wipes his nose.

'You must be Turhan Agha. I'm Shakaib, I'm the party's head of international finance. What do you do here?'

'Me? I…am…the voice of the Party.' Turhan says it like it's supposed to mean something, as if he's selling a soft drink rather than a political party. 'So, when can I have some money? I have thousands of ideas for the party. A series of protest concerts, and we can use holograms to livestream it in several places at the same time…'

'When can I get the money, Shakaib?'

'You can get it right away, Javed. But the only proviso that the donors have attached, is that you shouldn't be anybody's puppet.' Shakaib turns to look pointedly at Turhan Agha.

'I am not anyone's puppet.'

'Then what are you doing here, Javed? What is this protest of yours accomplishing? You've been inside this container for two weeks! It's getting ridiculous. People outside Pakistan are calling this a stunt, just to garner publicity.'

'It's that fucking Hamza! And that other cunt, Taimur! They guaranteed me that if I came here and did this protest for three days, the government would crumble.'

'Whoever suggested it, it was a stupid plan, based on an underlying premise of violence. Nothing is to be gained by staying here now. We've got the money, we can start planning a proper party structure, that will be in place and ready to roll by the time elections come about at the end of next year.'

'Next year! I'm not going to wait for a year! I was promised an election in the next month, and I want an election by next month!'

'That's right! Javed bhai was promised! And if we don't get it, our supporters will burn the parliament and the PM house to the ground! Can't these people see this is a revolution! And...I...am...the poet of a revolution! Come on, Javed bhai, let's forget all these penny pinchers. They're always going to try and hold you back. We need to start the revolution tonight!'

Turhan Agha gesticulates wildly during his outburst, knocking over the neat lines of cocaine and causing great annoyance to the YouTuber, who stares longingly at the white powder being dispersed in the air. Shakaib is more alarmed with Javed's expression, as he seems to nod along to Turhan's tirade.

'Javed, please listen to me. You cannot mount an insurrection against the government. Millions of Pakistanis, here and abroad, are rooting for you as their only hope for a democratic future. Whatever Taimur or Hamza told you, was a bad idea. Do you even know if they ever got approval from their superiors for this hare-brained plan? The best way out of this now is to announce the end of this protest, and then we can reassess our situation. This government is so stupid its shooting itself in the foot with its corruption and its suicidal economic policies. You are bound to win the next election. You've got the money now…'

'Why did they promise me? Why did they promise me if they didn't even have approval? If I move from here without doing anything, I'll be a joke. That bastard Prime Minister and his flunkies will laugh at me.'

'In politics, everyone changes strategies, based on what's happening on the ground. The current government has done dozens of about turns. And this is nothing as serious. You can just say that in the interests of maintaining public order, you restrained your supporters. It was a bad tactic. Besides, no one will be laughing at you with the war chest you now have. The donations I have gotten and the money that donors have pledged to keep sending us, will be a game changer.'

'It's not a bad tactic. It's just been implemented badly. Your man is correct, Afridi sahib. Better to withdraw, rethink and then come back much stronger. My followers do this all the time. You remember when we did the protests against the French cartoons? We gave an ultimatum, we said that unless the French ambassador was thrown out of the country, we would burn down the entire Diplomatic Enclave. And then when some 'friends' told us that our speeches were scaring people a little too much, we backed off. Got a meeting with the French ambassador, got some great pictures for our followers and all of us got five-year Schengen visas, and then we called it off. We told our followers that we had scared the government and that next time, we would have them on their knees. And remember, our protest was nationwide. Every major city was shut down. Nobody thought we were weak in backing off. That's just politics.'

The YouTuber seems to have awoken from his cocaine induced stupor. He leans back on the sofa, just as an attendant brings in a tray laden with food. He picks up a seekh kebab with his fist and fellates it into his mouth. He smiles at Turhan and Shakaib's disgusted expressions and gulps down another kebab in the same way. 'And by the way, you will never bring about a revolution by performing a pop concert, no matter how many holograms you use. Mr. Shakaib is right. You need money. Lots of money. And you need street power. Real street power, not this festival at D Chowk that your people have organised.'

Javed Afridi's expression is a mixture of despair and fascination. 'So what are you saying? That I don't have street power? That this isn't street power? To have been here for two weeks, and have the police cowering in front of us?'

'The police aren't cowering Afridi sahib. They are making money, off all the burger and bun kebab stalls outside, and the chai wallahs, and the unwed couples who are using the jalsa as an open dating venue. Your crowd is not the crowd that makes the police and their political masters cower. My crowd makes them cower. Rabid, bearded, muscular men burning flags and shouting 'death to America'. If you had that crowd with you these past two weeks, the government would have been performing on you what I just did to that kebab.'

As if horrified by his own vulgarity, the YouTuber smiles sheepishly and says sorry. But now Javed Afridi is too interested to take offence.

'So how do I get your crowd?'

'By making a deal with me.'

'What do you want? I got you on this platform, didn't I? You gave a speech to millions of people from the top of the container. You haven't ever received that kind of coverage before.'

'Speeches are fine, but they're remembered for about five minutes. I don't want much. My people do not hanker for cabinet positions. Nor do they want to sit in government Landcruisers, being followed by police escorts. Our demands are very small, and completely in your power to grant, on the day when you become Prime Minister. And believe me, with my people behind you, with every major city choked, and every national highway blocked, there will be an election, and you will become Prime Minister. You won't need any flimsy guarantee from our "friends".'

Javed Afridi looks at Shakaib and motions for him to sit down, seemingly ignoring the YouTuber's offer. He gets up and picks up a chicken tikka leg from the tray of food, and then turns to Turhan Agha, who is also reaching for a tikka.

'Oye, Turhan, the crowd is bored. Fuck off outside and sing a song.'

'Now, Javed bhai? But the food just came, and I thought we would discuss the financing of my hologram concert…'

'You don't need food, you have half a kilo of coke fuelling you. Get up there, I want to see you singing on the TV in the next five minutes!'

A disconcerted Turhan leaves the room. Only then does Javed turn to the YouTuber. 'Ok, what do you want?'

The YouTuber stretches himself in the armchair and plonks his bare feet on to the glass table, simultaneously scratching his balls as he does so. 'Afridi sahib, here is the problem. A few weeks ago, one of my followers came to see me. He brought with him his child's fourth class science textbook. Because it is a child's textbook, there were a lot of images in it. One of the images was of some female scientist called Isa Newton. She had invented something or the other. But that wasn't the shocking part. The shocking part was that the illustrator of this textbook had made a picture of her, with her blond hair showing, wearing no hijab, not even a dupatta covering her head. Now you tell me, how are children in fourth class supposed to deal with these pornographic cartoons in science textbooks??'

'There is no female scientist called Isa Newton. There never was. There was a male scientist called Sir Isaac Newton, and he came up with the laws of gravity, almost five hundred years ago.' Shakaib struggles to contain himself.

'Ishaq Newton? Are you sure? But the figure in the picture had long hair?'

'That's probably an illustration with his wig. It was the style in those days for men to have long hair, or wear wigs. There is nothing pornographic in any fourth class textbook. Our children need to study these concepts, in order to compete with the world. Please don't make an issue where none exists.'

'Wig? Dekho ji. Look at these *E-diot* followers of mine. But this exactly illuminates my point, Shakaib sahib. In order to avoid such needless controversies that are at times brought to me by over enthusiastic people, we need to have control over approving school textbooks in this country. I am telling you, such issues keep popping up. Sometimes someone is unhappy over what is in the Islamiat textbooks, sometimes people complain that some book is teaching children about that bloody Darwin and his monkeys. If my people had the final veto on all textbooks, these issues would never arise. And of course, we would be assisted by smart, learned people like Shakaib sahib. But the approval would come from us to ensure that each and everything being taught to our children, was one hundred percent morally safe.'

Shakaib is incredulous. 'Morally safe? You want morality safeguards while children learn about the laws of gravity, but you just inhaled five lines of cocaine in front of me! Where is the morality in that?!'

'Oh Shakaib sahib, don't be so old fashioned. There is no morality issue in having cocaine. It's just a chemical stimulant. No different than having, say a large dose of multivitamins. It's good for your health, good for your complexion, gives you energy...' the YouTuber pauses and looks down at his crotch, '...especially in the bedroom. I don't know why our government persists in these outdated prejudices against drugs.'

Shakaib is actually clueless about how to respond. He looks to Javed Afridi for help, but Afridi seems to be in some kind of zen-like meditative stance, staring straight at the television screen. Shakaib notices that he has changed the channel, and now, instead of the droning of various speakers from the container, the TV is showing coverage of the Republican party debate in Iowa. He recalls an email that Wajahat had sent him last week, recounting how he was preparing that ridiculous Ron Diamond for his first big test against the other contenders. He now looks at the screen and Diamond, looking almost red in his deep tan, with his windswept hairstyle, is aggressively pointing at one of the other candidates, a tall, slim man in a smart, fitted suit, who Shakaib recognises as having been the high profile American general in command of Afghanistan, a couple of years ago.

Diamond seems to be berating the General for not having done any real fighting, which seems absurd to Shakaib, since Ron Diamond doesn't seem to have had any military experience at all, ever in his life, while the General is acknowledged as one of the great American military commanders of this century, and one of the very few who came out of the twin morasses of Iraq and Afghanistan with their reputation enhanced.

Javed Afridi nods his head slowly at Diamond's outburst, as if appreciating the logic of the man. 'Shakaib, you know this Ron Diamond?'

'No, I don't know him personally. But my son, regrettably, is working for his campaign.'

'Really? That's a smart move. Good thinking on your part, to have your son placed in his campaign.'

'I didn't plan it. Frankly, I think this whole Ron Diamond campaign is crazy, but my son has a mind of his own.'

'Why is it crazy? He's going to win.'

'No Javed, I really don't think so. That's not how American politics works.'

'He's going to win. He's got guts, and he's totally unfiltered. None of this political correctness shit. People like politicians to be unfiltered. Trust me, he's going to win.' At length, he turns to the YouTuber. 'If I do this for you, if I hand over the approval of textbooks to your people when I become Prime Minister, what exactly will you do for me?'

'Ah, that's the easy part. First of all, let's finish off this silly protest. Call it off on any pretext. Shakaib sahib is wise. You can take his suggestion and say that you wanted to avoid bloodshed between your supporters and the police. Go home, and relax for a week. I will find an issue to galvanise my supporters against this government. It could even be the textbook issue. I will say you are the only morally upright leader in this country. We will come out on to the streets, and two weeks from today, we will shut down the country. With our street power harnessed to your political power, no government will be able to stand for long. I do not make idle promises like our khaki friends, and so I will not give you a guarantee that there will be elections in one month. But consider this: when every major city will come to a standstill, when no traffic will move on the motorways, when food will not be able to be brought from field to market, when oil will not be able to be transported from Karachi's port to the rest of the country, and when we will refuse to negotiate except through a call of fresh elections, do you think any government will be able to survive?'

Javed Afridi leans back and inhales deeply. 'No. They will not be able to survive. And you will also encourage your followers to vote for me in the election that follows, yes?'

'My people will vote for you only. Do you know how many votes that is? I have ten million YouTube followers. Multiply that by five, if you count their family members. That's fifty million votes, Afridi sahib. Without you having to lift a finger.'

Afridi stares at the TV for another long moment. Then he breaks into his trademark flashing grin, and profers his hand to the YouTuber. 'Deal.'

7.

THINGS TO DO IN DES MOINES WHEN YOU'RE DEAD (POLITICALLY)

'**WHO THE FUCK** is Balthazar Risotto?!'

'Who… the… fuck… is… Balthazar… Risotto!? What… the… actual… fuck??'

Long before she actually verbalises those words, Jessica May realises that the little voice in her head has been shouting them out for the past hour. Like someone watching an accident in slow motion, she stands in the middle of the living room of her suite in the Des Moines Sheraton and watches the sense of panic rise amongst her core team. This is supposed to be her campaign's nerve centre, her war room in the best-funded campaign in American political history. But over the past hour, she has seen what was supposed to be a mere formality, a victory lap on her inevitable march to the presidency, turn into a train wreck.

Like an out-of-body experience, she is physically present but a part of her is detached, floating above the room, observing the minutest of events. She watches her elite political team, the best that America has to offer and the best that money can buy, slowly disintegrate over the course of one hour. The first to go, predictably, is Maury, who starts screaming at anybody he speaks with on his phone, and then, as the fear spreads, screaming at anybody who approaches him in the room. Johnny Raines, usually so affable and approachable, constantly feeding his social media team eloquent articulations of the campaign's key talking points, at first grows quiet, and then disappears from the room altogether, leaving the team no answers to put out as the media begins a feeding frenzy.

Wolfson News anchors can barely contain their glee in proclaiming every five minutes that the 'message guns' of the May campaign have been silenced in the social mediaverse. Mike Cochrane, her old chief of staff, normally an immensely self-assured man, who always knows exactly what to say and how to respond in any situation, starts stuttering, and gives out contradictory instructions to panicked staffers, thus increasing the collective sense of dread. Only Shai maintains her cool. She continues to digest the incoming results from each caucus site, calmly asking pertinent questions as each result comes in and keeping her composure amidst the meltdown.

It is therefore only Shai who is able to decipher why the caucus results are going against them and in favour of a man whose name sounds like the Tuesday night special at an Italian restaurant in Cedar Rapids. And it is only Shai who is able to answer the question that she finally screams out, in her frustration.

'Balthazar 'Balt' Risotto is a local party activist and an old precinct captain from Davenport. No national footprint, no media footprint. Loony lefty. Virtually a socialist. Strictly local and strictly small time. He played the system to get his name on the ballot at a large number of caucus sites.'

'Then why is he winning?'

'He seems to have rigged the caucus system in a way in which his local name recognition is causing Democratic supporters to cast ballots in his favour.'

'Why? Why is he even in this race?'

Even Shai hesitates before answering this one. 'It, uh, seems as if he was encouraged to compete in the caucus by the…Vice President. He's a close confidant of the Veep. And, uh, as you know, the Veep is from…Iowa.'

'No shit. So he keeps reminding me every time we meet, when he talks of nothing but the fucking cornfields and ethanol.' Jessica May hates using profanity. It's just the way she was brought up. But when she does use it, you can tell that she's about to blow. But somehow, with great effort, she maintains her façade of composure. Instead, it's Maury who blows up.

'That motherfucker! Couldn't keep his dick out of this, could he? Not even after the President expressly told him not to run!'

'This isn't going to achieve anything, Maury. Jessica will still win and this Balt Risotto character isn't on the ballot in New Hampshire, South Carolina, or any other state. So why would the Veep do something so stupid? He knows it will alienate him within the party. What's his game?'

'His game, Mike, is to piss all over us. The Veep doesn't need Risotto to win. He just needs him to do well enough to muddy the waters. People start thinking that maybe Jessica doesn't have all the Infinity Stones and isn't inevitable after all. Party elders start worrying. And then that cocksucker flies in on Air Force 2 and offers himself as the best alternative. Gets the Party leadership to nominate him at the convention.'

'That's not exactly great optics, Maury. Now we're equating Jessica with a genocidal Marvel villain.'

'Listen, princess, I don't give a fuck about the optics. I need her to be our Thanos. I want her to be our Thanos. Because I know the Democratic party. If they start to believe that she ain't inevitable, you'll have cockroaches crawling out the walls to try and steal the nomination. The Democratic party are the world champions of rat fucking. Jessica has to kill this contest here or latest, in New Hampshire.'

'Do we actually think we're going to lose here?'

'Mike, I don't know. It's a fucking caucus, and everything hinges on party workers and organisers. With these numbers…'

'Can't we call the President and ask him to tell the Veep to keep his gun holstered? Get this Risotto guy to withdraw? Jessica, can you make the call?'

Jessica trains her steely grey eyes on her old chief of staff with a look of disappointment, as if the question he is asking her is one whose answer should be self-evident to him. 'Too late. Even if the President were to speak to the Vice President and got Risotto to withdraw, his name is already on the ballot. The media would say it was backroom politics, that I cut a deal to have the result overturned because it wasn't in my favour. If you think calling me inevitable makes me sound like a Marvel villain, this would be ten times worse. What do I have to do, to win here?'

Her question is met with stunned silence. Her elite team is speechless. Exasperated, she rolls her eyes and walks to her bedroom, slamming the door shut behind her.

'Fuck you all.'

* * *

It hadn't started like this. The beginning, as most beginnings are, was full of promise. She had started the campaign here in the summer, going from county fair to county fair, high school gymnasiums and community centres, and of course, cornfields, basking under a gentle Iowan sun. Jessica May had never felt as alive as she did during that summer and autumn.

This wasn't her first dance in Iowa. She had been here eight years ago. But that campaign had been trench warfare, slugging it out amongst a heavyweight Democratic field of seven other prospective candidates, including the mercurial Lincoln King and the Vice President who, as the sitting senator from Iowa at the time, had been the hometown favourite. That campaign had started with Mike Cochrane telling her that their aim wasn't to win. In fact, they couldn't win, not in the presence of a local boy in the race. All they had to do was to ensure that there were no gaffes, no fuck ups, and maintain an almost military discipline on their message, to ensure that they came second. In practical terms, that meant a campaign where she basically spun airy bromides and never said anything of any substance. Nothing too right-wing that would get her tagged as reactionary, nothing too lefty, certainly not in conservative Iowa, nothing too much about women, because she didn't want to be tagged as the 'feminist' candidate. In short, nothing that could be used to define her political convictions.

And she had done an excellent job. She never dropped the ball, she was ruthlessly on message, and came out of Iowa being as vanilla as possible. She also came out trailing fourth, behind not only the local boy, but also Lincoln King who, as an unknown black congressman came surprisingly second, and a former governor of Virginia, whose campaign would flame out three days after the Iowa Caucus when it was discovered that he had been having orgies with his wife's hairdresser and his children's au pair all over the state, including on election night, while his poor photogenic wife waited patiently for him on stage at one of the caucus sites as the results were announced.

Amidst the sordid tales of campaign threesomes involving strap-ons and PVC outfits, and the wow factor of Lincoln King's achievement, Jessica's efforts were completely overshadowed. She came across as a mere blip on the campaign trail, and she never recovered from that. Although she stayed in the race till well after Super Tuesday, and long after all the other contenders had dropped out, she could never bridge the gap between King's charisma and her own insipid efforts. Very few were willing to buy into Jessica May's bland meatloaf campaign, when Lincoln King's spicy enchilada was on offer.

Which is exactly why she had promised herself that this time would be different. This was going to be her campaign, headlined with her vision, not some talking points put together on a slide deck by a bunch of Beltway insiders and political hacks. She had made this very clear to Shai from the very first time that they talked about her running again.

Shai was the first, and for a long time, only person she had discussed the campaign with. She didn't even tell her husband until she was sure she was going to do it. She could trust Shai because her advice was unadulterated and entirely without personal ambition. Unlike Maury or John Raines, who were motivated by profit and a hefty slice of the campaign's budget, or Mike who, while an organisational genius at the department of Education, was inherently conservative when it came to election campaigns, and even more so because he valued his position as an *eminence grise* in the party, Shai would always tell it to her like she saw it. And as the only woman in her inner circle, Shai could see things the way that Jessica saw them.

Shai had come to her that evening, back in April, after the boys had left, and told her it was a green light. She had also told Jessica about their concerns about the rumours surrounding her marriage and their demand to dig into it before the other side did. As Shai knew she would, Jessica had absolutely refused. Not because she was afraid of some horrible discovery, but rather because this sort of thing felt exactly like the crap in her last campaign. Let's play defence before we do offence, let's do some opposition research on ourselves and then restrict ourselves to a campaign blander than buttermilk.

She knew the rumours about her marriage. She kept an ear out for what was being said, even though she never let on to anyone, even Shai, that she monitored such gossip. The truth was, no marriage is perfect. Hers' was as imperfect as anyone else's. When she had first met Tim, she had been swept off her feet. He was a brash, larger than life venture capitalist, always looking for the next big idea, and she the somewhat closeted and sheltered daughter of an ex-President. She had barely dated, let alone fallen in love with anyone before Tim, and thus was too inexperienced to realise that she was actually in love with the idea of Tim, rather than with the man himself.

He too had wanted a trophy instead of a marriage, and what better trophy than the daughter of President Jack May. He was a good man, just not a good husband. Her father had once commented that Tim was a great guy for his age. His only problem was that he was stuck at twenty-five. He did brash things, he philandered repeatedly, not because he didn't love Jessica or because he wanted to hurt her, but because that's what he did. It was in his DNA. To his credit, he had supported her ambition, never gotten in the way, and built an extremely comfortable life for them. He had also been discreet enough to ensure that his dalliances remained in the shadows. It now remained to be seen whether his efforts at discretion would survive the Klieg lights of a national campaign.

Jessica knew all of this. And yet, she would not countenance any forensic examination of her personal life. Perhaps it was naïve of her, but she wanted to fight a campaign of ideas.

That's the name Shai had come up with. A campaign of ideas. Healthcare, education, social security, foreign policy. She would build a narrative based on her ideas. She believed she deserved a shot at the big job on her terms. She was sure that, even if anything came out during the campaign, voters would find a way to look past it. After all, this was America in the 21st century, not the 1950's. Even the threesoming, PVC-wearing ex-Virginia governor had been validated by the voters, who had recently elected him as a senator. She would win, or she would lose, but it would be on the basis of her ideas, not on who her husband had slept with and when.

In Iowa, it all clicked for her. The crowds were electric. Women showed up in overwhelming numbers to support her. Everywhere she went, they wanted to shake her hand and tell her how she was an inspiration for all women. Everyone wanted to listen to her ideas about how to make their lives better. She had never felt so energised in her life.

And then her troubles began. It had started with a blip, the placement of an unknown political activist's name on the ballot. Nobody seemed to know who Balthazar Risotto was, but her team assured her it did not matter. Some local loon who had gotten his name on the ballot as a kind of last political wish. They all figured he'd get about five votes. The team wasn't even concerned when he started making speeches calling for a national health service, along the lines of the UK and the Scandinavian countries. It was only slightly inconvenient when lefty college students started heckling some of her events, asking her to commit to a national health service, as Risotto had.

Then, Ron Diamond intervened. In contrast to Jessica's lofty campaign of ideas, the Republican contest resembled a knife fight in a prison yard. The Reverend was favoured to win in Iowa due to the depth of his conservative base. But that prediction became a bit muddied once Ron Diamond started throwing some punches. He took his first swing at the General, berating his fighting abilities, and alleging that he had never really ever been under fire on a battlefield. This, despite the fact that the General had commanded armies in two theatres of war. But somehow, Ron put him on the defensive, claiming that the General's strategy in Afghanistan had been wrong because it was cooked up in a classroom. He had never done any real fighting, and so he didn't know what the reality on the ground was. Of course, Ron had never done any fighting either, indeed he probably had never even held a gun, but it didn't matter because, as he put it, he wasn't the one claiming to be a warrior.

He took his next swing at gay marriage. Before the Reverend could weaponise Ron's past and background, Ron Diamond, retired porn actor, came out against gay marriage. During a debate where he had already silenced the General, Ron matter-of-factly dropped his bombshell. As he put it to a somewhat stunned audience, he had no problem with gay people. He knew lots of them from show business, and he knew for a fact that there was a significant fan following for him in the gay community. But marriage should only be for a man and a woman. He knew that because he was an expert at marriage, having been through three of them already. As a shocked Reverend looked on, a deeply conservative audience in the middle of bumfuck, Iowa, had roared at Ron's response.

Normally, none of this should have been cause for concern for Jessica. Republicans cutting each other to pieces on national TV is just what she would have wanted. Except for the fact that Ron's shadow was so huge, his novelty and shock value so great, that he sucked all of the media oxygen out of her campaign. All of a sudden, Iowa wasn't about Jessica May's great ideas for childcare credits or increasing home ownership. It was all about Ron Diamond's latest soundbite. Her campaign was drowning in Ron's wake.

* * *

It's been a long night. Her best efforts at covering up, both physically and metaphorically, can't really conceal how rough it's been. Even her heavy makeup cannot hide the fatigue in Shai's eyes as she walks into the Sheraton's coffee shop at four in the morning. She hasn't slept all night, desperately trying to salvage something from the contest. But it's difficult to spin anything positive when a local nobody holds a comfortable four-point lead over one of the most recognisable faces in American politics. The boys have been no help. Shai has watched with horror as Maury, Mike and Johnny lost all coherence and the campaign crashed into a wall.

She can't bear to be in that war room any more, to look at the despondency on the faces of those once bright volunteers. And she hasn't yet attempted to do the most difficult thing, which is to inform Jessica that she has lost. There hasn't been any word from the Senator since she slammed her bedroom door in their faces. Shai doesn't blame her. They have all failed her. And so she sits in a corner booth of the coffee shop, pondering how to put the wheels back on the May campaign.

'Hi. You're… Shaiza Naqvi?'

She looks up to see a South Asian man standing in front of her. Which is a rarity in Iowa. But this one is vaguely familiar. He's dressed in an Iowa State sweatshirt and jeans, which seems a little out of place at 4am, the morning after the Iowa caucus, in a hotel that is overflowing with suited political operatives from both parties. He looks too young and not jaded enough to be a journalist. Besides, Shai has made it a point to personally know all the journalists who represent any major media outlet. So, unless this kid is some whizz reporter from Rolling Stone, he isn't part of the media pack. In other words, he doesn't matter in Shai's world right now.

'Yeah. How can I help you?' Her tone is curt and dismissive, hoping he will get the message and disappear.

'Hey. I recognised you from CNN. I'm Wajahat Shakaib, I work for the Diamond campaign. I'm sorry, I just…just wanted to say hello. You don't see a lot of desi…I mean, Pakistanis…South Asians… on the campaigns. Sorry for disturbing you.' Having sensed her tone, he retreats to another booth.

Now intrigued, Shai watches him go. He's a decent-looking guy. Tall, which she likes, with a nice head of dark hair and a sweet face, except for his very large, Roman nose. On a whim, she gets up and walks towards him.

'Wait, what did you say? You work for the Diamond campaign?'

'Uh, yeah.'

'And you're from Pakistan?'

'Yes.'

'So what are you doing on the Diamond campaign?'

'Oh, I'm his, like his body man cum speechwriter cum consultant.'

'No, I didn't mean what do you do on the campaign, I meant, what are you doing working on the Diamond campaign? He's against all Muslims.'

'No, no, that's a mischaracterisation. It's really not like that.'

'No? All his statements seem pretty clear on the subject. He wants the likes of you and me, out of this country.'

'No, no, it's just the newer migrants from Syria and places like that…it's to improve national security…' He can see from her raised eyebrows that his arguments have no impact. 'Look, I'm just here because I wanted a job in show business. I came up to you to say hi because I've seen you on TV and it's just really cool for someone… well someone like us, to be in politics. I'm sorry.'

She smiles and sits down, just as the waitress comes to the booth. She finds his shyness endearing. 'You know, you apologise a lot for a political consultant. Didn't they teach you that if you're apologising all the time, your strategy is wrong?'

'Can I get you folks something?'

'Coffee please.' Both of them say the words in unison, eliciting a weary smile from the waitress.

'Anything to eat? It's a bit early, but we got the kitchen running.'

Shai looks at Waj and shrugs. She hadn't really planned on having breakfast, but her curiosity hadn't been sated. Besides, the alternative is to go back upstairs and inform Jessica that she's lost Iowa. And, having avoided the junk food in the war room all night long, she is actually hungry.

'Yeah, sure. I'll have an egg white omelette with broccoli, peppers and mushrooms. Oh and instead of coffee, can I get a soy chai latte with almond milk?'

He shakes his head and speaks to her in Urdu. 'This isn't New York, you won't get a soy chai latte here. If she gets confused, she might end up getting you something totally different. Like almonds in milk.' He looks up at the waitress and smiles. 'Two fried eggs, sunny side up, and a side of Turkey bacon please.'

'I'll stick with the coffee thanks.' Shai can't help giggling and the waitress has a look of enormous relief at not having to interpret what a soy chai latte with almond milk is. 'How did you know I spoke Urdu?'

'You're from Pakistan, right?'

'My parents are. But I was born in New Jersey.'

'Even if you were born in Jersey, it's a safe bet that desi parents insisted on teaching you Urdu, to stay in touch with the old country. Let me guess, Saturday afternoon classes with some aunty?'

'An uncle, actually. A colleague of my mom's. He was a professor of Urdu literature at Princeton. Had me reciting Ghalib before I was a sophomore in high school.'

'Wow. That is seriously hardcore, even for desi parents.'

'And you? I take it, from your sweatshirt and your intimate knowledge of the characteristics of Iowan waitresses, that you're local?'

'Went to school here. My parents are back in Pakistan. I spent a lot of time in diners like this one, at least initially, trying to ask them to get me exotic concoctions, without much success. So I learnt that an easier strategy was to just blend in with what locals have.'

'Really? And turkey bacon is a real local specialty is it?'

'Come on, it's pretty common. It's not the same as asking for a soy chai latte with almond milk. The waitress knew what it was, didn't she?'

'Fair point. So tell me, Wajahat…'

'Waj. It's easier.'

'Waj. Did I hear you correct, when you said you got into this to get into show business?'

'When you say it like that, it sounds pretty weird.'

'I don't know if weird is how I'd describe it. So what's your deal?'

'My CV went to the wrong person.'

Shai laughs out so loud, her coffee comes out of her nose. 'What?!'

'I applied for a job in media, in the Diamond organisation. Somebody sent my resume to Mr. Diamond, just as he decided to run for President. So he hired me to be his body man.'

'Cum speechwriter, cum consultant. That's a lot of cums.'

'Since I'd studied in Iowa, I knew a little bit about local politics here.'

'And since you're a self-hating Muslim, you wrote those speeches excoriating all Muslims.' The waitress arrives with their order and Shai looks longingly at Waj's plate, with the bubbling golden egg yolks, the hashbrowns stacked high, and the crisp turkey bacon on the side. Her own healthy choice doesn't seem so appetising anymore.

'No, that wasn't me. That was all Mr. Diamond himself. He didn't consult anyone on that.'

'And yet you continue to work for him?'

'He doesn't really mean any of that. It gets him attention, and sucks the oxygen from the other Republican candidates. It worked here, didn't it?'

'Evidently. Got your guy to second place in a crowded field.'

'Actually, we've pulled dead even with the Reverend. It's a tie.'

'No shit? You're tied, for *first* place, in *Iowa*, with the most conservative Republican candidate?? What happened to all of his values voters?'

'I guess they voted for us. Especially after Ron came out against gay marriage and the war.'

'I guess Mr. Diamond was pretty smart to pick you as his guy. Have I walked into some strange twilight zone type alternative dimension? Ron Diamond ties for first with the Reverend in Iowa, and some unknown dipshit called Balt Risotto leads Jessica May?'

'You guys didn't do badly. You got a very large percentage of the vote…'

'Didn't get fifty-one percent, did we? Listen, first rule of politics, if you come second in a two-horse race, it's pretty difficult to say you did well.'

'Sorry.'

'Not your fault. We just need to work a lot harder in the next one. Listen, you gonna have all your turkey bacon?'

Waj grins and offers her his plate. 'So you decided to blend in with the locals, huh?'

She likes his unassuming grin, flashes him one of her own in return, and replies in Urdu.

'Let's just say that, I have to wake up my boss in the next twenty minutes and tell her that she's lost Iowa, and I'd rather do that with some crispy turkey bacon in my stomach.'

8.

HOW TO BUY FRIENDS AND INFLUENCE ELECTIONS
(EVERYTHING DALE CARNEGIE LEFT OUT OF HIS BOOK)

From: squreshi@yahoo.com

To: darkprinceSA@gmail.com

Your Highness,

It was an unexpected pleasure to receive your email yesterday. I am glad to see you are keeping well, despite the strain of your tremendous responsibilities as Crown Prince. And I am truly humbled that you took the time from your busy schedule to write and ask after me. It is good to see you reaching out to people directly, unlike so many others who have been in your position, who tend to become hostages to their staff. Although I would add a note of caution that perhaps you ought to consider changing your email address, in light of your present status. I know that this is your personal email and I also know you have had this one since you were a teenager and it was inspired by your obsession for playing Prince of Persia on your Playstation. But it may give people the wrong impression and these days I am told everyone is into hacking emails, whether it's the Russians, the Americans, the Chinese or the Israelis, so perhaps best to come up with a more unexciting moniker.

I was so happy to hear about your plans to diversify the economy. As you recall, this is something we used to talk about frequently, and it is a matter of some pride for me that some of my lectures that you found so boring at the time, did nevertheless rub off on you. You are absolutely doing the right thing. While oil will always remain a principal resource for your country, you also have to think about the country's future sustainability. I am totally for your ideas to invest in tourism, mining and alternative energy sources. However, I am not quite sure how feasible your plans for an underwater city are. Couldn't you just expand Jeddah, or make some offshore islands, like in Dubai? An underwater city seems a grand idea and so futuristic it's straight out of a Hollywood movie. But the cost of just building it, what to talk of running it, would be prohibitive in my opinion, even if you could power it by harnessing underwater currents for electricity. No doubt, it would be the wonder of the world, but just be careful that you don't dig a financial hole for yourself. When you are in the position you are in, many people will approach you with fantastic ideas because they want you to fund them but you must be careful and judicious in your selections. Your late uncle, you will recall, made many foolish investments when he was Crown Prince before your father, and he is not remembered kindly.

As for myself, I have recently gotten involved in politics. I know, I know, you will say I am the last person in the world who could be thought of as political. My wife tells me that every day. And it's true, I am not a political person. There's not much point in being political in Pakistan. But a few months ago, I met this man, this politician, Javed Afridi. Being a football fan, you will, of course, remember him. If I recall correctly, you were a huge fan of his. You once made me get you a huge poster of his from London. It was so big it wouldn't fit into my luggage, so I had to send it via the embassy's diplomatic bag. Well, I don't know about the man's footballing prowess, you would be a far better judge of that, but I know that since he has come into politics, there is a sincerity to him that is unmatched by any of our other kleptocratic politicians. I believe him when he says he wants to change our system, to help our people out of poverty. I believe him when he says he wants to break the wheel of politics in our country. It deserves to be broken. Just look at the state our government has dragged us into. If you hadn't helped them out by subsidising oil shipments and accepting deferred payments, we would have defaulted. Inflation is killing us, people are fighting in the streets over flour and bread, and yet the Prime Minister just appointed five new ministers to join the eighty-man cabinet he already has. And, he's authorised the purchase of brand-new SUVs for the entire cabinet.

It's just ridiculous. You remember that I used to be critical of the excesses of some of your distant relatives when they went on their eccentric shopping sprees. And I am glad that one of the first things you did as Crown Prince was to confiscate some of your cousins' most expensive toys. But at least your family had the money to indulge in the purchase of these super yachts and chateaus. We are a poor country, but our politicians keep acting like they are your cousins. This is what Javed Afridi is against. He says that this culture of corruption cannot go on like this. We have to make a better country for our children. That's what got me involved actually. A mutual friend introduced me to him and it was this appeal of his that motivated me. I have always wanted my children to come back to Pakistan, to live here, and to have the same opportunities here that they have abroad, but I could never make the case to them to move back, not under the current circumstances. But Javed has, for the first time, given me hope that we can have a better future. And it's not just me. I joined his party to help raise money from overseas Pakistanis. That was why I was in Dammam for a day. I was meeting with Pakistani labourers there. And Highness, I cannot tell you, there is such a groundswell of support for Javed Afridi. All of these people, whether they are construction workers in Dammam or bankers in New York, yearn for a better Pakistan. And Javed Afridi is like a breath of fresh air for them.

I don't say he is perfect. Like any politician, like any man seeking high office, he is a work in progress. Just as you are. But his heart is in the right place. And his message is finally beginning to resonate, not just among overseas Pakistanis, but with millions of people here as well. For the past two weeks, there have been protests against the government, led by a collection of groups, some right-wing and some left-wing. That is the beauty of Javed Afridi. His supporters are not bound by ideology. We have union leaders, we also have religious clerics, as well as moderate men and women who just want change in this country.

The government is really up against a wall. We are hoping, and hearing that the Prime Minister may just call it quits and announce a general election in the next 48 hours. If this happens, I am hopeful that our party will be able to make a very serious impact and we may well be moving towards a new phase in our history. And I am also very proud of the fact that I may play a small role in this historic process.

Anyway, that's what's going on with me. I am sorry we could not meet on my last trip to the Kingdom. Unfortunately, I was there for only a day, and your chief of protocol informed me that you were tied up on that date. Next time I come, I will be sure to plan ahead so that we can actually meet. It's been many years and I would love to see you again. I am very proud of all the work you are doing for your country, and proud of the man you have become.

Keep up the good work and give my regards to His Highness, your dear father. Umber and I send our love. And let me know if you still want chilli chips from Pakistan.

P.S. Do have a think about this underwater city. Fifty billion dollars is a huge price tag. Couldn't you find something else to spend that much money on?

Love, Shakaib.

'Shakaib, can you get off that damn laptop and come down. Dinner is on the table and your stupid friend is here.'

'Which stupid friend?'

'The idiot from Riyadh. Whatsisname, Hamza Hairylegs.'

'Umber, please. He might have heard you.'

'So? He hitches his shalwar up so high, the hairy legs are there for all to see. Besides, he's so dumb, he wouldn't be able to figure out what I was saying.'

'He's not that dumb, Umber. That's the other one. Taimur.'

'Right. Sorry, my mistake. This is the slightly less dumb one.'

'Umber, come on! They're my colleagues, for God's sake. At least try not to be openly contemptuous of them.'

'Uh huh. Did you get an email from Wajahat?'

'No. Wajahat is too busy, he's shuttling all over New Hampshire for the primary. It was from the Crown Prince. He sends his regards.'

'Any likelihood of cash, along with his regards?'

'Umber!'

'I'm just saying. The boy is happy to spend fifty billion on an underwater city, maybe he can send fifty thousand to us. I still need to run this house, even if you have decided to set aside consulting to go on this noble, Monty Pythonesque quest of yours.'

'It's not Monty Pythonesque! And don't worry about money. We'll get along just fine. I have savings. What's for dinner?'

'Karelay.'

'What? Again? It's the third time this week. How much bitter gourd do you want to feed me? I'm sick of it.'

'Well if you're sick of having karelay, take it up with your footballer friend. These damn protests have blocked the Highway. There's no fresh produce coming in. The vegetable man only has karelay, so you eat karelay. Or 'bitter gourd' as you like to call it, Mr. gora sahib.'

'Everything isn't Javed Afridi's fault.'

'Well, the protestors are saying the only leader that's acceptable to them is him. Whatever political excuse you want to give, the fact is that it's his fault that the cook has made karelay again. If you don't like it, you take it up with that idiot.'

'He's not an idiot. I wish you'd stop being so negative about him.'

'He is an idiot if he thinks he'll be able to control these nutters in the streets by cutting some deal with them. And did you know, he didn't even go to Oxford. He went to Oxford Brookes. Bloody fraud. Probably spent all his time chasing women there.'

'Ok, to be fair, he's never claimed to have gone to Oxford University.'

'In all his bloody speeches, he keeps shouting "When I was in Oxford, when I was in Oxford". For a while, I actually thought the musclebound moron may have had some brains. It was Kulsoom who told us the truth on my *Thandis* Whatsapp group. And bechari, the other *thandis* tore her to shreds, just for telling the truth. She actually had to leave the group. My God, those girls worship your bloody Javed Afridi. Won't hear a word against him. They're thinking of renaming the group Javed's GILFs. The minute they do that, I'm exiting. I don't care if they are my old college friends. I am neither a grandmother, nor a fan of Mr. *I never actually went to Oxford Afridi.'*

'Well, technically, Oxford Brookes is also in…Oxford. So he never said anything wrong.'

'Maybe you should join my friends. You sound just like them. Now go, Hairylegs is waiting.'

Downstairs, Hamza greets him with an angelic smile and a box of mithai. 'Shakaib bhai! The almighty has listened to our prayers! The government has folded. Protests worked. Elections announced for February 28th. Allah be praised. You are a political genius. This is all because of you.'

'Me? What did I do?'

'You talked him off that container.'

'Yes, but it's your radical YouTuber friend who brought the government to its knees. And I'm not convinced of the value of this Faustian bargain that Javed made.'

'Who's Frostian?'

'Faust, not Frost. It means, a deal with the devil. You know what, never mind.'

'That's good. I must remember that. Shakaib sahib, you worry too much. All politics consists of Fausty bargains. Don't take it so seriously. And besides, as long as there are smart people like you to advise Javed when he becomes Prime Minister, the YouTuber won't be able to do anything. But before that, we must ensure that he gets to that seat.'

'But, you said…the election's been called, hasn't it? The government's given up.'

'No government gives up in Pakistan. The protestors turned up the temperature, the economic tidings were bad, and so the government decided to make what we used to call in the Army, a tactical retreat. They figure they call a snap election, not giving us enough time to prepare, and though Javed Afridi will do well, he won't be able to get enough seats to form a government. Then the Prime Minister can build a coalition with all the other parties, come back into power, and start from zero. Khalaas. Javed will be out for another five years. We must ensure that doesn't happen. We have to throw him out of the game for good.'

'What do you mean?'

'Don't worry. This time the angels are with us. They will help us manage.'

'Angels will help you manage? Have you also started snorting now?'

'Not real angels, Shakaib bhai. Although their support is always welcome. Taimur's people.'

'But what will they do?'

'They will *manage*. But you and I need to do something first to ensure that the old man and his cohorts are knocked out properly.'

'What do we need to do?'

'You have to come with me right now to meet the chief anti-corruption judge. There is an old corruption case against the Prime Minister and his family pending in his court, but he needs to be convinced that Javed Afridi is a good man before he gives a ruling against them.'

'What does Javed have to do with the judge ruling against the Prime Minister? What are the merits of the case? Is there evidence to convict them?'

'He is very…what's the word? Accented. He's gotten very accented in his old age.'

'Accented? Oh God, you mean eccentric. But what does that have to do with the case? If he has solid evidence in front of him, he should convict them, irrespective of anything else.'

'Oh God Shakaib bhai, you are so gora in your outlook. This is not the west. Things don't work that way over here. There are so many other factors. If the judge rules against the PM, he will be disqualified from politics for life. Before that happens, he wants to make sure Afridi is up to the task of running the country, otherwise there will be chaos. He's a very spiritual man, the judge. He needs to be convinced spiritually. That's why we are meeting him in secret at the house of his Pir, who is also a friend. Please, don't ask so many questions and just come with me. You have to convince him, Shakaib bhai. Only you can do it.'

'Why me?'

'Because you are logical, not emotional. It's your gora training.'

'But you just said my gora outlook was a bad thing.'

'Sometimes it's good and sometimes it's bad. Like most things in this country. Please, we must go now.'

The judge's spiritual Pir lives in a magnificent old house some distance away, in one of the city's older cantons. Three Audi SUVs in the driveway testify to the fact that the Pir's spiritual followers have maintained him in the style he has been accustomed to for decades. The Pir's *gaddi* is an old one, with a large following. His grandfather was hung by the British for sedition, and his father chose to spend most of his life exploring the more sensual side of his spirituality by bedding over a thousand women in his lifetime, a figure that is a mark of great pride for his many devotees, even those ones who at times offered their own wives for Pir sahib's 'special' blessing.

The current incumbent has chosen to live a life between those two extremes, focusing on the acquisition of enormous personal wealth through the largesse of his followers. That largesse has manifested itself into a doubling of his landholdings in Sindh and southern Punjab, as well as the procurement of a manor house in Scotland and a penthouse opposite Harrods' in London. Like all spiritual men, the Pir has taken a great interest in cultivating men of power. His devotees include several senior generals, most of the Supreme Court, legions of senior civil servants and high-ranking police officials, and of course, the chief judge of the accountability court.

Inside, the Pir's men greet them deferentially and take them into a small side sitting room that is often used for their master's private meetings. A well-stocked bar takes up most of one side of the room, while the walls are adorned with prints of hunting scenes, and a couple of antique Jezail rifles. The Pir, looking less Rasputin and more Wolf of Wall Street in a bespoke tailored shirt and a very large gold wristwatch, meets Hamza like an old friend, hugging him effusively and guiding him to a seat next to his. He sizes up Shakaib in a glance, like a man well versed in evaluating people with one look. After all, the considerable increase in the Pir's net worth has not come just by passing on keepsakes and blessing prayer beads for his impoverished followers. It has come by expertly judging how valuable people, especially his more privileged devotees, can be to him. Evidently, having taken a look at Shakaib and concluded that he is not someone worth investing in, the Pir chooses to ignore him completely.

In one corner of the room, stands an older man, who Shakaib presumes must be the spiritual anti-corruption judge, who refuses to sit down until he is bidden to do so by the Pir. The older man grips the Pir's hands and kisses them reverentially. The Pir smiles indulgently, and then nods to Hamza to begin the conversation.

'Sir, thank you so much for agreeing to see us.'

'It is all because of my *murshid*. He asked me and I cannot refuse.' The judge once again makes a great show of kissing the Pir's hands a second time.

'Sir. Of course. Pir sahib is too kind. Sir, my friend Shakaib bhai and I are here, as you know, to discuss the important case that is in your court. Uh, the Prime Minister's corruption reference.'

The judge takes off his prince-nez glasses and closes his eyes in a kind of meditative way before answering. 'You know, the greatest burden that Allah can bestow upon a man, is to make him a judge over his fellow men. I did not want this case, or any other like it. You can ask my *murshid*. But one night, Hazrat Isa came to me in a dream. Jesus Christ himself. He was still nailed to the cross, but he spoke to me in my dream and said it was my destiny to save Pakistan. I could not interpret the dream, so I came to my *murshid* for his spiritual counsel, and he was the one who said I would be dispensing God's justice by becoming the head of the accountability court. And so I did. All thanks to the living saint who sits next to you.'

The living saint, who seems to be mentally calculating the financial, and other benefits he has accrued from those public servants who wish to be judged leniently by his disciple, smiles absent-mindedly.

'But this man, this Prime Minister and his family. They are the sons of the devil! I even told my *murshid*, that I would have to refuse even his counsel, if he chose to ever intercede on their behalf. They are beyond even his redemption.'

'So the evidence of their corruption is quite strong then?' Shakaib asks helpfully.

'Evidence? I have not really examined the evidence yet. But they are evil men. Do you know what they did?'

'Uh, no sir.'

'They cut down the trees!'

'The trees?'

'The trees of Multan! The mango trees! These devil spawns had them cut down. When I was young, there were mango orchards all around Multan. As young boys, we would often sit in the shade of the trees and in the summer months, enjoy the ripe mangoes. But now? They are gone. Now, you only have housing societies and flyovers and bypasses. It was all done by these sons of Iblis! In the name of 'development and progress'. What progress? We were much better off in the days of my youth, when we had mango trees to sit under. Now, where will the children sit in the hot summers? If there are no mango orchards to frolic in, obviously the children will turn to drugs and crime! These men are responsible for the moral degradation of our society. That's what happens when you have no trees!'

Shakaib looks at Hamza and the Pir in shock. Both men's faces are expressionless, Hamza nodding slowly, as if taking in some great secret of the universe that the judge has just divulged to him. And the Pir continues to stare into space, presumably continuing his byzantine financial calculations of how to monetise his disciple's decisions. Just as Shakaib is about to question the rationality of this conversation, Hamza pipes up.

'That's terrible sir. How can anybody be against trees? Trees are a gift from Allah. This is the cause of corruption in our society, sir. When you start cutting down the trees, you become a corrupt society.'

The judge nods, somewhat reassured that Hamza seems to share his worldview. 'That's exactly what I said to my clerk, when he brought me the case file. I don't need to read some case file to tell me the obvious. These people are corrupt. They have got to the top of the political system by cutting down the trees. This country cannot be saved from God's wrath until we plant the trees again. And these men will never do it. They will always want to make motorways and expressways and the petrol pumps on the side of the motorways and expressways.'

'So…you'll disqualify them then?'

'I don't know yet.'

'But…but sir, they're against the trees. They cut down the trees. You said so yourself. How can you not disqualify them?'

'Yes, but how do I know that the person who replaces them, will not also be against the trees? How do I know that your man, this Javed Afridi, will be on the right path? I told you at the beginning, Allah has imposed a terrible burden on me, and I must be judicious. I cannot remove one evil, only for the next lot to be even worse!'

'Well sir, my friend Shakaib here, is very close to Javed Afridi. He can speak to his character. You can ask him yourself. Shakaib is a fan of trees. When he lived in Saudia, he advised the King to plant date trees in Riyadh.'

The judge looks towards Shakaib with an inquiring eye. 'You like trees?'

Shakaib isn't sure how to answer that question. 'Well, my house is small so we don't have a lawn, but…my wife has a Japanese Bonsai in our courtyard.'

'Japanese Bonsai…that's a mini tree isn't it?'

'Uh, yes sir.'

'Yes. Bonsai. Very neat. Very symmetrical. Very good. And Javed Afridi? What does he think about trees and corruption?'

'Uh, well sir, he is totally against corruption. Firmly against it. He definitely thinks the Prime Minister and his family are corrupt. As for trees…he has a big garden. With big Eucalyptus trees. That's a good thing, isn't it?'

'Eucalyptus. Yes, yes, I suppose. But what will he do to keep the children away from the drugs, now that they don't have trees to climb on? Does he have a plan?'

Shakaib stares at Hamza incredulously, but Hamza purses his lips and mouths a silent 'please'. 'Well, uh sir, as you know, Javed Afridi is…was…a footballer. He is very keen for the youth to be engaged in sport and outdoor activities. He has mentioned wanting to construct…football grounds across the country for youngsters to play in. I mean…I know it's not a mango orchard, but…'

'Football. Yes, football isn't bad. At least there's some grass. But I want more than that.'

'More? More than football grounds? What more…'

'I want a commitment that he will plant trees. Thousands of trees. Millions of trees. The Prime Minister has billions of rupees in funds. When your man becomes Prime Minister, I want him to spend on planting trees. Will you make the commitment on his behalf?'

'I…sir…I am not authorised…'

'Of course, we will, sir. Just convict these scoundrels and let Javed Afridi become Prime Minister once, and he will plant not millions, but billions of trees. Don't you worry, sir. We guarantee it, Shakaib and I.'

The judge looks towards the Pir, who nods in agreement. 'And one more thing. I have meditated long and hard on this and have, of course, asked for my *murshid*'s guidance. He and I feel that the mission I have been entrusted with can only be fully realised if I am made a High Court Judge. There are some…hypocrites, senior judges, even the Chief Justice, who oppose me. They don't want me to progress because they are afraid that I will expose their hypocrisy. They will try and block my elevation. But you will arrange it.'

'And if we arrange it…'

'The Prime Minister will be convicted.'

* * *

He has never seen anything like it. Standing at the base of the Minar-e-Pakistan in Lahore, looking out on an expanse of the park named after a poet philosopher, there is an ocean of humanity as far as the eye can see. This is as different an experience from the D-Chowk protest as can be imagined. And yet, at the centre of it is the same man. Javed Afridi, now charged, all signs of desperation and despondency erased from his visage, is greeted by a roar so loud that Shakaib is sure it must have been audible all the way to the Indian border, some 17 miles away. Standing at the back of the stage, Shakaib is privy, for the first time, to the full range of Javed Afridi's not inconsiderable skills. Like all great orators, he senses what the crowd wants, and gives it to them. He makes them laugh with his earthy humour, he makes them angry by telling and retelling stories of the obscene corruption of the government, and finally, he makes them believe. In a better future. In him.

A beaming Afridi greets him with a bear hug as he walks off the stage at the end of the speech. 'So? Amazing isn't it? God, I love these crowds. And they say this isn't even the biggest one. The ones in Karachi and Peshawar were even bigger! This…' he turns and points to the roaring multitude, '…this is better than any drug.'

Afridi wraps his arm around Shakaib and guides him off the stage to another version of The Lair. This one, Shakaib is relieved to see, is far less hedonistic than the D Chowk version.

Afridi firmly pushes him into a chair, while at the same time signalling several flunkies to leave the room.

'You've done it! You've done it again, Shakaib! You know, you remind me of this little guy who used to play with me at Real Madrid. Little black guy, from the Ivory Coast or Liberia or some place. A real *pidda*, I forget his name, but he was short and compact. I would set up the ball for him, and he would always be there, in just the right position to score. Never failed. He would be surrounded by these big, bulky European defenders, but he always scored. He used to come on as a substitute, just for ten or twenty minutes, but his impact on the game was massive. That's you! You're the *pidda*! First, you went and got me all those donations. And then, you go and talk to the judge, and lo and behold, he's indicted those bastards today! There's no way we can lose now!'

'It's still a long way to a conviction, Javed…'

'Yes, but it's the first step. And what timing! That fucker tried to wrong foot me by calling a snap election, but he got trapped himself. With just four weeks to go, he doesn't have enough time to salvage the situation. Not with the media ripping him apart. The channels are running wall-to-wall, minute-to-minute coverage of the scandal. And our social media people are going to town on his flunkies. It's the first thing that those two cunts, Hamza and Taimur have got right.'

'To be fair, Hamza was with me when we went to see the judge. And I'm still not a hundred percent comfortable with what happened there. I don't think we should be promising High Court judgeships for convictions of our political opponents.'

'You didn't offer anything. Ok, so the judge was a bit cuckoo and wanted more trees planted. What's wrong with that? Didn't you write me a memo in which you said we should focus more on issues like climate change? Well, planting trees will be a cornerstone of my climate change policy. Trees are good for climate change aren't they?'

'Yes, but that's not all that was promised, and you know that.'

Afridi waves his hand in the air dismissively. 'Nothing was promised. It may have been implied, but many things can be implied. And it's not like he's going to convict those bastards for me. He knows they're corrupt, there's evidence against them. Plus, he doesn't like them. You had a frank exchange of views with the judge. He was on the fence, and your 'frank exchange' convinced him he was on the right path. And besides, what do I have to do with appointing judges? The Chief Justice and judicial council do that. If this judge is good enough, he'll make it anyway. And if Hamza's people want to put in a word for him, they'll do it. Good for him, good for them. Like I said, nothing to do with us.'

'I should never have gone to see him. Hamza dragged me along, but it was my fault. We want to bring a new future to this country. We should be different from all the others who came before us. We can't get in the mud like this Prime Minister and all the others who've been screwing this country for decades.'

Afridi smiles indulgently. 'How can you be such a smart man and so naïve at the same time? You want me to do great things for this country, but I've got to get elected first. You don't think the government was doing everything they could, to stop me? Do you remember the container at D Chowk? It was bugged. The government had ordered the intelligence agencies to listen in on me. On my private life. That idiot Turhan didn't check when he got the contractor who set up the container. He had been paid off to install listening devices in the main office.'

'But … you … and that young woman … the … substances …'

'Yes, lucky for me, I always use the bathroom to shag. The idiots hadn't thought of bugging the loo. But that poor girl Seema, or Saima, whatever her name was, the fucking PM sent his flunkies to her house and tried to force her to give a statement saying I had forced myself on her. And they're saying this to her, in front of her parents. That's how ruthless these people are. And you're worried that you did something wrong by having a passing conversation with a judge. Ha! You know, I'm definitely going to make her a Minister of State or something, in my government. Poor girl.'

'But … the cocaine … was in the room …'

'And it was largely Turhan and his friends who were snorting it. I like to fuck, and I don't need coke to get it up like Turhan does. Trust me, I've never had a problem getting it up.'

'But Hamza said you were … indulging …'

'Hamza and Taimur are double dealing cunts. I like to smoke charas occasionally, but I wasn't on some kind of drugs binge. I was angry because they were the ones who came up with the stupid D chowk plan, they promised I would be Prime Minister in a matter of weeks, and then when they couldn't deliver, they started saying I was on some kind of bender with Turhan. I bet they were the ones who told you Turhan was pumping me full of coke, right? Well, now they're begging me to give Turhan a reserved MNA seat, so he won't have to go through with the uncertainty of actually contesting an election. Hamza and Taimur, are in this for their own purposes. And I use them for my purposes. Not like you. You want a better country for your children. You're pure. You're the sort of person I want in my cabinet when I win.'

A half-hour later, a somewhat stunned Shakaib steps out of the container office. His phone has been ringing incessantly and when he takes it out of his pocket, he finds twenty-seven missed calls from the Haircut. He is about to put his phone back when it rings for the 28th time. In spite of his deepening anger, some instinct prompts him to pick up.

'Shakaib sahib, welcome to Lahore sir! It is very important that we meet. I know you are at the jalsa, I can arrange for you to be brought to one of my safe houses.'

'I don't think I really want to see you, Taimur.'

'Sir, please. I know there are many misconceptions, but please, just five minutes of your time. It is a matter of critical importance. Everything will be cleared up. Please sir.'

Against his better judgement, Shakaib agrees. A party volunteer drives him to a central point in the Cantonment, where another car and driver are waiting for him. The second car drives him to a very large, but nondescript compound close by. Inside, in a simple yet tastefully furnished living room, he finds Taimur, dressed formally in a suit and tie, waiting for him.

'Shakaib sahib, thank you for coming. You would have seen, mashallah, that the jalsa was a huge success.'

'Is that another thing that you're going to take false credit for?'

A uniformed waiter brings in a tray ladled with tea and snacks. 'Shakaib sahib, you and I have gotten off on the wrong foot from the beginning. Hamza often tells me that I come across as very rude and anti-social when I first meet people. But I assure you, it's not my intention to do so. I have seen you with Mr. Afridi and I can say, hand on heart, that it was one of Hamza's best decisions to bring you on board. You have brought a much-needed seriousness not only to Javed Afridi, but to all of us. I have personally learnt a lot from you, these past few months.'

'But?'

'No buts. I mean it. I asked you here today to allay any reservations you have about my role in this endeavour. Javed is mercurial. There are times when he comes to me, asking me to do everything for him, and other times, when he blames me for everything that goes wrong, irrespective of whether I had a hand in it or not. I need you to understand the truth, so that whenever he gets into one of his moods, you can be the one to control him.'

'Control him? You speak of him as if he's some untamed animal. Hamza lied to me about his having a drug problem. Where is that little shit anyway?'

'Hamza is out on a mission connected to the campaign. We are trying to ensure as big a margin of victory as possible for Mr. Afridi. And he didn't lie. Turhan Agha was a bad influence. In the past, Javed Afridi had succumbed to his temptations. He didn't this time, because we were able to send you to intervene at the right time. You saved our entire enterprise. If you had not come when you did, there was a high probability that Javed would have done…something with Turhan, and the former government would have used it against him.'

'If Turhan is such a bad influence, why are you lobbying for him to get a reserved MNA's seat? What's your game?'

'Not my game, sir. Turhan is a leech. He was a leech with his bandmates in Mash n' Bangers, and he's a leech with Javed Afridi. A freeloader. If it were up to me, I would take him to the desert and make him disappear for good. Or at the very least I would publicly expose the recordings of him snorting cocaine and having orgies at D-Chowk. But unfortunately, my boss is a huge fan. *Soda Pop*

Pakistan is his favourite song. He says he used to listen to it non-stop when he was deployed on an isolated post during the Kargil War. He says it's what got him back alive. It was my boss who interceded with his counterpart in another service to ensure that the recordings of Turhan disappeared. And it's my boss who is insisting that Turhan should be given a seat from the reserved list, instead of having to fight an electoral contest which he will most likely lose. Turhan knows my boss is a fanboy, and so he is using him to lobby Javed Afridi. I'm just a tool in all of this.'

'Don't expect me to lobby for Turhan. Javed doesn't want to give him a seat and I'm not going to recommend that he get one.'

'Fair enough. If I had the same freedom of action that you do, I would probably do the same. I just want to stress that at this point in time, my boss's support is critical. The people in my organisation weren't convinced that Javed Afridi was a good bet. There was a lot of internal debate. You see, the current lot of politicians may be corrupt, but they are predictable. In our profession, we value predictability. It took me some time to convince my superiors that Mr. Afridi was a good bet. One of the sceptics was my boss, but now he's been won over. Largely due to the fact that his idol, Turhan Agha, worships Javed Afridi. So, in the larger context of the support we will provide to ensure Mr. Afridi's election, giving Turhan a reserved seat is a very small price to pay.'

'What support are you talking about? You've seen the TV channels. You've seen the polls. The nation is for Javed Afridi. Inshallah we will win this election. How will you add to the momentum we already have?'

'Elections are not such a simple business. Yes, Javed Afridi is very popular. And yes, I admit that he played a masterstroke by allying himself with our YouTube friend and his followers. They gave him muscle, and it's a move I should have thought of earlier. But the support you see on the TV channels is our doing. We have pushed the channel owners to give blanket coverage to the corruption scandals of the previous government. It's that blanket coverage that has swung the polls in his favour. But even that will not be enough. If Mr. Afridi wants an outright victory, instead of being hobbled in some coalition with a group of greedy smaller parties who will keep blackmailing him and will ultimately cause him to lose his very limited patience, we need to work on a number of constituencies.'

'What do you mean, 'work on' a number of constituencies?'

'We will need to manage the results from there. That's what Hamza is working on currently. Phase one will consist of pre-poll alliances. We will talk to local notables and electables and ensure that they either vote for our candidates or refrain from voting altogether. Phase two will involve reaching out to the local police and administration to ensure they favour us on all marginal outcomes.'

'That's election fraud! My God, how many constituencies are you planning to do this in?'

'It's not election fraud. It's risk mitigation. An integral part of any operation. And the good thing is, due to Javed Afridi's soaring popularity, we won't have to do this in very many constituencies. Hamza is working out the actual math on this, but it won't be more than a handful.'

'We don't need any of this. We will win naturally. If you do this, the entire process will become controversial. You will ruin everything, don't you see that?'

'But this is what Javed Afridi wanted. This is the support he kept saying we didn't give him in the last election. He wants this. He has asked us, in fact instructed us, to do this.'

'You expect me to believe that? You expect me to believe that you people will take orders from Javed Afridi? Why would Javed want this?'

'These are the conditions he laid down to work with us. He said he didn't want to be burdened with messy coalition partners who would keep nagging and irritating him. It would have been far easier for us to do none of this. We could have just waited for whomever emerged with the most seats, and then encouraged smaller parties to join a coalition. A coalition whom we would have defacto control over. It would all have been on merit. But Mr. Afridi said that for him to change things, to 'break the wheel' of corruption of the current political parties, he needed absolute power. This is why so many within my institution were sceptical. Because it's a radical departure from past practice. But the current lot needed to be changed. It wasn't enough to just keep swapping the opposition and government. They're all the same. Mr. Afridi certainly has charisma and popularity, both locally and internationally, as you saw on your last visit overseas. A number of our senior people were big fans of his sporting achievements. The only question mark was over his political … maturity. And that reservation has been largely shelved thanks to you. Your presence by his side, the gravitas you lend to him and to the party, the international contacts that you bring into play, whether it be the Crown Prince or your son, has really reassured a lot of important people that Javed Afridi is the way to go. It's certainly reassured me, I can tell you.'

'My son is hardly an international contact. He's a fresh college graduate who's interning for a crazy fool who's decided to run for President of the United States.'

'Maybe, but I don't know any other political figure in Pakistan who has someone working for an American presidential campaign. At the very least, your son has direct access to this Ron Diamond fellow. And he may not be as crazy as you think. CNN is saying that he is going to win the upcoming electoral contest in New Hampshire next week.'

9.
NEW HAMPSHIRE

SHE REPLAYS THE footage on a loop in the darkened studio, her anger rising with each replay. For all his pretentious arrogance, Leonard Wolfson has never asked her to do anything like this ever before. An audit of her own performance as moderator of the last Republican debate before the New Hampshire primary, to assess whether there was any truth to allegations of bias against a candidate.

The candidate in question is on the screen in front of her, in his ill-fitting suit and garish yellow tie, his paunch distended over his belt like a rocky overhang that Tom Cruise would jump off from, his tanned face framed by his windswept hairstyle, staring daggers at her seated in the moderator's chair during the debate. Amanda curses him silently as she turns up the volume on the feed.

Amanda Spano (Moderator): Mr. Diamond, General Patrakis has said that with regards to the war in Afghanistan, the best policy is to stay the course. What is your response to this?

Ron Diamond: Stay the course? How many courses is he gonna stay for? We've been there for twenty years and people like General Patty Cakes keep saying things like that. Let me tell you, if this guy worked for me, I'd fire his ass. Stay the course just sounds like covering up for not knowing how to do your job.

General Patrakis: Can you please ask him to refer to me either as General, or by my name. Patrakis. P.A.T.R.A.K.I.S. I'd appreciate it if he didn't use these childish nicknames and how dare he say I don't know how to do my job!

Amanda Spano: Mr. Diamond, I will remind you that under the terms of this debate, you are obliged to remain civil towards your opponents. As you well know, General Patrakis has had a distinguished forty-year career in the US military, during which time he was the commanding general of US forces in both Iraq and Afghanistan. He is a highly decorated soldier, the recipient of a Purple Heart, a Silver Star, and an Army Distinguished Service Cross. Are you sure you want to accuse him of not knowing how to do his job?

Ron Diamond: Hey, I know he's a fancy general with a whole fruit salad of medals on his uniform. And I respect that. I call him Patty Cakes out of affection (*laughter from the audience*). My take on the war is simple. I like my wars to be like action movies. Two, three hours, and we blow up a lot of stuff and win. We have the best military in the world, with the best technology in the world! (*Audience cheers*). A war can't be like a Netflix series, with like ten seasons. That's not how America fights! (*Audience cheers again*). I got a lot of respect for the General. A lotta respect. In the old days, I would have taken him to one of my clubs and asked the girls to show him a real good time. But, he hasn't done his job in Afghanistan. He was the General there, but he never did any fighting. He doesn't know what was going on in the trenches, in the front lines. He has to defend this lousy policy because he made it. Stay the course? What crap! I got a newsflash for you, General Patty Cakes. If you're still fighting after twenty years, you aren't winning (*Audience cheers wildly*).

General Patrakis: It's PATRAKIS!!!

Reverend Stark: I think it's shameful frankly, all this talk of having a good time with girls. It's a real sign of the crisis of morality that this country faces...

Ron Diamond: Who are you gonna have a good time with, if you don't like girls, Reverend? Boys? (*Audience laughs*) I thought you already came out in agreement with my stand against gay marriage?

Reverend Stark: It's not your stand, it's mine!! It's God's stand!

Ron Diamond: As I recall, in Iowa I was the one who came out and said it first, and a few hours later you put out a wishy-washy press release saying you were against it too. That doesn't sound like moral leadership to me. Sounds like someone's trying to jump on my bandwagon.

Amanda Spano: Mr. Diamond, you raise an interesting question about moral leadership. You, of course, have been a very popular and successful actor in the adult film industry. In the course of this campaign, you have taken a number of moral positions, including coming out against gay marriage. How do your current positions square off with your background, because it does seem as if some of your positions have been inspired by political expediency. Do you think you are equipped to be a moral leader for America?

Ron Diamond: It's my background that has prepared me for leadership of our great country. I've been out there, on those streets, working hard like all the working stiffs. Like all the people in here! (*Audience cheers*). Nobody else on this podium has done what I've done. Nobody else up here has lived like a real American. I wasn't handed anything on a silver platter. You think my buddy the Reverend over here has ever worried about a mortgage payment, or a credit card bill? Hell no! I worked hard for everything I've got. You can be snooty about my background, but I know American morality, because I've lived the American dream! (*Audience cheers loudly*).

Amanda Spano: Mr. Diamond, you didn't really answer my question. In this campaign so far, you have made objectionable comments about minority communities, especially Muslims, potentially putting at risk the country's foreign relations with Muslim states and also potentially endangering American citizens in those countries. You haven't ever held any political office or even run for election. Would you agree with the characterisation that you are too reckless and inexperienced to become President?

Ron Diamond: Wow, I feel like you're the one I'm running against Ms. Spano. Maybe you should be on this stage instead of over there in the moderator's chair. You sure as hell aren't moderate. I gotta tell you guys, I've been married three times, and I've never been given such a tough time from any of my wives as I've gotten here today from this girl! And trust me, if you've ever met any of my wives, you'll know, they ain't no picnic! (*Audience laughs*)

Amanda Spano: Excuse me, Mr. Diamond, but I think your comment is extremely misogynistic and insulting to women. I'm doing my job here sir, and the fact is, you still haven't really answered my questions. You're going to have to answer these questions if you want to be taken seriously as a candidate.

Ron Diamond: The fact is you're not acting as a particularly fair moderator. You're acting as a mouthpiece for the Republican party establishment. They don't want a real American to win this race. You guys just want your phoney governors and Senators, who line their own pockets and keep the gravy train running. I'm too inexperienced to run for President?? What experience does General Patty Cakes have? Knowing how to lose a war? What's Reverend Pork Chops' experience? Cashing cheques from his mega church franchises? You guys don't give a damn about the common man, the real Americans who are out there, busting their asses every day! I'm not the one who's insulting women, you're the one who's insulting not only women, but all Americans, with your shameless bias!

'Fuck you, Ron.' She stops the video feed, and scrolls down on her phone to the email from Wolfson. She still can't get over the fact that the old man threatened her with an external audit by Phil Rorschach, if she didn't audit herself and come up with a formula for a non-apology apology. Everybody knows Phil's so far up Ron Diamond's ass these days, he's practically an intestine. Might as well hand over the network to Ron Diamond.

Further stretching the credulity of the situation, today is election day in New Hampshire, and early indicators point to an overwhelming win for the Diamond campaign. In two contests, he's silenced the blowhard Reverend, and bitch slapped the General. What the fuck is wrong with the Republican party, she wonders.

She is jolted out of her musing by a short sharp knock on the door. 'Come in!'

'Ms. Amanda Spano, as I live and breathe. I do declare, you look ravishing ma dear!'

'Congressman Herrera. You do know it's not PC to quote from *Gone with the Wind* anymore.'

'It's still your favourite movie, isn't it? Or have you changed your preferences to be more in sync with the times?'

She smiles as she looks at him. He still has his boyish good looks, despite being a four-term congressman from Florida. It's that impish smile and those dimples and the outdoorsy, athletic body that have continued to bewitch South Miami's voters time and again. They certainly bewitched her. She could swim in those dimples.

'It's still my favourite movie. I just don't publicise that fact as much. How've you been Ryan?'

'I've been good. Washington's treated me well. But I heard there's some tough talk going on in the party about you. Leonard made a very public announcement about looking into allegations of favouritism in the debate. Kinda threw you under the bus.'

'Leonard wouldn't be Leonard if he wasn't screwing someone over. For some reason, he's fallen madly in love with Ron Diamond, and Phil Rorshach is practically masturbating to pictures of his daughter, but I didn't realise there were others too?'

'The party loves a winner. And Diamond's numbers look good in New Hampshire. I don't know how far he'll go, but he's certainly gutted both the General and the Reverend. Don't see them coming back.'

'And what do you think about him?'

'He's repulsive. Can't stand him. He wouldn't have lasted five seconds if this weren't the social media age. But, I figure he's a good suicide bomber. He's knocked out two establishment dinosaurs, and if he becomes the nominee, this is a good year to have a loser like him. Jessica May is going to whip his ass. Might as well save the really good candidates for the next cycle. Or the one after that.'

'And you still consider yourself one of the 'really good' candidates?'

'Come on, Amanda. You know this stuff better than anyone. Better than my wife. This is all we used to talk about, after having sex, for two years.'

'Yeah. And I want to know if you still have that burning ambition that attracted me to you, or was it all just pillow talk?'

He smiles sheepishly, and then suddenly turns serious. 'Yes. I am one of the really good candidates. Four years from now, I will be the future of the Republican party. Another two terms in Congress, and then hopefully I get picked as the Veep candidate for our nominee, whomever decides to run against Jessica's second term. As a Latino from Florida, I would be the perfect pick for vice president. If the ticket wins, I would become the youngest vice president since John

C. Breckinridge, or one of those other 19th century fuckers. And if we lose, I'll be the front runner for the Republican nomination eight years from now and an almost certain winner, especially after 16 years of King and May.'

'Looks like you've got it all mapped out. What does your lovely wife have to say about your plans?'

'My wife is the richest and best-looking heiress I could find in the Florida Keys. I married her because together, we're the most telegenic couple in Congress. I don't concern her with my plans. Besides, what would she have to object to? Who wouldn't want to be the First Lady of the United States?'

He says it with his inherent cockiness. She remembers it well. It was the thing that was least attractive about him. 'What if you ran now? In this election cycle?'

'What? Why the fuck would I do that?'

'You said it yourself. Diamond's mortally wounded your competition, and he will self-destruct himself sooner or later. It's an open field this year. And Jessica May's not as invulnerable as everyone thinks. Iowa showed her weakness. She's not good at retail politics. She's got enemies. The Vice President is quietly gunning for her. If he knocks her out in a convention battle, he'll have turned 80 by the day he accepts the nomination. I would fancy your chances against an octogenarian Democrat. Even if Jessica survives, like I said, she has vulnerabilities. Why settle for becoming the youngest Vice President since John C. Breckinridge, when you could become the youngest President since JFK?'

'I think I know what this is about, my little Pink Taco. Ron Diamond sullied your reputation and he's gotten under your skin. You want your ex-boyfriend to get into the race, rough him up a little? Even the score?'

'Don't call me that. I'm not your fucking Pink Taco, and I don't need my ex-boyfriend to fight my battles for me.'

'You never had a problem with me calling you that when we were in bed together.'

'That was twenty years ago, back in Boston. For one thing, you weren't married, and for another, I hadn't developed better taste in men back then.'

'Ouch. That was a bit harsh.'

'I wasn't the one who decided to move back to Florida to become the Latino gigolo of the Keys.'

'That's unfair, Amanda. I've worked very hard to get to where I am. I work hard for all my constituents.'

'Yeah. You work some harder than others, if the tabloids are to be believed.'

'Fuck you, Amanda. That was before I got married. I haven't messed around since I met Veronica.'

'How commendable. It's good to know that you only felt the compulsion to cheat on me.'

'I don't owe you an explanation for anything. You were the one who was obsessed with your career at the time. Desperate to get to New York, not really giving a thought about what would happen to us. Did you really call me here to give me the same bullshit?'

'Look… sorry. No, that's not why I called you here. I'm serious about you taking a shot at the nomination.'

'Why Amanda? Why would I stake everything I've built up, for a long shot that would serve no purpose other than to boost your ego.'

'It's not about my ego, Goddamnit! Doesn't he piss you off, as a Republican? You want this party to become a joke? Because that's what we will be if he's the nominee. Forget about your next two election cycles. We'll be tagged forever as the party who nominated a fucking clown! This is supposed to be the party of Lincoln and Reagan, for fuck's sakes! What are you so scared of?'

'I'm not scared! It's just not worth risking my reputation…'

'What reputation are you risking? You're a congressman from Miami. Nobody knows you outside of South Florida! This could be your chance to become a national figure.'

'I've done good work in the House…'

'Voters don't give a shit about what kind of deals you've cut in the

House. Voters want to see a gutsy politician. These assholes are losing to Diamond because they don't have guts. He's a bully, and they're cowering in front of him. The man that stands up to a bully, is a man that the American people don't forget.'

'He's going to win in New Hampshire, which will give him the first two contests. He's got momentum. There would be no point in getting into the fight at this point.'

'Do you still care about this party? Or were all those late night discussions that we had about compassionate conservatism just lines to get me to blow you? This man will destroy the Republican party. We owe it to ourselves to try and stop this catastrophe. And besides, why do you assume that he has irreversible momentum? He's a paper tiger. He's got no strategy and no policies to get this country out of the mess we're in. He's just an empty talking head. The right candidate, at the right time, could wipe the floor with Ron Diamond.'

'You really think I'm the right candidate? Genuinely?'

'You think I called you just because we were lovers twenty years ago? Please. I'm a political professional, not some dewy-eyed college senior. I called you because, in my professional opinion, you have all the ingredients to be the candidate to topple not only Ron Diamond, but also, potentially, Jessica May in the general. You're a young Latino congressman from a swing state, you can easily become the party's Great Brown Hope. You're fiscally conservative but socially moderate enough that you could appeal to independents and Democrats, especially those hardcore Lincoln King supporters who aren't getting excited about Jessica May as their party's standard bearer. And you are right, you do have an incredibly telegenic family, one that America would very easily fall in love with. You're not a hypocrite like the Reverend and unlike the General, when you speak it doesn't sound like you're reading off a PowerPoint. And let's see, where do I start with Ron Diamond? Oh yeah, you're not a two-hundred pound piece of human excrement. I think those are pretty promising prospects for someone looking to get into the White House.'

'Wow. That's some pretty sharp analysis. Ok, hypothetically, if, and a big if, I were to listen to you and get in the race, how would it work?'

'The next contest is South Carolina. You've missed the filing deadline for that, but that's not a bad thing. You've got just about enough time to get on the ballot in Nevada. Get national Latino organisations excited. You have a natural advantage starting the race in a state with a huge Latino population. You win Nevada, and the big money and social conservatives that had been backing either the Reverend or the General, start climbing onto your bandwagon. You go after Ron, and go after him hard, calling him out for all the shit he's been saying. You show voters that you're not afraid to speak up and call him out. I've gotten to know him a bit, these past couple of months. He's got a short fuse. You saw him in the debate. He lost his shit just because I took off the kid gloves for five minutes. You bait him and wait for him to blow himself up, leaving you as the only viable, and logical candidate for the general election.'

'Easy as that, huh?'

'It could be. If you play it right.'

'And if I lose, despite this perfect strategy of yours?'

'If you lose, Ron Diamond goes up in flames against Jessica May and leaves you as the front runner, four years from now. Which was your plan anyway, right? So what have you got to lose?'

'I need to talk to my wife first.'

'I thought you said you don't concern her with your plans? Besides, she'll love this. I've seen enough interviews of the woman to know she's got ambition coming out of her perfectly bleached ass.'

Ryan grins. 'You always had a way with a phrase. And for your information, nobody bleaches in South Florida. Our asses are all tanned. No, I gotta talk to her because she's the one who's gonna be funding this campaign from her inherited millions.'

'So you'll do it?'

'If the most respected conservative political commentator in America thinks I can do this, then…yeah. Why the fuck not?'

* * *

I had never in my life felt the pure elation of winning anything, prior to tonight. I know that makes me sound like some poor, deprived loser, but you know what I mean. I wasn't a jock in school or college, I wasn't an academic genius or a debater, in short, I had never before put myself in a position to compete with others. So the feeling I experienced when the networks called New Hampshire for Ron Diamond, was a joy I had never really felt before.

Granted, it was hardly my success. It was his. But that feeling, of having been an integral part of a winning team, was just something else. And make no mistake, I had been an integral part of the team. Starting in Iowa, Ron had insisted on keeping me close. He would call me to his room, or his cabin on the plane, late at night, just to chat. Sometimes he would talk politics, but not always. He had a stream of consciousness way of talking that could transport you from how we could benefit from our rivals' precinct captains feuding in Nashua, to the moral fallout of the Holocaust on the German people (or as he put it, you think those Germans were actually sad about what happened to the Jews?), to whether Tootsie rolls were better than Junior mints. Often, this was all in the same five minutes.

Sometimes it didn't make a lot of sense, but when Ron was on a roll he liked to talk, and I was a good listener. Occasionally, I would interject with a thought or suggestion of my own. And occasionally, Ron would even take on one of my suggestions. For instance, it had been my idea to hit the General with political jujitsu, inferring that despite his time as commander in Afghanistan, he was out of touch with the ground realities of the conflict.

Boy, did that work in our favour. I knew Ron Diamond would never publically credit me with the strategy. In Ron's world, all good stratagems came from him alone. But I knew that he kept score of which one of his minions had been helpful and who hadn't, and I knew that from that point on, my personal stock had risen tremendously in Ron's book.

Others knew it too. It was the way of the Diamond court. Everybody studied gestures and intonations, to figure out who was in and who was out. I know that my late night sessions were looked upon with great envy by both of Ron's sons, but especially by my erstwhile culinary assailant Luke. I saw the looks he gave me when I was on the move with Ron, but I didn't care anymore. Harvey had been right when he said Ron had bred Rottweilers. And if that's the way it was, then I was going to treat them like dogs too.

Therefore, the New Hampshire win was a truly special moment for me. Not just for playing on a winning team, but for the knowledge that I had provided a key assist in one of the goals. And so, as I looked around the hotel suite at the very moment Ron's victory was called, I grinned from ear to ear like some delirious raver hopped up on Ecstasy. I wasn't the only one in delirium. All the members of Ron's court were in various stages of jubilation.

Erika Diamond alternated between a semi-comatose state and cheering for Ron in what could only be described as sexual moaning; Han and his girlfriend took the opportunity to shove their tongues down each other's throats; Luke lurked in a corner, and I couldn't figure out if he was happy or sad at the result; Harvey and Ron fist-bumped each other like a pair of deranged, overaged frat boys and bellowed the chorus from the campaign theme song, Journey's *Don't Stop Believing*, which someone had decided to play at full volume on a loop.

Only Krystal maintained a semblance of composure, sipping a glass of champagne, which she tilted towards me in silent acknowledgement when I turned to look at her.

Was I imagining things in my ecstatic state, or was there a hint of a smile towards me? Till now she had been the one Diamond offspring who hadn't shown any reaction to me, positive or negative. I had continued to not exist for her. And now, suddenly, I saw her smiling and, wonder of wonders walking across the room towards me. I turned and looked behind me to check if there was somebody behind me that she may have been acknowledging.

'Who are you looking for, Waj?'

'No, I…uh…hey, Krystal…I just thought you may have been waving at someone behind me…wait, you know my name??'

'Yeah, did you really think I didn't know your name? I'm not an idiot like my brothers. Besides, dad doesn't stop talking about you.'

'Uh…really?'

'Yeah. He thinks you're real smart. Believe me, in this family, that's a huge compliment. You did a really good job here.'

'Thanks…I guess.'

'My dad's not the only one who likes smart people. I do too. They're useful to have around. And they gel really well with other smart people. I think you and I could really gel together, don't you think?'

I must have stared at her like a moron for what seemed to me like an age. So much for all that talk of me being smart. But I couldn't really figure out what was happening here. Was she coming on to me? And why?

'On projects. Campaign projects. Dad has me doing so many things because he thinks Han and Luke can't handle them, that it would be really good if you and I were to collaborate…on stuff. Don't you think so?'

'Campaign projects. Yeah, absolutely, we should collaborate…'

'Awesome. Let's do coffee tomorrow morning, when we've all recovered from this craziness. We can talk about areas of mutual interest then. Give me your phone.'

'My phone?' I took it out of my pocket and held it in front of her, not really comprehending her request. She snatched it out of my hand and typed something on it. She then bent close to me and brought her lips close to my ear, her perfume filling my nostrils.

'I've put in my private number. Only dad and a few of my ex-boyfriends have it. So we can be in touch directly. Give me a call. I'll be waiting.' She whispered huskily, or at least I thought it was husky. By this point, my hormones were so hyperactive that Harvey could have whispered in my ear in his gravelly voice and I would have probably thought that was erotic too.

She slipped the phone back into my palm without my really noticing, and walked away, turning and smiling at me as she did so. I finally understood why Ron had assigned her the task of charming Phil from Wolfson. Damn, she was good. No wonder the next time I had seen Phil on the campaign trail, he had been reduced to a drooling idiot every time Krystal came within a ten-metre radius of him.

I was so enamoured watching her go that my phone's incessant buzzing in my hand didn't momentarily register. When I finally saw the number on my screen, it brought another smile to my face. I stepped out of the suite into the relative quiet of the hallway to take the call.

'Hey, Shai.'

This had become one of the more pleasant rituals of the New Hampshire campaign. Late at night, usually very late, after we had put our principals to bed physically and metaphorically, we would reach out to each other, just to shoot the shit. We would talk about everything and nothing in particular: Events on the campaign trail, Bollywood movies, our respective taste in music (Gangster rap and Taylor Swift in my case, western classical and 80's/90's hard rock for her, though we both agreed that we couldn't stand Billy Eilish, but were both huge Springsteen fans. As Shai put it, you couldn't grow up in New Jersey and not be a fan of the Boss.), and elaborate debates about where to source the best desi food on the East Coast. Every few days when the May and Diamond campaigns happened to be in the same city, we would ditch our phone conversations in favour of face-to-face meetings at all-night diners and coffee shops near or in our respective hotels. I found myself looking forward to these encounters more and more as the campaign had worn on. Of course, who doesn't enjoy talking to an attractive, intelligent woman of a similar social and ethnic background.

But it was more than that. There was something about Shai that really got my heart racing. It wasn't who she was or what she did. It was how she went about everything she did. She was a goddess, and part of my excitement at our meetings was a sense of incredulity at my luck, that this woman actually wanted to spend time with me. I mean honestly, what did I bring to the table? But she kept coming back. And my heart raced ever faster.

As luck would have it, the two campaigns were both ensconced in the Manchester Hilton for the night. This was great for me, as it meant I just had to walk down to the coffee shop to see Shai, but it did briefly cause some logistical problems for the hotel staff. While the May campaign nerve centre was centred on the fifth floor and the Diamond dugout was on the second, the fact that both campaigns had won caused some consternation since there was only one ballroom and both campaigns wanted to use it to announce their victories, and both obviously wanted to do it in prime time. This caused the management of the Double Tree Hilton to indulge in all sorts of mathematical equations of how much time it would take for the followers of one campaign to empty out of the ballroom and how long it would take for the second campaign to file in, and whether both feats could be successfully managed in the brief window between 9 and 11 pm, which was the only time when most of America was actually paying attention to the election.

The matter could have become a major issue, knowing Ron's historic prickliness, but it had been Shai who amicably resolved things by graciously bowing out and selecting a nearby community centre as the location for Jessica May's victory speech. By the end of it both campaigns were in such a heady and gracious mood towards each other (How that would change in the future!) that even the notoriously miserly Ron had plumped for a couple of cases of champagne to be sent across to the May campaign for them to toast their success. Although he did insist that the champagne be from one of the vineyards under his brand.

Shai had called me as soon as she wrapped up the victory announcement to tell me she was heading back to the hotel. By the time I came down to the coffee shop, she was already sitting in a corner booth, holding up one of Ron's champagne bottles.

'Couldn't he have come up with a better name than Ron's Fizz?' She poured two glasses as I sat down across from her.

'I think the marketing consultants wanted to call it Ron's Jizz since that was in line with his former career, but better sense prevailed. So they decided on the closest sounding thing.'

'Eww!! You are sick, Waj! I just ingested that stuff!'

'It's not actually…you know…jizz. It's just a marketing thing. It's not like you're actually having some of his…you know…'

'You are disgusting! Shut the fuck up and join me in drinking some of your boss' jizz. That's what staffers are supposed to do.'

I delighted in her brazen high spiritedness. There was a raunchy boldness to Shai that I had never experienced in any other woman I had met in America, or anywhere else for that matter. I assumed it came from the inner self-confidence of someone who had achieved a lot at a young age.

'How did the victory announcement go? Your boss wasn't too pissed at having to do it in a community centre instead of the hotel?'

'Listen, after what we went through in Iowa, we would have been happy to do it at the city dump, just as long as we won. Jessica's over the moon at the comfortable win. Besides, she leaves these things to me. I convinced her that making her speech from the community centre on Bingo night, surrounded by middle-aged women, would make her look far more genuine as a candidate, compared to just having the typical party volunteers cheering her. And it's true. The press got some great photos. Tomorrow's headlines will read 'Jessica May fights for average Americans'. So, in a strange way, we have you guys to thank for our good press.'

'So, Jessica's got a lock on it now, right? The nomination? No more surprises like in Iowa?'

'My little Jedi Padawan, how much you have to learn about politics. It's never going to be easy for her. There are always going to be party bosses in smoke-filled rooms conspiring to trip her up. Somebody, the Vice President, or some other old white guy thinking she won't be able to cut it. One sub-par performance in any of the remaining primaries and you'll find another couple of Balthazar Risottos popping out of the woodwork. We can't drop the ball, even for an instant.'

'But, there's no credible opposition left, right? I mean you have a couple of C-listers still in the contest, but it isn't a real fight, like our nomination.'

'In your case, you guys are exceeding expectations. That means you have the insurance that even if you slip up in one or two states, it doesn't matter. You guys are the underdogs. Jessica's the one everyone wants to knock off the block. We lose one primary to some non-entity congressman by half a percentage point, and everyone will start questioning her legitimacy to take the nomination. Trust me, it isn't easy being Jessica May.'

'You really look up to her. She isn't just a job for you.'

She took a contemplative sip of Ron's champagne and gave me a funny look.

'You know, my parents were all about academic achievement. Since that was what had gotten them from Pakistan to America, they couldn't get it if someone wasn't an overachiever. Like, at the end of my senior year in high school, my mom went into depression because I didn't get into Princeton or Harvard. I got into Yale, fucking Yale, but for her, I might as well have gotten into some state college.'

'I went to a state university. It was great.'

'I'm sorry. I didn't mean it like that. That made me sound like a real bitch. Actually made me sound just like my mom. But she was actually that fucked up. I had a bit of a breakdown because of her, the summer before I left for college. By the time I got to Yale, I had totally lost my confidence.'

'I find it hard to believe that you could ever lose your confidence.'

'I did, Waj. The person you see today, is all because of Jessica. My freshman year, I was a mess. Nothing I did was good enough for my parents. Can you imagine a household where my mom thought I had ruined my life by going to Yale, and my dad, before having any conversation, would have me recite randomly assigned couplets from Ghalib or Faiz, and if I got one pronunciation wrong, would refuse to speak to me? That's all that mattered to him, that I retained my cultural identity. He didn't give a shit about anything that was happening in my life. I almost didn't apply for the internship with Jessica's office. Working for her, watching her, is what gave me my confidence back. She made me what I am today.'

'Wow. I'm sorry. I didn't know.'

'Not your fault. How could you? That's why this campaign is so special to me. She isn't a boss. I'm not some political pollster who'll move on to the next campaign. Her struggle is my struggle. Jessica standing on that stage, giving that victory speech, is like me giving the victory speech. She's my alter ego.'

'If it's any consolation, not getting into Harvard did a number on my sister as well.'

'Really?'

'Yeah. Except in her case, it wasn't our parents, it was self-inflicted. She had convinced herself that Harvard was where she was supposed to be. When she didn't make it, her world went to pieces.'

'Holy shit. What did she do? Where did she get in?'

'Stanford. She cried for a week or so. And she was very touchy about the whole thing all through freshman year. I used to mess with her by ordering Harvard merch online and mailing it to her in Palo Alto. She would lose her shit every time. But then she got over it. Now she acts like the civilised world begins and ends in California and the rest of us unfortunate rubes may as well be barbarians living in Outer Mongolia.'

'Huh. So there actually are people in the world as fucked up as my mom.'

'Absolutely. But it all works out in the end. My sister ended up loving Stanford. She found a really nice guy, she got a great job. And as for you, you could quite possibly be at the threshold of becoming one of the most powerful persons in the world. Certainly the most powerful South Asian. So there you go. Fuck Harvard.'

I raised my glass in a toast. The champagne wasn't as bad as I had thought and it was beginning to have an impact.

'Fuck Harvard.' She touched her glass to mine and smiled. 'So how come you turned out so normal?'

'Things like grades and college admissions never bothered me much. I just wanted to get to America and wanted to work in showbiz. Which is what led me to Ron Diamond.'

'Yeah. And what a story that is. How does it feel now, the guy who sent his CV for a job in a porn production company, ends up winning the New Hampshire primary six months later?'

'I gotta tell you, it's almost orgasmic.'

'Orgasmic, huh? That's an interesting way of putting it. Never thought of it in those terms.'

'Sorry. I mean…you know what I mean.'

'No, I don't. But I'd like to.'

She smiled invitingly, got up and took the half-finished champagne bottle with her. As she passed my side of the table, she handed me her spare room key card, and then walked away towards the elevators.

* * *

It was four in the morning by the time I snuck out of Shai's room and made my way back to mine. The combination of cheap champagne and the incredulity of the situation was making my head spin. I could barely believe that I had just had sex with her. Three times.

For me, it was virtually star fucking. Shai Naqvi was a name that had been lighting up American desi blogs, chat boards and websites for the past couple of years. She was the shining light of the community, the girl who had Senator Jessica May's ear. The fact that she was attractive and well put together didn't hurt her appeal either. Pictures of her in smart, sexy outfits, walking in and out of the halls of Congress with Jessica May had been a staple on various desi Instagram and Facebook fan pages. I admit, even though it makes me sound like a pig, that I had thirsted over her and actually even voted for her in an online 'Which desi celeb would you like to have a one-night stand with?' poll. She had beaten out the likes of Priyanka Chopra Jonas and Mindy Kaling, such was the esteem I held her in. And now, in addition to winning the New Hampshire primary, I had spent the last three hours fucking her. I could not believe my good fortune. Three times in one night.

I was so buzzed I couldn't sleep, so I opened my laptop. I had been thinking of replying to a message I had gotten from my dad. He was so pissed off that I was working for Ron. He had given me a whole sanctimonious spiel about what a dick Ron was, and how could I work for a man who was not only a pornographer, but who had said all these racist things about Muslims being terrorists, and how they should be deported from America. He had really gotten under my skin and earlier in the day, I was going to send him a nasty reply which would have served no purpose other than to get him even more pissed at me. I was saved by the networks calling New Hampshire for Ron. Now, in my post-coital zen mood, I decided to write out a far more reasoned email than the one I had been contemplating hours earlier.

10.
THE REPUBLIC OF TWITTER/X

From: Waj@diamondforpresident.com

To: Squreshi@yahoo.com

Hey dad. Apologies for not responding to your email earlier. We've been a part of something special here in New Hampshire tonight. I mean I was getting the polls that said that we were likely to win, but until we actually did it, I didn't really believe it would happen. And that too by such an overwhelming margin! I don't know if you've been following the coverage back home, but Ron has won by a massive 15 points. This wasn't a win, this was an ass-kicking.

People often misunderstand Ron. There's a lot of negativity about him here in mainstream Republican party circles because of his background. But it's not just that. He keeps saying that they don't like him because he says it like it is. And you know, it's true. On the campaign trail, I saw all the candidates interact with normal people. Ron is the most genuine person amongst all of them. He comes from a working-class background, made it big on his own, and he connects with average folks. The rest of these candidates are so plastic. Other than generalised talking points, they don't even bother to try and come up with solutions for the problems this country faces.

I know you have an issue with Ron's background. A lot of people do.

But honestly, in this day and age, isn't that just reflective of your own biases? So what if he was an adult entertainer? Shouldn't it count for something that he's a self-made man? You always go on about the importance of merit and being able to pull yourself up by your own bootstraps. This guy has done exactly that. He first made himself a gazillionaire, and now he's not only running in the presidential primaries, he's winning them! What more do you want from him? Didn't you and Ma always say that aunty Huma's grandmother was from Lahore's red light area? And yet when we lived in Riyadh, everyone used to suck up to her because she was loaded and super connected to the royal family. I don't recall anyone having a problem with aunty Huma because of what her grandmother was. So why is Ron different? It's a new world out there, dad. Your thinking is outdated. I mean, just look at your guy Javed Afridi. He slept with thousands of women in the '80s and '90s, if the internet is to be believed. He was also very open about it. There used to be pictures of him and his conquests in all the tabloids back then. How is he different from Ron?

I have also taken up the other issue you raised with Ron. Like you, a lot of people are concerned about his rhetoric with regard to Muslims. I admit, it was shocking at first to hear him talk about deporting Muslims and locking them up and all that stuff. I asked him about it, even before Iowa. I asked him if these were his actual views. He said, if they had been, he would never have hired me. Problem is dad, and Ron identifies this completely accurately, all of these other candidates feel the exact same way but they don't say it. You think the Reverend isn't an anti-Muslim bigot? I've seen some of his campaign's talking points to their own supporters. They read like something Goebbels would have written about the Jews. And General Patrakis was the one who was in favour of unrestricted drone attacks in Pakistani cities if there was even a 20% chance of hitting an al Qaeda target. These douche bags are actually racist. Ron isn't. We talked about this stuff three nights ago, after he had doubled down on his rhetoric against Muslims. I asked him again, Ron is this how you actually feel? Because if that's the case, then I don't know what I'm doing here.

He turned to me and said: 'The problem with you Muslims is that you're the new blacks. No matter what you guys do, somebody is going to have a problem with you. The same way most white people think a young black guy with a Ferrari must be a drug dealer, they think a Muslim with a beard must be a terrorist. That's the way it is in America. That's the way it was when my people first came to this country. They were treated like shit. You gotta take it until the next group of shmucks come along. America is all about waiting to find the next guy to shit on, so that you stop getting shat on. I didn't make the rules and I may not like those rules, but that's the way the game is played. I'm not a racist. I'm the only one out of all these lilly white motherfuckers standing on that stage who has lived with, worked with, eaten with and fucked, people of colour. But if I don't say what I say, these fucks will try and tag me as being soft, liberal, cosmopolitan. They'll wolf whistle me out of this fight. That's not going to happen to me. The only way to knock these pricks out is to attack them from the right. Once I win, I can take any position I want. I can make you my fucking Secretary of State if I want. I got no problems with that. How will that go down in terms of promoting tolerance towards Muslims? But I've got to win first.'

I hadn't thought about it in those terms, and the more I did, the more I am convinced that Ron is right. Politics in America is all about hypocrisy. Ron's message resonates because he isn't a hypocrite. If he wins, he can be a real game changer. Can you imagine if Ron actually made a Muslim Secretary of State, or Director of the CIA, or any of those big jobs? Can you imagine the message that will send, after all of his rhetoric? Somebody like Jessica May will never have that impact. My friend Shai has been her chief of staff for years. No one can be better at her job than Shai. But everyone dismisses her because they say she's there either because of tokenism or she's directing Jessica's uber-liberal agenda. Some of the stuff they say about Shai is so contradictory, it doesn't even make logical sense. But the right wing channels like Wolfson go on and on about it. They can't do that with Ron. If he wins the whole thing, he will have proved his conservative credentials. I mean come on, he outfoxed the Reverend by flanking him on gay marriage. Conservative bible-toting voters went for Ron over the Reverend in Iowa. He's that good. It may not look like it from a distance but he really understands politics. Because he understands the common man. That's his strength, dad. And I am learning so much from this job. I have never worked harder or learned more on a daily basis. If you could only see me here, dad, you'd be proud of me.

Anyway, I gotta go. Give Ma my love. And congrats on your guy winning the election. Sounds like a pretty big deal. Almost two-thirds of the seats in the assembly. Good for you. But does this mean you guys will move to Islamabad?

Love, Waj

Shakaib shakes his head as he finishes reading the email. The simplicity of his son is sometimes mind-boggling. He appreciates how the young can get carried away with a cause.

But this is different. Wajahat seems to be not just drinking the Kool-Aid, he's injected it into his veins. Totally brainwashed by this mad, Quixotic campaign of Ron Diamond.

And how does his son have the gall to compare that deviant sex fiend to Javed Afridi? This is a man who literally let it all hang out, on film, for more than a decade. A man who marketed a dildo made from a mould of his penis! Javed Afridi never did anything close to that!

Shakaib pauses for a moment, reflecting. Well, not that he knew of. He hadn't been with Javed Afridi long enough to have insight into such things. It was true that Javed had never bothered to hide any of his bedroom exploits. And his memory seems to recall some highly objectionable, and extremely candid, photoshoots that Javed had happily done for some British tabloid back in the day. Who knows? It wasn't beyond the realm of possibility that he too may have marketed his genitals for a commercial enterprise.

Shakaib shudders at the thought, hoping and praying that the tabloid photos haven't made it onto the internet and that any dubious mercantile endeavour is similarly buried deep in a pre-internet past. It would be disastrous if it were to pop up now of all times, what with the election victory and Javed's very public alliance with right-wing religious elements. What would the YouTuber say if such salacious stories ever surfaced? Shakaib smiles. That dirty bastard would probably love it.

He looks up from his phone and surveys the scene outside as his official car whizzes past largely empty streets. A wintry drizzle has made temperatures drop drastically in Islamabad and Shakaib, dressed in a cotton Shalwar Kameez that is highly unsuitable for this weather, is thankful that the driver has turned the car heater up.

'Why is there no traffic today?'

The driver smiles at him through the rear view mirror. 'Oh, Sunday, sir. Half of Islamabad still isn't back from the election holidays and those that are here have gone to Murree to enjoy the cold weather. Are you ok, back there, sir? I knew you were coming in from Karachi, so I turned the heating up. You Karachi people feel very cold here. Normally swearing in ceremonies are held on weekdays. You must be really special to be getting sworn in on the weekend, sir.'

'Yes, thank you. It's very comfortable. Have you served with a lot of ministers who were from Karachi?'

'Not many, sir. The last lot were mostly from around here. A lot of driving to their villages. Ruined the shocks on the car. But a couple of governments ago, there was a gentleman from Karachi. I forget his name, but he used to feel very cold. He would keep a shawl in the car, all through the winter. He was also constantly chugging from a hip flask. He was locked up after leaving from here, if I recall. Terrorism charges or something.'

'Comforting to know that my predecessor ended up in jail.'

'Oh, don't worry sir. It's very normal. A lot of ministers go straight from the minister's enclave to prison. You'll like it there, sir.'

'Where? Prison?'

The driver lets out a jolly chuckle. 'Oh no, sir. The Ministers' enclave. You will get a house there, I expect. It's really nice, a gated compound, no crowds, the electricity never goes, and there are some great walking tracks. You can often see the monkeys coming out from the Prime Minister House's gardens as you walk.'

Shakaib hopes that doesn't become a metaphor for this

administration. It seems apt somehow. Things have been moving so fast, he hasn't really gotten a chance to take stock. It's taken him over a week just to get around to reading Wajahat's email. But he knows that some of Javed Afridi's moves have been hasty and ill-thought-out. Of course, everyone acknowledges that the new government is short on experience. That was exactly why they got so many votes, because they weren't the usual lot of politicians. But he just hopes they don't crash into a wall before they've even had a chance to take off.

Exactly ten days ago, a day before the New Hampshire primary, Javed Afridi's party won a historic victory in the general election. Out of nearly 350 parliamentary seats, they had secured 200, thus proving Shakaib's theory that there was a genuine popular groundswell of support for Afridi across the country. However, there also seemed to be circumstantial evidence of Taimur and Hamza's hand at work in a number of marginal seats. Certainly, that's what the former government, now the opposition, was screaming about. It did seem curious that virtually every seat where the result had been categorised as being too close to call, or neck and neck, had been won by Afridi's candidates. By Shakaib's analysis, there had been 50-60 such seats. The former Prime Minister was of course screaming that the 'angels' had been at work in over one hundred constituencies, thus fundamentally altering the result of the election. But after four and a half years of their economic mismanagement, interspersed with stories of their epic shopping escapades in Knightsbridge and 5th Avenue during state visits, few in the media were paying serious attention to their claims. Shakaib suspects this may also have been due to 'helpful' suggestions made by Taimur to the TV channel owners.

He doesn't know if there is any truth to the allegations. Since he himself was not a candidate, he spent most of the campaign at home, trying to fine tune policies that Javed Afridi could enact upon taking office. He had not expected any kind of official position in the government. More so since he has been distanced from both the coterie of office seekers who have trailed Javed Afridi on the campaign trail, and Hamza and Taimur, whom he has steered clear of since his last disturbing conversation in Taimur's office. He had assumed that the spoils of victory would likely go to individuals in those two categories. Certainly, the first round of appointments that came just 48 hours after Afridi's victory had been confirmed by the Election Commission, seemed to be indicative of this. Not only was Turhan Agha nominated for the reserved parliamentary seat he had craved, but his name has also found its way on to the first list of cabinet appointees, as minister of education and culture. Shakaib wonders if this means that the national chemistry syllabus will now include a recipe for crystal meth.

Turhan Agha's appointment is one of several that he has been apprehensive about. The cabinet remains desperately short of experience and gravitas, as evidenced by the pair of newly minted ministers whose celebratory Tik Tok video, firing AK-47s indiscriminately in a residential neighbourhood to acknowledge their promotion to high office, has gone viral. Still, all is not doom and gloom. Two days ago, Javed Afridi suddenly and unexpectedly told him to fly to Islamabad immediately as he wanted him to work as an advisor in the Prime Minister's secretariat.

Needless to say, Umber is not happy. The prospect of giving up his lucrative private consulting work and moving to Islamabad is not a glowing one for her. She has flatly refused to make the move. Not for her the subtle pleasures of uninterrupted electricity and monkeys from the PM House on her walking path. Just because you feel the need to babysit a grown man and a bunch of other delinquents who barely know how to tie their own shoelaces, leave along run a government, does not mean I have to accompany you on this fool's errand, were her exact words. And while he may not have liked how she had termed it, he fears that may be the reality of his new role.

The car drives up a winding path through a forest towards the porch of the PM House. As the driver pulls to a stop just in front of an awning that leads up a set of steps to a doorway guarded by two six-foot plus bearers in crisp Shalwar kameez and green waistcoats emblazoned with the Prime Minister's crest, Shakaib is received by an Army captain in ceremonial dress uniform. He feels the sharp cold as he steps out of the car, and wishes he had brought a jacket instead of his light blazer.

'Welcome to the Prime Minister House, sir. Or, the house on the Hill, as we like to call it. I'm captain Salman. I'm the PM's ADC.'

'Nice to meet you, captain. I'm…'

'I know who you are, sir. We've been waiting for you. If you'll come this way with me, they're waiting on you to start the SAPM swearing in ceremony.'

'Sapum? What's that?'

'Oh, sorry sir, that's our internal lingo. S.A.P.M. Special Assistant to the Prime Minister. SAPM for short. There are three other SAPMs apart from you, and they're already here, but the PM thought it was better for all of you to get sworn in together, in one go. We've got the Senate Chairman drinking cup after cup of coffee and getting cranky waiting to start, hence my rushing you in.'

'Oh, I'm sorry if I delayed you.'

'Not at all, sir. Not your fault. You had to fly in from Karachi. The PM however, is keen to have you settled in as soon as possible. He's asked me to take you in to see him as soon as the ceremony is done. We've also found an office for you here on the Hill. It's not very big. Unfortunately, we're a bit short on space up here. We had to convert an old storage closet.

But still, you're going to be the envy of all the other SAPMs, not to mention most of the cabinet.'

'Why? Are the others not based here as well?'

'Oh no, sir. Only the MS, SPM, and ADC have permanent offices here. SAPMs are never given offices on the Hill. They're all usually down in town in the secretariat, but the PM specifically insisted that you should work from here, so you have access to him at all times. It's quite a big deal, sir.'

'Those are a lot of acronyms and I don't know any of them.'

'Oh, don't worry sir, it's just the way we speak around here. Makes it quicker than actually saying the whole title. You'll pick it up in no time, sir.'

The ADC ushers him in to a small hall, where a bank of TV cameras have been set up, and a man with a remarkable resemblance to Groucho Marx, wearing a ceremonial robe, frowns at Shakaib with barely concealed irritation. He sets down his cup of coffee on a table which already has half a dozen empty cups on it, and urges the other three SAPMs to rise. Shakaib has no idea who the Groucho lookalike is but the captain whispers in his ear, informing him that it's the Chairman of the Senate.

Chairman Groucho shakes his hand perfunctorily and like an impatient teacher waiting to start, rushes to take his spot to start proceedings. It's only once Shakaib joins in the oath taking that he has a look around the room. Apart from the camera teams, there are a handful of other persons in the room, families or loved ones of his fellow oath takers, from the looks of it. He has been so out of touch with the whole process of government formation in the last ten days that he has to admit with a degree of shame, that he does not recognise any of his new colleagues. Only one of them, an attractive young woman in a smart outfit and six-inch heels that somehow feel a little out of place in such a sober setting, her peroxide blonde hair covered loosely with a dupatta, seems familiar. She smiles shyly at him, indicating some recognition. He assumes she must be someone he's met at a party event. It isn't till the conclusion of the ceremony, when she passes by him and flashes him another, broader grin, that he finally recognises her.

'Hello, sir. So good to see you again. You remember me?' She speaks with a sudden injection of confidence that seems to have come with her elevation as a SAPM.

Shakaib stammers, not knowing how to address the question. Of course, he remembers her. The last time he saw her, she had been brazenly parading around Javed Afridi's container in nothing but her bra and panties. 'Uh...'

'Seema. From the D chowk protest. I was the party's head of

young women. We met in Afridi sahib's container. Remember? Before I went to give my speech. After…'

She seems to be almost egging him on to remember the unusual circumstances of their last encounter. The fact that it occurred literally three minutes after she had fucked Javed Afridi doesn't seem to faze her at all. A mumbled 'yes' is all he can manage in reply.

'I just wanted to thank you, sir. Javed sahib has been so kind, and I'm sure you put in a good word for me as well. My parents are so proud that I've become a special assistant to the Prime Minister.'

'Very kind of you, but I assure you, I had no input…'

'Oh sir, everybody in the party knows you are Javed sahib's top advisor. That's why we never see you in public gatherings. Everyone says you and he have private meetings to discuss important things, like the list of ministers.' She nudges him suggestively as she says it.

'No, no, it's not like that…'

'Oh sir, you're so modest. But you're the only one who's getting an office here in the PM house. Even *I* didn't get that, after all my *services*. You are going to be a very important person in this government. We must get to know each other better. What is your portfolio, sir?'

'Uh…I don't know. What's yours'?'

'Special assistant for youth affairs. My God, if you haven't been assigned a portfolio, that means the PM wants a roving role for you. You're probably going to be overseeing all of us! Sir, please, you must give me some time. I want to discuss my ideas for reaching out to the youth of the country.'

Shakaib smiles weakly and luckily before he can answer, he is rescued by the ADC who drags him away to another corridor.

'Apologies sir, just had to see off the Senate Chairman. You'll have to get used to that, sir. A lot of ministers and SAPMs and other hangers on, clinging to you because of your position, wanting you to put their ideas in front of the PM, wanting you to get them face time with the PM.'

'But that's ridiculous, captain. I have no authority to get anyone any time. I'm a nobody. I don't even know what the PM has in mind for me, leave alone anyone else. They're crazy if they think that way.'

'In my experience, sir, this job is all about real estate. They all know the PM has given you, and only you, an office here on the Hill. You're on the *premises*. You're the only one he's asked to see after the ceremony. You can walk into his office. They need an appointment from me just to drive up the Hill. In this town, that's power, sir.'

The ADC walks Shakaib right past a door that has, in bold letters, the words *Prime Minister* emblazoned on it, and leads him up a flight of stairs and into another wing of the building. There, in a lavishly decorated lounge, sits Javed Afridi, wearing a pair of 1980's style short football shorts and a training hoodie. Two giant TV screens are turned on in front of him, one displaying the feed from the five top news channels, and the other showing a National Geographic documentary on the mating habits of lions. Javed is engrossed in his mobile phone and doesn't initially respond to the ADC's subtle clearing of his throat to catch his attention. Finally, after thirty seconds, he looks up and grunts at them.

'So? Did you get him sworn in?' He nods to the ADC.

'Yes sir. Shakaib sahib is all set.'

'And has that bastard Senate Chairman left, or is he still wanting to meet?'

'I saw him off, sir. But he was very persistent in his request for five minutes of your time.'

'What the hell does he want? Bloody paedophile. I don't want to see him. Every time I see him, I picture him fucking some thirteen-year-old. Sick old fuck.' Javed suddenly turns to the two of them. 'He is a paedo, isn't he?'

Both the ADC and Shakaib turn to each other and shrug their shoulders in unison. 'I don't know for sure, sir. All I know is that he is very keen for a photo opportunity with you. Shall I slot him for some time next week, or would you like me to continue to stonewall?'

'Fuck that. I'm not having my picture taken with that cunt. Stonewall him for the next six months, for all I care.'

'Uh, Javed…I'm sorry…Prime Minister…don't you think it

would be unwise to stonewall him for six months? He is, after all, the Chairman of the Senate, and an ally of our government.'

'Fine. You meet him then, Shakaib. ADC, tell the paedo he can meet with Shakaib. The SAPM can sort out whatever his issue is.'

'Yes, sir.' The ADC salutes smartly, and turns to leave.

'Oh, and get someone to take away all these files.' Javed points to a pile of official folders lying on the table in front of him. 'They're so confusing, they're driving me crazy. Why doesn't anyone in the government write things in plain, simple English? What's with all this bureaucratic jargon? Tell the Principal Secretary to go through them and address them as he thinks best. I have more important things to do.' He flings himself on to the couch again and starts watching the documentary in which the male lion now seems to be taking part in what can only be described as a kind of feline orgy, with rapt attention.

'Uh Javed… sorry, Prime Minister… I'm so sorry, this will take a little getting used to… Prime Minister, don't you think you should at least take a look at the files? Some of the issues may well be of supreme national importance. I'm sure you would like to weigh in on them, before the Principal Secretary takes actions in your name?'

Afridi momentarily breaks away from his lion fucking marathon. 'ADC, in future, tell the Principal Secretary to send the files to the SAPM for vetting. He will take a look at them and will bring whatever he feels is important, to my attention. You can start with this lot here, Shakaib.'

The ADC nods and leaves the room as a bewildered Shakaib fumbles to pick up the first file from the top of the pile. 'Thank you Prime Minister, this is very generous of you and I will do the best I can, but don't you think you should be looking at some of these? I mean this one, for instance, is calling for a hike in petrol prices. That could become a major issue because it'll trigger inflation, but we may have to do it if we want to appear fiscally responsible in front of the IMF…'

'Listen, don't tell me all this boring shit. This is your job. This is why I brought you in to the party and this is why I've appointed you my special assistant. You sort this stuff out. You make these decisions.'

'But…this is the crux of your job, Prime Minister. Making informed decisions. That's literally why they pay you.'

'No. My job is to be a leader. I have a vision to change the destiny of this country. I have to reach out to the people directly and through the media to build our narrative. To do that, I have to do two things constantly: Jalsas, every week, every ten days, more than we had during the election campaign, to educate the public about our mission; and dominance over social media, to make sure our narrative is being reinforced each and every minute, on Twitter, on Facebook, on Instagram, on Tik Tok and on every other platform. You see, the problem with the previous bastards was, they were disconnected from the people and so they lost the people.'

'Prime Minister, surely you realise that continuing to have public meetings at a rate equal to, or greater than during the election campaign, will be financially ruinous to the party, and extremely distracting for governance. The campaign's over. We won. Now, we must buckle down and govern, to show the country how much better we are than the previous lot. As it is, they've left us in a precarious state. The economy is on the brink of ruin, and the war in Afghanistan is becoming more and more unstable. If it were to spill over, it would be disastrous. Now, some of our ministers haven't made the best of starts, and considering that we have a very young and…eccentric lot of cabinet members, perhaps it would be good to give them time to focus on learning how to run their ministries, instead of running around in their constituencies arranging jalsas.'

Afridi laughs sardonically. 'You think idiots like Turhan will ever learn how to run a ministry, no matter how much time you force them to spend there? They're morons and job chasers, like that Seema girl. She selflessly offered to move in to my living quarters, to 'service' my every need. I think in her mind the stupid bitch was contemplating marriage or some kind of long-term relationship. And these are the sorts of people that you think will become good ministers, after a bit of training?'

'But, if they're all so bad, why did you appoint them? It was your discretion, no one could force your hand!'

Afridi waves his hand dismissively. 'They're clickbait. Fodder. I needed some idiots to fill the seats in the cabinet. Might as well be these ones. They only need to be good at one thing: Remaining absolutely and unquestioningly loyal to me. Besides, what's the big deal? We'll run the government, you and I. You work on these files, come up with good policies, and I will enlighten the people about them. And as far as money is concerned, well, now that we run things, any expenses incurred on arranging jalsas or expanding our social media outreach will come from the government coffers. It's a much better use of public money than the shopping sprees at Harvey Nicks that the last lot used to do.' He pauses for a moment. 'Oh, but just keep in mind one thing. Any policy you come up, you must be able to explain it either in a 240-character tweet, or in a single sentence in a stump speech. I can't do complicated policies, like this IMF, YMF crap that you were just mentioning. It goes over my head, and if it goes over my head, our supporters won't understand it either.'

'You want policies…in 240 characters…'

'Yeah. Like, CHEAPER FUEL. See, that's a great policy. Well within our character limit, easy to understand, easy for me to sell. Or something like, LOCK UP THE LEADER OF THE OPPOSITION AND FORCE HIM TO RETURN THE MONEY HE HAS PLUNDERED FROM THE GOVERNMENT. #LOCKTHEMALLUP. Yeah, that's a really good one. Must send that to the social media guys immediately.'

He grabs his mobile phone and starts typing furiously, completely missing the look of utter exasperation on Shakaib's face. 'Prime Minister, are you seriously thinking of locking up the opposition leadership, who I must remind you, are still members of parliament, just because it's a good hashtag?'

'Well, not just because it's a good hashtag. It's a good policy too. All those bastards were corrupt to their core. You know this. You spoke to the judge.'

'Yes, but the judge has only indicted the former Prime Minister and his cousin. The case is under trial, they haven't been convicted yet. And there aren't any corruption cases against the rest of the opposition leadership. Why would we lock them all up?'

'Why wouldn't we lock them all up? They're all cocksuckers.'

Shakaib sighs, trying very hard not to lose his composure. 'In a democracy, it's generally not a good idea to lock up your political opponents.'

'Stop siding with those corrupt cunts, Shakaib. Its beneath you. The entire opposition leadership, the whole lot, is rotten to the core. I can't change this country until I make them accountable for what they've been doing all these years. If we don't sort them out, there's no point in our being in government. Either you're with me on this, or you're against me.'

'Prime Minister, I'm not against you. You are right, but if we want to bring about accountability, we have to do it within the bounds of the law. You want to go after the rest of the opposition leadership? Fine. But the way to do it is to announce that we will be investigating allegations of widespread corruption in the previous government, and the one before that. Let's start building a case against these parasites. When we have the requisite evidence, then we can legally arrest any or all of them, and then we can ensure that they are convicted properly. All I'm saying is, let's do this right.'

'Hmmm.' Afridi picks his nose thoughtfully. 'OK. We can do it your way. So we say, JAVED AFRIDI WILL ROOT OUT CORRUPTION FROM PAKISTAN. ALL OLD CASES WILL BE OPENED AND INVESTIGATED. NO MERCY FOR THOSE WHO PLUNDERED THE NATION. #JUSTSAYNOTOCORRUPTION. Yeah, that works.' And then he dives back into feverishly typing on his phone.

11.
POLITICAL TSUNAMIS

NEW YORK CITY (Seven days before Super Tuesday)

Ok, so I'm going to be a little gross here. Or 'ungentlemanly' at the very least. But I don't care. When you're lying naked in a hotel bed with a woman as hot as Shai Naqvi and she's stroking your crotch with her bare legs, no matter how nice a guy you may be, you're going to talk about it.

Admittedly, I had become a little obsessed with her. I couldn't believe that someone as cool as her would want to be with someone like me. I couldn't believe how well we got on when we were together, how electric it felt just to be with her and the fact that we had hooked up on seven other occasions since our first time in New Hampshire just blew my mind. While the two campaigns crisscrossed the nation trying to discover more votes, Shai and I discovered each other sexually. She went down on me for the first time in Nevada, I rimmed her in California, we did doggy in Michigan. She was older than me and far more experienced than either me or any of my previous lovers. Every time I was with her was an erotic journey of discovery.

This morning in New York was another first for us. It was the first time we had actually spent the entire night together. It was still ridiculously early, but we were both up. As the soft sunlight streamed through the curtains illuminating her body, I couldn't take my eyes off her. Maybe it was just me, getting hornier with each caress of her toes, but as we lay there in bed, too lazy to get up, I thought I saw her look at me in a different light, more boyfriend than fuck buddy perhaps.

'What are you thinking about?' Her voice was soft and inviting.

I looked down at her toes on my crotch. 'You really want me to spell it out for you?'

She laughed and threw a pillow at me. 'You need to go into therapy. You're a sex addict. You want to go again, after we did it what, like five times last night?'

'Listen, I'm 23, I'm in my sexual prime, and you're an incredibly hot, older woman. That's the ultimate twentysomething fantasy come true. Besides, it takes two to tango. As I recall, it was you who initiated sessions number four and five. And you're the one playing footsie with my dick even now.'

'You are such a perv. All right then, I guess you're right.' She shrugged dramatically as she said that and her hands and mouth moved on my cock. As I started floating towards seventh heaven, I absentmindedly reached for my phone to put on some mood music and accidentally pressed the TV remote.

'Once again, we bring you breaking news from Afghanistan. The Afghan government has acknowledged that three major cities, Mazar Sharif, Kandahar and Herat, have fallen to Taliban forces in the last 24 hours. Our Kabul correspondent Marc Overmars is reporting that Taliban units have been spotted 50 miles from the capital. Local sources are also claiming that members of the government have started to flee the country. The location of the Afghan president is also currently unknown. We are getting some reports that he may already have left for Dubai.'

Now, for future reference, you should never, ever, turn on the TV to listen to sensational breaking news of the collapse of a country, while receiving a blowjob. Ever. The reflexive jaw clamping caused by the shock of hearing of Kabul's downfall really fucking hurt.

'Ouch!' As I yelped in pain and withdrew from Shai as rapidly as possible, she ignored my predicament and stared at the TV.

'What the fuck!?! How can this be happening?'

I was too preoccupied by my pain to give a coherent response to her question. As I got up to look for some ice or cold water, she frantically tried to call members of the May campaign. Standing under the freezing shower in the bathroom in an attempt to numb my pain, I could hear a stream of *what the fucks, how could this happens*, and *did you fucking knows* punctuating her conversation. By the time I stepped back out into the room, Shai had her blouse and panties back on and was pulling her leggings up, while her eyes remained transfixed on the screen. The TV now had visuals of a plane on the tarmac at Kabul airport with people swarming the wheels and trying to climb on to the wings like an army of ants.

On the split screen, a Pentagon spokesperson was announcing that all US troops were being evacuated from Afghanistan immediately. The next visual turned to another split screen, this time showing old footage of Jessica May and General Patrakis saying that America would never abandon Afghanistan. Ouch.

'What a fucking shitshow. This is really bad for you guys.'

'You think?!'

'Sorry. Didn't mean to sound so dickish.'

'No, I'm sorry for snapping. And for…you know. Is it ok?' She got up and kissed me.

'No permanent damage.' I didn't add the word 'hopefully'.

'But the media's gonna go much harder on the General for this stuff, so it may not be that bad for you guys.'

'Yeah, the General is toast. All the momentum he picked up from winning South Carolina just went up in smoke. Between your guy and the Taliban, he's been hit by a two by four. But Jessica's taking hits because she always supported the President's line on Afghanistan.'

'Why?'

'Ok, this may come as a novel idea for someone who's

spearheading a subversive, anti-establishment guerilla campaign for president, but in regular, non-Ron Diamond politics, you normally support your party leader's actions. You show your loyalty, so that when it's your turn, that loyalty is repaid.'

'But King has a bullshit position. It's the equivalent of shutting your eyes and wishing the bogeyman away. He says no one will be left behind and that the United States will never falter in its support for the Afghan government, but he doesn't do anything to back that up. No extra troops, no funding. He even cut back on counter narcotics programs. If they didn't want to pay for it, they should have pulled the troops out years ago. The Taliban were never going to disappear just by the President wishing them away. You and I are from the region, we know this. King had to either put up or shut up, and he chose to twiddle his thumbs and now the country's fucked. Jessica's got to ditch him. She's got to throw King under the bus. That's just smart politics. You guys are getting punished for a policy you never contributed to.'

'Jessica's not going to ditch the President. You don't know her. It may be smart politics but that's not the way she operates.'

'You're not getting it. You know the one thing I remember from my Junior year American History class? There was a picture, in the class notes, of the last helicopter on the roof of the US embassy in Saigon. That picture we just saw, of the kids hanging on to the wheels of the plane? That's going to be in the history books for the next 50 years, with a note underneath explaining that the fall of Kabul cost Senator Jessica May the presidency because she continued to support the idiotic policy of President King! This will define your campaign unless you ditch King now.'

She was fuming. I could tell, because she finished dressing and started packing her things in complete silence. I didn't know if she was angry at the predicament her team was in, or over the fact that I had pointed out that predicament to her so bluntly.

'Shai, where are you going? It's 6am.'

'Jessica wants us all back in DC for a huddle ASAP. She and

Mike think she should take to the floor of the Senate and be seen consulting with her Senate colleagues to work out some kind of salvage operation for Afghanistan. Wheels up on the campaign plane at 7:30, so I gotta run. Don't worry, take your time, grab some breakfast, I'll clear the bill as I check out.'

I went to hold her. 'Have I done something wrong?' I was unused to this version of Shai, the super-efficient, uber competent, emotionless staffer. I knew that side of her existed, but I had never experienced it ever before.

She pushed me away. 'Yeah Waj, relax. It's not always about you. Jessica needs me and I need to go. Right now.' My expression must have been that of a kicked puppy, so she relented after a moment. 'Look, I'm sorry. I'll call you tonight. I'll have a look at the campaign schedule and we can figure out where our next hookup will be.'

'Next hookup. That's all this is to you?'

She arched her eyebrows. 'Oh. Do we need to have that talk?'

'Nope. No need. Call me and we'll 'schedule' the next hookup. I'll make sure it doesn't clash with my teeth cleaning appointment.'

'Waj, come on. I didn't mean it like that. You're not just a hookup…you know that…I…I can't do this right now. Jessica needs me and I have to go. I'm sorry.'

She came close and kissed me passionately, and then walked out the door, leaving me in perhaps more pain than when she had bitten down on my dick.

* * *

WASHINGTON DC (48 hours before Super Tuesday)

Washington looks like a ghost town. An unseasonal snowfall covers the ground and remains virginally white, untouched by man or snow plough. The Kalorama neighbourhood where Jessica May's townhouse is located is eerily quiet as Shai steps out of her car, wearing a surgical mask, face shield and rubber gloves. Two

Secret Service men in full Hazmat gear step out of a side door to intercept her on Jessica's driveway. She has to stand outside for a full ten minutes, shivering despite her thick Patagonia parka, as the men administer a finger prick test and wait for its results on a laptop set up on the porch. Only when the test returns a confirmed negative, is she allowed inside.

Jessica's normally pristine townhouse has the look of a college fraternity. Since the lockdown was announced 96 hours ago, Jessica's core team, including Mike, Maury, John and a couple of junior aides have been crashing here as part of her pod, with predictable results. Shai is greeted by Maury roaming the foyer in his underpants, drinking coffee.

'Hey, Princess! Welcome back! What news of the world outside? Is the President gonna grow a pair of balls and allow all of us out of here?'

'Can you please put on a pair of pants, Maury? I can see little Maury peeking out, and I really am in no mood to *see that.*'

'Listen, sweetheart, not everyone is as lucky as you, being able to frolic back and forth from your apartment on a special White House pass. The rest of us have to rough it out.'

Shai grunts as she takes off her protective gear and throws her coat in a corner. 'Listen, Maury, putting on all this shit every time I step out, and getting a goddamn finger prick test every time I come back here isn't exactly a fucking picnic. Here, make yourself useful and put away the groceries.'

'What's the White House saying, Shai?' Mike Cochrane emerges from Jessica's living room, unshaven and looking more than a little dishevelled.

'They've been able to confirm that the outbreak started from the one CDC scientist who flew back from The Congo. He was exposed to Ebola over there and brought it back with him. The two hospital workers who treated him were directly infected and died, along with patient zero. CDC has his family members in isolation but they're ok so far. They've also managed to track down all the other passengers and crew from the flight and so far nobody else is showing any symptoms.'

'Great Shai, but I didn't need to send you to the White House for this information. The networks have been repeating these facts since yesterday. Even Ron Diamond is going on about the 'Muslim' government official who brought Ebola to America. Was he really a Muslim, and what was a CDC guy doing flying into Washington anyway? Shouldn't he have gone back to Atlanta from the DRC?'

'Yeah, he was a Muslim. Ethiopian-American. He had family here in DC. He tagged on a couple of vacation days before he got back to Atlanta. I can't believe Ron Diamond is doing the 'Muslim' angle on this. What does that have to do with anything? And why isn't the Diamond campaign still not in lockdown?'

'Ron believes there is no immediate risk of the Ebola virus spreading outside the metropolitan Washington area and he believes it is more important than ever, at this difficult time, to keep meeting and reassuring the American people. Furthermore, President King's lockdown orders are only compulsory for the District of Columbia, and are only recommended for the rest of the country. We don't believe in adhering to the recommendations of an administration that is responsible for this act of biological terrorism, due to their own failures and is now trying to cover it up. Ron Diamond will continue to fight for a better, and safer, America. Spokesman for the Diamond campaign.' John Raines greets them in Jessica's living room. Her ornate coffee table is covered with plastic cups and fast food wrappers.

'He's actually pushing this ridiculous line? That the poor dead man deliberately brought Ebola into the United States?'

'He called him a biological suicide bomber in last night's debate with Herrera in San Diego.'

'What the fuck are his staff thinking?'

Maury sidles up to her, thankfully wearing pants now, and whispers in her ear. 'Well, you're the one who has the inside track on that one, Princess.'

'Fuck you, Maury!' The forcefulness of her reaction startles

Mike and John, who she realises, hadn't heard what Maury had said to her. To the best of her knowledge, no one in the campaign knows about her and Waj. But Maury was always a sneaky little shit.

'The Muslim angle works for him, Shai. Diamond's had a rough month. Military voters got the General over the line in South Carolina, and then Ryan Herrera bushwhacked him in Nevada. Herrera is really beginning to hurt him in the polls. Who doesn't like a tall, handsome Congressman from Florida with an even better looking wife? But the debacle in Afghanistan took care of the General, and this Muslim story that Ron's pushing so hard is gaining traction. Republican social media can't get enough of his claims. Rumour is, Leonard Wolfson has told Rorschach to devote his entire show tonight to debate this allegation. Ron's really putting the President's feet to the fire.'

'Diamond is absolutely right to dismiss the President's lockdown recommendation. It's 48 hours to fifteen states holding their primaries. That's a whole lot of votes. He's got the media all to himself while we're holed up here. We should do the same thing. Break out of lockdown and make a run for the endzone. Who's stupid fucking idea was it to come to Washington anyway?'

'It was my stupid fucking idea, Maury.' Jessica walks into her living room, the only one of them looking immaculate in her slacks and pullover, make up on and not a hair out of place. 'And it was the right thing to do at the time. A Senator has to be in the Senate in times of national emergency. And five days ago there was no greater emergency than Afghanistan.'

'With due respect, Jessica, you aren't just a senator anymore. You're the frontrunner for the Democratic presidential nomination, two days before Super Tuesday. You need to be out there in the country, not hanging out with your colleagues in the Senate cloakroom.'

'The United States Senate is still paying my salary, and I will continue to discharge my duties as a senator from Connecticut until I'm voted out, or voted in to something bigger. There are

American troops still on the ground in Afghanistan. Not to mention the thousands of Afghans who worked with us over the past twenty years, who don't know if they'll still be alive next week, now that the Taliban have taken Kabul.'

Maury makes a face and is about to reply when Mike interrupts. 'Listen Maury, what's done is done. No one could have predicted this Ebola lockdown. It is what it is. We're doing ok in the polls, we're ahead in most of the Super Tuesday states. Shai, when does the White House anticipate the lockdown ending?'

'They're not sure, Mike. If there are no more reported cases in the next couple of days, they may open up by Friday. But the President will call a meeting before they make a final deliberation.'

'So the soonest is another four days. We'll lose our victory lap for the primaries. All that free media, going to waste. Johnny, what do you think the impact will be for us?'

'Well, our not being out there is making us disappear from social and regular media. It's all about Ron and the secret al Qaeda plan to spread Ebola in America. Or its Afghanistan and the administration's paralysis over what to do there. Until voting happens on Super Tuesday, no way to judge whether this has hurt us a lot, or whether it'll just be a blip. In some ways, it's not bad to be isolated. We don't have to respond to questions about Afghanistan and Jessica's support for the President's non-existent position.'

'Anyone figured out what our position on Afghanistan is, or are we just standing around, pissin' in the wind?'

'You know Maury, instead of being critical of every single thing I do, why don't you do something useful for a change? Like your job! I told you to run a poll on our stance in Afghanistan. Where are the results?' It's the first time Shai has seen Jessica lose her temper since the Iowa Caucus.

'Jessica, I can't.'

'What do you mean, you can't? if you can't run a simple goddamn poll, then what are you doing here?'

'Jessica, I can't run a poll on Afghanistan, because we don't know what your stance is. Other than your generalised position, that we would never leave anyone behind, nobody knows where you stand. And that position is outdated, now that the Taliban are doing cannonball dives in the pool of the Presidential palace in Kabul.'

'I stand for serious deliberations across the government, about the impact of this Taliban surge. I stand for the United States coming up with a reasoned policy that will accomplish all of our objectives and ensure a minimal loss in terms of both lives and reputation.'

'Ok, I can't do anything with that. I need to put out a soundbite if you want a poll. This is just all Senate jargon.'

'It's not Senate jargon goddamnit, this is how policies are made in the real world!'

'That's not how politics works in the real world and you know it, Jessica. People need to understand your stance. Ron Diamond has a stance. He says we should have left a long fucking time ago. Fair enough. I may not agree with it, but people know where he stands. That crazy Republican Congressman from Texas, who wants to abolish the State Department, has a stance. Batshit crazy, but it's a clear stance. I can't run a poll based on what you just said, about 'deliberations across the government'. Nobody knows what the fuck that's supposed to mean.'

Jessica bristles at Maury's criticism, and Shai senses that a line has been crossed. Jessica May will be the easiest person to work for 90% of the time, but Shai knows that when she thinks someone is being disloyal, she can be as tribal as the most reactionary politician. She has to stop this before Maury talks himself out of a job. 'Listen, what if... what if we broke with the President on Afghanistan?' They all turn to her as if she just announced that she was pregnant. 'I mean... we all agree that the President has a bullshit position, right? It's the equivalent of shutting your eyes and wishing the bogeyman away.' As she says his words, Waj's face comes in front of her eyes, and she feels an intense need to see him right away.

'Break with the President.' Mike says the words slowly, considering each one carefully. 'How?'

'Look, we don't even necessarily have to come up with our own policy. We're not part of the administration, that's not our job. But what if we said that Jessica disagreed with the President's current stance, and that we feel that the administration needs to do more, and quickly. We still have troops in Kabul holding the fort at ISAF HQ and at the embassy, who are in a very precarious position. So we all agree that more needs to be done, right? I mean, I'm not talking about invading the country again, but in terms of securing our people in Kabul or diplomatic initiatives with the Taliban. All we say is, Jessica is concerned and we feel that the President needs to understand the urgency of the situation.'

'Actually, that's not a bad idea. Shai is right. We don't have to come up with our own policy, which, whatever it may be, might go to shit within hours, considering the situation on the ground. We just need to spell out that Jessica is concerned about the gravity of the situation and she has reservations about the way the President has handled it so far. It shows military families in key swing states that Jessica hasn't forgotten about Afghanistan despite the lockdown. That she firmly has her eyes on the ball. I think its brilliant.'

'Johnny, you think its brilliant to rebuke the President, 48 hours before Super Tuesday? You really think that's the best time to show disloyalty to the party leader? What does that say about me? You think the Vice President won't whisper poison in Lincoln King's ear about me not being dependable? You think the axes that the party is hiding, won't come out for me? No, we have to stick to our position. We're deliberating and we support the President.'

'Jessica, I know how you feel about loyalty, but I really think we should do this. We need to come out with something that differentiates us from him. As long as we're stuck here and can't change the visuals, the networks will keep running that old footage of you saying we'll never leave anyone behind, right alongside the feed of US troops flying out of Bagram having abandoned all their local allies.'

Shai can see Jessica is thinking. She's perplexed. Shai rarely goes out on a limb for any issue. She's the one who usually reflects Jessica's inner thinking. So for her to be so vocal about Afghanistan raises questions in Jessica's mind. Wordlessly, she motions Shai to come to the kitchen, to talk alone.

'You really think I should break with the President on this?'

Waj's face comes in front of her eyes again. 'You remember that old photo, of the last helicopter leaving Saigon from the roof of the US embassy? Jessica this Afghanistan thing could become the same poisoned chalice. Those visuals coming out of Kabul are going to end up in all the history books for the next fifty years, as a symbol of American impotence. You don't want to get tagged with what everyone will call Lincoln King's disaster. You don't want to be Hubert Humphrey to his LBJ. I don't want you to regret later that you didn't break with the President on this.'

Jessica paces in the elegant kitchen, now overrun with old takeout cartons and empty drinks cans. She does it for a full five minutes, as Shai watches the expression on her face like a hawk. Finally, she shakes her head. 'No, Shai. It's too big a risk. What if he withdraws his endorsement before Super Tuesday? What if the Vice President uses it as an excuse to jump into the race, with King's blessing? Look, we're too close. We need to get past the next three days. If my current lead in the Super Tuesday states holds and I win, I'll have secured the nomination. I will officially be the next leader of the Democratic party. After that, we can fine tune our stance on Afghanistan, we can urge Lincoln privately to do more, and we can speak for veterans' groups or whatever. But not before I've secured the nomination. Until then, I have to continue to be the good soldier, even if there are a few bumps along the way.'

* * *

Los Angeles, California (17 hours before polls close on the West Coast on Super Tuesday)

I had to quit. After deliberating on the issue for the last three days, that's the conclusion I had come to. I had tried everything else. I had dissected Ron's statement about 'Islamic Ebola' in every way I could, to come up with some valid justification. There was none. This wasn't even wolf-whistle racism. This was just regular, in your face, racism.

When Ron first said it during the last debate with Herrera, it took me a couple of minutes to register exactly what he had said. Herrera had given us a hard time. He had swept into the race in Nevada and taken full advantage of the state's Hispanic voters to bitch slap us. But it wasn't just that. Herrera was eloquent, was good on the stump and an excellent debater. And he came hard for us. It rattled Ron. The Republican establishment, shaken by the way both the Reverend and the General had been brought down, needed a rallying point. The Reverend had packed up, even if he hadn't formally announced his withdrawal. The General had been kept in the race just barely by a narrow victory in South Carolina. But then the Taliban took Kabul and took a dump on his campaign. His military reputation was in tatters and his judgement had become a laughing stock. It was clear that, short of a miracle greater than Moses' parting of the Red Sea, he would be out as well.

But Herrera leapt over both those losers with his performance in Nevada. At first, it had only been Amanda Spano backing his cause. I say only, but having Amanda Spano in your corner in Republican politics was a huge deal. I mean, for all Ron's private claims that he had Leonard Wolfson in his pocket, the only Wolfson anchor singing for us was Phil Rorschach, or Horny Phil, as Krystal and I had started referring to him privately. Phil was the same guy who couldn't stop staring at Krystal's legs during dinner all those months ago. And he hadn't changed since. Problem was, while Phil would parrot anything Ron said, he didn't have the clout of Amanda Spano. So when Amanda started talking up Ryan Herrera, people started listening.

Truth be told, Ron hadn't been tested this way in the campaign up till now. We had been the underdogs, throwing punches at these caricature candidates. It was like shooting fish in a barrel. That was easy, but now we were top dogs. We didn't know how to deal with a hungry contender, and especially one who wasn't so easily mocked as Herrera. He was from a working-class background, good-looking (a point that I know really irked Ron, even though he didn't say it out loud), with an even better-looking wife (I once spied Luke hiding backstage at one of our debates, staring at her and (it seemed like touching himself), and worst of all, he slammed us on the issues. By my count, of the three debates prior to the one in California where Ron blew up, we had clearly lost two and tied the third, at best.

So we all knew Ron was fuming. Even the reaffirmation of his position on Afghanistan by most of the media, was cold comfort. Something was going to give in this last debate. I had just never expected this. Many of my Muslim friends in America and Pakistan later accused me of having foreknowledge of what Ron was going to say. But, hand on heart, swear to God, I didn't. The Ebola issue had only come up in so far as we had decided we weren't going to stop campaigning. I mean, we were on the West Coast, and had no plans to go anywhere near Washington. Besides, Herrera wasn't stopping either. He was shaking hands with every goddamn farm worker and avocado picker he could find from Sacramento to Bakersfield. Only the Reverend and the General heeded the President's recommendation. The Rev did it mainly because he realised that since he was out of the race anyway, he could pocket the money that his campaign would otherwise have spent on travelling. And the General was getting so much shit for his errors in Afghanistan, that going into lockdown for an Ebola outbreak was actually a more palatable option than remaining on the campaign trail and being asked at every stop whether he still thought the war was winnable.

I didn't think much of it even when, just before the debate, Han Diamond gave his father a printout from some whack job, right-wing website that had disclosed that the CDC official who had brought the virus into the country was a Muslim. But even the website hadn't reached the conclusion that Ron came to during the debate. During a particularly jarring segment, in which Herrera had hit us for being light on policies, Ron came out of the gate swinging. He had said he had plenty of policies ready, especially when it came to national security. He just hoped that there was a country left for him to take over, because Lincoln King was driving us into the ground and leaving us more vulnerable than ever before. And then Ron popped his line about the CDC official being a biological suicide bomber and how it was a major security gaffe on the part of the administration for not having flagged this individual ages ago.

I wasn't the only one totally flummoxed by Ron's allegation. I could tell the shock registering on Herrera's face, live on TV. How was he expected to respond to something so ridiculous? He couldn't downplay it, and he could hardly support the President. That would be suicide in a Republican primary debate. Ron saw his confusion and pounced, and from then on, the rest of the debate was all about Ebola terrorism, and Herrera was reduced to nodding his head like a pliant flunkey.

I was so stunned, that when Ron came off the stage and walked directly past me, winking as he did so, it still didn't register. I couldn't believe that he would be so irresponsible. It must have been some kind of error, an incorrect fact that had been fed to him. With a little dexterity, we could walk it back. All night, I sat up alone in my hotel room and tried to figure out an elegant way to extricate ourselves. First thing in the morning, I decided to go to the source of the erroneous information. I grabbed Han as we were checking out of the hotel, and asked to speak with him privately. I wanted to take him to task for giving Ron unverified information.

'Hey Han, what was the story that you gave Ron before he went on stage?'

'Oh, that. That was gold dust, Waj. Pure gold. They've found a link between al Qaeda and that guy who brought the Ebola into the country.'

'Han, I've spent all of last night checking virtually every news source on the planet. There is no link between the CDC guy who contracted Ebola in Africa and al Qaeda, other than the fact that incidentally he happened to be a Muslim.'

'Exactly. There you go. You're getting smarter, Waj. Beginning to connect the dots for yourself.'

I strongly resisted the urge to punch him in the face. 'Han, there is no link. We cannot make allegations like that. It's extremely irresponsible, you can't give Ron made-up facts like that. What he says from that podium carries a lot of weight. We've got to find a way to walk this back.'

'Walk it back? Are you fucking nuts? Did you see that crowd? They ate it up. Look at your X feed. It's been blowing up since last night. The base is going crazy. We made Herrera look like an idiot. Why would we walk it back?'

'Because it isn't fucking true! We can't make shit up and have Ron say it.'

'We didn't make anything up. It was reported in a credible publication.'

'It's a fucking right-wing nut job website!! The same site also suggests that the Ku Klux Klan wasn't as bad as they're made out to be, and that the federal government is hiding aliens in Area 51!'

He gave me a weird smile. 'You know Waj, I think I know what the problem is. Look, I like you, but I think your Muslim cultural biases are coming out here. You've got to be very careful with that. You're a little too close to this situation, don't you think? Just because you're a good Muslim, doesn't mean everybody else in the country is the same.'

'What?! My Muslim cultural biases??'

'Look, if it were say, someone from my prep school who had been accused of bringing Ebola into the country, I'd be very touchy about it too. But at this level, you've got to be able to think about these things objectively. That's what I always tell dad about you. You're a great guy, but still too fiery, too passionate. You need a little seasoning before you become really top drawer.'

'These are fucking lies that you just made Ron say.'

'He doesn't think so. I don't think so. Millions of Americans who are going to vote on Super Tuesday, don't think so. You seem to be the only one who thinks there is absolutely no possibility that this man deliberately contracted a deadly virus, on the orders of his radical Islamist colleagues, and weaponised his own body to strike at the United States. Can you honestly say that this isn't a possibility that is at least worth investigating? Can you give me a guarantee, as a fellow Muslim, that there is zero probability of such an event ever happening?'

I couldn't believe my ears. I had always taken Han as a bumbling, but generally harmless buffoon, unlike his younger brother, who was a genuine douchebag. He could even be endearing, especially when his weather girl girlfriend was around. I had never imagined that he could store this kind of venom inside himself. I knew if I stayed there a second longer, I would do something I would regret. Or perhaps it was fear. Fear of being portrayed exactly as Han was trying to frame me as: the irrational, violent Muslim male. And so, without answering his question, I turned my back on him and walked away.

I was so mad, and so on edge, that I tried to stay away from everybody the entire day. For some reason, Ron didn't call me for anything either, so it was relatively easy to disappear within the frenzied atmosphere of the campaign. I thought a lot about what Han had said and the more I thought about it, the madder I got. The prick was right about one thing. Ron wasn't a child. Nobody, least of all Han, could dupe him into saying something like that.

Either Ron believed some part of this crazy allegation, or he had said it for political advantage, with deliberate disregard for any consequences. Either way, that put me in a very difficult position. If I didn't do something, I was in danger of becoming the Muslim Uncle Tom of the Diamond campaign.

It was pretty late by the time I came to a decision. I hadn't eaten, and I barely remembered even checking in to the hotel in LA. But I was determined to do something. So I took the elevator straight up to the floor where Ron's suite was.

But I didn't go to Ron's suite. I wasn't sure how I would handle myself in front of Ron, who, I was realising, was a master manipulator in any situation. Instead, I knocked on the door next to Ron's. After a minute, an ugly man wearing a short hotel robe which displayed his spindly legs to the full, opened the door.

'What d'ya want?' Harvey Calzone was, as usual, to the point.

'Harvey, I need to talk about something.'

'Yeah? Go on.'

'Can I come in? This is a little complicated.'

Harvey paused, as if actually considering my request. 'No. Whatever you gotta say, you can say in five minutes from out there. If you can't do that, it's a waste of my time anyway. Go on sport. You're on the clock.'

'Harvey, Ron has to pull back what he said on stage during the debate.'

'About what?'

'You know about what. The whole Ebola terrorism bit. He's got to retract it.'

'Or what?'

'Or we'll be a laughingstock by tomorrow morning.'

'I don't think you've seen any of the network coverage. Wolfson is eating it up. Snap polls after the debate also indicate a hugely positive response. So what's the downside?'

'The downside is, it's not true, Harvey.'

'Last I checked, we weren't in the truth business, we were in politics. All's fair, and all that sort a' thing, sport.'

'Harvey, we don't want to go down this path.'

'This is politics, kid. We go down whichever path leads to victory. What's your beef?'

'My beef? My beef is that I'm a Muslim and by saying this stuff, we are making ourselves into an openly racist, anti-Muslim campaign! How can I work for somebody like that?'

'That's not at all how I read it. We've raised questions about national security. We ain't saying that's the way it is. We're just sayin'' it's something the government should look into, and by not looking into it, the current administration is being negligent. We're not accusing anybody of anything. You shouldn't take it so personally.'

'How the fuck can I not take it personally, Harvey? Han just asked me to give a personal guarantee, on behalf of all Muslims in the fucking world, that something like this could never happen! How is that not racist?'

'Han's a fucking idiot, and you know that already. Talking to him is like me talking to my toilet seat and expecting it to spout some Confucian wisdom. So why waste your time?'

'Harvey, please, we've got to talk to Ron about this. We have to convince him that this is a bad idea.'

'I'm not touching this issue with a ten-foot pole. And neither should you. Besides, I'm not convinced that this is a bad idea, politically.'

'Harvey, you've got to say something to him. Otherwise… otherwise, I'll have to resign.'

'Let me tell you something, kid. A bit of free advice. Never give Ron an ultimatum. Get some sleep, you look like shit. You'll look at the world different once we've won the nomination on Super Tuesday. Now fuck off.'

I went down to my room, but I couldn't sleep. I just sat there, upright in the chair and stared at the wall for hours. I thought and thought and thought, but I still couldn't muster up the courage to go and talk to Ron directly. As dawn broke, I flipped on the TV. CNN was reporting incidents of violence against Muslims in Illinois and Michigan, and somebody had beaten up a Sikh gas station attendant in Tennessee. It wasn't clear whether it was because his assailants thought he was Muslim or whether they just didn't want to pay the extra five dollars they owed for the gas they had bought.

At seven am, I finally got out of the chair. I had one card left to play. I took the elevator up to the floor above mine and knocked on another hotel room door.

'Waj! What are you doing here so early? I thought we were

meeting to go over today's media engagements at eight?' Despite the early hour, Krystal was fully dressed and made up, and as usual, looked stunning. I had grown close to Krystal since she had approached me in New Hampshire. She was really intelligent, light years ahead of the Diamond boys. Ron was right to put her on a pedestal above them. I guess, growing up as the attractive daughter of a porn actor-turned real estate developer, she had to develop some defences to ensure she didn't come across as too available, but under that armour I had found a really, really nice person.

For some reason, in the last few days since I had my fight with Shai, Krystal and I seemed to be spending more time together. It was almost as if she sensed that I was hurting. Of course, that was ridiculous, there was no way she could have known that Shai and I were…well, whatever we were, leave alone that we had fought. It was probably just the highly pressurised environment of the campaign running on full steam in the lead up to Super Tuesday. Whatever it was, I had felt in her a kindred spirit over these last days. And I think she sensed the same in me. That's why I thought she was my ace in the hole.

'Krystal, what Han made Ron do during the debate…'

'Was horrible. Yeah, I don't know where that asshole gets this rubbish from?'

There. I knew it. We were kindred spirits. 'Krystal, we've got to find a way to retract that statement.'

'Forty-eight hours before Super Tuesday? Waj, that's crazy. Everything's locked. We do something stupid like retracting the statement, and that gives Ryan Herrera a huge advantage. We'll look indecisive, and voters will still have enough time to rethink their decision. Specially here, in California, where it's going to be a close race anyway.'

'Krystal, I know, but there are some things that are morally right and morally wrong. What Han made Ron say, was wrong. It's going to have repercussions. CNN says there have already been attacks on Muslims…'

'Oh Waj, you can hardly believe CNN. They're always looking to connect these sorts of things, no matter how outlandish that may be.'

'Krystal, this isn't about right-wing or left-wing media. What Ron said, was just wrong. I feel that way, as a Muslim. We have to be better than this. You have to convince him. Everyone is saying its good politics, but you've got to tell him that he has to rise above the politics of the issue.'

'Waj, if everyone else is telling him this was a good idea, then why would I put myself out on a limb to say the opposite? Why would I burn all my credit with him, on something like this? What do I get out of this?'

'You get to do the right thing, Krystal! This isn't some kind of 'Let's make a deal' parody! I've told Harvey already, and I'm telling you, that if Ron doesn't walk this one back, I'm resigning from the campaign.'

She paused for a long moment, looking me up and down, evaluating me, perhaps trying to judge my sanity, perhaps trying to evaluate if I was in fact the emotional kind of Muslim that Han tried to paint me as. 'Waj, that would not be a smart thing to do. You've got all this leverage with Ron (for some reason she always called him Ron instead of dad), why would you throw it away so childishly? I'm sorry but that's the kind of idiotic thing Luke would do. Be mature about this, Waj. Use it to your advantage. Add to your leverage.'

'I'm not leveraging this, Krystal. I'm walking.'

'I'm sorry to hear that. I truly am. I guess we won't be going over the media engagements then. Goodbye.' And with that extremely curt reply, she banged her door on my face like I had never mattered.

The next 48 hours were a blur. I didn't go in to work, I turned off my cell phone, and requested a change of room in the hotel so that no one could come looking for me. From the rumpled sheets of notepaper in my room, I apparently took several hundred stabs at writing a resignation letter. I snuck out of the hotel for long walks in the city late at night, even though LA is probably the worst city in the world to walk in. I was utterly defeated and, as Krystal had made abundantly clear, utterly disposable as well. Acknowledging my defeat, I did the only thing any reasonable person would do in my situation. I raided my minibar and got absolutely shitfaced.

I must have been passed out through all of Super Tuesday, because it was pitch dark when I was awoken by a heavy pounding on my door. As the smell hit me, I retched, and then realised it was coming from me. The pounding only got harder as I fumbled for the light and staggered to the door.

Of all the people that I imagined to be knocking on my door, the last one I expected was Ron Diamond, alongwith two of his security guys, holding a gigantic bucket of KFC, looking like the cat that ate all the cream. Or chicken wings, in his case.

'Looks like you've been on a real bender, Iowa State. Haven't shown up for work in two days either. Either you're shacked up in there with the best piece of ass this side of the Rio Grande, or you're looking to quit or be fired.'

'Ron...I'm sorry...I was going to come to you...'

'But you thought you should hit the minibar a few hundred times before you did. Krystal and Harvey tell me you're pissed about what I said during the debate.'

'Ron...I'm a Muslim. I may not be a good one, but I am one...'

'I didn't call you a terrorist.'

'Yeah but Ron...'

'Listen Iowa, let me enlighten you about certain facts, since it looks like you haven't emerged from your Batcave for a while. You're standing here, talking to the Republican nominee for President of the United States.'

'We won?'

'Fourteen out of fifteen states. Swept Ryan fucking Herrera straight out, along with yesterday's garbage. I beat him by five points here in California. He's only won his home state, and he's hanging on to his lead there by a thread. And I managed to do all this, because of my Ebola terrorism line. You ever seen The Godfather III? Probably before your time. Lousy movie, but it has one good line. This mafia don tells Andy Garcia "Finance is a gun. Politics is knowing when to pull the trigger." You're right, I don't know whether the story Han gave me was true or not. All I know is, it's a weapon. And if politics is knowing when to pull the trigger, I'm the quickest draw in the West. I told you before, I don't make the rules, I just play the game. And right now, I'm winning. Which means you're winning. So why would you want to jump off, just when things are starting to get good? Over an issue that's going to disappear in another couple of days? You've studied American politics. People have said all sorts of shit to get elected. None of it matters. Only thing that matters is what they did once they got elected. So sober up, eat something,' he shoved the KFC bucket into my hands, 'And for God's sake, take a shower. You stink worse than my second wife after a gang bang. And your ass better be on the plane tomorrow morning. We've got a lot of campaigning to do.'

12.

FOREIGN POLICY CREDENTIALS
(OR HOW TO CHANNEL YOUR INNER KISSINGER)

MAKKAH, SAUDI ARABIA

'Disaster. An absolute disaster.'

The floor-to-ceiling windows give a panoramic view of the grand mosque complex. The décor is typically flashy, what can be classified as Saudi royal chic, with lots of gold trim and overstuffed cushions reeking of oudh. The room, as befits a royal guesthouse, is massive but curiously furnished, with all the furniture placed in one corner and all the space near the windows overlooking the Haram lying vacant. Shakaib had initially thought this was just bad decorating, probably done by some royal flunkey or minor princess in need of a project, but at prayer time it all made sense. Years ago, the Crown Prince's uncle had petitioned the caretakers of the holy mosque to designate the room as part of the mosque complex, since it had a breathtaking view of Islam's holiest site and would eliminate the requirement for royal guests to actually step outside of these gilded walls and join the proletarian masses for prayer. The slightly old fashioned and stuffy caretakers had very fixed ideas that pilgrims ought to actually physically join the congregation, irrespective of their exalted status. And so, for many years the petition was refused until recently, when the Crown Prince came along and offered a

"

sharp word and a lavish refurbishment of the caretakers' apartments. Suddenly, a fatwa appeared which enabled all VIP guests to say their prayers from the comfort of this room, as long as the guests had a line of sight to the Ka'aba. Which explained the lack of furniture in front of the windows, since that area became a defacto extension of the holy mosque at prayer time.

'Total disaster.'

Shakaib looks around the room at the sizeable delegation. And this, the ADC tells him, is the smallest entourage ever taken by a Prime Minister on a foreign visit. In recent years, it has become tradition for newly minted PMs to inaugurate their foreign policy by going on a holy pilgrimage. The convention serves the dual purpose of displaying the new PM's piety and also allows him or her to pay obeisance to the Saudi monarchs, upon whom the country is heavily dependent for subsidised oil and remittances from expatriates. This year's 'shrunken' delegation nevertheless still includes the foreign minister (whom Javed Afridi hates), the finance minister (who Javed Afridi barely tolerates), the religious affairs minister (a nominee of the YouTuber who has so far on this trip been more interested in the buffet table than in any religious observance), Seema, the special assistant for youth affairs (No one is quite sure why she is on this trip, except for speculation that she is focusing on the affairs part of her title more than anything else), Hamza and Taimur, (who seem to have grown into the role of jesters for the Afridi court, always around but not particularly helpful in any given situation), the military secretary, the ADC, the PM's security staff and Shakaib. And of course, the Prime Minister, who is the only one not present in the room.

'Utter disaster.'

'Yes, Hamza, we've heard what a disaster it's been, there's no use repeating it.'

'Shakaib sahib, you don't understand. This is going to turn from an unmitigated disaster into a complete catastrophe. Social media has gotten hold of the footage, not only of the PM not knowing how to perform Umrah, but also they are reporting that the Crown Prince snubbed him by just giving him an audience for twenty minutes. The previous Prime Minister got an hour and a half on his first visit. And he got invited back for dinner that night.'

'OK, it wasn't twenty minutes. More like…twenty-five. And as for the Umrah gaffe, why didn't you coach the PM on what to do? I mean, you did like 500 Umrahs when you were posted here.'

'That wasn't my job. That's why we brought along the minister for religious affairs.'

The minister looks up from the buffet at the mention of his name. 'Listen, I am a minister. It's not part of my responsibilities to teach the PM about the basics of doing an Umrah.'

'Technically, you are the minister for religious affairs, so this is literally your job description.'

Stung by the criticism, the minister's face turns red and he puts down the glazed donut he's been holding. 'Well, I mean…if I had gotten a little forewarning…I mean, I had to do my own Umrah as well, you know.'

'You could have just told him to follow what you were doing.'

'Well…I was looking it up on my app. Between that and taking selfies in the holy mosque for my Instagram account, I was a little tied up.'

Taimur speaks up. 'This is irrelevant. This will be forgotten, and our dear minister can always give a ringing endorsement of the examples of the PM's piety on his Instagram. The bigger issue is the story about the Crown Prince's snub. The minute the PM finds out about that, he's going to blow up.'

As if on cue, a rattled security officer runs into the room and says the PM has summoned Shakaib. Everyone can gauge from the security officer's expression that its unlikely to be a pleasant meeting. Shakaib follows the officer out of the room to another suite on the same floor. This suite is more luxurious than the viewing room, with an equally magnificent view of the Ka'aba and an even more private prayer area. One look at the expression on Javed Afridi's face makes it evident that he is fuming.

'Shakaib! This was your idea, wasn't it? To meet this bloody Crown Prince!'

'Prime Minister, you were scheduled to travel here for pilgrimage. Every Prime Minister in the last twenty years has made this journey and each of them has met the Saudi head of state on that trip. For you to have not met him would have looked bad. Besides, he was very keen to meet you. He specifically asked me about it.'

'This is how he shows his keenness? This bullshit meeting?! Who the hell does this asshole think he is?'

'Prime Minister, I would advise that we choose our language very carefully here in this room. The Saudis probably listen in on their guests and we wouldn't want to say anything undiplomatic that may cause us problems in the future.'

'Fuck diplomacy. And fuck this brat of yours! He may be a Crown Prince, but I'm Javed Afridi! I was a superstar when this whelp was in diapers! How dare he make me wait for twenty minutes! Nobody has ever made me wait!'

'Prime Minister, I understand your irritation, but we have to acknowledge that there is a fundamental disparity in the relationship between our two countries. Sometimes, that will manifest itself at inopportune moments. I think you should draw solace from the fact that the Crown Prince was personally very eager to meet you. And it wasn't just a pro forma meeting. He has been a fan of yours since he was a boy.'

'He was eager to meet me, for just twenty minutes! And that also not to discuss any important geopolitical issues but to ask my opinion on whether he should buy Manchester United or not! I'm not some bloody football scout! I'm the Prime Minister of Pakistan! And now his people have deliberately leaked this story about him having met me for only twenty minutes. My opponents are having a field day on social media, saying the Saudis have 'downgraded' us since I became Prime Minister, and that my bloody predecessor had a much better standing internationally! It would have been better had we not come on this tour!'

'Prime Minister, I think you're giving too much weightage to what is being said on social media. We should focus on policy, and policy-wise, the good thing is that the Crown Prince pledged that nothing would change in our relationship. At a time when they are cutting loose others like Egypt and Lebanon, they will maintain their commitments with us. That's what we came here for, and we got that. This social media garbage about the Crown Prince meeting you for twenty minutes instead of an hour, is a storm in a teacup. It'll be forgotten in a day.'

'I didn't come here to beg him for crumbs off his table. I came here to give him my advice on important issues of regional importance! This was supposed to be my launching pad on the international stage! And he tries to brush me off? Me? Well, two can play this game. I'm going to tweet about our meeting as well. I'm going to say that I was the one who cut short the meeting because unfortunately, I felt that the Crown Prince was not a person of substance.'

Shakaib knows that in his current mood, Javed Afridi is capable of anything. 'Prime Minister, before doing anything rash, why don't you discuss it with your cabinet? Or at least the key members? The foreign, finance and religious affairs ministers are here. Call them in and debate the issue with them, so you can benefit from their collective wisdom.'

'Why the hell would I take advice from that bloody police inspector's son? Just because he's learned how to wear a suit, doesn't mean he knows anything about foreign affairs. I made him the foreign minister and I can take it away from him in an instant.'

Shakaib grits his teeth. In the past two months, he has learnt that there is no arguing with Javed Afridi when he's in this kind of mood. He tries to think of something to say that will somehow avert what is sure to be a debacle greater than all the adjectives Hamza can think of. And then suddenly, it comes to him. Something Wajahat mentioned in his last email. A long shot, one reeking of desperation, but anything to circumvent Afridi trashing the Crown Prince on Twitter.

'There is something else we can do, Prime Minister. Something that may solve our social media issues and satisfy your desire to play a bigger role on the international stage.'

'What?'

'My son wrote to me two days ago and informed me that Ron Diamond, the Republican presidential candidate, was departing for Europe on a short foreign tour. Now that he's won the nomination, his advisors want to shore up his foreign policy credentials, since many people believe he's a lunatic, myself included. Nevertheless, as you had once predicted, he has won the nomination and has to be taken seriously now. Maybe we can arrange a meeting between the two of you. A photo op, a short exchange of views on key issues, something like that. Perhaps we could meet him somewhere in Europe. Wajahat's email said they were going to go to Poland first, because of Diamond's ethnic origins, but they are due to be in London over the weekend. If we could fly there directly, I could maybe get my son to arrange a meeting…'

'That's perfect! It's the perfect rebound from this Clown Prince! Why should I bother with him when I can speak to the next President of the United States! You've got to arrange this! You're the only one I trust! These buffoons outside can't do anything right. Get it done, Shakaib.'

* * *

It's well past midnight by the time Shakaib manages to get to the royal palace. The Chief Usher informs him that the Crown Prince was scheduled to return to Riyadh that evening, but extended his stay just to meet with him. Even in his heavily accented English, the Usher's tone has a degree of deference and wonder, as if he is awestruck by this foreigner who can compel the prince to delay his plans.

Unlike the earlier official meeting with Afridi, Shakaib is whisked through the palace and taken into its innermost sanctums, the private royal apartments. The one used by the Crown Prince is devoid of any of the usual royal trappings. It looks more like a teenager's man cave.

Taylor Swift blares on the speakers while a fast food feast, featuring burgers, pizzas, french fries, hoagies and milkshakes is laid out on a pool table. The Crown Prince himself sits on a comfortable couch, playing the latest version of FIFA on a video wall. Gone are the official robes and headdress of a prince, and in their stead, he is dressed in a Manchester United kit. As Shakaib enters, he drops his controller and gives the older man a bear hug, thus further raising Shakaib in the estimation of the Usher.

'Uncle! I am so glad you came! I wasn't able to meet you properly at the official get-together.'

'Your Highness, don't you think you are taking your love of fast food a little too far? You told me you were eating healthy, but I see you have now had a Coke dispensing fountain installed here.'

On cue, the Crown Prince burps. 'It's fantastic. Dispenses 18 different flavours. You should try the raspberry. The Coca-Cola people send it specially for me.' He laughs at Shakaib's disapproving look. 'Oh come on, a little fast food never hurt anybody. I end up working so late, I need something fun to eat. Besides, I bet you haven't given up your ice cream. I hear they have Baskin Robbins now in Pakistan. You must be in heaven. Come on, have something to eat. Aunty is not here.'

Shakaib laughs and picks up a Big Mac container. 'How is your father?'

'His health is not what it used to be. He's often ill, which means I increasingly have to carry the burden of his responsibilities. He misses the old days, though. He misses you a lot. He mentions you often.'

'It is very kind of him to do so.'

'It's not kind. It's just the truth. We all miss you. Why don't you take some time out and stay on for a few days? We can fly to Riyadh tomorrow and go meet him. If you like, I can send a jet for Aunty. She can enjoy a few days shopping and relaxing. It will be a good break for her.'

'Your Highness, not all of us are princes who can just drop everything and jet off on a whim. I have grave responsibilities as well.'

'Yes, I saw your responsibility. He is a grave one.' The prince laughs and inhales half a packet of French fries.

'Highness, in all the years I have known you, I have never seen you be unkind or rude. Then why did you make the Prime Minister wait? You were the one who was keen to meet him. You messaged me yourself. But then you got rid of him in twenty minutes and to top it all off, announced that fact on social media. He feels very cut up about it.'

'Uncle, I assure you, I did not mean to be rude. I was genuinely held up. My father called just before the meeting to discuss something. And as for meeting him, yes I did want to meet him, because I wanted his advice on whether I should buy Manchester United or not. I want to do it, you know I have been a fan since I was a boy, but my sovereign wealth fund guys want me to buy Chelsea instead.'

'He came here ready to discuss regional politics.'

'Uncle, with due respect, the man is a moron. If I want to discuss regional politics, I will call Henry Kissinger. Truth be told, even the discussion I had with him about Manchester United was out of respect for you. I've already decided to buy the club and as much as I idolised Javed Afridi the player, he knows as much about buying football clubs as he does about regional politics. However, I will definitely consult him when I am picking my fantasy football squad for the weekend.'

'Highness, your brush-off has become a political issue for us. Our political opponents are claiming that they had better relations with your late uncle, and this is your way of indicating a downgrading of the relationship between the two countries. This is a major problem for us. You know Pakistanis feel a special affinity for the Guardian of the two holy mosques.'

'Uncle, it was not a brush-off. I didn't know what else to say to the man after twenty minutes! He is the most vacant person I have ever met. And so pompous! It is Allah's grace that he made him talented at football, otherwise Afridi wouldn't have known how to get through life. And as for your previous rulers, my uncle spent hours with them because they were involved in corrupt businesses together.

Businesses I have ordered shut down, at great loss to both my 'dear' cousins and to your opponents. Perhaps you should highlight that fact in your media.'

'Thank you, Highness. I will certainly inform the PM that he can use this information to counter the social media narrative.'

'Of course. But uncle, you look tired. This politics does not suit you.'

'It's been a rollercoaster day. After the meeting with you, I had to really hustle to set up an alternative meeting with the American presidential candidate Ron Diamond. Wajahat is working for him these days. To be honest, it has been a rollercoaster couple of months. But I guess new governments always have a tough time initially.'

'Waj is working for Ron Diamond? Wow, I didn't know that. And you didn't object? I would have thought you would have had objections to him working for a porn star, and an anti-Muslim bigot at that.'

Shakaib shrugs his shoulders. 'When kids grow up, they make their own choices. Between your father and myself, we have never managed to get you to quit fast food either. I was extremely reluctant initially, but obviously this campaign seems to have turned into a serious one, and Wajahat, by all accounts, is at the heart of it. I have told him several times to get out, especially with this garbage that Diamond keeps spewing about Muslims, but my son has his own logic.'

'Well, I wish him the best. Next time I go to America, I must meet up with Waj. It's been too long. Tell me, what can I do for you?'

'I have one request, Highness.'

'Name it.'

'We…the Prime Minister's delegation…need to borrow your plane. You see, Diamond has agreed to meet with Javed Afridi in London, but he is only there for the next 24 hours. There is no way we can get a commercial flight that will get us there in time. Chartering a plane from Pakistan, in these days of economic crisis, will become a huge political issue for us. And we have to meet Diamond to change the narrative of the last day. Will you help?'

The Crown Prince sighs. 'Of course you can have my plane. But uncle, what is this man doing to you? You are jumping through hoops for him. He is not worth it.'

'What he wants to do for the country makes it worthwhile.'

'Uncle, I have been Crown Prince now for four years. I see all sorts of people and I have met dozens of world leaders, so I have developed a sense for this. Afridi is not someone who will change things. He doesn't have it in him. He is a megalomaniac. He will only make things worse.'

'I believe he will change things for the better. I have to believe that, for my children. I want them to come back to a country they can be proud of.'

'Uncle, this is not your age to struggle like this. Why don't you come back here and work with me? We are doing some amazing things. And every time I take a decision, I always try and think back to the lessons and values that you taught me. You will be invaluable to me. And the King would be overjoyed. Your family will be happy and comfortable.'

'I know you are doing amazing things. You are building a city under the water! Who would have thought it possible! I am so proud of you. But it's my country, and I have to fight for it. And I believe that Javed Afridi, for all his shortcomings, is the best man for us.'

'My prayers are with you, uncle. And remember, if you need anything, you let me know. I have informed my chief of protocol that he is to facilitate you in every way possible. Javed Afridi may be an idiot, but you are the one who matters to me.'

* * *

LONDON (12 hours later)

Shakaib marvels at how grown-up his son looks. Gone is the boy with ruffled, overgrown hair, with his perpetual uniform of hoodies and tracks. In his place is a young man in a smart suit and tie, his hair cut stylishly with not a strand out of place, confidently firing off various instructions to campaign staffers as he walks towards his father. He may not agree with Ron Diamond's politics, but Shakaib cannot deny that being part of the campaign has made a man out of his son.

'How was Poland?' Father and son embrace in front of the side entrance of the Ritz in Piccadilly.

'Cold, even though its April. Bad food. I was stuck eating fries most of the time, because there was pork in everything. I'm too used to New York, where virtually everything's kosher.'

'And how did your Mr. Diamond do, on his first foreign trip?'

'OK, I guess. It was an easy one, relatively speaking. We went to Lodz, where his ancestors were from, and the Polish PM was good enough to do a meet and greet. That's what we wanted. It's much harder here. The Brits don't want to see us for fear of looking like they're favouring one party over the other. Plus, I think they expect us to lose in November to Jessica May, so they probably figure it's a waste of their time.'

'And how about you? I recall getting a barely legible email from you a few weeks back which, once I had deciphered your garbled syntax, seemed to indicate that you were quitting.'

Waj looks at his father sheepishly. 'Yeah, about that. I guess I had a little too much to drink that night.'

'I hope you're not drinking that much on a regular basis.'

'Dad. Come on. I'm not. I'm responsible, you know that.'

'I know. You must have been very upset to have gotten that drunk. What happened? Are you OK?'

'I…yeah…I just had a moment. I wasn't sure if I was pursuing the right path.'

'And now? Ron Diamond has convinced you that his ravings are somehow the gospel truth?'

'If he wins, he can be a real game changer. Isn't that what you say about your guy? From what I hear, he's been in a number of gaffes recently. Apparently, Mo brushed him off after just twenty minutes.'

'It was more like twenty-five. And they had a constructive

discussion on matters of mutual interest.'

'Yeah. Like buying Manchester United.' Waj snickers.

'Who told you that?'

'I saw a tweet about it, I think. Or was it a blog? These things always leak.'

'Look at my son, the political professional.'

'You had a problem when I wanted to go into showbiz, and now you have a problem with me being in politics? I recall you're the one who called me for this meeting.'

'I… I'm sorry. That was out of line. I'm very proud of you. I may not be thrilled with your choice of candidate, but I am very proud of how you've created a niche for yourself. You're a powerful man. All of my colleagues are in awe of my son, the advisor to a US presidential candidate. And thank you for this meeting. We were in a tight spot and this has helped.'

Waj shrugs. 'Not a problem, Dad. It suits us too. Since the Brits weren't willing to play ball, we get to say our trip didn't go emptyhanded. Ron meets up with another world leader, the head of a country of 250 million people, a nuclear power, and a Muslim to boot. So, when's your guy coming?'

'On his way. How do we do this?'

'Don't worry, I've got it in hand.'

Once again, Shakaib stands aside and marvels as Wajahat handles the meeting like a seasoned pro. Afridi is received with all due deference and whisked off to a special meeting room in the hotel. Wajahat manages it down to ensuring that both men enter the room at the same time from different doors, thus ensuring no ruffled egos on either side. Afridi brings with him Shakaib, his much maligned foreign minister, Taimur and the High Commissioner, whereas Ron's delegation is smaller, with Waj, Harvey, Han and Krystal who Waj notices, has once again dressed for effect, her long legs on display in a short skirt and stiletto heels. But Afridi isn't Phil. He is a skilled apex predator when it comes to the opposite sex. He takes it all in, silently admiring but completely composed.

It's when the two men sit down across from each other that one can almost smell the testosterone in the air. Both men stare at each other wordlessly, two stags sizing each other up. There is a pregnant pause which extends well after the photographers have snapped the official photos of the meeting, and Wajahat and Shakaib share a worried look, unsure of how to proceed. Afridi appears chastened by his experience with the Crown Prince and holds his tongue, but does not break his gaze away from Ron. Finally, Ron breaks the silence with a smile.

'I heard a lot about you, back in the 80s' and 90s'. Is it true, the story about you and the Princess of Wales having a thing?'

Both father and son wear shocked expressions but before anyone can intervene, Afridi flashes Ron the widest of smiles. 'Are the rumours about you and Farah Fawcett true?'

Ron nods his head slowly. 'Yeah. I fucked her. I fucked her till she was bow legged. She said her boyfriend couldn't satisfy her because he had a small dick.'

'That's what the princess said about the Prince of Wales.'

Both men break out into raucous laughter, completely defusing the tension in the room.

'They used to tell me you had quite a score, back in the day.' Ron takes two bottles of soda from the bucket in front of them and tosses one to Afridi.

'What can I say? I enjoy sex. But you're quite a connoisseur yourself. I've even used some of your products.'

'Yeah? Which ones?'

'Uh, Prime Minister, perhaps we could move on to more substantial matters …' Shakaib tries to interject before the conversation becomes completely lurid, but Afridi ignores him.

'The penis enlarger. And various creams and lubes.'

'Did it work for you?'

'Actually, yes. My partners always enjoyed it when I used it.'

'There you go. Another satisfied customer. See what I always say, Harvey? Customer feedback is key.' Harvey nods as if the conversation is as normal as any between a sales rep and a consumer. 'I never watched a lot of soccer, but I was envious of your conquests. There were at least two British models, they were sisters I think, who I had heard you banged. I really wanted to get with them and I remember chasing them all over New York the summer of '89, but I couldn't close the deal.'

'The Ashleys. Trust me, you didn't miss much. Nice to look at, but both were lousy in bed. And the younger one had BO issues too.'

The two men laugh again while the two delegations, stunned at this unorthodox turn of events, look at each other and smile nervously.

'Listen, what do I call you? I'm terrible with pronunciations.'

'Jim. That's what all my teammates used to call me.'

'Jim. That's easy. Call me Ron. Hey Jim, you wanna get rid of the suits? Let's get some food in here. I don't know about you, but I'm starving. We can keep the father and son, but the rest of you can all fuck off.'

The foreign minister bristles at the profanity and is about to say something, when Afridi gives him a withering look. 'You heard him. Get out. My lot are all incompetent anyway, Ron. Except for Shakaib. He's the only dependable one.'

'Welcome to the club. Sometimes I doubt whether my sons are actually even mine, they're so dumb. But these two,' Ron gets up and puts his arms around Krystal and Waj, 'These two are my stars. So, this is your old man, huh Waj?'

'Dad, Ron. Ron, my father, Shakaib.'

'You got a good kid here, Shak. Real good. Still a little green, but he's coming along nicely.'

'Thank you … Mr. Diamond.'

'You know Ron, I predicted your victory. Very early on. I saw you in one of your debates, before the first contest, and I told Shakaib that this man will win because he understands what the people want. They want someone unfiltered, not some on-message robot.'

'You're a man of great vision, Jim. From what I hear, you've done pretty well too, overthrowing the existing elites in your country.'

'They were real cunts. Never worked a day in their lives but became billionaires through years and years of corruption.'

'All elites are cunts. They always act as if their shit don't stink. It's the same in America. My rival, Jessica May, is part of the old elite establishment. Like you said, these people have never worked for anything in their lives. Got handed everything on a silver platter, but they act like they're doing the country a favour by running it. Not like you and me. Whatever we have in life, we made it ourselves by swimming in the gutter.'

'She sounds just like my rivals. Let me know if I can do anything to help you get elected.'

'Uh, Prime Minister, we cannot interfere in the election of another country.'

'Why not, Shak? We Americans do it all the time. Been doing it for decades in your part of the world. Iraq, Iran, Afghanistan. We're very good at going into places, but not as good getting out of them. If people like Jessica May and that asshole President of ours ever lived in the real world, they would have understood the need to always have an exit strategy. I'd appreciate it if your people are able to get something on her.'

'Listen, Ron, I have an idea. I've been monitoring the Taliban takeover in Afghanistan. My people, some of my political allies and members of my intelligence services, have very good relations with the Taliban. Plus, I have a lot of goodwill with them because many of the Talibs are football fans. I know you have some troops stuck in Kabul, right Shakaib?'

'Yes, Prime Minister. There are American troops at the embassy and the ISAF headquarters, and some at the airport. They are trying to evacuate, but the process is slow and the Taliban aren't very helpful.'

'Ron, I can talk to the Taliban. I can get them to agree to allowing the American troops out without any hassle. I offered my assistance to your ambassador in Islamabad, but he was an idiot. He ignored me. Gave me some line about 'checking with Washington first.' I could have solved this problem for you guys six weeks ago.'

'Typical, fucking foreign service bureaucrat. Hey Waj, make a note of this. The minute we get in to the White House, I'm firing the ambassador in Islamabad. Jim, can you still make a deal with them?'

'Of course. But your bloody President should at least be willing to answer my calls.'

'King is an absolute disaster. We're going to solve this problem, you and I, Jim.'

'Uh, Ron, we can't do anything. We're not part of the US government. You're just the Republican nominee. If we try and negotiate with the Taliban, it'll be seen as interfering with US foreign policy.'

Ron looks at Waj and smiles, and then turns to Afridi and winks. 'You see, Jim? This kid. Bright as fuck, but he's got a lot to learn about the real world. I'm not going to negotiate with the Taliban. Jim is, and he can because he's Prime Minister of Pakistan. He can do whatever the fuck he likes. Isn't that right, Jim?'

'Of course.'

'Exactly. All we do is publicly acknowledge what a great job Jim has done, what fantastic efforts he's made in trying to extricate American soldiers from Afghanistan, and what a shame it is that no one in the King administration has paid any attention to his efforts. It's not interfering with foreign policy to say that if I was President, I would immediately use the good offices of my friend Jim to get those boys home as quickly as possible. That's just politics.'

Javed Afridi lifts the bottle of Coke in his hands and toasts Ron Diamond. 'What's the line from that film? I think this is the beginning of a beautiful friendship.'

13.
THE
HUSBAND PROBLEM

'**SHAI, YOU SAID** we didn't have a problem on the husband front.'

Shai picks up her head from the old log table in Jessica's barn. She wishes she could ingest a whole bottle of aspirin to rid her of the piercing headache that she's had for the past three hours. It just won't go away, a bit like the problems of the May campaign. The past two months have been relentless trench warfare. Jessica's inability to decisively kill off challengers despite an impressive showing on Super Tuesday, coupled with the now incontrovertible evidence that the Vice President is conducting a proxy war against them, has dragged the campaign on much longer than any of the people now assembled in the barn had hoped.

The hours have been long and the work unending. They had all thought a Memorial Day weekend spent with family and loved ones would be restorative, before the frenzy of the conventions and the general election campaign. For Shai personally, she still hasn't been able to sort out her relationship with Waj. Things between them remain as they left them that early morning in a New York hotel room. There have been no further hookups, just the occasionally exchanged text or WhatsApp message. Even she, for all her hard headed practicality, has had to acknowledge that he was more than just a passing pleasure for her. She has missed him in a way she has never missed or yearned for any previous lover. This is a new sensation for her. In the past, her relationships, even the ones that grew beyond pure physical gratification, were firmly controlled by her. She has always known how much emotional investment to make and when to pull back. But Waj has surprised her. There's something about him. Something that makes her, for the first time in her life, covet a deeper relationship. She had hoped to use this weekend to reconnect with him, to talk things out. But all such hopes have been dashed by the news of Jessica's husband, which has hit the campaign like the atom bomb on Hiroshima.

'I'm sorry, Mike. That's what she told me. I have to accept that. What did you want me to do, get a private eye to follow him around to see if he was going to sex parties?'

'What I wouldn't give for this to have just been a regular sex scandal.'

'Come on, Johnny, he wasn't involved in anything.'

'Yet. The operative word is yet. But his business partner, with whom he went on vacations, whose corporate jet he shared, whose house in Martha's Vineyard was used by both Jessica and Tim, has been exposed as a serial paedophile. So we can't say with any degree of surety that he isn't involved. And why can't we say that? Because we never fucking bothered to vet him when we started this campaign!'

'Mike, that was a no-go area for her. That was her express wish. What were we supposed to say to her? 'Sorry ma'am, but we're going to stick our noses into your marriage by force?' Come on.'

'We should have. You and I should have, Shai. That's what you do in presidential campaigns. Had we done so, at least we wouldn't be having a crisis meeting about what to do now that the candidate's husband's business partner has been arrested and indicted by the US Attorney for having sex on 200 separate occasions with underage girls, over a five-year period.'

'Two hundred separate occasions. Jesus Christ, when did this guy get the time to make all that money? Looks like he was partying all the time.'

'I suspect a lot of the 'partying' was business development. You'll probably find a lot of his clients and partners were around when this stuff happened.'

'Come on, Mike, there's no proof of that yet! Maybe we're all jumping the gun here. It may not turn out to be as bad as we fear.'

'*No proof yet, that Senator Jessica May's husband was involved in the sex trafficking of underage girls on 200 separate occasions, along with his business partner.* Now that's a press release you never want to send out Johnny boy. Even Ron Diamond for all his fucking luck, would have difficulties coming back from that one.' Maury chuckles.

'Look Mike, there's no use crying over what's done. Jessica wanted things a certain way and we ensured that for her. Unfortunately, it's gone wrong for us. But Jessica wants us to look past this. What's our strategy for the general election? I cannot believe that Ron Diamond is coming off looking like Henry Kissinger, with his plan to get US troops out of Afghanistan! I mean, where are our plans to thwart him? He's scoring goal after goal, and we're throwing up air balls.'

'You can't make a strategy if you're constantly playing defence, Shai. Diamond clinched a decisive victory on Super Tuesday and became the unquestioned nominee of his party. Up until a week ago, we were still fighting off challenges from deadbeat Congressmen and small-time mayors.'

'Meanwhile, Ronny boy is getting on the shortlist for the Nobel Peace Prize, for his 'selfless' encouragement of peace talks with the Taliban. And getting his dick sucked by the editorial board of the *New York Times* for doing so.'

'I thought you always said foreign policy didn't matter in American politics, Maury.'

'Well, what can I tell you, Princess, that was before 5000 American troops got stuck in Kabul, while the Taliban swept the table. And Ron was the only prick who came up with a practical solution to get them out safely, while President King sat on his ass and twiddled his dick! How did he pull this off anyway? He must have a lucky charm stuck up his ass. I mean, how the fuck did Ron get a line to the Pakistani President?'

'It's the Pakistani Prime Minister, not the President. And he has a guy…' Shai bites her tongue for almost taking Waj's name, '…he has a Pakistani connection.'

Maury raises his eyebrows quizzically. 'He's not the same as… your Pakistani connection??'

'Fuck off, Maury!'

'That cocksucking motherfucker!!'

Their squabbling is ended abruptly by the outburst from Jessica. Each of them have, separately and together, spent a lot of time with Jessica May during the course of her political career. They have seen her wrestle through all sorts of crises, whether it was her first Senate campaign, her resignation from the cabinet on account of President's Baird's predilection for receiving fellatio from interns, her frustrations at not being able to match the charisma of Lincoln King eight years ago, and of course her travails over the past year. They have all seen her show displeasure in various ways, sarcastic, cutting, bitchy, but always reserved and controlled. They have even heard her curse a handful of times, and then also only in the face of the greatest provocation, like her 'Who the fuck is Balthazar Risotto?' in Iowa. But the three men and one woman who represent Jessica May's brains trust, have never, in their collective experience, heard her call anyone a cocksucking motherfucker.

They don't have to wait very long to learn the identity of her target. 'That motherfucker thinks he can just sit in the White House and shovel shit on me, and I'm just going to keep bending over and taking it? Fuck him!'

By this point, while Maury continues to enjoy the tirade, Mike and Shai grow concerned at Jessica's lashing out against the President. 'Jessica, what's he done?'

'Fuck my life! He's nuked us! The President's nuked us! I can't believe it.' John Raines' distress increases with every scroll of his mobile phone. '*POTUS has expressed his horror and utter disgust at the allegations of serial child molestation and sex trafficking levelled against Mr. Brendan Bracken. Mr. Bracken, who is a partner in Bracken-Regan*

Investments, a private equity fund he runs along with Mr. Tim Regan, the spouse of Democratic presidential candidate Senator Jessica May, has been indicted by the US Attorney for the southern district of New York on 200 separate counts of trafficking and having sex with minors. Responding to suggestions from some media outlets that the King administration would look to hush up the case as it involves an individual connected to the circle of the Democratic frontrunner, the President in his weekly press conference, responded to such concerns by making it clear that there would be no deals offered to Mr. Bracken and no pressure on the US Attorney's office from any quarter. The President remarked that he expected the Justice Department to prosecute the case to the fullest extent of the law, and, if required, to look into any other individuals who may have been involved, irrespective of their closeness to any public figure. I mean, why doesn't he just come out and demand that Jessica should be handcuffed and hauled down to the US Attorney's office!'

'Holy shit. I can't believe King would stab us in the back like this.'

'It's that motherfucker from Iowa who's fondling his balls! This is his way of torpedoing me.'

Shai is shocked once again at the level of profanity spewing from Jessica's lips. 'You think the Veep put him up to it?'

'Of course! Those bastards just can't stand that I'm going to be the next leader of the Democratic party. They'll do anything to fuck me! I bet that cocksucker pushed the US Attorney to go after Brendan, just because it would embarrass me! If that's the way they want to play, that's fine. I'm done being the good soldier. I'm going to shit all over those motherfuckers! Maury, give me a policy area. I'm going to go after him. He thinks just because he's the first black president, he's got some kind of immunity? He's a politician like the rest of us, and I'm going to tear him down, just like any other pol. Give me a policy Maury. Shall I fuck him on this Afghanistan mess? Tell me, Maury!'

'Well, uh, Jessica, a bit late to go after King on Afghanistan. Ron Diamond's already taken the lead on that one. We go after the President now, and you look like you're the girly cheerleader for big, bad Ron, the quarterback. That's not a great image for you to have, especially with all the fucking misogynist assholes who are already sceptical about a female presidential candidate.'

'Fuck!! Give me something, Maury!'

'Well…how about crime? The Republicans are statistically correct. Crime rates have gone up in King's eight years in office. We can argue that his focus on civil liberties has made law enforcement soft on crime.'

'Maury, how can a Democrat argue against civil liberties?'

'We're not arguing against anything, Princess. We're just saying that Jessica is going to get tough on crime once she's in the White House. It's a great issue for us. We're trailing Ron Diamond in support among white males, and a tougher anti-crime stance will pull some of those voters back to us. Plus, we get to dog whistle that King was soft on crime because of his background.'

'Because he's black?!?'

'Because he's a liberal from Los Angeles, Princess. On the black thing, I'm not saying anything. But if the shoe fits…'

'How does that make us different from Ron Diamond, Maury?'

'Well, I hate to burst your bubble, Johnny boy, but if King keeps giving press conferences insinuating that Jessica's surrounded by a gang of serial paedos, then I'm afraid we won't have much of a campaign left. And by signalling a tougher stance on crime, we also distance ourselves from this controversy. No one can accuse us of trying to cut any backroom deals with the US Attorney if we're blasting away that we're tough on crime. Unless, of course, there are any backroom deals being cut. We should know about that…'

'There are no backroom deals, Maury. All of you can be very clear on that. There are no deals now, nor will there be at any point in the future.'

'What about Tim, Jessica? What if some evidence comes out… you know…'

'My husband is not a part of this campaign. Johnny, I want you to make that very clear to the press. He doesn't travel with us, he doesn't fund us, he doesn't advise us. If the US Attorney has any questions for him, that's between them and him. We will not defend or offer any clarifications on his behalf. There's a firewall between us and him.'

'What firewall?'

'Me.'

'No one is going to believe that, Jessica.'

'They better believe it, Mike. Because it's the truth. And you people better do a damn good job of selling this, because I have never been more serious about anything. If any evidence emerges of his criminal involvement with Brendan, I'm going to publicly announce that I'm divorcing him.'

'Jessica, are you sure that's the best course?'

'Yes, Shai. From now on, I'm all in. I'm not going to get bushwhacked by the likes of Lincoln King or Tim Regan. This is my campaign and I am going to win. So you just start preparing that offensive on crime, Maury. I'm going to carpet bomb Lincoln King and his cocksucking Vice President.'

* * *

They say the universe sends out signals at times, portents of momentous events and warnings before catastrophic ones. Throughout history, leaders, great and small, have invested heavily in trying to interpret these omens. The poet-mathematician Omar Khayyam financed his studies of cubic equations and binomial theorems, as well as his remarkably accurate calculations for the solar year, by casting horoscopes like an eleventh-century astrologer to the stars for the Seljuk sultan Malikshah, advising him when was a particularly propitious time to embark on his next rape and pillage venture. It is said that all of history is divided up into those that read the signals correctly, and those who didn't. Haley's Comet flashed over the English Channel in 1066, and while King Harold in London thought it was an unfavourable sign, across the water in Normandy, Willy the Bastard took it as confirmation of his destiny, and soon after became William the Conqueror. Even in modern times, Nancy Reagan always kept her astrologer on speed dial, and it is claimed that the Great Communicator rarely issued a key pronouncement or policy statement without first checking the star signs. Nancy claimed in later life that if White House Chief of Staff Don Regan had followed her astrologer's recommendations, the Iran Contra affair could have been completely avoided.

Jessica May had no Nancy Reagan and no astrologer advising her campaign. But looking back in retrospect, perhaps keeping one on the campaign payroll would have been the smart thing to do. An astrologer would have perhaps informed her that the missteps that seemed to plague her campaign from the beginning were a result of Mercury being in conflict with Mars, or Venus being blocked by Uranus. If the stars were indeed aligning against Jessica May, their culmination seemed to occur in the first three weeks of June.

It starts in Tulsa, Oklahoma, the unlikeliest of all celestial locations. Three days after the May campaign unleashes its broadside alleging the King administration's softness on crime, Ade Onitolo, a Nigerian immigrant with a prior arrest record for possession of three and a half ounces of marijuana, is stopped by Tulsa police officer Don Pence during a routine patrol. With his airpods soundly lodged in both ears and his head bent down towards the ground, Onitolo at first misses Officer Pence's instruction and then, fearful of the discovery of the spliff in his jacket pocket, tries to cross the road while reaching inside his jacket to change the song on his iPhone. Pence, already on edge after having been on patrol for the past six hours in the dangerous Valleyview neighbourhood, interprets this as Onitolo attempting to pull a weapon, and empties an entire pistol clip in the Nigerian man's back.

Even at that point, things could have perhaps been salvageable. But Pence, a former Marine with two tours in Iraq, but a rookie cop, sees Onitolo's body twitch and fires his last round into him at point blank range while standing over the body. This act of his is captured for all posterity by Blanka Kolenikova, a forty-five-year-old Ukrainian mother of three, on her way to the local 7/11 to buy a box of Fruit Loops for her kids. Having spent the first four decades of her life under totalitarian regimes, she films the incident as insurance, in case the cops ever come looking for her. She has no intention of releasing the video, but on her return home, finding her boyfriend eager for a quickie, she leaves her phone outside her bedroom to distract her twelve-year-old, who immediately finds the video and uploads it on to his Instagram feed. The video has the impact of throwing gasoline on a lit barbecue. It sparks anti-police riots in fifteen major American cities over the next two weeks, ultimately resulting in injuries to 123 civilians and 65 cops. Fortunately, there are no fatalities, unless you count the May campaign.

Timing is everything in politics. It could be argued that till this point, the timing of the announcement of Jessica May's new tough on crime stance is simply unfortunate. Claiming that the police have been hamstrung by an overemphasis on civil rights, two days before an unarmed black man is shot in the back by a police officer may be ill-fated, but what makes the campaign's strategy feckless and stupid, is the several U-turns they take in the aftermath of the shooting. On Thursday, the day after the incident, the campaign signals its support for the police officer, marking the event as a victory in the war on drugs, based on the Tulsa police department's murky initial claim of the incident involving a 'major' drug dealer. By Saturday, when it becomes clear that the drugs in Mr. Onitolo's possession would barely get a Chihuahua high, the May campaign changes its tone, calling for the Justice department to initiate a civil rights investigation. But by Monday morning, after a weekend in which Newark, Detroit, Chicago, Houston, Los Angeles and Minneapolis all burn, the campaign once again tries to walk back from its position, calling for all citizens to stay within the bounds of the law.

The first person to hit the May campaign with a pile driver is Amanda Spano, who points out the obvious hypocrisy of their positions. Spano is soon joined by the entire right-wing media, and after Monday, by seventy-five percent of left-wing media as well, in their condemnations of Jessica May's opportunistic and insincere stance, and her attempts to play politics with a national crisis. By Wednesday, on the one-week anniversary of the incident, as thousands lay condolence wreaths on the spot where Ade Onitolo breathed his last, most pundits agree that metaphorical wreaths are also being laid for Jessica May's campaign, which is officially in freefall. The white, male voters that the campaign had been targeting in its get tough on crime approach have withdrawn, convinced that Jessica May is a phoney. Middle of the road independents are turned off by the continuing rumours of her husband's active involvement in his partner's sex trafficking operation. And large segments of the Democratic base including, crucially, black voters, have turned against her in droves for her strategy of going after Lincoln King. Nowhere is this more evident than when the President announces his intention to attend Ade Onitolo's funeral, accompanied by the Vice President. The May campaign's attempts to gain an invitation are firmly and not so politely, rebuffed. By the 20th of June, the date of the funeral, the latest polls show Ron Diamond with a ten-point lead over Jessica May.

* * *

GRAND CAYMAN (20th June)

The twentieth of June will go down as one of those dates in history, like the moon landing or the day Kennedy was shot, that people will always think back on and remember exactly where they were that day. I found myself, strangely, considering we were in the middle of a presidential election campaign, on a tropical island paradise. Ten days ago, when the violence around American cities really started to spike, Ron announced a suspension of the campaign and decided to take a well-deserved vacation. Some of us didn't understand his logic. When I say some of us, I mean primarily me. I didn't understand why, at such a crucial moment, the candidate would simply suspend his campaign and quietly slip out of the country with his entourage.

Especially when someone from the May campaign was commenting virtually every day about the crisis. I thought we would be left far behind if we allowed the other side to monopolise free air time. I only understood the wisdom of Ron's decision much later, when the media sharks decided to maul Jessica May.

Thus, I found myself in a five-star resort on Grand Cayman. Ron had an investment interest in the resort, which hadn't opened its doors to the public yet. And so we had the place all to ourselves. I had been conflicted about going. I thought it was the wrong move politically, and personally as I was also hoping for some kind of resolution to the Shai situation. We had reached out to each other before and acknowledged that we both missed each other tremendously. I thought about her all the time. There was a point during the campaign, when every time I saw a South Asian girl, I would yearn for Shai. We had hoped to meet up on Memorial Day to try and work things out, but of course, that was the weekend that Paedogate broke. And then afterward, the Onitolo shooting happened. And then Jessica's campaign went into a tail spin. That was why I initially wanted to stay in New York. I figured with Ron and the gang away, I could go and meet Shai and talk about where we saw this thing going. But the crisis engulfing the May campaign was so dire that she couldn't commit to meeting up. That rankled me. No matter what Shai wrote in her messages about caring for me or being serious about this relationship, there was always something else that she had to do for Jessica, something bigger, more critical. Jessica's every need seemed more important than any opportunity to talk about us. So I finally said fuck it, and got on board Ron's plane.

That morning, I had been out for an early morning swim and had then showered and breakfasted, so that I was ready to check in on Ron by midday, which was around the time he woke up. As I entered Ron's deluxe cabin suite, I found him already dressed in his standard vacation uniform of oversized Ron Diamond signature collection Hawaiian shirt and baggy shorts, with his pasty and surprisingly thin (considering the rest of his frame) legs on display. He was sitting up with Harvey, who was also wearing a matching shirt, but thankfully with a pair of slacks instead of shorts (Having seen them on display once, Harvey's legs were not a sight I ever wanted to revisit). There was a tray with Ron's favourite snacks laid out, really any and every form of candy and junk that you could think of, along with several cans of Ron's preferred Cherry Coke. Harvey had a glass of something stronger in his hand, and both men were intently watching the live coverage of Ade Onitolo's funeral on a large-screen TV.

'Pull up a chair, kid. You want some Cheetos or somethin'?'

'No thanks, Ron. I just had breakfast.'

'You kids. I'll never understand this generation with all their healthy bullshit. The world's going to shit, Iowa State. Doesn't matter if you eat vegan or gluten-free or whatever. We're all going to be dead in fifty years, so who gives a fuck?' he tossed me a packet of Doritos as I sat down.

The TV was showing footage of the President's motorcade pulling up at the graveyard. The Vice President received him and led him to a group of people who I assumed were Mr. Onitolo's family. 'Don't you think we should have made an effort to be there? At the funeral?'

'What would we have done there, Iowa? Sat waiting in attendance for Lincoln fucking King? No fucking way.'

'But you know, as a symbolic gesture? Maybe we could have gone to their house after the President left. Just to show solidarity with their grief.'

'Look how that worked out for Jessie May.' Harvey sneered. 'She was beggin' for an invite and was told to fuck off, on national TV. How's that for symbolic gestures?'

'There's no upside to goin' there Iowa. Somebody's gonna shove a mike under my nose and ask, was this right or wrong? Even King is taking fire from the police unions for attending the funeral. Why should I piss anyone off by taking any position on this issue? Jessica's working overtime taking it up the ass as it is, why should I bother to get my hands dirty, when I could be sittin' here sippin' Pina coladas?'

'How did you know?'

'How did I know what?'

'Not to take a position on this issue. There's been complete radio silence from our side for the past ten days and we've gone up six points in the polls. We haven't moved, and we're winning.'

'You never played baseball, did you Iowa?'

'Uh, no.'

'Neither did I, but when I was a struggling actor, I liked to go to the games occasionally. I used to live in the Bronx, just a couple of streets down from Yankee stadium. I knew a guy who worked there. I'd get him the videotapes of the latest pornos that we had shot, and he would sneak me into the stadium for games. And I learned somethin' from watching all those games. Sometimes, the best batters, they wouldn't swing on every pitch. Sometimes they'd let a few go, ones that were wide, or had a low percentage. The next one, the pitcher would inevitably pitch in the batter's wheelhouse, and he'd slug the shit out of it. Same thing in politics. You don't need to chase every pitch, especially those ones that are a little out of your zone. Wait for the one that comes to you. That's what we did with this shooting issue and that's why we're on top right now. Jessica and her people are under so much pressure, they're swinging twice at every pitch, and they're getting struck out. Always wait for the one in your wheelhouse, Iowa.'

Wolfson juxtaposed coverage of the funeral with footage of angry police union officials berating the President for having taken a side without having had all the facts in hand. There was footage of more extremist groups calling the President a racist and anti-white, which I didn't know was a thing. To his credit, King didn't try to milk his presence. He spoke a few words, eloquently I thought, although Ron and Harvey let out little exclamations when he started speaking. And then, as the funeral emptied out, the world turned upside down.

The footage of the next three minutes would be replayed on an endless loop for the next few weeks. Indeed, it would become as historically relevant as the Zapruder film. But looking at it live, I couldn't make any sense of what was happening. We saw the President walk towards his vehicle, flanked by his Secret Service detail. And then, a sharp sound, like dozens of firecrackers going off together. The camera lost focus, pointing first skyward, and then it swung equally rapidly downwards. It was Harvey who first realised that the loss of focus was a result of the cameraman ducking suddenly, and that the cracker sound was probably gunfire. Thirty seconds later, when the camera was able to refocus, we found several Secret Service agents hugging the spot where the President had been, in a kind of rugby scrum. The same scrum seemed to move in unison towards the open door of the presidential limousine, dragging something, which was then shoved into the car, along with a couple of the agents. We still couldn't figure out what had happened, but I did notice that there was a thick pool of a dark liquid in the spot where the scrum had been standing. In slow motion, the Wolfson anchor and I simultaneously had the same epiphany. 'That's blood!' we both shouted in unison.

Ron, who till this point had been distracted by whether to open a packet of peanut M&Ms or Twizzlers, suddenly looked up and stared with rapt attention at the screen without saying a word. None of us said anything. Over the next few minutes, what we had surmised by ourselves was confirmed by the networks. President King had been shot and wounded.

Over the next three hours, we sat in complete silence and watched a national tragedy unfold live on TV. We saw the presidential motorcade head to Saint Francis Hospital, where the networks, barred from entering, gave endless footage of the hospital parking lot overflowing with Secret Service agents brandishing their weapons. We followed the unfolding investigation, where Tulsa police claimed that a team of shooters armed with high-powered laser scope sniper rifles had hidden in the trees within the cemetery to carry out the attack. We monitored stories about one of the shooters having been apprehended by local police as he tried to leave the cemetery. We were as dumbfounded as the rest of the country to learn that the apprehended shooter was actually an ex-Tulsa police officer who had only been arrested because absurdly, having just shot the President, he refused to draw his weapon on the fellow police officers who ordered him to surrender. And approximately four hours after the first shots had been fired inside the cemetery, we listened in stunned silence as the Chief Medical officer of the hospital, a short squat man who looked like a middle school principal, came out to the parking lot and read a short statement in which he pronounced the President of the United States dead.

I looked towards Ron, who took the news no differently than if the Chief Medical Officer had read off the day's baseball scores. His only reaction was to shut the TV and down the Cherry Coke he had been nursing for a while. 'Harv, those fucks better invite me to the funeral.'

As Ron left the room, I took it as my cue to leave as well. I needed to get out. The tension of the last few hours had been overwhelming and I was relieved to feel the evening ocean breeze hit my face as I stepped out. I stood on the path outside Ron's cabin and looked around for some noise, some movement, some reaction, but there was absolute silence. Of course, I realised that we were in Grand Cayman and not in America, and that the resort was empty bar our entourage, but still, the silence felt strange. I don't know what I expected, that perhaps the death of a great leader should have set off spontaneous wailing across the globe, or something similarly dramatic. But the silence was unnerving.

As I stood there in the failing light, I saw Han walking towards me. We had largely ignored each other since San Diego, but our mutual contempt for each other was now on display at each and every campaign meeting. Since I decided to stick around after the Ebola controversy, I had also decided that I had nothing left to lose. I wasn't going to kowtow to these pricks. I knew exactly how much faith Ron placed in both his sons, and having been on the verge of quitting myself, I was no longer worried about getting fired. So I had started giving as good as I got. But I found that my new, take it or leave it attitude, far from being detrimental to my position in the Diamond camp, became a huge plus. Ron and Harvey seemed to enjoy the spectacle of me going toe to toe with the two idiot brothers, and the rest of the campaign thought that anyone who trashed the boss's sons the way I did was the ballsiest fucker alive. I became a beacon of hope for anyone who had been bullied by Han and Luke.

But there was none of the usual derision in Han's eyes today. He looked panicked. He almost seemed relieved to see me, and rushed towards me. He stood in front of me trembling, not knowing what to say.

'Han, are you OK?'

'Waj. Oh God, Waj. It's horrible. What am I going to do?'

'About what?'

'About the President's death.'

'What do you have to do about it?'

'Oh God, Waj, you don't understand. They'll think I did it.'

'What? Who will think that, and why? What does this have to do with you? You're in Grand Cayman, the President was assassinated in Tulsa.'

'My friends. All my New York friends. They'll think I'm involved in King's death. It's because I'm Ron Diamond's son, and dad's been so critical of King. They're all Democrats, they'll all blame me and they'll boycott me socially. Oh God, Waj, what will I do?'

'Han, that's ridiculous. Why would anyone blame you for the President's death, just because you're Ron's son? Just because Ron is his political opponent doesn't mean you, or anyone on the campaign, has anything to do with his death. Come on, this is America. This isn't…', I bit my tongue, as what I was about to say would sound exactly like the kind of condescending, borderline racist comment that Han and Luke would make, but I couldn't think of anything else. '…This isn't like Pakistan. you're being paranoid Han, just calm down, have a drink. You're going to be fine. You haven't done anything wrong. You haven't committed a crime.'

He stared at me, and then he did something totally unexpected. He started weeping. Not the sort of subtle, tear running down your cheek, throat getting choked up sort of thing, but the crying like a baby version. Literally. He hugged me and bawled. 'What if I have, Waj?'

'What if you have what?'

'What if I've committed a crime. Oh God, that fucking shit for brains Luke, I should never have listened to him. Oh God, Waj, he's fucked us all.'

'Wait, what are you talking about?'

'There was a Twitter Space forum last week about the election. It was a right-wing thing and Luke and I were on it to court the radicals. Somebody on the forum said King should be shot for the crap he'd pulled. Luke light-heartedly suggested that we should set up a shooting contest to see who could pop the President. And I put up a thumbs up emoji in support of Luke's message. And a happy face. Oh Fuck oh fuck oh fuck.'

'Jeez, Han, why were you guys on those sorts of nutty forums?'

'We wanted to court the right-wingers. We thought dad would be happy.'

'Happy that his sons were on a forum where the members suggested killing the President as a policy solution? Fuck!'

My reaction seemed to be the last straw. Han completely broke down. He fell to his knees on the path and started wailing again. I honestly didn't know what I could do for him. I stood around uncomfortably for a couple of minutes, but there was nothing I could say. I mean, I know it was a stupid thing and I'm sure there must be hundreds of social media forums where people say such crap. Nobody expects the President to actually be killed. And if something like that does happen, who knows to what extent the FBI and Secret Service look into these things. I mean, it wasn't like presidential assassinations were so commonplace in this country that we had an established SOP for them. Besides, after all the crap Han and Luke had put me through, I didn't want to end up being his emotional crutch, at a time when he was shitting a brick. Let the jerk stew. So I decided to leave him on the path, and started walking towards the beach.

It was dusk. The rays of the setting sun illuminated the sea in bright orange light. I was so distracted by the image that I saw a missed call from Shai on my phone, but ignored it because I couldn't take my eyes off the scene in front of me. I stood there for a long moment, and then as I turned towards my cabin and raised my phone to dial Shai, I saw Krystal sitting on the sand, right in front of my hammock. We hadn't really spoken since the night when she had slammed the door in my face. Perhaps she had thought at that moment that I was finished and subsequently, after my so-called 'resurrection' inside the campaign, after the triumphs in meeting Javed Afridi and my dad, she felt sheepish at having written me off so quickly. Or perhaps that was just wishful thinking on my part, and she genuinely didn't give a shit. Unlike her brothers, there had been no overt hostility between us, just a distance. Even when we flew back from Europe, we had sat together on the plane for hours without saying a word. So it was strange to find her, at this moment, sitting on the beach outside my room.

She had obviously heard the news. Her eyes had a vacant look, staring out at the ocean. She was still in the bikini that she must have worn while out swimming. Her hair was wet and droplets of water covered her arms and legs. She was without an inch of makeup and I thought I had never seen her look so beautiful and vulnerable at the same time.

'Krystal?'

'Waj.' She shivered visibly in the fast-cooling evening breeze. I ran past her to my hammock and grabbed a set of towels to drape over her. Wordlessly, she hugged the towel to her body.

'You must be freezing.' I had a penchant for stating the obvious, and to cover it up I awkwardly rubbed her back. I was about to ask her if she wanted to come in, but for some reason I thought that would sound very forward, so instead, I shuffled past her back into my room and got another, larger towel to drape over her.

'The sea. It's blood red. Looks like the sun's bleeding into it. It's somehow fitting. As if the heavens are bleeding for the President.'

I sat down next to her on the sand and kept absentmindedly rubbing her back. 'Yeah. It's one of the most beautiful things I've ever seen, and it feels so weird to witness such beauty on such a sad day.'

She broke off her gaze from the horizon and looked at me intently. 'I didn't know you were such a poet, Waj.'

'What? Oh no, I'm not. I just…I don't know…it's just a really depressing day for the country.' My voice cracked a little as I said the words. I turned to see if she had noticed my un-macho act, but she had tears in her own eyes.

Wordlessly, we hugged each other, for what seemed like an eternity. As she withdrew from the embrace, I put my arm around her and she rested her head on my shoulder.

'What's going to happen now, Waj?'

'I don't know.'

'You're the smartest one out of all of us. How can you not know? You've been right about everything. That day when you came to my room to ask for help in shutting down Ron's Ebola comments, you were right. I was so stupid, worried about not wanting to be singled out. But you were right. It was the morally correct thing to do, and I wish I had gone with you.'

'I guess it worked out in the end.'

'Yeah, but we wouldn't have had all this ugliness. You're a good man, Waj. I haven't known many good men in my life, but you're one of the genuine good guys.'

She raised her head from my shoulder and kissed me. I didn't know what it was, the emotion of the day, the fact of snuggling with a stunningly attractive woman, or just the moment, but I responded enthusiastically. Soon, the draped towels were being shunted aside and our hands were exploring each other's bodies. Her fingers trailed over my chest, down to my stomach, and then lower, till she felt the full extent of my arousal.

'I've thought about you so many times, Waj. Have you thought about me?'

In truth, I hadn't. There are some women who are so gorgeous, so sexy and so unattainable, that you don't ever really think about them. Krystal Diamond was in this category. She was the boss's daughter, for one. Had I ever had an unchaste thought about her, that simple fact would have killed my libido. Apart from that, she had never displayed any interest in me for the longest time, and then despite our brief intimacy on the campaign trail, she had frozen me out again just as quickly. Besides, for the past six months, the only woman I had thought about had been Shai. That was the truth. But circumstances are everything in life. And if the circumstances happen to be that a woman as hot as Krystal is fondling your balls while asking you if you've ever thought of her, *in that way,* you tend to improvise your answers.

'Yes. I've thought about you a lot.'

14.

WE DON'T NEED NO EDUCATION, WE JUST NEED SOME THOUGHT CONTROL
(WITH APOLOGIES TO PINK FLOYD)

'**WHAT THE HELL** is The Save Pakistan From Evil Thoughts Act?'

'Sir? Oh, you mean TSP-FETA.'

'Huh?'

'That's the acronym, Shakaib sahib. All files on the subject are marked TSP-FETA. It saves us from writing the whole name of the bill.'

'What is it with this place and acronyms? You people feel some kind of compulsion to reduce everything to alphabet soup.'

The Principal Secretary to the Prime Minister puts on the fakest of fake smiles and looks around the small, but elegant library of the Prime Minister House. Shakaib has been using the library as an office while his own janitor's closet-size office is refurbished. Shakaib and the SPM (to give him his own rightful acronym) often meet here towards the end of the day to discuss what files need to be personally reviewed by the Prime Minister, and what issues need to be brought to his attention. Shakaib likes the SPM. He's a quiet, learned man, who was a Master's gold medallist in English literature a lifetime ago. He chose the civil service over academia, probably at the insistence of his family, who didn't see how a measly literature professor would ever garner respect in a society obsessed with rank and status.

But he ended up spending most of the next thirty years in dead end government jobs that were scantly more notable than the lost literature professorship. Javed Afridi had chosen him as his SPM because he was a political orphan, not tagged by any association to either the previous PM or his political opponents, which was the reason for his having spent his career on the sidelines in politically unimportant postings. Shakaib and he have formed a good team, managing the flow of work to and from the Prime Minister's office in an orderly manner, which is a real achievement in a government that is becoming famous for its dysfunction.

'So, what is it? Sounds like a bill that either legitimises the practice of voodoo, or will restrain teenage boys from having wet dreams. How does one save a country from evil thoughts?'

'The Prime Minister insisted upon that name, sir. He felt it captured the true spirit of the law.'

'Wait, he's seen this rubbish? I thought this gibberish had been sent to us by the Law Ministry.'

'The PM personally tasked the Law Ministry to draft this bill as a priority.'

'Have you read this draft? It's an incredibly repressive law. It basically says that anyone can be arrested if it is deemed that they have criticised or brought into disrepute the Prime Minister, the President, the ruling party, the military, the judiciary, and any policy that is considered essential to national security. Including this act itself. Considering that it is the job of the parliamentary opposition to criticise the government's policies, this is essentially a licence to lock up all your political opponents and throw away the keys. It's ridiculous. What was the Law Minister smoking when he drafted this?'

'Well sir, notwithstanding the Minister's proclivity for hashish, I am told that the draft has also been approved by members of the Deep State.'

'You were told this by whom?'

'By the same members of the Deep State.'

'You mean Taimur.'

'He is the one who is the official liaison between this office and the Deep State.'

'And the Prime Minister is aware of all this?'

'Yes, sir. Like I said, he is the one who commissioned the draft.'

'Well, I think a law like this seems to be a patently bad idea in a democracy. Look, the PM is a good man. You and I both know that. We've worked with him long enough to know his heart is in the right place. This whole bill smells of Hamza and Taimur. They must have riled the PM up about something, and to cover their own inadequacies, they must have suggested this kind of repressive legislation. This is a bit like when he first came in and wanted to introduce prison terms for smoking. You and I should handle this one the same way.'

'As I recall sir, that situation was handled by your direct intervention with the PM. He seems a bit more serious about this bill. It's the only time I can recall in his seven months in office, that he has been so…enthusiastic…about any bit of government work. He's called me several times to check on the progress of this bill. He is quite keen that it should be voted on by the National Assembly in their current parliamentary session, before they break for the summer recess.'

Shakaib picks up the file and shoves it at the bottom of a tall pile of similar-looking files.

'Well, let's just leave that there, shall we? If the PM asks again, we will say it's in the pipeline. I mean, it's taken this country's bureaucracy 75 years and we still haven't gotten universal electricity, so it's not exactly unheard of for a piece of legislation like this to get mired in red tape. Meanwhile, parliament will go off on its recess in two days' time, and it's another three months or so before they come back. By that time, I will have had the opportunity to talk the PM out of another 'misguided' idea. And then we can bid adieu to The Save Pakistan from Devious Ideas Act.'

'Evil Thoughts sir, not Devious Ideas.'

'Whatever.'

* * *

Cabinet meetings are often a measure of a government's capability, competence, and direction. Most developed democracies make regular use of this system of consultative, collective wisdom. In such countries, cabinet meetings are regular, usually weekly and in times of crisis, even more frequent. Often, the first indicator of a ruler's bent towards a more dictatorial approach is the reduction in the number of cabinet meetings. All rulers presume that if they know best, why spoil it by listening to the pesky, and potentially contradictory views of other, lesser individuals. Fewer cabinet meetings also often reflect a growing dysfunction in government. In the six months preceding the elections, as his government lurched from crisis to crisis, Javed Afridi's predecessor conducted only two cabinet meetings, one of them for barely ten minutes on his last day in office, where he formally announced the dissolution of the government.

In the Afridi government, cabinet meetings are viewed differently. Their frequency continues to climb through the roof, even as Javed Afridi becomes more and more autocratic. There are two scheduled every week, and some weeks the cabinet meets virtually every day. And despite the meetings multiplying faster than rabbits, the dysfunction within the government only grows worse. In the Afridi government, the purpose of a cabinet meeting is less an exercise in consultative governance, and more a free-wheeling mix of improvisational theatre, pep rally, gossip session and group therapy. The advertised agenda is so rarely followed that after the first three months, the Cabinet Secretary stopped even bothering to distribute it in advance.

Today's meeting promises to be no different. The first hour is dominated by Javed Afridi's histrionics, berating the performance of his ministers. He even shoos away the bearers bringing in tea and samosas, saying that a cabinet this incompetent doesn't deserve to stuff their mouths with samosas. Afridi is soon distracted from his rant by Turhan Agha sharing a spicy piece of gossip that's he's heard from a friend of a friend whose aunt lives in the same apartment building as the former Prime Minister in London, about how his younger daughter has eloped with one of her white bodyguards. As if that wasn't bad enough, Agha confirms with absolute certainty that he's heard the bodyguard is Jewish, which elicits a series of *tauba taubas* and *astaghfirullahs* from the YouTuber, now firmly enthroned as Minister for Housing.

The foreign minister then begins to brief on the situation in America, in the ten days since the assassination of President King. Shakaib sits up and starts paying attention. He still hasn't figured out whether he likes the foreign minister or not. He's articulate and well-spoken, as foreign ministers should be but, having made his fortune from investments that were initially funded from the ill-gotten gains that his father accrued during his record tenure as the officer in charge of the most lucrative police post on the Punjab-Balochistan border, he still carries the chips of the newly wealthy on his otherwise immaculately tailored shoulders. He has reminded Shakaib on no less than six separate occasions about his seven-bedroom apartment off 'Band' street in London, and on another four occasions has told him about the incredibly expensive professional wine-tasting course in one of the most prestigious vineyards in Bordeaux that he has enrolled his son in.

'Sir, the situation in Washington remains very precarious. The rioting in black neighbourhoods has not abated, even after ten days. And our embassy is reporting that now there is a backlash against the rioters in predominantly white areas.'

'What does this mean for my friend Ron Diamond? Is it good for his election prospects or bad?' Having been the only one in the room to receive a plate of samosas, Afridi chews one thoughtfully.

'Sir? I'm...not sure. The embassy says the political scenario is so muddled after the death of President King that it is impossible to predict who will benefit. Initially, Senator Jessica May had received a lot of criticism, but her very dignified conduct in the aftermath of the assassination and her speech at the President's funeral, which I attended on your behalf, has caused a slight surge in her popularity. Ron Diamond obviously was not accorded the same opportunity, as he was not invited to the funeral, and some of his disparaging comments towards the Vice President…I mean the new President, have gone against him in this time of heightened emotionality. But at the same time, his calls for law and order to be restored in the country have also found a sympathetic ear amongst many voters, not just Republicans. People are tired of being stuck in their homes for the past week, under conditions of virtual curfew in some cities. But again, we cannot say what the long term impact of this will be as election day is still over four months away. We may have a better picture next week when the Republican convention kicks off in Kansas City.'

'Yaar, what do you know? You know nothing about American politics or foreign affairs. I don't know why I appointed you foreign minister. You seem to just be doing junket trips around the world. I watched CNN's Crossfire last night as well. You haven't told me anything I didn't pick up from that, or from Amanda Spano's show. I might as well appoint my Samsung Smart TV in your place.'

Shakaib prepares to step in, in case the retort from the foreign minister is a sharp one in the face of Afridi's provocation. But the foreign minister, instead of standing up for himself, grows more obsequious.

'Yes sir, I mean, of course it is a great honour you have awarded me by making me the foreign minister. What I forgot to mention, and which has not been reported widely in the media, is the level of gratitude that American policymakers had for our…I mean your… intervention in Afghanistan. I was approached by several Senators and Congressmen, from both parties, who sit on key committees, who told me that Pakistan's efforts were greatly appreciated in allowing the American troops to get evacuated without any issue. It was unfortunate that the new President chose not to raise this issue in my very short interaction with him. But the embassy reports that the current administration is still smarting over the fact that it was Ron Diamond who received credit for this in the media, and not them. I did try and raise with the President the issue of recognising the Taliban government, especially in light of their cooperation in allowing the American troops to pull out. But my impression was that the Taliban were still a sore point in Washington and nobody was in a hurry to shake hands with the people who after all, inflicted a defeat on the US forces.'

'Who told you to raise the issue of the Taliban? This is an extremely sensitive issue. I don't want Ron's opponents to jump on his case as being friendly with the Taliban. We discussed it the other night, we have to tread very carefully...'

'Excuse me sir, but did you say you discussed this? With Ron Diamond?' For the first time, Shakaib sits up in his chair.

'Yes. We WhatsApp each other regularly, and we discuss various issues. So what?'

'Sir, do you think it wise to be discussing policy matters with him? He is not yet a part of the US government, and these kinds of communications could easily be misconstrued.'

That gives Afridi some pause. 'Well, perhaps I should set up some kind of secure channel with him. Taimur!' Taimur, who has been slumped unobtrusively, half asleep, in a chair along the wall with the other aides and department heads, suddenly comes to attention. 'Can you not establish a secret channel with Ron Diamond?'

'Uh...we can certainly try, Prime Minister.'

'Maybe we can get a separate new phone for Shakaib's son and communicate through that. There's a name for this. Burner phones? I saw it on Netflix. Shakaib, let's get your son a burner phone.'

'Uh...'

'You know, speaking of phones, Prime Minister, the new taxes imposed by the finance ministry have made mobile phones prohibitively expensive. I wanted to get the new iPhone 14, but it's costing me almost five hundred thousand rupees. Shouldn't cabinet ministers get some kind of duty waiver for the purchase of mobile phones?'

'Five hundred thousand? I was quoted a price of almost six hundred thousand. Who is your mobile phone dealer, maulana sahib?'

The price of mobile phones is hotly debated for the next five minutes, with several ministers expressing their displeasure particularly passionately, forcing the besieged finance minister to defend the tax hike as a necessary measure to counter the financial mess left by the previous government. Javed Afridi, who has happily allowed the cabinet meeting to drift, snaps out of his reverie at the mention of the previous government. Their reference is like a red rag to a bull for him.

'Those bastards! They've really screwed us! They deliberately left me a shattered economy. Do you know how dangerous that can be? I mean, if we don't stabilise the economy, we are literally inches away from having the kind of unrest over here that they are having in America. I mean, all of it is being generated by social inequality. But those bastards who were sitting in these chairs before us didn't care. All they wanted to do was loot as much as they could! And we can't even get them arrested! Whose stupid idea was it to use legal procedures to prosecute those bastards! Shakaib, it was yours, wasn't it? Why haven't we made any progress in the corruption cases? Every time I ask why so and so hasn't been arrested, I am told that they got bail from the courts! This is why I told you, we should have just locked them up when we first came in!'

'Prime Minister, we can still do it. Let's just lock them up! Lock them up! Lock them up!' Bizarrely, Turhan Agha stands up and raises his fist, chanting louder and encouraging the other cabinet members to join him. Shakaib is shocked to see that Javed Afridi raises his fist like Turhan, prompting several other participants to raise their fists and take up the chant.

It takes another couple of minutes before order is restored to the meeting. As Shakaib is preparing to mount a defence of rule of law and due process, the YouTuber steps in and takes the meeting in yet another direction.

'Prime Minister, you are right that your predecessor and his cronies were criminals, and should be taken to task, but we should also examine some other criminal behaviour that is going on, right under our noses, in this government!'

'What? Corruption?'

'Worse! Industrial size pornography!'

'Where?' Several cabinet ministers perk up at the mention of pornography.

'In our text books! My representatives, whom you appointed to the text book boards, have pointed out that if we continue to allow our children to learn from these filthy books, we might as well allow the young boys and girls to start copulating in the streets! I mean, just look at the biology text book. They have diagrams of the dirtiest things in the world: Uteruses and pen…men's genitals. I mean, there are thousands of young girls, our daughters, studying to become doctors and nurses. How are they supposed to look at these diabolical images! And that also, in open classrooms with hundreds of their fellow students looking on, judging them for their immorality. I tell you Prime Minister, I don't agree with the Taliban on a lot of issues because they are from a different sect, but I think they're on to something with this idea of banning girls from coming to schools and colleges. At least they are protecting the chastity of the next generation of mothers! I propose that we also consider banning co-educational institutions.'

'Hmm.' Afridi contemplates the suggestion. 'I don't think that's a bad idea. Especially nowadays, with all this online learning shearning. The girls can stay home and learn everything they need to from the safety of their bedrooms. Then we wouldn't have this problem.'

'Exactly sir! That's what the Taliban also wanted to do. Their problem is that internet connectivity in Afghanistan is not so good. But we have no such issues. We can easily implement this here. Thank God for a fast internet!'

'The only problem is we will get a critical backlash from the west.

I know these bloody Europeans very well from my footballing years. Bloody hypocrites. If they promote online learning for children during the corona lockdown, it's considered smart for health and safety, but if we do the same thing to protect impressionable young girls, they'll brand us religious fundamentalists. They'll say we are being influenced by the Taliban. They'll start calling me Taliban Jim. I know the mentality of their tabloid reporters. And it will become a problem for Ron as well. They'll try and attack him because he's friends with me. His opponents will try and say he has links to extremists. And we've got to do everything we can to help him win. Once he's in office, it will be a different world. But until then, we have to shelve these sorts of ideas.'

Several members of the cabinet, including the YouTuber, nod in agreement, as if appreciating Afridi's deep logic. Shakaib waits for a minute to see if anyone else will speak up, but to his utter exasperation, no one does. Finally, he can hold back no longer.

'Are we seriously discussing banning girls from schools? Have we gone collectively insane?'

'Shakaib sahib, we are not talking of banning girls from schools. They just need extra shelter. You know, like when it is hot and you go sit under a tree for shade. We just want to be the tree that provides shade to our girls.'

'And how do you expect young women who are training to become doctors and nurses to study without looking at diagrams of the uterus, or male genitalia?'

'I mean, it shouldn't be so brazen Shakaib sahib. You are also on the text book committee. Even you will agree that these textbooks are full porno.'

'They are the same textbooks and diagrams that medical students have been using to learn about the human body for the last 150 years. Please tell me what part of them is 'full porno' as you call it?'

'The diagrams of the male penis!!'

'If these students don't look at the bloody diagram, then ten years down the road, when one of them is operating on your penis, he or she won't know where and what to cut! Would you prefer that?!?'

A look of absolute horror covers the YouTuber's face, as he visualises Shakaib's comments.

'Shakaib, he isn't wrong. Maybe we do need more safeguards for the young girls in the country. We don't want them corrupted by western values.' Javed Afridi smiles indulgently.

'You are saying this?!? You, of all people, Prime Minister? You, who spent half your life living and working in the west?'

'That's exactly why I'm saying it. I'm an expert on western corruption.'

'Is that what you were doing when you were sleeping with half the girls in England? Becoming an expert on western corruption?'

'How dare you speak to me like that! How dare you! Who the hell do you think you are! You sit in this cabinet because of me, Shakaib! Don't you dare forget that!'

'I serve at your pleasure, Prime Minister. I neither wanted this nor did I ask for it. If you feel my advice is something you no longer wish to listen to, as seems evident, then I will happily resign.'

Afridi glares at him, a look of pure malevolence that Shakaib has never seen before and that, frankly, unnerves him. However, before the confrontation proceeds any further, the SPM intervenes with a note, and accompanies Afridi out of the room, bringing the meeting to its conclusion.

* * *

Shakaib is already half awake when the phone rings. He can hear the storm outside, the rain coming down in sheets, the gusts of wind knocking on the windows of his house in the Minister's enclave. He hasn't slept much, tossing and turning and contemplating his next move. He doesn't want to resign, because he still believes he can do good things. But his ability to do good is dependent on his ability to influence Javed Afridi and prod him in the right direction. And after the cabinet meeting from hell, that ability looks unlikely to be sustainable in the future. Besides, he fully expects Afridi to fire him before he resigns.

He looks at the phone as it rings, its ringtone shrill and old fashioned. The houses in the Minister's enclave seem to be the only ones left that actually still use landlines. He wonders why the caller hasn't called him on his mobile phone and then realises that he had turned it off as soon as he got home.

'Yes?' An operator asks him to hold for the SPM. He understands. This is it. The metaphorical equivalent of a firing squad.

'Ah, good evening sir. I do apologise for the lateness of the hour.' Shakaib looks at the bedside clock. The SPM sounds as fresh at 1am as he had at 1pm.

'Not at all. I expect you've called to give me my marching orders. No problems, I just have a couple of personal items in my office, I'll come by in the morning and clear them out. I didn't bring too many things with me, so I can pack up in a day. I'll try and catch the evening flight to Karachi. Shall I just hand over the keys of the house to the caretaker, or someone in your office?'

'Keys? What keys? Oh good heavens, no sir, why would you do that?'

'You've called me to fire me, right? That's what the PM must have told you to do. That's the only reason anyone calls up at one in the morning. So if I'm fired, I can hardly keep staying in a minister's bungalow, can I?'

'Not at all sir. I've not called to fire you. Neither has the PM given any such instruction. He was momentarily upset but he had completely calmed down fifteen minutes after I pulled him from the meeting. In fact, later in the day he marked several files and instructed me to discuss them with you tomorrow.'

'What? Then why are you calling me?'

'You had said to keep you in the loop. I wanted to inform you that TSP-FETA has been passed by the National Assembly.'

'TSP what?'

'The Save Pakistan From Evil Thoughts Act.'

'When did this happen?'

'Earlier this evening. Actually about half an hour ago. The Speaker and Senate Chairman were asked to call a special joint session. It didn't take very long. There was just one agenda item, and the entire thing was over in about ten minutes.'

'But we had shelved the bill. We put it at the bottom of the stack. How did it get out?'

'When I took the PM out of the cabinet meeting, he asked me about the status of the bill. I told him, as you had instructed, that it was under review. He called Taimur into his office, and ordered him to ensure immediate passage of the bill. It was Taimur who cracked the whip on the Speaker and Chairman.'

'You mean that crazy bill has become law? But we had agreed that it was mad. It's an abhorrent law in a democracy.'

'The PM wanted it done pronto. There was nothing I could do. I'm sorry sir. Anyway, thought I'd check up on you and let you know. See you in the morning, sir.'

* * *

It is still early, barely seven, when the houseboy knocks gingerly on his door to inform Shakaib of Taimur's arrival. He hasn't slept since the SPM's call, brooding all night and mulling over his resignation. So it's somewhat surprising to find the Haircut in his sitting room that morning, sipping coffee.

'What are you doing here? I was going to come and see you.'

Taimur smiles. The haircut is no longer as severe as it was when Shakaib first met him. Gone also is the air of uncertainty and fidgetiness. There is a greater calm, a confidence gleaned from his success in this government.

'I know. I thought I should save you the visit.'

'The SPM told you, did he?'

'No. I haven't spoken with him.'

'Then how...Oh. You're listening to my phone calls. Real classy.'

'Nothing personal. All the phones in the minister's enclave are bugged. It's been standard procedure since the 60's. Every ruler wants to know if his colleagues are conspiring against him. And rightly so, since all of them do, sooner or later.'

'Then why are you telling me? Shouldn't you have kept it secret? Cat's out of the bag now.'

'Shakaib sahib, we have nothing to fear from you. I have observed you all these months. You are the only genuinely straightforward person I have ever come across. You say what's on your mind, you don't conceal it. Even now that you know we're listening, you won't change. That's not who you are. Like yesterday. All of us were thinking the same thing, but you were the one who came out and said it.'

'You also think Javed Afridi was being hypocritical?'

'Of course! How can a man whose exploits made the front pages of the British and Spanish tabloids a record 356 times, more than Princess Diana and Cristiano Ronaldo put together, now say that girls should be banned from educational institutions?'

'Then why the hell didn't you say anything?'

'It's not my job to. It's the cabinet's job to decide policies.'

'Right. So what's your job then? Strong-arming members of parliament to do a midnight vote for the most repressive law in this country's history?'

'I was instructed to do that.'

'Your superiors actually think this is a good idea? To ban all dissent?'

'Not my superiors. The Prime Minister.'

'Taimur, why are you people doing this? Why are you indulging him like this? This will lead to no good. Do you really want to be that despotic?'

'Shakaib sahib, I told you a long time ago, if it was my choice, I would never have made Javed Afridi Prime Minister. We were happy with the previous lot. They kept bickering among themselves and stayed out of our business. Yes, they were corrupt, but what country in this part of the world isn't? For that matter, in any part of the world? But I was instructed to make this Afridi experiment work, and that's what I'm doing. It's a pain in my ass, frankly. He is far too demanding.'

'That's convenient, Taimur, but you and I both know you're an enabler. You are running him, putting bad ideas in his head.'

'Shakaib sahib, you really think, after working with him all these months, that Javed Afridi is that innocent? That Hamza or I, or you for that matter, can just put an idea in his head and he will run with it? There is a purpose in everything he does. An agenda. Now, either you are playing the fool deliberately or you are actually that naïve, in which case I am sorry that you haven't figured Afridi out yet. He uses us. We know this. He uses everyone around him, including you. He used you to get to Ron Diamond, didn't he? It was your son who was the contact, it was your idea to get them to meet after our disastrous trip to Saudi Arabia. But you were as surprised as everyone else when Afridi told us that he was in regular contact with Diamond. I was looking at your face, and you were absolutely shocked. You can't fake that kind of reaction. Which means that he kept you out of the loop of his communications, just as he kept us out.'

'You're seriously going to tell me that this bloody law isn't beneficial for your work?'

'Of course, it's beneficial. That doesn't mean I initiated it. But if it has been passed at the express insistence of the PM, then I will use it. You keep wanting to make me the bad guy in all of this. But I'm really not. The SPM told you that the PM called me and ordered me to ensure that the Speaker and Senate Chairman got together and passed the bill immediately. What he didn't tell you, what he doesn't know, is that the PM has personally prepared a list of people that he believes should be targeted under the new law. The list runs to 5000 names. Opposition leaders, journalists, bloggers, lawyers. There's even a football critic who was never kind to Afridi in his playing days. Although even I think that one's a bit unfair.'

'I don't believe you.'

'I can show you the list. You can even check with my superiors. Don't you get it? He wanted the bill passed ASAP because he knew you would try to block it. And he knew that, given a chance, you would probably be able to talk him down from it. He didn't want that to happen. He wanted to have the power in his hands. I'm just a tool in this equation. I'm the plumber who unclogs the toilet, but it's Afridi who's designing an entire sewage system and filling it with shit.'

15.
MARANZANOGATE

KANSAS CITY (Day one of the Republican National Convention)

'Yes Waj, yes!! Oh God yes!!'

Krystal's screaming brought me out of my cocaine-induced trance. I was suddenly very aware of my surroundings. My senses seemed enhanced to a supernatural level. The scene that unfolded before my eyes blew my mind. Krystal was pushed up against the floor-length windows of her suite, completely naked as I took her from behind, staring at her slender spine curving from the golden hair at the back of her head right down to the crack of her ass. I could feel every twitch of her body as I entered her, even as I inhaled her natural smell, sweat mixed with the sweet scent of her own signature brand perfume.

'Harder, Waj, harder! Fuck me harder!'

If anyone had described this scene to me a year ago, hell, six months ago, I would have told them to check into a mental hospital. I could not believe that the woman who was so passionately urging me to fuck her harder was Krystal Diamond. Krystal, fucking Diamond. I mean, it had been barely believable for me to have hooked up with Shai. But now, I was doing Krystal as well? Was I also going to win the lottery next week?

Shai. I hadn't thought about her in a while. I had actually never bothered to return her missed call from the day the President was assassinated. The weeks since had been so hectic as we got back on the campaign trail with a renewed vigour, that I had just not had the time. I had worked 18-hour days, and at night, usually the only time I was alone with my thoughts, Krystal would come over to relieve her tension and mine. Wake, work, fuck Krystal, sleep, and repeat. That had been my routine for the past month.

Today was a little different. Krystal and I had flown to the convention as part of Ron's advance team, while the candidate himself waited in New York till the final night of the convention, when he would fly in directly to accept the nomination. The novelty of not having Ron or anyone else from the senior campaign team around, had stirred me to tear her clothes off and jump her as soon as we entered her suite. Krystal had been equally, if not more enthusiastic, initiating the encounter in the elevator and offering me a line of coke off her bare belly as soon as we had discarded our clothes. Now, I had never done cocaine before and I honestly confessed this to her. She had smiled, snorted a line herself and laid back invitingly on the bed, totally naked except for the short trail of white powder on her stomach. I felt funny as it first hit me, but she said it would take the edge off after what had happened earlier. In any case, with Krystal posing against the window and inviting me to take her from behind, all other thoughts were put aside.

What had happened earlier. That was a pretty anodyne way of describing my first racist attack. I was pretty shaken up. Truth be told, I don't know if the cocaine actually helped to take the edge of or made the memory more vivid. I could still smell the guard's stinking breath, all stale tobacco, and early-onset halitosis, as he had shoved me up against the wall of the convention centre and screamed at me, saying 'Are you a Muslim, boy? We don't want your kind here!' It had happened during our visit to the venue where Ron would be crowned as master of the Republican party in 48 hours. The first thing that had struck me was the palpable air of menace in the place. True, the primaries had been bitter, but the nomination had been contested vigorously in the past as well.

This time, there was real malice. You could sense it in the demeanour of the delegates who walked past us, even the ones pledged to us; you could see it in the nastiness of the heavily armed private security guards, whose overwhelming presence gave the entire convention centre the feel of a super max prison. I could even feel the malevolence from the looks I got from the fast food vendors.

It was very much a me thing. People were significantly nicer when Krystal was with me. Whether that was because she was the instantly recognisable daughter of the candidate, or whether it had something to do with the fact that I seemed to be the only brown man within a five-kilometre radius, I honestly could not say. But the stares grew significantly in number and intensity when she went to have a word with the convention chair while I wandered around the vendor area on my own. That's where I had been accosted by a heavy set man wearing wraparound sunglasses, Khakis and a camo T-shirt, with his AR-15 slung by his side. He was about to punch me in the face when, to my great fortune, Krystal came running back with several members of the organising committee to restrain him. He later claimed to be a private security contractor, deployed for extra protection at the venue in light of the heightened threat after President King's assassination, and also claimed that he had questioned me only when he saw me acting in a 'suspicious' manner. Considering that I had been eating a hot dog at the time, I could only speculate as to how that appeared suspicious to him.

'Waj! Why are you slowing down? Keep going, baby! Fuck me hard!'

I focused on the issue at hand, gripping her ass tightly and increasing my pace and rhythm. It was almost dark, and as I stared down from the 17th floor window, the skyline of Kansas City slowly became illuminated. I could see the convention centre from here, with its big neon sign proclaiming it to be the venue of the Republican convention, with a smaller sign welcoming the next President of the United States, Ron Diamond. It was weird, seeing those words actually spelled out in neon. I mean, of course, that is what we had all been hoping for when we started the campaign, but I wondered if anyone thought we would get as far as we had.

'Waj, you're going soft. Wait, let me work on it.' Krystal turned to face me and went down on her knees. I was reminded of the last time Shai had done that. The morning of our last time together. Shai. I couldn't believe, despite my wildest fantasies coming true with Krystal, how much I was missing her. No matter how nice this was, I ached for her.

'That's never happened before.' Krystal's remark was directed at my complete loss of arousal. 'Are you OK, Waj?'

'Sorry. I'm so sorry. It must be the coke. I'm not used to it…'

She rose from her kneeling position and kissed me gently. 'Poor Waj. It's been a stressful day. Don't worry about it.' She gave my dick a supportive tug, casually walked to the bed and flipped on the TV while opening a bottle of Perrier, as if the act of carnal congress we had been engaged in just moments before was no different than say, a particularly intense Peloton session.

Still feeling a little ashamed of my performance failure, despite Krystal's reassurance, I slumped and sat down on the edge of the bed. The incident from this morning and the memory of Shai made me feel acutely vulnerable.

'I can't believe that guy was actually going to hit me.'

'Yeah, the conventions really drag all the crazies out of the closet, don't they?' She responded to me absentmindedly as she scrolled through her phone, still not bothering to put on any clothes.

'Do they? Do they really? Or is it us?'

'Sorry. What do you mean?' She still didn't look up from her phone.

'I've never been part of a presidential campaign before, so I have nothing to compare this with. But I don't think it's ever been this crazy out there. The anger, the open racism. And this stuff isn't happening on the fringes somewhere, it's happening here, at the very venue where my candidate, the man I helped to make the nominee, is going to be confirmed as leader of the party. And it's happening to me. Do you think, at some level, Ron's gone too far? That he's ended up stoking genuine hatred?'

Krystal finally looked up from her phone and stared at me as if I was a particularly slow puppy. 'Of course, he has, Waj. There's nothing subtle about it. And you've contributed to it more than most.'

'What? I have never advocated that Ron take a racist stance against Muslims, or anyone else!'

'You didn't stop him either, Waj.'

'Krystal, I came to you, literally begging for your help, before Super Tuesday. I was ready to quit. But you slammed your door in my face! You even conceded that I had been right, when we were in Grand Cayman. How the fuck can you now say I didn't stop him!'

'Well, you didn't quit, did you? Ron has said a lot of things and you've signed off on those because it fulfils some kind of tactical objective in the race. And you know he listens to you more than anybody else.'

'What about you Krystal? Why the fuck haven't you said anything to him? Why am I the one who's supposed to bear the burden? He's your father. You're closer to him than anyone, why haven't you moderated him? Unless you believe in this crap!'

'Don't be so dramatic, Waj. Of course, I don't believe in any of this shit. If I did, why would I be sleeping with you? The truth is, this was the campaign we had to fight, considering where we came from and all our baggage. This is what's gotten us here. You can be in denial all you want Waj, but this is the bargain we all made. Say anything, do anything, to win. Whether it was attacking Muslims, or me titillating sleazy network anchors. And we won big. My father is about to become the nominee of the Republican party. Can you believe it? A porn star will fight it out with a US Senator from one of the oldest families in the country, over who becomes the next President. I spent my entire school life with people pointing to me and snickering at me because I was the porno king's daughter. In High School, guys would come up to me and describe my father's latest sex scenes to me in graphic detail, in the belief that since my dad was a porn star, it was logical that I was also some kind of slut who was gagging for it. The Porn Princess. That's what they called me through high school. I can't wait to see their faces now. So you ask me, why I didn't object to Ron's tactics. That's why. Why should I be the one to sacrifice my position in this campaign, arguing against the game plan that got us here?'

'Doesn't that make us bad people? By endorsing this?'

'No, it doesn't make us bad people. It makes us smart people. Do you really think, that if he gets elected, he will ever do even one of the crazy things he's talked about during the campaign?'

'I don't know, Krystal.'

'Of course, you do. Ron's not going to do any of that. But by the time anyone figures that out, we'll be in the White House.'

'You think we can actually win?'

'You're the smart one. You're the one who's made him believe. You're the one he listens to, ahead of all his children, including me. All of a sudden, you're having a crisis of confidence? Just because some redneck picked on you? Is that why that happened?' She pointed to my dick.

I looked away and didn't answer. In truth, there were no simple answers. Krystal wasn't wrong. Perhaps I just didn't want to acknowledge the reality. That all of us were complicit in creating Ron the candidate. And that, having come so close to winning, nobody wanted to walk away now. All of us wanted a share of the spoils. We had started joking about things like what posters we would hang on the walls of our West Wing offices. But at what price would that victory come?

I got up and got dressed. Suddenly, I didn't want to be here. Not just in this room with Krystal, but in this city. At this convention. Sitting at the edge of the bed, struggling to put my socks on, I had an epiphany. There was only one thing I could think of that would soothe the witch's brew of raw emotions that were bubbling up inside of me. I needed Shai back in my life. Krystal and I had amazing sex. She was an even better lover than Shai. But we both knew that this was a campaign situation. Two people blowing off steam on the road by fucking each other's brains out. It was never going to be sustainable and perhaps, neither one of us even wanted anything long-term out of it. But Shai and I had been at the precipice of something special, maybe. I wanted to explore that maybe.

* * *

'Amanda. Good to finally meet in person.'

'Senator May.' Amanda takes the outstretched hand and shakes it, automatically scanning the older woman for any outward signs of panic or hostility. But Jessica May is a professional's professional, greeting Amanda as breezily as if they were meeting at a summer garden party, instead of in the midst of one of the most dramatic and contentious nominating contests in American political history. 'I'm glad we could finally tie up this interview. I was very keen to do this last time round, but events kind of overtook us.'

Jessica flashes an absolutely brilliant, 100-watt smile. 'Yes, Ron Diamond announced his candidacy and took a pole axe to the Republican party. And here we are, fifteen months later. Since you are part of the party establishment that he keeps hammering, I should really ask how you're feeling.'

Amanda can't help laughing. It's true, since the day of her last scheduled interview with Jessica May, the same day that Ron Diamond announced he was running for President, her party has been turned upside down by the human tsunami that is Ron. The wreckage of other candidates' campaigns lies scattered like flotsam in the political arena. The Reverend has gone so completely underground since dropping out of the race that Amanda is sure he must have entered the FBI's witness protection program. General Patrakis has gone in the opposite direction. He's become a kind of joke, a caricature general like the one in Dr Strangelove, someone who is invited on talk shows by hosts wanting to gain rating points by excoriating him on air for his stupidity and hubris over Afghanistan, and in the campaign. Memes abound of him spelling his name out during the debate with Ron Diamond.

And then, there is Ryan Herrera, Amanda's creation and the party's great brown hope for about two weeks, between his victory in Nevada and the shellacking he got on Super Tuesday. The fallout from that one could fill a book, but Amanda doesn't want to think about it now. Not when she has to put on her game face to interview Jessica May.

'Shall we start? Where's your assistant? Shai, right?'

'My chief of staff. She's around, she came in with us, but I think she's taking a personal call outside.'

'Smart girl. Tough as nails. Gave me a real tough time when I was negotiating with her for your last interview.'

'Shai is amazing. She's the one who keeps the trains running on time. I call her my mini Mussolini. But seriously, how are things with you? We've heard a lot of rumours about the Wolfson executives turning against you after you took on Ron in the debates. I saw the footage and as a woman, I think the way he spoke to you was reprehensible. Good for you for not taking his crap. I mean that sincerely, all politics aside. Even now, there are too few of us in politics and media. We need you to be out there.'

'Thank you. Coming from you, that means a lot.' Amanda decides she likes Jessica May. There is a quiet dignity to her, despite all the shit that's been thrown at her by her own party. If the Republicans have committed *harakiri* by nominating Ron Diamond as many serious pundits are now saying, the Democrats and the new President, are trying very hard to have a 'hold my beer' moment by trying to steal the nomination from her.

Amanda waits for the technician to mic up Jessica, and checks the video monitor. The Senator's yellow dress catches the eye and brightens up the otherwise drab background. The cameras start to roll.

Amanda Spano: Senator May, welcome to the show. It's a real pleasure having you here with us today. And may I add that you are also the first nominee from the

Democratic party who has agreed to come on air here at Wolfson. That's highly commendable, because other Democratic candidates are quick to brand this network as reactionary and 'an arm of the Republican party', to quote the President from when he was Vice President. What made you get past that bias?

Senator May: Well, Amanda, it's a pleasure to be here, and I can go back and tell all of my Democratic colleagues that the Devil does not, in fact, reside within the Wolfson building. I can't speak for other Democrats, but I believe in respecting all the institutions of the media, whether they agree with my politics or not. And by my coming here, maybe, just maybe, some of your colleagues may grudgingly accept that I am not in fact, a witch.

Amanda Spano: I think some Republicans have used much harsher language than that to describe you. Especially certain Republican candidates.

Senator May (laughing): Well, I can't say those words. I've always been a PG-13 kind of girl, while some of my opponents have enjoyed significantly more 'graphic' ratings.

Amanda Spano: Well put, Senator. Well, let me come straight to the point. There are many within your own party, who seem to be dissatisfied with your selection as the nominee. They point to the fact that you have struggled as a campaigner throughout the primaries, and there is a growing body of opinion that feels that in light of the killing of President King, the President, who had as Vice President, ruled himself out of contention as a candidate, may be a better choice for the Democratic party. How do you address these concerns?

Senator May: First of all, Amanda, these are certainly not 'concerns' from my point of view. I am the only candidate who has fought each and every primary contest and won an overwhelming majority of them. I personally believe that in a democracy, that's how you should win nominations, by contesting elections, rather than being selected in some smoky backroom by a group of party bosses. And as far as the President is concerned, he has not publically made any statement that would indicate that his stance on running has changed.

Amanda Spano: Would you step aside if he did change his stance? For the good of the party?

Senator May (pausing): I will repeat what I said earlier, Amanda. I think I'm the best candidate to win in November, I have gone through the gruelling process of primaries, and I have outlined my vision for America in these past months. People know where I stand. I think the President made a very well-reasoned decision when he chose not to run, and I don't think those reasons have changed too much.

Amanda Spano: People say one of the reasons he chose not to run was his age. He will turn 80 in September. Do you think he's too old to be President?

Senator May: I think experience matters a lot in this job. I have tons of it, as a Senator, and a former cabinet officer. I also believe that we have more young people in America at this point in our nation's history than ever before, and that we as politicians have to cater to their aspirations and dreams. We see violence in our streets, we see racial tensions, we're divided between red states and blue states. We need someone who is able to bring us together.

Amanda Spano: What if, as some are suggesting will happen during the Democratic convention next week, the President forces himself onto the ballot? What would you do in that situation? Are you going to take a back seat in the interests of party unity, or are you going to fight it out on the convention floor?

Senator May (pausing again, but looking straight at the camera with great determination): Let me say this as unequivocally as possible, Amanda. I believe I am the best candidate, I believe I have earned the right, after fighting in every primary, to contest the election in November, and I have a very strong belief that I can win. So if anyone wants to try and take that nomination from me through some kind of backroom deal, they'll have to prise it out of my cold, dead hands.

* * *

'Shai, where the fuck have you been? You missed the whole interview. Jessie hit it out of the park! Even gave that old octogenarian cocksucker in the White House a nice kick in his sagging balls! Never thought she'd do it. And you missed the whole … wait, why are you crying?'

She doesn't look up. She can't take her eyes off her screen, even as the tears stream freely down her cheeks. For the past hour, Shai has tried to keep up the pretence, tried to project her usual Olympian calm, tried to somehow wrest back control of her emotions so that she could get back inside the studio to watch Jessica's interview. But she has failed and now the floodgates are open.

'I'm sorry, Maury … I … can't …'

'Shai, what the fuck's happened? Come on, you can tell me.'

She hesitates for an instant. But she knows that she has to tell somebody, otherwise it will keep eating her from the inside. Her parents aren't an option. Since blossoming into Jessica May's alter ego, a position so elevated in the eyes of her immigrant parents that it has finally eclipsed their disappointment over Harvard, she has finally obtained the upper hand in her relationship with them. She now maintains formally pleasant contact with them, without any sharing of true intimacy. As for friends, she decided long ago to sacrifice anyone outside Jessica's inner circle for the greater national interest. And as for Jessica herself, she cannot fathom going to her with this problem, in the middle of an election, one week from the convention. Shai would never forgive this act of weakness and unprofessionalism in herself, even if Jessica did. That leaves the three men, Mike, Maury and Johnny, who have for better or worse, become her real family and only friends over the past year.

Unable to speak, she hands her phone to Maury, who reads the message without expression.

'This is your Pakistani connection?' She nods her head. 'I'm impressed. He hooked up with you and Krystal Diamond in the space of the last six months. Boy's got some game.'

'Fuck you, Maury.' The tears well up in her eyes again.

'Look Princess, I'm sorry, I'm not trying to be facetious. But, what's the problem here? He seems obviously in love with you. He wants to commit and he's being very honest in telling you about Krystal. I've been in a lot of campaigns. That kind of stuff happens. It doesn't mean anything. What matters is that he's figured out that you're the one he wants to be with. If you want to be with him, and I assume by your tears that you are not exactly untouched by this guy emotionally, then the rest is just logistics. You know, inter-party relationships are more common than you think. My ex-wife was a Republican. Worst case scenario, you two wait till the campaign's over. Three months. It'll be a breeze.'

'Why did he have to be so honest with me? Why did he have to tell me about her?'

* * *

'How would you like your steak, Amanda?'

'Wow Leonard, you really do know how to impress a girl. Clearing out the executive canteen for a one-on-one meal, corner table with a stunning view of the Potomac, and on top of that you ordered for me as well. Can I expect chocolates and flowers when I get home?'

The expression on Leonard Wolfson's face is humourless. Amanda fears the worst, since he's never invited her to lunch before. But her Jessica May interview has broken all viewership records, so she figures even Leonard Wolfson wouldn't be that stupid as to try and fire her at this point.

'Medium rare.' Wolfson instructs the waiter without waiting for her reply, another one of his petty power plays to show everyone who's boss.

'Well done, actually. In fact, just burn it.' She relishes the look of utter disgust on his face as she takes the seat opposite him. 'What's the matter, Leonard? I heard that's the way Ron Diamond likes his steaks, so I thought I'd try it too. Besides, the chef's got to practice before Ronny comes swinging through here next week. We wouldn't want him to leave DC saying the food at Wolfson was pretentious and "un-American".'

Leonard Wolfson's lips break out into the thinnest of smiles. With his eyes, he sends the waiter scurrying to the kitchen. 'I thought it would be nice if we spoke privately.'

'You're the boss, Leonard. Although you do realise you're going to have a bunch of pissed off executives who've had to line up at the falafel cart downstairs. You could have just called me to your office.'

'Some things are best discussed outside the office.'

'Fair enough. What would you like to discuss?'

'You did quite an interview with Jessica May. Turned her into the 'belle of the ball'. Even my focus groups in the heartland have softened towards her. They're calling her a real fighter, standing up against the unelected and illegitimate President. Twenty-five percent of Wolfson viewers say they will vote for her. That's massive. The best King ever got from us was eleven percent.'

'Well, she is an impressive lady. And everybody saw through that crap the President tried to pull at the convention, trying to force his way onto the ballot with the 'spontaneous' acclamation from the floor. He should have realised it isn't 1956 anymore. People don't buy that. He's singlehandedly made her a much stronger candidate.'

'Well, not singlehandedly. Your interview raised her to the stratosphere. I was watching it again this morning and I couldn't tell if it was supposed to be a tough, journalistic interrogation or a May campaign PR event.'

'Are you questioning my integrity? You, of all people?'

'What's that supposed to mean?'

'Leonard, I'm not the one who sent Phil Rorschach to hump Ron Diamond's leg like a horny little media puppy.'

'It is the policy of this network to support the Republican candidate. A policy you are clearly not in line with.'

'Supporting the Republican candidate. Do you even know what Phil did on his last show? He invited several of the 'candidate's' former female co-stars to come on air to give testimonials about Ron, scantily clad as if they were going to a pyjama party at the Playboy mansion. With all the tits and bare thighs on display on Phil's show these days, you might as well shift him to Skinemax. Come on, Leonard. You're pissed that I gave Jessica May a fair interview, instead of coming out and accusing her of being at the centre of a den of child abusers. But my interview has raised your network's profile. My show isn't being watched just by hardcore Republicans. Independents and Democrats are also tuning in and lest you forget, they buy Ford trucks and Viagra just as much as your beloved base does. The marketing guys are having a field day since my interview and you know it. Our ratings are through the roof.'

'You've made her look statesmanlike. In contrast, Ron looks like a boorish amateur.'

'That's because he is a boorish amateur, Leonard! That's not my doing.'

'You have to fix this, Amanda. I won't hear of anything else. That's an order.'

'What do you want me to fix, Leonard? I can't fix the fact that the Republican candidate is a con man, that he doesn't have substance, that he doesn't know squat about policy. These are things that the party should have seen a long time ago, before they, and you, became enraptured by the great Ron Diamond. He beat out the Republican field in the primaries because he figured out, accurately as it turned out, that the so-called darlings of the party were all paper tigers. Jessica May is the real deal and you may not like my saying it, but she is going to kick Ron's ass in November.'

'You've had a personal thing against him since that debate you moderated. You haven't sold him as well as you could have.'

'If by "personal thing", you mean I have a problem with a misogynist, sexist asshole, then yes, like all right-thinking women, of course I have a problem with that. And it's not my job to sell your pet Frankenstein project.'

'I am announcing that when he comes here next week, you are going to do an interview with him. You're right, Phil has become too obsequious. But you will lend some of your vaunted gravitas to Ron. Do a family interview, get his wife and children on air as well, show them as the happy family they are, in contrast to Jessica May, whose husband has become so toxic that she can't be in the same room as him. And to clear up any misconceptions that your viewers may have about your commitment to the Republican cause, you will do a "clear the air" segment, not necessarily an apology, but a kind of "both of you regret what's happened between you in the past", sort of thing. You say you got us a load of new viewership thanks to your May interview, fine. Let's use this opportunity to introduce a new, more serious side of Ron Diamond to your enlarged audience.'

'You're a smart man, Leonard, I'm sure you've figured out my answer already. You'll have my resignation letter on your desk in the next thirty minutes. And I'll simultaneously release the text of the letter on all my social media accounts, in which I will discuss in some detail the reasons why my continuing to work at Wolfson is no longer tenable.'

Amanda rises from her seat, just as the nonplussed waiter brings her steak.

'I'm certain you won't do that, Amanda. Please sit down and eat your steak and I'll tell you why you will do exactly what I tell you to do in this matter. I'm well aware that you feel that you can walk away from the network, because you think you are somehow bigger than us. But you're not. You may be the biggest star in the right-wing universe, but that universe exists because of me. I will happily accept your resignation letter, but then what will you do? None of the other right-wing networks will take you. They'll view you as a traitor, someone who sabotaged us due to her own hubris in the middle of the election. Do you think NBC, CNN or any of the other loony left media houses are going to welcome you with open arms? They despise us. The best you can hope for is your own YouTube channel, with you filming yourself from your pathetic little living room, debasing yourself by asking viewers to "click and subscribe", earning $10,000 a month with your 50,000 followers.'

'I'll take my chances, thanks, and you can take your steak and shove it.'

'Brave. Of course, that is a key part of your image, isn't it? The ballsy Bostonian, always ready for a scrap. I respect that. That's why I pay you so much. But I wonder how well your tough guy image will hold up when the world finds out how you tried to meddle in the primaries by thrusting your ex-lover into the race to divide the party? And how you shamelessly lobbied for him behind the scenes, even when it was patently obvious that he didn't have what it takes. An attempt to reignite the old flame, at the expense of the party. If I was sentimental or soft-headed, I might even find it romantic. But I wonder what Congressman Herrera's pretty wife would make of all this? Did she know? Was she complicit, or was it just a plan contrived while the two of you were canoodling? All very interesting questions, well worthy of thorough journalistic investigation. Of course, it's only right that this network look into this exhaustively. I mean, we wouldn't want to be accused of, how did you put it? "Humping your leg like a horny media puppy". You have set very high ethical standards for us, we can't be seen to not uphold those same standards in your case. That wouldn't be right, would it?'

'This is between me and you, Leonard. Leave Herrera out of it.'

'Happy to. I happen to think that he is one of the future stars of this party and I won't take any pleasure in demolishing his career. Just do the goddamn Diamond interview.'

Amanda storms out, almost toppling the waiter and his carefully perched steak. Such is the intensity of her anger that she decides to walk down the ten flights of stairs to her office, rather than standing alongside other corporate douchebags waiting for the elevator. The effort makes her break into a sweat, but the cardio calms her down. By the time she reaches her office, she is no longer fantasising about a violent death for Leonard Wolfson, just grievous bodily harm. Oddly, as she enters her corner office, she finds Gary Patton already sitting inside. Has Leonard alerted her team in advance, another not-so-subtle humiliation to put her in her place? Not only is he forcing her to eat shit, but he's also dictating production content, as if she were some newbie nobody? As if she was Phil fucking Rorschach. What's even more disconcerting is the wide shit eating grin on Gary's face.

'What the fuck are you so happy about?'

'How badly do you want to piss all over Ron Diamond?'

'What? Haven't you spoken to…wait, what are you talking about?'

'Ever heard of a YouTuber called Mr. Sully? Don't expect you have. The guy has about 500 subscribers. He's a prankster, looking to increase his subscribers. Calls up C-list celebrities pretending to be someone else and pranks them. So, he decides, after the President's killing, to prank Luke Diamond. Calls him up, gets through to him, and records the conversation.'

'Ok, so what?'

'So, Mr. Sully pretends to be from the FBI and tells Luke that he's part of the team investigating the President's killing, and would he have any information about it. I admit, it's a bit crass, but like I said, Mr. Sully is hardly highbrow. He's in it for a few cheap laughs. The best he's hoping for is maybe Luke Diamond losing his shit and cussing him out. What he doesn't anticipate is a complete meltdown. Luke starts crying, panicking, and blurts out that although he did advocate playing a game called 'Shoot the President' on an online right-wing forum, he had nothing to do with the assassination. But the conversation doesn't end there. Emboldened by Luke's verbal diarrhoea, Mr. Sully continues to quiz him, asking if he is aware of criminality on the part of anyone else in the Diamond campaign. Luke then admits that Han was also on the same nutty forum and supported his call for 'shooting the President.' Not only that, but he 'fesses up to virtually everything illegal he, or anyone else in the Diamond family has done, including Han and him soliciting hookers, industrial level cocaine use by everyone in the family, filing false expense claims with the Diamond organisation, and the fact that Erika Diamond was an illegal in this country for six months before she married Ron, and that the Diamond organisation falsified her papers to cover up that little gem.'

'Wow. How stupid is Luke Diamond?'

'Oh, very fucking stupid. There are Cherry blossoms planted along the Potomac that have a higher IQ than this guy. But all of this is peanuts compared to the next nugget of information that Luke vomited out. Shit scared that he would leave out any relevant fact and that would land him in trouble with the FBI, Luke disclosed that early in his career, Ron Diamond had been involved in allegedly raping one of his co-stars. It had been the girl's first or second film and Ron was a more established star, so the matter was hushed up within the adult film fraternity. It was written off as a kind of, "She said no, but actually meant yes" deal. Besides, it was the 70s' and this kind of behaviour was fairly common in that industry back then.'

'But how do we know it happened? Did he get a name for the girl? Please tell me he got a name?'

'God bless him, Mr. Sully did. A Janet Maranzano. She left the industry after the incident. Never acted again, in adult or regular films, and generally disappeared from the map.'

'Can you find her?'

'If by that you mean have I acquired her current address, phone number and social security number, then yes.'

'At this point in time, I am ready to have your babies.'

'You're not my type. So? We go for it? I know he's the Republican candidate, but this shit is too good. And if I was able to dig out Mr. Sully, someone else from the other side can do it too. So it might as well be us. What was the meeting upstairs about, by the way? Rumour is old man Wolfson had the executive canteen emptied out to have a private chat with you.'

'He's pissed that we made Jessica May look like Abe Lincoln. He wants me to do a puff-piece interview with the Diamond family, to show off Ron the family man. Says if I say no, I'm out.' Tactfully, she leaves out the part about Ryan Herrera and her.

'Shit. So we can't do this, then.'

'Why? I want to do it.'

'Amanda, you're playing with fire. You pull this shit and Wolfson is going to fire your ass.'

'Leonard Wolfson ordered me to do an interview with the Diamond family. I'll do an interview with them. I'll even ask them a bunch of softball questions. But I'm going to ask Ron about this Janet Maranzano, live on national TV.'

'What do you think he'll do to you? To us?'

'Once this story breaks, it's going to spread like wildfire. A presidential candidate, accused of rape in the middle of the campaign? This is going to go supernova. What's Leonard going to do, fire us for doing our jobs? That'll create an even bigger backlash.'

'You sure about this one?'

'Exposing this son of a bitch is worth anything. We're journalists, that's what we do. If Leonard Wolfson doesn't like it, he can kiss my ass.'

16.
THE
INTERROGATION

CRIMINALITY BRINGS WITH it a degree of courage. This is not to say that those who choose to live outside the bounds of the law have no fear of those who enforce it. But experience gives them a certain familiarity with the processes of the law. Thus, the midnight knock on the door, the handcuffed ride to the police station or the stench of a prison cell no longer hold the same terror for the hardened criminal as they do for the law-abiding.

Therefore, the events of the last night of August came as a rude awakening for the Qureshi household, whose adherence to the law had till then, been so absolute that neither Shakaib nor Umber had ever even spoken to a policeman, let alone been accosted by one.

The night in question is a sweltering one in Karachi, days of incessant monsoon rain interrupted by a weather pattern that stops the sea breeze and brings an intense stillness and extreme humidity. The hum of the air conditioner on full blast prevents Shakaib from hearing the commotion at the gate, as armed men in plain clothes swarm into his house. It is only when the house boy comes running and knocks on his bedroom door half a second before an armed man kicks it in, that Shakaib receives his first inkling of what is going on.

'Are you Shakaib Qureshi? Get up!' The armed man prods him roughly with his automatic weapon.

'Who the hell are you and what are you doing in my house!'

Shakaib turns to see Umber pick up her slipper and throw it in the direction of the intruder. The armed man is momentarily stunned and retreats to the bedroom door.

'Shakaib Qureshi, you are to come with us!' The man looks in Umber's direction, not certain whether to expect another flying slipper to his face. 'We're the police!' He says it unsteadily, as if not convinced himself that he is.

'You're not police! Where are your uniforms! What sort of police runs around dressing and behaving like hoodlums!' Umber's second shoe is raised and ready to fire, but Shakaib is aware of the gun in the man's hands, and he motions Umber to calm down.

'We're…special police. Shakaib Qureshi, you are to come with us!'

'What special police? Can you show me some identification? And why should I come with you?'

The man is clearly not used to his arrestees throwing a barrage of such questions at him.

'We're…uh…special. We don't need identification. You're to come with us.'

'For what? I'm a former Special Assistant to the Prime Minister! And I'm not going anywhere until you tell me the reason.'

'We know you're a former minister. You are being arrested under TSP-FETA, for corruption. Now either you come with us, or we arrest everyone in this house!'

'The hell he will come with you!' Umber readies her shoe but Shakaib puts his hands up in front of Umber and calms her down.

'This is some sort of misunderstanding, Umber. Let me go and sort it out. I'll come with you, but let me get changed first. And please leave my bedroom.'

The armed man grudgingly accepts and walks downstairs, past a terrified houseboy. Shakaib hurriedly changes while a concerned Umber looks on.

'Shakaib I am not letting you go anywhere with that thug.'

'There's been some kind of mistake. I don't want these people in the house, around you. Look, if I don't come back by the morning, call this number. It's the SPM's number, he will inform Javed Afridi. Don't worry.'

'What an absolutely moronic thing to say.'

Shakaib walks downstairs and out the gate to find the house surrounded by armed men and police escorts. Most are in plain clothes, but a few are wearing camouflage trousers and tight-fitting commando T-shirts. The armed man who broke down his door, who is presumably the leader of this rabble, guides him to an unmarked sedan. As soon as the car pulls away from his house with the other vehicles escorting it, the man hits Shakaib hard in the face while grabbing his hands to bind them. Before Shakaib has had the time to recover, the man has placed a hood over his head and punches him in the ribs just for good measure.

At this point, time loses all relevance. Shakaib cannot recall how long it takes for the car to get to its destination, nor does he have a clue as to what that destination is. He can only judge, based on the time he spends in the car, that it is unlikely that he has been taken to the local police station. Even when they dismount, his eyes remain covered and so he cannot say if he is in a police establishment or anywhere else. He is led down an interminable number of steps, to what he imagines must be the deepest basement in Karachi, and it is only when he reaches the bottom of the stairs that the smell hits him. That mixture of stale sweat, urine and vomit that seems to be the standard aroma of incarceration.

The hood on his head is only removed once he is inside his cell which, upon finally being able to see, he finds is not even large enough for him to either stand erect or pace in circles. A flea-ridden blanket and a pillow that is clearly on its last legs and barely recognisable as a pillow, is placed on the cool floor right next to the stinking three-foot partition that separates the toilet area for modesty purposes. There is no tap, just an old and grimy plastic litre bottle that is filled every day and is meant for both drinking and what little washing one can do with a litre bottle.

Shakaib has no conception of how much time he spends in there. There is no natural light in his cellar-prison, just tube lights adorning the narrow corridor that divides the cells, and no light in the cells themselves. The tube lights are left on perpetually, thus making it impossible to judge the passage of time. The only conceivable way to do that would be to literally count the hours. This Shakaib attempts to do initially, but loses count after the first six. He then tries to make note of meal timings, but these seem almost random, with meals sometimes following quickly one after the other, and at other times interspersed by extremely long gaps. He tries to speak to his captors at every meal time, but they remain silent.

Over the next few days, every time he hears the rattling of the metal door that seals off the stairs from this cellblock, Shakaib readies himself for an interrogation, for someone to come down and at least ask him something. But no one ever does. After a couple of days, thinking that perhaps he has been forgotten in some kind of clerical error by his captors, he repeatedly asks his jailor to inform the 'people upstairs' of his presence, as if he were stuck in some madcap waiting room. But the jailor never waivers in his silence, shovelling a tray of food into his cell and moving on to the next. Shakaib then tries communicating with his other cellmates. He knows there are others here, he can hear them when they pray, he can hear a couple of them whimpering, and he can even hear one snoring loudly. But they seem petrified to say anything. Once, one of the men tries to respond, but the jailor immediately enters the cell block and in a harsh voice, forces them into silence.

His utter isolation begins to eat away at him. He worries about Umber, whether she made a call to the SPM as he had instructed her. And then he worries that if she has made the call, will that cause a repeat visit to her from his captors? And what if it causes a visit from them to him? What if they revert to more violent methods? The bruise on his forehead from the man's punch swells and hurts constantly. The worst bit of being locked up, Shakaib learns, is not the physical pain, nor the torrid living conditions. It is the thinking. Hours and hours of thinking, pondering over what has gone wrong, why he is here and what will become of him. It can drive a man mad. He starts to feel as if his sanity is slipping away in the silence of his cell.

And then all of a sudden, it happens. One day, he is lying on his filthy blanket, in and out of a restless sleep, when the doors open and three men order him out of the cell. He is not manacled, but held and guided up the stairs to a brightly lit room with a steel table and two chairs placed across from each other. He is placed on one of the chairs and handed a small, cool bottle of mineral water, which he thirstily gulps down. At length, the door of the interrogation room opens and a face he would never have imagined in a million years, confronts him.

'Shakaib bhai!! How good to see you! Oh my God, you stink! Here, use some of this.' Hamza sprinkles some of his signature oudh cologne straight in Shakaib's face, making him cough. He sits down on the chair opposite and looks solicitously at Shakaib. 'Have they told you why you are here?'

'How long have I been here?'

'Oh my God, these idiots! You mean they haven't even spoken with you? Idiots! Absolute Idiots! Shakaib bhai, it's been four days since you were arrested.'

'Four…days? But no one has spoken to me. No policeman has informed me of the charges. I haven't been produced before a magistrate. The law says I have to be brought before a judge within 24 hours of my arrest. This is blatantly illegal…I don't even know why I'm here!'

'Uh, Shakaib bhai, under TSP-FETA, the authorities don't have to disclose your apprehension for fifteen days.'

'The fellow who came to my house said something about corruption and TSP-FETA, but what has any of that got to do with me?'

'Idiots! Absolute idiots. Basic things they can't do. This is what happens when you don't invest in education. The quality of public service declines dramatically. Imagine, not even having the simple courtesy to inform you of the charges.' He turns to the wall, speaking to an invisible audience. 'Bhai, we are not telling you to go catch Ayman al Zawahiri, but at least you can tell someone why they are here!'

'Hamza, what is this all about?'

Hamza places a file folder on the table in front of him and with some ceremony, takes out a pair of reading glasses from his pocket. 'You have been arrested under section 7 of The Save Pakistan From Evil Thoughts Act, for abuse of your official position while you were Special Assistant to the Prime Minister, corrupt practices while in office, and bringing the country into disrepute. If convicted on these charges, you could face up to fourteen years' imprisonment, as well as a fine of a minimum of one million rupees.'

'I didn't do anything when I was SAPM! I was the one who resigned, remember? I walked out six weeks ago. Besides, everything I did there was logged and recorded by the Prime Minister's Office. The Prime Minister and the SPM are fully aware of all my work. These charges don't even make any sense. "Bringing the country into disrepute?" What the hell does that even mean? These are bogus charges. Any judge will throw them out in five minutes.'

'You are absolutely correct. However, it was the SPM who initiated the complaint against you after getting approval from the Prime Minister. It's all been done with the proper noting and minuting on the file. And as for judges, well I have learnt confidentially that our friend from the anti-corruption court has been contacted and briefed on the case. He is willing to take it on. You see, he still hasn't been elevated to the High Court, so if that asparagus is dangled in front of him, and I am told there has been much dangling, he will bite.'

'Carrots. You dangle carrots, not asparagus.'

'Shakaib bhai, even now you can't give up your English remedial classes! I am telling you, you are in serious hot water boiling!'

'If things are as you say and the judge, who was originally your source, is involved, then I can presume that this has to do with you and Taimur and one of your infernal schemes. You must have turned Javed Afridi against me!'

'Shakaib bhai, Taimur told you this earlier, and I am also saying it. We have nothing to do with this. God promise. We are not in the loop in any of these things. I am even barred from entering the PM House. Javed Afridi has new friends who advise him, and not as wisely as you once did. This is why I told you not to resign. No matter what. We had a voice of sanity in the House.'

'If you aren't advising the PM, then who is?'

'His old friend. His excellency, Turhan Agha, Federal Minister of the Interior.'

'What?! Not possible! Turhan could barely run the education ministry. And Javed hated him! Why would he make him the interior minister? When did this happen?'

'Officially, the notification was issued earlier the same evening that you were arrested. Unofficially, he has been weaselling his way into Afridi's graces since the day you left. He kept pushing Afridi, saying the accountability process was too slow and he could speed it up, if given he was given the chance. He even contacted the judge through his spiritual pir. So, he was given his opportunity. And to prove his efficiency, his first order of business was ordering your arrest. Along with about 500 other opponents of the regime, all in the same night. Your dear wife has been calling the PM office from the day you were picked up, but they have been giving her the runaround.'

'Why? What did I do to deserve such treatment?'

'Your mistake, Shakaib bhai, was to upset the man-child. You upset him by walking out in such a dignified manner. It made him look small and made you look heroic. You were his pet and you barked at him. So he decided to punish you. It's a habit of Javed Afridi's. He wants the world to think that he is the only shining knight in white armour.'

'White knight in shining armour.'

'Yes, what you said.'

'Then why did he even bother to make me a minister? He should have stuck to the likes of Turhan Agha from the beginning.'

'Javed Afridi, if you haven't noticed already, is a complicated personality. Your desire to do good, your decency, reflects one side of his personality. Turhan reflects another, darker side.'

'And you and Taimur and your people are just sitting around, watching the circus?'

Hamza sighs and turns towards the wall. 'Get us some tea! And biscuits!' In less than a minute, the door opens and a bearer brings in two steaming cups and a plate of Sooper cookies. After four days of ingesting nothing but dirty water and watery daal, the tea and biscuits taste like heaven to Shakaib.

'Frankly, Shakaib bhai, we are at our wit's end. This experiment has turned out to be an utter disaster. You know how all of this started, why we decided to support Javed Afridi. There were many within us who admired his sporting achievements and his straightforwardness. He didn't look like a politician, with that hair, with that fit body, the way he walked, the way he talked, the stories about the women he had slept with. What a guy he was!'

'If that was your criterion for choosing to back Javed Afridi, then you lot were stupider than I thought. That's the dumbest thing I've ever heard.'

'No, Shakaib bhai, it's not. That's where you are wrong. You think people choose who they will follow or who they will vote for, based on issues? You do that, but most people don't. Most people's criteria is a lot more frivolous. Look at the American election. You think Jessica May wouldn't get more support if she was more attractive? If she dressed a little provocatively rather than in the dowdy fashion she has? You don't think that at least some of the support Ron Diamond has generated is due to the fact that people are in awe of his sexual prowess? People are shallow Shakaib bhai. So were we, when we chose to support Javed Afridi. We were sold on his image, not just his message. The problem, as Taimur has explained to you in the past as well was, Afridi demanded that he be given the complete authority to clean up the system. And so we indulged him even in that, helping him to secure a parliamentary majority, assisting him above and beyond anything we would have done for anybody else. Shakaib bhai, I myself went to meet candidates of his party who were so clueless, they couldn't believe they had won on election day. We also swallowed the fantasy that Javed Afridi was a messiah, just like you did.'

'I was sold on him by you. Because I trusted you. I didn't know all this other stuff about him, about his dark side. But you should have known all this. You should have done a proper risk assessment on him.'

'We never thought he would go out of our control. We genuinely believed that as long as there were a few good men whispering sage advice in his ears, he would change the destiny of this country. And so we gave him everything. We gave him the election, we gave him the judges, we got him the laws he wanted. Like a bright child who is given everything because the parent believes he or she will go far, we spoiled him. And like a true spoilt child, now he has started snapping at us.'

'What do you mean? What can he do to you? He can't lock you up like he has me.'

'Yes, but that's just about the only thing he can't do. He refuses to listen to us, he refuses to even meet with us. Last week when Taimur's boss went to see him, he refused to meet him. He operates through the SPM and Turhan Agha. He has cleverly co-opted the contacts that we made for him. You put him in touch with Ron Diamond and we connected him to the Afghan Taliban leadership. Now he's in direct WhatsApp contact with both, leaving us out of the loop.'

'I thought they were your pets. Why don't you tell them to stop picking up his phone?'

'They were never our pets, Shakaib bhai. They worked with

us only when it suited them. And why would they stop speaking to him, when he constantly tells them we've been double-crossing them for years? Of course, they will believe him. He is the Prime Minister, why on earth would they not talk to him? Why don't you tell your son to tell Ron Diamond to stop speaking to him?'

'I didn't even know he was talking to Ron Diamond. I'm not sure my son did, either.'

'That's exactly our point. He is conducting his own foreign policy, without keeping any of us in the loop. This bloody WhatsApp will be the death of all of us.'

'You expect me to believe that you people, with all of your levers, cannot control Javed Afridi?'

'Did you ever teach your son how to ride a bicycle? I did. At first, I had to get him training wheels and even then, I had to sometimes hold the handle. But then he kept growing and kept cycling and now he is much better than me, and now he doesn't like to cycle with me. That's us and Javed Afridi in a nutshell.' Hamza looks towards the wall again and lowers his voice to a whisper. 'Shakaib bhai, we have credible information that Afridi is thinking about sacking Taimur's boss.'

'Why?'

'To show everyone that he can.'

'Can't you stop him?'

'Well, short of a coup, no. Every week he insists on having a mass rally and gets massive coverage for it in the media. We even tried to cut back his media coverage. But Afridi threatens everyone with TSP-FETA. It allows him to play God. And he controls social media. His supporters flood Twitter, Facebook, and TikTok. May Allah put ants on this bloody Zuckerberg fellow! No, a coup would be disastrous under these conditions.'

'When I told Taimur, when I pleaded with you people not to allow the passage of this law, you didn't listen! Taimur told me he was just following orders! And now we're all stuck. If you can't do anything, then why are you here? If you're not even allowed into the

PM House, you certainly can't get me out of here! So I'm stuck in here, while God knows what happens to my family!'

'Shakaib bhai, don't be so despondent. Maybe we can do something to help get you out of here. If you do something for us.'

'There it is. Always some bloody angle, playing me for a fool again, like when you took me to see Afridi the first time, like when you took me to that bloody judge! Every time you had a problem, you used me! I'm in here because of you! I had a perfectly good life, until you dragged Javed Afridi into it!'

'Shakaib bhai, please hear me out! This is an extremely sensitive matter. A couple of weeks ago, we were approached by the Russians, through our Chinese friends. Now, this happened just as the mood in America turned against Ron Diamond, with that interview where he was accused of raping some actress. The Russians and Chinese were both concerned over the fact that Jessica May had taken the lead. They believe a Ron Diamond victory will suit them because it will expand the current internal divisions in America. And they think since he doesn't have a lot of experience in foreign policy, or any sort of experience except pornography, he will be easier for them to manipulate. They know, of course, that Javed Afridi is friendly with Ron Diamond. I mean Afridi boasts about his 'special relationship' to whomever he meets. When he went to China, he actually showed the Chinese President his WhatsApp conversations with Ron Diamond. Unfortunately, he accidentally opened a link where he and Diamond had shared some pornographic pictures. It was very embarrassing. Anyway, like I said, the Russians and Chinese know of the 'relationship', and so they approached us with some information. Apparently, Jessica May's husband's business partner, who has as you know, been accused of being a paediatrician…'

'Paedophile, not paediatrician.'

'Really? What's the difference?'

'One is a children's doctor, the other is a child molester. Quite a bit of difference.'

'Right. Of course, well that makes sense. Now I know why the

Chinese intelligence officer gave me such a strange look when I used that word. Anyway, as I was saying, this partner is a paedia…paedo… well he likes to have sex with children, and is often in contact with other such…people. There was a Russian businessman whom the partners wanted a contract from, and this man, the Paed…the child rapist, he knew that the Russian had similar tastes. So he discussed the matter with May's husband and both partners agreed to fly in a 13-year-old girl to London, where they had a meeting with the Russian. Now, Russian intelligence already monitors all such high profile businessmen because, well, because that's what they do, and since this contract was sensitive, they also started monitoring the communications of May's husband's partner. They have a record of all the conversations in which the two partners discuss offering the Russian the girl as a sex slave. It's proof that May's husband was directly involved in the sex trafficking. There are also some hints in the conversations they recorded, that Jessica May also may have had some knowledge about her husband's activities. If this information is passed on to Ron Diamond, it can turn the election around. He will rebound from his current negative position and sink May.'

'So why do you need me? I'm sure the Russians have ways to pass on this information directly.'

'They don't want their fingerprints on this. That's why they contacted us. If it is passed on through a third party, they will be able to protect their anonymity and also, presumably will continue to be able to monitor whomever they want to monitor without it becoming public.'

'So go to your old friend Afridi. This can be a game changer for your relationship. Perhaps by giving him this intelligence to pass on to Diamond, you can save Taimur's boss's job.'

'Giving this information to Javed Afridi is like handing a child a loaded Kalashnikov. We don't trust him for a minute. He has turned out to be such a snake in the grass, there is no guarantee that he still won't fire our boss. No, we don't want Afridi anywhere near this information. That's why I thought the best way to do this was for you to pass this on to your son Wajahat, and he can then give it to Ron Diamond. If you agree, we can arrange for you to get out of here. We will even ensure that the charges against you are quietly dropped.'

'You lying bastard! If Javed Afridi put me in here, and you can't even speak with Afridi anymore, how are you going to get me out!'

'We will manage it at a lower level. We'll prevail upon the investigative agency to quietly slip you off the system. They are having to process so many arrestees due to Turhan's daily directives, it's not very difficult to lose count of a couple of targets. I mean, they haven't even gotten around to informing you of the charges in four days. How diligent can the system be?'

'What about the cases? And the judge?'

'The judge was our man. We can speak to him again and tell him you are engaged in some highly sensitive national security work for us.'

'Yes, but Turhan will find out. And he will tell Javed Afridi.'

'Turhan is high as a kite most days. And Afridi won't find out as long as you keep a low profile. Maybe leave the country for a few months. In the meantime, we will try and find a solution to the Afridi problem.'

'You expect me to cooperate with you, after I was locked up and humiliated like this? My wife doesn't know whether I am alive or dead. All of my friends and family know I was picked up. You have destroyed my reputation.'

'Not us, Shakaib bhai. Javed Afridi. He did all of this.'

'That's convenient, isn't it? Blame Afridi because it suits you to do that now. "Everything was Afridi's fault, it had nothing to do with us." But if you held me in such high regard, you could have done all of this for me before I was locked in that stinking cell like a common criminal! You could have pulled all the levers that you are now offering to pull. You could have done it because I was your friend, and you know that I am innocent! But you were happy to sit back for four days and let me suffer, so that you would have some negotiating leverage over me. I'll rot in this cell, but I won't do another "favour" for you.'

'Shakaib bhai, you are right in all of this. You are right to be angry. But what can I do? This is the way this business works. Please don't be emotional. Think rationally. It's easy to say you will prefer rotting in this jail, but these people are ruthless. They will make up more cases against you. You will be paying for lawyers and for bail for years. Whether you rot in here or not, bhabi and the kids will rot outside trying to get you freed. Please take my deal. It's simple, if you don't want to directly pass on the information, just arrange a meeting between me and Wajahat. I will fly to America to hand him this material. That's all you have to do. Please.'

17.
OCTOBER SURPRISES

WHEN I FIRST got a call from my dad, telling me to meet his friend Hamza, I thought it a little strange. Dad had never asked me to meet any of his friends ever before, even though several of his old college buddies lived in the Tri-state area. He knew I hated meeting random uncles and aunties, with their questions about where I was working and their ceaseless attempts to play matchmaker. But this uncle, I suspected, was quite different. He didn't seem the matchmaking type.

Dad hadn't given me any details. The only thing he told me was that this guy was someone he used to work with, and that I should meet him in a public place, and listen to him. In fact, dad didn't talk very long at all, which was again unusual. I had been really slack in calling my parents over the summer because the campaign had hit a new intensity, especially after the Amanda Spano interview. With our numbers dipping for the first time, we went into full crisis mode. Whatever my doubts about what we were doing, this wasn't the time to ponder quitting again. Besides, Ron and Harvey had thrown so much work at me that I barely had any time to think. I suspected that may have been Krystal's doing. She may have spoken to them about my reservations, and they decided the best way to get me over my hump was to work me like a dog. Or maybe she was just getting them to dole out some punishment to me for not sleeping with her anymore. Because, irrespective of my feelings about our campaign, coming out of Kansas City I was very clear about my feelings for Shai. I wanted her back, I wanted something real with her, regardless of how good the sex was with Krystal.

I had spoken to both women, explaining to Krystal that I didn't think it was a good idea for us to hook up anymore because it would cause complications going forward. And I had written to Shai, expressing my desire for us to try again and also making a full disclosure about Krystal. I didn't want to keep any secrets from her. Neither had taken my efforts at truth and reconciliation in the spirit that they had been intended. Krystal reverted to her ice queen setting, ignoring my existence altogether. Things with Shai were a little more complicated. While she acknowledged, in our back and forth messaging, that she felt something deeper for me as well, nevertheless she also admitted to being hurt over my admission about Krystal and besides, with the craziness of the campaign, she needed time to think things over in her head.

My soap opera life had ensured that I hadn't really been following events back home. The only time I actually spoke to my mom over the summer was when, after several missed calls, I got a frantic voice message from her one day, stating that my father had 'been taken'. By the time I heard the message and called her back several hours later, her demeanour had completely changed. She chalked it up to a misunderstanding and told me not to worry about it. My sister had gotten the same treatment from mom. I didn't think much of it and continued with work. I didn't even know dad had resigned until this last call. But again, he assured me it was nothing to worry about, just some political differences, and that it was most important to ensure that I met with his friend and heard what he had to say.

Which was why I found myself entering the Red Lobster in Times Square shortly before noon on a Wednesday. When dad's friend called me, the campaign was back in New York, taking a break for a few days to prep for the first debate which was scheduled for next week in Cleveland. The team had been sequestered in The

Erection doing debate prep. With our numbers tanking, the first debate had garnered a far greater importance for us. It was a strange time over all. There had been an edginess in the air, a tension you could almost taste around the country in the last month. Some of it had to do with the Janet Maranzano allegations. So far, we had been the bad boys of the election, bullying every candidate who stood in our way with our rhetoric and our obnoxious supporters. But after the Spano interview, we started getting a hefty dose of our own medicine. We often found women (and some men) protestors shouting 'rapist!' at all our events, and there was a constant fear that a potential criminal case could be filed against Ron any day.

But Maranzano wasn't the only issue. The trial of the police officer who had shot Ade Onitolo in Tulsa began in September and with each passing day, you could sense an increasing agitation across America about the outcome. I wasn't a legal expert by any stretch of the imagination, but watching the proceedings on TV, the impression everybody got was that the judge, jury and prosecutors in Tulsa didn't seem too interested in convicting the officer. As the trial moved to its conclusion, the talking heads on TV couldn't shut up about the racial tensions in the country and what the verdict would signify. No shit, Sherlock. Walking to the corner of Central Park from The Erection to get a cup of coffee from the street cart, I could tell you that. Most black people saw things one way, and most white people saw things very differently.

The day I got the call from "uncle" Hamza was the day the verdict was due to be announced. Following dad's instructions, I chose Red Lobster because firstly, it was a very public place and second, you never knew with Pakistani uncles and their degree of halal compliance. A fish restaurant was safe for him to get a bite to eat and not to make any nosy judgements about me.

When I walked in, he was already seated at a table that overlooked Times Square from behind a big Hershey's billboard. He wore a shalwar kameez which would no doubt make him stand out, and had what I referred to as a topless beard, with the 'tache shaved off the upper lip. He seemed vaguely familiar and obviously recognised me immediately, as he waved me over.

'Salamaleikum, uncle.'

'Waleikum, Wajahat. I'm Hamza, your father's friend. You may remember, we met briefly in London. I had accompanied the Prime Minister to his meeting with your Mr. Ron.'

'Of course.' I had no recollection, but over a year of working for a politician and meeting hundreds of people every day who expected you to remember them, had made me an accomplished liar. 'How are you, uncle Hamza?'

'I am good. But we are all very concerned with Mr. Ron's recent fall in the polls. How is your campaign going?'

'Yeah, it's been a bit tougher in recent weeks after the Amanda Spano interview. We've lost a lot of women voters, but it could have been worse, frankly. The Janet Maranzano story could have hurt us a lot more. We may be down by a few points, but at least we're still in the race.'

'Oh, that is good to hear. Thank God. Curse this Marzipano woman! First, she has the shamelessness to display her naked body in films, and then she cries about it later. These pornographic people are filthy! No values!'

'Well, uh, it's a little bit more complicated than that. And her name's Maranzano. Besides, Ron is also one of the 'pornographic people', as you call them.'

'Yes, but he is a good man, a God-fearing man. Look at how he came out against gay marriage. Great man. Great. He has a lot of supporters in Pakistan. All of us are praying for his victory.'

'Uh … thanks, I guess?'

There was a moment of silence between us as neither of us were sure how to proceed. "Uncle" Hamza noisily slurped from the giant glass of Coke the waitress had brought, and smiled at me.

'What has your father told you?'

'Nothing. He was very mysterious. He just asked me to meet with you and said it was very important.'

'That is true. What we are about to discuss is critically important. For your father and for Ron Diamond.' He took out a USB from his pocket and surreptitiously slid it across the table to me. 'Put that in your pocket. Your father's life may depend on it.'

'What?!?'

'I must tell you that Shakaib bhai was arrested three weeks ago in Pakistan. He has now been released temporarily, but there are many people who are against him. His continued liberty depends on you giving the information on that USB to Ron Diamond. We believe if your campaign uses this information correctly, it could turn around the entire election and guarantee you a win in November.'

'What does this have to do with my father? Why was he arrested?'

'He was accused of anti-state activities.'

'My dad? Anti-state? That's a laugh. He still cries during the national anthem.'

'The charges against him were very serious. And the atmosphere back home has become toxic. The Prime Minister, Javed Afridi, made these accusations against Shakaib bhai…'

'But that guy loved dad! He couldn't tie his shoelaces without him. How…'

'Politics, my boy. It is a terrible thing. Suffice it to say, Javed Afridi has now completely turned against your father and will use the entire resources of the State to lock him up. But some of us are working to get Shakaib bhai out of this mess. My bosses… are very powerful men. They wish to help Ron Diamond and they wish to have their own relationship with Mr. Ron, separate from his friendship with Javed Afridi. They have agreed to get Shakaib bhai off the hook if you will pass this on to Mr. Ron, and… well put in a good word for us.'

'Who are you people?'

'We are called many things. You and Mr. Ron will understand everything once you have reviewed the USB. It's all on there. But please, do this as quickly as possible.'

'Where is my father now?'

'He is safe. For the moment. We managed to get him out of custody without Afridi finding out. But he has to keep a very low profile because they are watching everything. We asked him not to say much on the phone and we are trying to get him safely out of the country, but my bosses first want you to deliver that, before they make Shakaib bhai completely secure.'

I stared at the USB in some wonderment, this little device that now controlled my father's future. I was about to ask Hamza more details, but I was interrupted by a commotion outside. As Hamza and I, and a number of the other patrons of Red Lobster turned to look outside the window, we saw a crowd gathering in Times Square. The big screens had moved off their commercials and were showing live news coverage from Tulsa. It didn't take a genius to figure out that the commotion was in response to the Not Guilty verdict that had just been announced. The crowd, now largely made up of black people, grew more incensed as details of the verdict were flashed on screen. Many started shouting "Fuck the police!"

From my vantage point, I could see a visibly nervous bunch of police officers forming a phalanx at the police post at one end of the Square. A loud shout of "Yeah!!!" which seemed to come from a predominantly white construction crew, arose when the acquitted police officer was shown on the screen, further angering the crowd. An incendiary was thrown in the direction of the police from somewhere, and then all hell seemed to break loose. In minutes, Times Square was ablaze as America went to war with itself.

I would have continued to stand there by the window, mesmerised by the orgy of violence that unleashed itself below me, but soon enough we too became targets, as a couple of bricks came hurtling towards us, shattering the windows of the Red Lobster and covering us in glass. Suddenly awakened to the unfolding carnage, the patrons started rushing out the front door.

'It's time to go. Things over here are becoming just like Pakistan. Please, Wajahat, keep that USB safe. Contact me on the number I called you from. I'll check in on it, no matter where in the world I am.'

'My parents will be ok?'

'Yes. Just get this to Mr. Ron.'

* * *

RIDGEFIELD, CONNECTICUT

'So? What's it going to be? We condemning the rioting or no? It's been three days and we haven't put out a statement on this. We're kind'a missing the bus.'

'We're not missing anything, Maury, because we're not catching this bus. The last time round, I got slammed, first for coming out for a tougher law and order stance, and then again for calling for a civil rights investigation into the Onitolo killing. Meanwhile, Ron Diamond sat on his fat ass in the Caymans, soaking up the sun and avoiding the issue altogether. That's what I'm going to do. We are not touching this thing, we are locking down and prepping for the debate. If we have to, we can say that since it's a matter under judicial review, we won't comment on it as it's still an active legal issue.'

'Jessica, you can't say you won't comment because it's a legal issue. Abortion is a legal issue, and half of our campaign is based around it. And Diamond's come out hard on the law and order side this time. He spoke out four hours after the verdict, and he didn't pull his punches. He slammed the President hard, blaming him for the violence.'

'Well, he had to do it because he's behind in the race. He's got to say and do anything to stay alive. We have the luxury of floating above the fray, right Johnny? And blaming the President for this doesn't even make sense. The President wasn't the one who decided the verdict, and the federal government isn't responsible for local law and order.'

'It's stabilised Diamond's numbers. In some polls, they're

even ticking upwards. Both sides are angry. People are angry at the injustice, and they're angry at the almost constant rioting that has made us look like a banana republic. Violence in 50 American cities. In the public eye, the President seems to be a dithering old man, fiddling while Rome burns. Unfortunately, he's from our party so despite our personal animosity with the White House, we still get tagged with his ineffectualness.'

'So what are you telling me now, Johnny? That our numbers are dropping? Again?'

'No. Not dropping… not yet. Ron's picked up a lot of favourables because of his strong anti-rioting stance…'

'Well Godamnit, it's not like I'm handing out Molotov cocktails in the Bronx! You make me sound like I'm for the rioting!'

'You're not… obviously. All I'm saying is, he's harvested a popular surge because of his unambiguous stance. The negative impact of Maranzanogate has been stopped. The race is going to get closer. He may even pull to within the margin of error. People admire his forthrightness, even if some of them feel he's done unsavoury things in the past.'

'Oh, ok. So it's ok to rape someone, as long as you shout "Shoot the looters!" at the top of your voice!'

'Look, Jessica, I'm just the numbers guy. I don't agree with it, but this is the way it is.'

'Come out against the rioting. Tackle Ron Diamond from the right.'

'And risk losing the entire minority vote?! Which at this point, is our bedrock?? Have you lost your mind, Mike? And as if that wasn't bad enough, I'll get tagged as a flip-flopper again, like when Onitolo was shot! No way! I'm not going through that crap again! I'm staying silent on this issue. I can't win on it. We've got to find another way of damaging Ron. We've got to remind people, as bluntly as possible, about what a douchebag he is. Can someone in this fucking room start thinking out of the box, for a change?'

'Ok. I've got an idea. I wasn't going to say it, because I thought all of you would shout it down and say "Are you crazy, Maury??" but I guess…whatever else it is, it's certainly out of the box…'

'Spit it out, Maury. What is it?'

'Give me a second, Princess. Ok, so we wanna remind America that Ron Diamond is a misogynist, date-raping bastard, right?'

'Well, we don't know if he actually date-raped Maranzano, legally speaking…'

'Legally speaking, shut the fuck up, Johnny. So, here's what we do. We get Maranzano to sit in the audience during the debate. We put her right up front, in our VIP seats, so he has to look at her every time he tries to speak. He's gonna fumble, he's gonna look guilty, he's not gonna look like some fucking strongman who says he's tough on law and order. Meanwhile, we kick the shit out of him in the debate. We win the debate on the issues, which is what Jessica wants to do anyway, and we make him look like a fucking putz.'

'Won't people call us out for being shamelessly opportunistic for using Maranzano in this way? I mean, this could backfire on us big time.'

'Jessica May is proving that she does what she says. She stands up for women and the underprivileged. She brought Janet Maranzano here to this debate to show solidarity with her, and to remind the world to never forget the crimes of this man, Ron Diamond. In fact, we even make a point of calling for a police investigation into the matter.'

'But Maranzano apparently signed those NDAs and waived her rights to any legal action, years ago.'

'NDA, ShmenDA. Whether it happens or not, doesn't matter. We call for him to be locked up. Our supporters can even chant it during the debate: Lock him up, Lock him up! We really give it to that motherfucker.'

Silence. A long pause in the room, as everyone looks towards Jessica, who finally speaks after a long contemplation. 'You really think this can work, Maury?'

'We clean this asshole's clock in Cleveland, and trust me, this race is over.'

* * *

I didn't do what "uncle" Hamza had told me to do. At least, not immediately. Of course, events, in the shape of The Great New York riot, came in the way. I barely managed to make it back to my apartment. None of us left the building for the next few days, and as I looked out of my window at the view that had so captivated me when I first walked into this apartment, I could see a line of burning police cruisers and taxi cabs down the length of Broadway. You could smell the fumes from fifty floors up.

I took this opportunity to look at the data that Hamza had handed to me. It was obvious that he was trying to play me, with all that talk of my father being in trouble. It's not that I wasn't worried about my dad. But I wanted to be certain that Hamza and his people would actually help dad and not just ditch him when they got what they wanted. Besides, even when dad had called me to set up the meeting with Hamza, he had said something that stuck with me. He told me to listen to Hamza. And then he said, just listen to him. He was sending me a message in his own way. Hamza was not to be trusted. So, I took my time, reading everything on the USB, trying to understand it, and most importantly, summarising it in a way that would ensure that there wasn't a knee-jerk reaction from Ron. I had to control the flow of this story as much as I could.

Besides, this was hardly the top priority at Diamond headquarters. Ron had felt the heat from the Maranzanogate backlash, and the riots had afforded him another chance to get back in the game and put the sexual misconduct allegations behind him. He was in full warrior mode, calling out the rioters and calling out the President for being asleep at the wheel. When the President did finally awaken to the gravity of the problem, it was too late, and the sight of M1-Abrams tanks and Armoured Personnel Carriers being parked at Columbus Circle, or on the Mall in Washington, or on the Loop in Chicago, just drove home to millions of people Ron's point, that the government had lost all control.

By the evening of the fourth day of rioting, I was ready. I asked Ron and Harvey to convene a meeting so I could brief them on a key development. The meeting was in the conference room on the 69th floor, the same place where I had started my journey with Ron Diamond.

When I got there that evening, five minutes earlier than the given time, I found that the key team, which included Ron, Harvey, the three siblings and Erika, were already seated and waiting. I had expected only Ron and Harvey and was surprised to see the entire family arrayed across the table from me in an interrogatory manner, the same as when I had first interviewed here.

'Uh, Ron, are you sure you want everyone in on this? What I have to say is top secret and cannot leak from this room.' I tilted my head subtly towards Luke and Han.

'Everyone who needs to be here, is here. Now, what's this all about, Iowa State?'

'OK.' I took a deep breath. 'Here goes. Four days ago, I was approached by a Pakistani man, who claimed to be a friend of my dad's. He handed me information that he said could be critical to this campaign.'

'What was the information, and if it's so critical to this campaign, why did you delay four days before informing us?'

Han never let an opportunity pass where he could play the role of a prick. 'The information is highly sensitive and was given to me unedited. I had to work to put it together properly before I told Ron. I can't stress enough that this cannot be used frivolously or incorrectly. This stuff has national security implications and is unverified by American sources.'

'So what is it, Iowa State? Give us the big fucking reveal.'

'Basically, there's a document, a transcript, that claims that Brendan Bracken and Tim Regan trafficked an underage girl, flew her to London and made her have sex with a Russian businessman whom they wanted to get a contract out of. The documentation makes it very clear that this wasn't just something Bracken was doing. Regan was fully aware and facilitated the transaction. There may even be an indication that Jessica May was also aware of this kind of behaviour from her husband and his partner.'

I could see from the expressions on their faces that this had blown everyone's mind. There was pin-drop silence in the room for several seconds. Harvey, with his acute legal brain, was the first to recover.

'Where's the information from? What does your dad's friend do and how has he gotten his hands on this little nugget?'

'I'm not exactly sure what he does but I think he works in intelligence. And this information was passed on to the Pakistanis by the Russians and Chinese. The Russians were monitoring their businessman, and I guess, once these sorts of conversations happened, they also started monitoring Tim Regan and Brendan Bracken. They didn't want this stuff to be connected to them, so they filtered it and passed it on through the Chinese and Pakistanis.'

'Does Jim know about this? He hasn't mentioned it to me. Have the Pakistanians told him?'

'I don't think so. The... Pakistanis... their intelligence people, want to give this to you directly because they want to establish a direct liaison with you, independent of Javed... of Jim.'

'We could blow that bitch out of the water! We could...'

'Shut the fuck up, Han. How good is your information, Iowa?'

'Like I said at the start Ron, it's unverifiable. It could be true, it certainly looks legit. But it could also be the Pakistanis, the Russians, the Chinese, or all of the above, trying to trick you and creating an issue in the election.'

'You're not sold on this, Iowa. That's why you took your time coming to me. What's your gut say?'

The moment of truth. I had thought long and hard about what I would say when Ron inevitably asked me this question. Logic dictated, and I'm sure "uncle" Hamza and his friends hoped, that with the threat to my father, I would come down hard on their side. The information would establish their bona fides with Ron and he would buy it, they presumed, because I did a convincing job selling it. Truth be told, having done a forensic study of everything on the USB, I was convinced that this stuff was the real deal. But I didn't want them to have their nails in me, or Ron. My commitment to them had been to the extent of bringing this to Ron's attention. Having done that, they would have to fulfil their part of the bargain to protect dad. I wasn't obliged to sell their story, certainly not at first drop.

'My gut tells me to stay away from this. It's too risky. It's unverifiable information, no matter how juicy it may appear, and it's basically being handed to us by a foreign intelligence service. If the media were to find out about this, they and the May campaign would hit us so hard, we wouldn't be able to recover.'

For once, Ron's usually expressive face was inscrutable. He turned towards Harvey, but before he could speak, Han let out his tirade.

'Dad, I told you, didn't I? Every time there is a decision that has to be taken in the greater interest of the campaign, Waj is against it. He actually wanted you to take back your comments on Ebola terrorism! That's what won us Super Tuesday. No surprise here that once again, he opposes the thing that will win you the election. I don't know why you rate his political acumen. Either he's wrong all the time, or he's deliberately trying to sabotage this campaign. I mean, you can go out on the street and ask ten people on 9th Avenue and they'd all tell you, the obvious play is to use this information to blow Jessica May out of the water. Hell, even Luke can figure that out.'

'Hey! Fuck you, Han!'

'Shut up, Luke. Harvey, what do you say?'

'I don't buy the kid's reasoning. So what if this information hasn't been vetted by American sources? Intel is intel. Doesn't matter where it comes from. This is the game changer. We make this public, and we win. Everyone forgets about some broad called Janet Maranzano. A week from now, they'll all be saying Janet who? It'll all be about Jessie May and her gang of international child molesters. We get to go on the offensive and we bury this problem. This'll be our October surprise.'

'Ron, your stance on the riots has already made your numbers go up. Don't you see, what's happening outside, that's your October surprise. You don't need to use this stuff. We can't be irresponsible about this. It has foreign policy implications. It's hostile foreign powers interfering in an American election. We can't play fast and loose with this information, just because we think it'll get us over Maranzanogate…'

'Don't call it that! I fucking hate when these fucking media jerks call it that! Makes it sound like I was doing a bunch of illegal shit like Richard fucking Nixon!'

Luke, as was his wont, couldn't resist snickering. Even worse, he had to go and open his mouth. 'Well, Dad, you kinda' did.'

'Fuck you, you little cocksucker! We're in this mess because of you, shit-for-brains! Don't you dare talk to me about anything. I should have had the good sense to have you aborted! I'm sure that cunt mother of yours was fucking a retard on the side, because no way are you my son!'

Luke's face crumpled as the venomous bile of Ron's words sank in. He first started to shake uncontrollably, and then began to weep hysterically. The meeting was threatening to turn into a farce worthy of any episode of *Reality Losers*. I decided to put in a final plea before we descended into absolute chaos. 'Ron, please listen to me. It's bad politics to use this, it will come back to haunt us…' My entreaty was interrupted by Luke, stumbling out of his chair and leaving the room, his wails still audible in the hall outside.

'Your desperation to have us not use such explosive political information wouldn't have anything to do with your relationship status, would it, Waj?'

'Excuse me?' I turned to Krystal and tried to read her face to understand how far she wanted to go in this. I wasn't sure which of the people in this room knew about us. I had personally always maintained a "Don't ask, don't tell" policy, but I was very cognisant of the fact that this was probably not the best place for Ron to find out that I had been fucking his daughter.

'Well, I mean it's fairly common knowledge on the campaign circuit that you have a relationship with Shai Naqvi. Is it have, or had? I can't be sure. Nonetheless Waj, you have to admit, that places you in a conflict of interest in this situation. Are you trying to protect the May campaign, or perhaps certain individuals within the May campaign from the fallout of this political nuclear bomb? Is that why you're so vehement that we shouldn't use this stuff, even when logic clearly dictates that we should?'

There it was. Revenge. The whole "woman scorned" bit. Krystal was willing to walk a high wire, risking exposure of our trysts, just to kick me in the balls. She was daring me to come out and say something. I had half a mind to do it. If I had been one of her dickhead brothers, I would have too. Gentlemanly conduct be damned. But I just couldn't do it. I couldn't tell everyone assembled in the room that Krystal had chosen to attack me in this way because I had refused to sleep with her anymore.

'Hang on. Iowa State's been fucking Jessica May's girl?? How come I don't know about this? And how'd you find out, Krystal?'

'Reporters on the campaign trail often cover both campaigns. And they all talk, especially after a couple of drinks. You see Ron, for all his talk of not wanting to be irresponsible with this information he's given us, Waj has had no issues being extremely irresponsible all through the campaign. He's literally been sleeping with the enemy.'

I had to give it to Krystal, she was the perfect assassin. She knew exactly where and when to stick the knife for maximum impact. Her strike hit its mark, as that was the spark that ignited Ron. He went ballistic on me in a way that he hadn't done since the first day I met him, all those months ago. What he said exactly didn't matter anymore. It was all bad anyway. What he did though, took me by surprise because I did not expect him to become so unhinged. He fired me on the spot.

I guess it was naïve of me to have thought that I was immune from Ron being Ron. If I had spoken to anybody else working on the campaign other than the group assembled in the 69th floor boardroom, they would have told me that getting humiliated and then fired was a given when you joined RonDiamondForPresident. If it wasn't Ron blowing up and doing the firing, then it was Harvey not liking your tie or some other ridiculous reason, or Han shitting on you just for the heck of it, because it made him feel like more of a man. It was a toxic environment and I had been living and breathing that toxicity for the past year without recognising what was staring me in the face.

I was frog marched down to my apartment, made to pack while two security goons watched over me and Harvey personally took possession of the USB. And then I was kicked out onto the street. I didn't know where to go. As I stood there on 9th Avenue listening to the constant wail of police sirens, I realised that despite living in this city for so long, I didn't know anyone here, apart from the people in the building that I had just been thrown out of. The only other person I knew was my ex Sonya, and I had burned my bridges with her a long time ago. I couldn't even get a cab, because the rioters' appetite for setting fire to taxis had forced all remaining cabbies off the streets. Not knowing what else to do, I called the only number I could think of, that would come to my help.

'Hi Shai. I need you.'

18.
THE
CHOICE

SHE CURSES HERSELF for the umpteenth time. And then she curses him. Why did she have to look at his laptop? And why did he leave the Russian file open on his screen? That one fateful decision has turned Shai's world upside down.

'Frankly Shai, I never thought I'd say this to you, but I'm disappointed in your judgement. Or lack thereof. How could you get involved with this boy?'

The woman standing in front of her is Jessica May, but in her words and in her tone, Shai hears her mother, with her myriad and constant disappointments. The first 19 years of her life flash before her, when, certainly in her mother's eyes, she could do no right. The next seven years have been the opposite and that has all been due to Jessica. Jessica, who constantly encouraged and nurtured her, who became more of a mother than her real mother ever could, in whose eyes Shai could do no wrong. Which is why this rebuke hurts particularly deeply. *How could you get involved with this boy?* Eight words that are tearing her apart.

Was it such a crime to "get involved?" She's been around politics long enough to know that romantic liaisons between staffers in Congress or during campaigns, are nothing new. Even the ones that cross party lines are fairly commonplace. So what was her crime? That she answered his call last night? What else was she supposed to do?

'What? I can't understand what you're saying Shai. Speak up.'

She realises she has been mumbling unintelligibly. 'I didn't think I did anything wrong.'

'You didn't think you did anything wrong? My God, girl, what world are you living in? Has this boy robbed you of all sense?'

'Jessica, let's get to that part later. I'm more interested in the discovery from last night. Shai, go through it one more time.' She sees Mike from the corner of her eye. It's the first time he has spoken up since coming into the room. They're in Jessica's hotel suite in Cleveland. With the debate just two nights away and the rioting finally dying down after the President's declaration of a national emergency, the campaign has moved to Ohio to stump through what is likely to be a swing state once again. Ever since she got back from Waj's hotel early in the morning, armed or as she now considers it, cursed with the information she stumbled across, she had debated how to share it with Jessica. In her mind, there had never been a question of not sharing it. Regardless of what transpired between Waj and her last night, regardless of the passion that she felt in their lovemaking, a passion she has never felt with anyone before, regardless of the intensity of feeling for him that is making her ache physically, her loyalty never wavered. The problem for her had been how to tell Jessica that she, Shai Naqvi, the perfect staffer, the immaculate political operative, had fallen in love.

'Shai? Can you repeat what you told Jessica before she asked me to come in? I've only heard a summary of your discussion.'

'Sorry, Mike. Of course. So…uh…I was in the city…I went there last night, and came back this morning…'

'Why were you there, Shai? Start from the beginning.'

'Right. Waj…Wajahat…called me last evening. He asked me to meet him, because he had just been fired by Ron Diamond and thrown out of his apartment in Diamond's building. He didn't have any place to go. So I drove down from Ridgefield and picked him up, and we went to a hotel.'

'And he called you because you've been having a relationship with him?'

'Yes…well, no…I mean, we were having a relationship, and then we kind of broke up…for a few months…but he wanted to get back together and we had been talking things out for the past few weeks. But we hadn't gotten back together.'

'Until last night.'

'Yeah. I guess.'

'OK. So you went to a hotel and talked.'

'Right.'

'And had intercourse.'

Trust Mike the Machine to make her tryst sound like a visit to the gynaecologist. 'Yes.'

'And then what happened? Did he tell you why he was fired?'

'He was evasive. He just said he would tell me one day, but it was basically because Ron was in one of his moods and Waj…Wajahat… disagreed with something Ron wanted to do.'

'Did you think it was normal for Waj…is it ok to call him Waj? Did you think it was normal for Waj to be so evasive? If he cares for you this much, why wouldn't he tell you about why he got fired? I mean, considering that he called you to come and pick him up.'

'I…things have been a bit complicated between us. In the past, we both strictly compartmentalised our personal and professional sides. I assumed he was being evasive because his firing may have had something to do with Krystal…'

'Krystal Diamond? How is she connected to this?'

'When we broke up…Waj started hooking up…they slept together a few times…he told me because when he called me to admit his feelings for me…he said he didn't want to hide anything from me…'

'Oh Jesus! He's been banging you and Krystal Diamond?? Am I the only one who isn't getting laid around here? Is this an election campaign, or a goddamn orgy??' Jessica throws her hands up in the air in exasperation.

'Jessica, please. Shai, if he didn't want to hide anything from you, why was he trying to hide why he got fired?'

'I thought…I thought she may have gotten him fired. When he got back in touch with me, he ended things with her. He told her they couldn't continue…doing it. When he first told me about her, I had been very hurt…I couldn't deal with it. So that's why I figured he was being evasive because he didn't want to tell me that his firing was some kind of revenge move on her part.'

'OK. So how did you get this information?'

'After we…you know…he went for a shower. His laptop was on the bedside table. I picked it up to check my email because my phone was in my pant pocket, and my pants were…lying some distance away. When I turned on the screen, the information…was right there, in an open document.'

'And what exactly did you see?'

'It was a kind of summary…I presume he had made it for Diamond…it said that the Russians had passed on some intelligence to the Diamond campaign, through the Pakistanis and Chinese, about Tim and Brendan. Claims that the two of them were actively and knowingly involved in sex trafficking.'

'Did you see the actual intelligence?'

'No. I just saw the summary. He came out of the shower before I could look further.'

'And then what happened? Did you confront him?'

'No.'

'Did he see you with the laptop?'

'No, I put it down when I heard him shut off the shower.'

'So what did you do then?'

'I…we…had sex for a second time, and then he dozed off and I snuck out of the room and drove back to Ridgefield.'

'A second time?!? Jesus, what are you, rabbits??'

'Jessica, please. Shai, then you got on the plane with the rest of us, and told Jessica about this, right now?'

'Yeah, Mike.'

'Did you tell anyone else? Message anyone? Maury, or Johnny? Anything at all?'

'No. I wanted to tell Jessica before anyone else.'

'Have you considered that this may be a plan to trap you? They must know that you would tell Jessica about anything you might come across when you were with Waj. Maybe they're setting us up.'

'What do you mean, Mike? Are you saying what Shai saw was false?'

'We can't rule out that possibility. You've got to admit, it's a pretty juicy story. Isn't it too much of a coincidence that the guy from the other side, whom Shai is…you know…just happens to leave these crumbs on his laptop? Some fantastic story about the Russians and Pakistanis trying to intervene on Ron's behalf in the election? If we go public with it and it isn't true, they've got us. It'll be all about Jessica May being the candidate who will say anything, no matter how outrageous or untrue, to get elected.'

'But if it is true, then this is a federal indictment against Ron Diamond. It's foreign interference in an election. It's game over for the Republicans.'

'But how did we find out, Jessica? We don't have any proof, just a word document that Shai saw on this boy's laptop for a couple of minutes. How can we go public with something so slim? The press would never buy it.'

'We don't go to the press, Mike. I'll speak to the FBI Director. I'll explain to him the 'special circumstances' under which a member of our campaign came across this information, and that we weren't sure whether it was a prank or a national security issue. I mean after all, it's hardly something the FBI should ignore, and besides, there's some circumstantial evidence that points to its veracity, like this boy being a Pakistani and his father working for the government there. All we need to do is nudge the FBI in the right direction. Once they announce an investigation, we will leak some of the details to loyal media people and condemn the Diamond campaign for being in bed with Russia, or China, or whoever.'

'But Jessica, what if…the stuff about Tim is true? That'll hurt us.'

'Not if we've already gone and said the information came from foreign powers. In fact, we can play it as a positive, that the Russians and Chinese are so scared of my becoming President because they know I'll be tough with them, that they are digging up false intelligence against me and passing it on to my rival to try and stop me. It's perfect. We look like the victims, but we also get to show off that our foreign policy creds are much better than Diamond's.'

'Ok, but what if the FBI investigation concludes that Tim was … involved in these activities with Brendan?'

'Look, Mike, it's the 11th of October today. The election is less than a month away. No way the FBI finishes what I am sure will be a complex investigation, in less than a month. By the time they finish, we would already have won. Don't you see, this is the silver bullet. This is the thing that gets us past everything. We keep hitting Ron Diamond but he keeps coming back. With this, he goes down for the count. Once he's dead and buried and we've won the White House, we can evaluate the results of the investigation and what we should do with it. Maybe there's nothing there and it just quietly goes away. Maybe, if there is something serious, I'll divorce Tim. I've told you guys before, I will walk away from that son of a bitch if I have to. It's a problem doing it before the election, but once I'm in office, it will make me look even tougher. It will be great for my image. The President who was even willing to sacrifice her marriage in the fight against the Russians.'

'OK. Yeah, I think that's workable. Let's bring Maury and Johnny in on this, but no one else. We'll craft our message and responses, and of course, we'll have to coach Shai on exactly what to say…'

'Wait. Mike, Jessica, I can't do this.'

'What?!? Why??'

'If I speak to the FBI, I'll have to tell them about Waj. And they'll arrest him…'

'So? It is a serious breach of national security.'

'But … I love him, Jessica.'

'For Christ's sakes, Shai! Get a grip! What the hell has this boy done to you?'

'I can't throw him under the bus, Jessica. We've got to figure out some other way.'

'Grow up! This is the election! You think I'm going to jeopardise my presidential campaign over your teeny-bopper romance? It's a crime if you don't cooperate with the FBI. And apart from that, it will be a betrayal of me, one that I will never forget. So get your shit together, Shai.'

* * *

The one thing you should know about federal prison is that the food is actually as bad as you see in the movies. I read a report once, that was written by some prison consulting firm (Only in America would that be an actual thing), in which they tried to prove that prison food was as tasty and nutritious as anything that came out of the average high school cafeteria. Not that the average American high school cafeteria was a great metric to compare with, but I can state from personal experience that when they wrote that report, the prison consultants were lying through their extremely well-compensated asses. And I'll bet good money that none of the authors had ever personally faced the business end of a meal tray consisting of two pieces of slightly stale Wonder bread, a portion of undetermined brown slop (which was supposed to be the meat choice) and a smaller portion of undetermined yellow slop (which was supposed to be your vegetable choice), topped off with the one redeeming feature of the meal, an intolerably small portion of Jello, obviously designed by sadistic jailors to enhance the inmates' sense of hopelessness.

But let me rewind a bit, to explain how and why I was on my way to becoming the world's foremost gastronome of prison food. I was arrested two days after my last encounter with Shai. I was still in the same hotel where we had spent that night but surprisingly, I had lost all contact with Shai after that morning. She was already gone by the time I woke up. She had told me that the campaign team was moving to Cleveland ahead of the debate, so I expected that she would be incommunicado for a bit, but I didn't expect to find myself blocked on her phone when I did call her later that same night. I was still trying to figure out what had happened and what my next moves were, since I no longer had a job and hence no more work visa, when the feds came bursting through my door.

The interrogation was short and sharp. They asked me about the Russia files. I couldn't lie, after all, they had my laptop and the summary that I had typed for Ron was lying open on my screen. The only choice I had was how much I should reveal. Having asked for my one phone call, I had three options: I could try Shai again, but since she had blocked me, it wasn't a promising prospect. I could call my parents back home, but what exactly they could do immediately to help me, and keeping in mind the fact that my dad was also barely managing to keep himself out of a Pakistani jail, was a huge question mark. The third option, which I did take, was to call someone in the Diamond organisation. I decided to call Harvey, but I only got as far as his PA. She heard my plight for about five minutes and then, having put me on hold to presumably confer with Harvey, promptly hung up on me.

I was totally isolated. I told the FBI agents that a man named Hamza had handed me the information, but I concealed his relationship with my father, choosing to say that I knew him from Ron's meeting with Javed Afridi, as a member of the Prime Minister's entourage. On everything else I stonewalled, asking for a lawyer. For my troubles I was given some pimple-faced newbie from the Defender's office who at times seemed to be more interested in prosecuting me than defending me. Due to what was termed as my 'non-cooperative' attitude, the feds threw me into the Manhattan Metropolitan Correctional Centre, where past inmates had famously included luminaries like El Chapo, Jeffrey Epstein and Khalid Sheikh Mohammed. Clearly the US government felt I was on the same level as the world's biggest drugs trafficker, a serial paedophile and the mastermind of 9/11.

I knew I was going to be stuck there for a while, thanks to the ineptitude of my lawyer and my inability to raise the two hundred thousand dollars for my bail. The feds insisted on such a hefty amount, since they categorised me as a "dangerous alien" who could flee the country. As I heard the arguments in court, it amazed me how, in the space of about five days, I had gone from being a top political operative in the presidential campaign of the Republican party's candidate, to being categorised as a "dangerous alien", which made it sound as if I was a creature from a Ridley Scott movie.

It took me about a week of sitting in my solitary cell and staring at the toilet bowl to figure out that the only way the FBI had gotten wind of this was through Shai. Ron and Krystal and co. may have been pissed at me, but they would never risk implicating themselves by fingering me. Besides, they had been wanting to use this information themselves, so why would they involve the FBI. The only other explanation was that Shai had somehow seen my summary while we were together that night, and reported me. That was why I was blocked on her phone. That's the only thing that made sense.

The problem before me was an acute one and my options were narrowing with each passing day. Like the bit about my father's involvement, I had chosen to hold back the part of the story in which the original USB was now with the Diamond campaign. In fact, I hadn't even confirmed to the FBI agents whether I had in fact informed anyone else about the information. That was why I had been desperate to reach out to Harvey, so I could maybe leverage my silence for some legal assistance. Also, weirdly enough, Ron Diamond still had a hold over me. I had been betrayed by Shai, I had lost my job, and in all probability would end up spending some time in jail. I didn't see the point of bringing down Ron as well. It still wouldn't save me. Besides, the way the feds were going, they would probably end up establishing a link to Ron without my help. Between this and Maranzanogate, all the space he had regained during the riots would disappear. As far as I knew, he was already toast.

I had no access to the outside world anymore. The Manhattan Metropolitan Correctional Centre was a high-security prison, which meant that all inmates were in solitary cells, and completely isolated from each other. There weren't any Hollywood-style prison yard conferences, where you could catch up on what was going on outside. The only ones who could keep you in the loop were the prison guards. Now prison guards on the whole are a pretty reticent, douchebaggy group, but in my case they were especially unfriendly on account of my being a brown, Muslim, entitled, twenty-something. I found out, to no great surprise, that Ron Diamond was a huge favourite of the prison staff and probably won 90% of the vote in the MMCC. Suffice it to say, despite my campaign credentials, I wasn't a favourite of the guards and none of them saw fit to keep me in the loop about the news.

I was therefore surprised to be informed on my fifteenth day of captivity that I had a visitor, and that in fact, the visitor was my lawyer. Since my court appointed counsel had never bothered checking in on me, I was somewhat stupefied. That surprise turned to outright bewilderment when, as I entered the meeting room, I saw a kid who must have been younger than me, dressed in a suit he had obviously just purchased for this meeting, since the price tags were still attached to his tie. The kid was vaguely familiar, but I couldn't quite place him.

'Mr. Waj-a-hat Shak-abe?' The kid rose nervously from his chair and extended his hand, before realising that there was a glass partition between us.

I looked at him quizzically. 'Who are you?'

'I'm your… I'm your lawyer.'

'I don't recall hiring you. And you don't even look old enough to have passed the Bar exam.'

He looked around the room, which was empty, and then lowered his voice to a whisper. 'I'm actually waiting for the results. But the Oracle said it would be ok for me to come down here.'

'The Oracle?' In my jailhouse musings, I had momentarily forgotten Harvey's nickname. 'Oh, you mean Harvey!'

'Shhh! You can't say the name. He instructed me that, no matter what, we are not to take his name.'

'Who are you?'

'I'm Scott Styris. I used to work on the campaign. I was taking a gap year after law school and figured it might help my CV. Then I got fired a couple of months ago because the coffee I got for Mr. Cal … for the Oracle, was too hot. So I decided to sit my Bar exams.'

'You … worked on the campaign?? And you got fired and decided to sit for the Bar? So you're not a real lawyer? Why did Har … the Oracle, send you?'

He looked furtively around the room again. 'Because I'm deniable. I'm not connected to the campaign anymore, so no one can say that they sent me. If anyone asks, you're supposed to say that we met when I was working for the campaign, and since you knew I was a lawyer, you decided to hire me.'

'But you're not a fucking lawyer!'

'The Oracle says I don't have to be. I'm just here to pass a message.'

'What's the message?'

'If you try and implicate Ron or any of the senior campaign staff in your legal troubles, the organisation will deny any and all knowledge of you. They've already held a press conference denying that you had ever been in touch with any of the senior staff. It will be your word against the entire organisation's. Furthermore …'

'I haven't said anything. They don't have to worry. I'm not a rat. That's why I'm in here.'

'Oh. Ok. Phew. Well, that's good. So I don't have to do the threat bit, I can just skip to the other stuff. I wasn't very comfortable with that …'

'What's the other stuff?'

'Well, the Oracle said that … wait, I wrote this bit down …' he took out a little notebook from his pocket and started to read from it. 'If you keep your mouth shut and take it like a man, we'll help you out.'

'How? Will he get me a lawyer? A real one?'

'Well … no. Not directly. The campaign can't be seen to do anything that would link you to them. But the Oracle said he would get word to your parents and sort something out. He thinks that if you haven't said anything, the government case isn't that strong. You could easily get out with minimal jail time if you copped a plea and took it all on yourself. He said that might be the best outcome for all concerned.'

My shoulders slumped. Great. I was having a conversation with a cut-out, fake lawyer who may possibly have actually been even younger than me, about pleading guilty for the good of everyone. I felt like I had joined the mafia. The saddest bit was that this probably was the best course of action for me. Shai was gone and if I turned on the Diamond campaign, they would crush me. After all, who was I? An immigrant Pakistani who worked on a presidential campaign for about five minutes? And if I chose to talk, I would have to implicate my dad as well, and that was something I was just not prepared to do. I had no choice but to stay quiet.

'Tell me something. What's going on outside? In the campaign? How has my situation impacted the election?'

'Well, it was bad for a few days when it first came out. But then the campaign managed to turn it around.'

'What? How?'

'When the FBI announced its investigation, the May campaign leaked that the Russia files had been meant to target them. But then Krystal held her press conference where she claimed you had just been an intern who had been fired and that the campaign knew nothing about this.'

'Just an intern.'

'Yeah. Sorry. That must hurt. I remember what a big deal it was for any of us in the volunteers' pool just to speak to you, when I was working on the campaign.'

'What happened after Krystal's press conference?'

'Well, it took off some of the heat from the media. But then the real game changer was when they announced a couple of days later that an internal investigation had revealed that you had been in a relationship with one of Senator May's staffers and you had made some boasts to your…girlfriend. That's how the May campaign had gotten hold of this and used it to politically victimise Ron.'

'What?!? They actually said that!?'

'Yeah. Unfortunately, quite a few details from your personal life are now out there in the media.'

'Like what? What else?'

'Well, that you were in a relationship with one of Senator May's top staffers, and that you had been sleeping together for a while, probably since the Primaries. That you had made these kinds of big boasts to her while you were in bed together, to pretend that you were a big shot. And that when this staffer informed Senator May of your boasts, she decided to spring a trap for the Diamond campaign and influenced the FBI to start a witch hunt.'

'Did they name the staffer?'

'Yeah. Shai Naqavi, or Naqvi, or something like that. Apparently, she's also a Pakistani like you.'

* * *

November the fifth is a date I will never forget in my life. It was the day I finally got out of the nightmare that was the Manhattan Metropolitan Correctional Centre.

The week that followed my meeting with my "lawyer" passed in a blur. Just a day later, I got another visitor, this time a real lawyer and a hotshot one, judging by the beautifully tailored bespoke suit he wore, the Audemars Piguet watch on his wrist, and his business card, which had the letterhead of one of those three-name law firms whose poshness can be judged by their exclusivity. This guy was no ambulance chaser. He told me that his firm had been engaged by the Saudi Crown Prince at the request of my father, to act as my counsel. He also said he would have me out in a week.

He was true to his word. On exactly the seventh day after his visit, he showed up again, this time with a court order for my release. As I walked out into the soft autumn sunlight, having finally shed my orange prison jumpsuit for my own clothes, scarcely able to believe that I was free, I was greeted by a sight I had never been happier to see: my dad, standing there in the parking lot, waiting for me.

I was so overwhelmed with emotion, that I had no words. I ran to him and hugged him in a way that I probably hadn't hugged him since I was twelve.

'Why the hell didn't you call us and tell us what had happened, Waj?'

'Dad, I…didn't want to get you involved. You had your own problems.'

'How can I not be involved? You're my son.' He hugged me tighter. 'Why did you pass on Hamza's information? I told you to just listen to Hamza, not to do anything else.'

'Hamza said the only way his people were going to be able to get you out was if I passed on their information to Ron.'

'Hamza was a bloody lying snake. He manipulated both of us to get us to do what he wanted. You look thin. Come on, let's get some real food in you. If American prisons are anything like Pakistani ones, I'm sure the food was lousy.'

I had to laugh. 'But Dad, how are you here? How did you get out? And how could you afford this lawyer?'

'Well, you never bothered to tell us that you were in trouble, but CNN did. We found out after the story broke. But we had no way of contacting you. Your sister offered to fly here, but I didn't want to involve her. All of this was a dirty business and I didn't want both of my children to be caught up in it. I feel bad enough as it is that you ended up in there because of me.'

'It's not because of you, Dad.'

'It is. You would never have met Hamza if I hadn't asked you to. And this mess would never have kicked off.'

'I did it because I wanted to get you out of whatever trouble you were in, in Pakistan. What happened with that?'

'It's done. The charges against me were dropped. They would have been dropped anyway because they had no substance, so Hamza and his friends didn't exactly do me any favours. They just expedited the process a little. That was the other reason why I couldn't come sooner. I was on the Exit Control List and couldn't leave the country until I had been cleared.'

'And the lawyer? Please don't tell me you did something stupid like sell the house to raise the money?'

'No. And trust me, selling our house still wouldn't get us this lawyer, with the exchange rate the way it is. No, I turned to the only person who I knew would genuinely help.'

'Mo!'

'Yes. I contacted him and asked for his help. Not only did he immediately order his embassy to engage the best law firm in the city, but he also flew me here in his private jet. His ambassador will not only be monitoring the case personally, he will also lobby the US government on your behalf. So, where do you want to go to eat? Or do you want to go to my hotel first?'

'It's election day today, isn't it?'

'Yes. That's all the media's talking about. How close it will be, how it's a dead heat between Ron Diamond and Jessica May. God, I'm sick of politics. The sooner we get back home, the better. I don't want you staying in this godawful country one day more than you have to.'

'I have to face the case against me, Dad. I can't run from that. Everybody would think I'm guilty. Besides, what difference does it make, whether I'm here or in Pakistan? Both places are the same now. There's a ruthless megalomaniac in charge there and irrespective of who wins today, there's going to be a ruthless megalomaniac in charge here too.'

19.
THE
ELECTION

ELECTION DAY (Four hours before polls close on the East Coast)

'Hey Amanda, should we run the Pakistanian coup at the top of the hour?'

'Firstly, it's not Pakistanian, it's Pakistani. And secondly, their Prime Minister has fired his intelligence chief. Generally, that's not considered a coup, that's an administrative action. How long have you been working here? This is very basic stuff.'

'Well, Ron Diamond calls it Pakistanian.'

'Oh well, that's just great. If Ron Diamond does it, why don't we all just do it? I didn't realise that in addition to being the Republican presidential candidate, he's also become the God of Grammar.'

'But it's still a pretty big deal, right? BBC website's saying its linked to the Russia files leak. That apparently the Pakistanian... sorry, Pakistani, intel guys tried to pass on the files without checking with the PM first. And Pakistani social media is going crazy over this, saying it's all connected to Ron Diamond because Ron is friends with their PM.'

'Well, Kirsten, this is not the BBC and this is not Pakistani social media. This is Wolfson News, and the only story any of our viewers give a shit about on election day, is the fucking election! So let's stick with that, shall we? The top-of-the-hour story, as on every election day since the founding of television, will be the latest polls. Where are we on that?'

'Too close to call. Gallup has Ron 50.5 to 49.5, CNN-USA Today has May 51-49, and FiveThirtyEight has a dead tie nationally, with Pennsylvania, Ohio and Illinois too close to call.'

'Illinois? Why is it that close in Illinois? May should win that easy. President King took it by 19 or 20, both times.'

'Apparently, Ron's got quite a bit of home state support, because he keeps talking about his Chicago origins. Jessica's losing black support because she didn't speak up after the Pence trial. And she's losing voters in rural Illinois because there's a strong perception that she will say or do anything to get elected, especially after the way her campaign tried to play the Russia files. It has turned voters off her in massive numbers.'

Amanda looks out from the conference room's glass partition onto the newsroom. There's a buzz around the place, an almost infectious nervous energy. But she senses it's more than just the regular anticipation of election day. It comes from the uncertainty of the situation, of even hardened, experienced media people not being able to predict what will happen in the next few hours. This election has been the craziest Amanda Spano has ever covered. Both candidates have set themselves on fire repeatedly, only to recover and then torch themselves again, almost like a moth that keeps hovering close to the flame despite burning its wings. She was sure Ron Diamond would not be able to survive Maranzanogate. But then fate intervened in the shape of the riots. After almost a year of burning and looting each other, America seemed less concerned with injustice, and more with restoring law and order. And when Americans had wanted someone to speak out for them, Jessica had remained silent. Then fate ridiculously gave her another opportunity with the Russia files leak. But Jessica May hadn't been able to close the deal. And somehow, implausibly, Ron Diamond has held his ground. The stakes are so high for the country and the differences between the candidates so stark, that it's no wonder everyone is on edge today.

She takes another look around the newsroom and finds one seat, the one that is the most important one in her mind, still empty. 'Can someone find out where the fuck Gary is? We are two hours and forty-seven minutes from starting our election broadcast.'

'I'm here. Sorry, I'm late. It was unavoidable. Ok, Kirsten, you've got the roster. We start with the latest polls, voter turnout and all of that, and then go to the mood in both camps. And we highlight the negative mood towards Jessica May in swing states, especially after the Russia files. My sources are telling me the FBI may be close to making an announcement shutting down their investigation. If it is true, that's also going to reinforce the image that she will make up anything to get elected. So we put in a line on that as well. Got it?'

'Right Gary. And Pakistan?'

'Hold it for today. Do some more digging. Let's focus on the election. Now get out of here, I need to speak with Amanda.'

The room clears and Amanda gives Gary a withering look. 'I haven't heard anything about an FBI announcement. That's impossible. Last I heard, they were going to prosecute that kid, Wajahat whatsisname. Nobody's shutting down anything, so why are we saying something that is false and will blatantly help Ron Diamond, while polls remain open on the West Coast for another few hours? Whose Kool-Aid have you been drinking and where the fuck have you been, Gary?'

Gary shuts the door and smiles. 'We are a right-wing news channel, Amanda. It is our stated policy to support the Republican candidate.'

'Oh, I get it now. The Kool-Aid is Leonard flavoured. Is that where you were? Leonard's too scared of me, so now he's calling in my producer?'

'Relax Amanda, it's nothing like that. If you really want to dig up something else on Ron, look closely at the Pakistan story. My sources in Langley are telling me there's a lot there. According to them, the Pak establishment started getting jitters after Ron and their Prime Minister became pals following their London meeting.

Both men seemed to be working out policies and ideas on their own. The Paks started really freaking out when Afridi, their PM, started totally ignoring his intelligence chief. They were shut out of the loop between Ron and Afridi. That's why they went to the Diamond campaign directly, through this Pakistani kid, to pass on the Tim Regan information. They wanted Ron to owe them if he won. But Afridi was pissed when he found out that they were trying to undercut him. So he fired his very powerful intelligence chief, who according to my friends, played a huge part in bringing him to power, to show everyone who's boss.'

'I didn't realise the implications were so…complex and tied so intimately to the Diamond camp.'

'Oh yeah, Ron is all over this story. Langley is even sceptical about the Diamond campaign's claims that they were unaware of Wajahat Shakaib's actions. They're pretty sure the kid brought the information to senior staff, including Ron. He wasn't just an intern, like Krystal Diamond claimed. He was quite close to Ron and involved in decision-making in the campaign. Everyone knew him. There's even a rumour that he had a scene with Krystal.'

'Wait, you're telling me this kid, this twenty-three-year-old, fresh out of college kid, was a key voice in the Diamond campaign? And that he was considered reliable enough by foreign agencies to approach to pass on sensitive intelligence? And on top of that, he was allegedly involved with both Shai Naqvi and Krystal Diamond? Are you serious? Who is this Wajahat Shakaib?'

'That's the story, isn't it? Everybody's writin' him off as some horny intern who was showing off about some information that he got through his dad's government connections, just to lay Shai Naqvi. But it ain't that simple. My Langley sources believe he was the one who arranged the first meeting between Diamond and Afridi in London. And do you know who his lawyer is?'

'I don't know. Some public defender type?'

'He started with that. But now the kid's got a gold-plated legal team, from Parker, Cochrane Matheson. That's some serious artillery.

They start billing at $1000 an hour, and they're used by a number of foreign governments, including the Saudis, the Malaysians and the Chinese. He's probably gonna get bailed out today or tomorrow.'

'You think the Chinese or Russians got a lawyer for the kid? Or do you think it was Ron?'

'Don't know. Could be either. Ron's always used Harvey Calzone for his legal stuff but in this case, he would need deniability, so he would need to outsource. Or it could be the Russians or the Chinese. Either way, there's a lot of meat to explore in that story.'

'So is that what you've been doing since the morning?'

'No. I've been interviewing at the Home Shopping Network.'

'Who have you been interviewing? Is there some huge expose we're doing of how they rip people off?'

Gary laughs. 'No. I've been giving an interview. For a job. Tonight is going to be my last broadcast for Wolfson.'

'Ok, you know what Gary, it's the most fucked up election day in American history and I have to spend the next eight hours sitting next to Phil fucking Rorshach, wondering if he's jacking himself off under the table every time Krystal Diamond comes on screen, so I'm in no mood for your jokes.'

'I'm not joking. I'm out after tonight.'

'You're not out till I say. You and I are going to walk out of here together. Is this Leonard? You did see him, didn't you? That fucking prick doesn't have the balls to come after me, so he starts going after you! I'm going to call him out on this one, on air, during the show…'

'No, Amanda, you are not. If there's one thing you will do for me, you will not call out Leonard Wolfson for anything during the election broadcast. Not for me. You have to stay on here. You have to keep your bully pulpit. You have a voice here, you can do a lot of good. Look at what we achieved with the Janet Maranzano story. Wolfson has hated us ever since that interview with Ron. We embarrassed his guy. He wasn't ever going to forget. He can't touch you because of your popularity, so obviously he was going to come after me. No big deal. But you've got to keep fighting.'

'I can protect you…'

'No, you can't. Old Lenny isn't stupid. He isn't firing me. He's making me resign.'

'What? How?'

'You remember that intern we had? The Twinkie? Legal got statements from her and a bunch of our other interns from over the years, alleging that I had exhibited patterns of lewd and inappropriate behaviour. Wolfson showed me the sexual harassment case they had prepared against me. He said if I didn't go voluntarily, he would use the case to fire me and that would also ensure that I never worked in media ever again.'

'Sexual harassment? But you've never harassed anyone! That's complete bullshit. I can vouch for you! They can't prove anything!'

'Is that really the way we want this to go? That they can't prove sexual harassment? You don't need proof to get cancelled in this age. You just need enough smoke for people to believe there was a fire. I probably said a lot of things over the years that would be considered inappropriate. I don't want to put my family through that. So I've already handed over my resignation to Leonard. If you protest this now, he'll take it as my reneging on our agreement, and then he'll revive the allegations.'

'Christ, Gary, how can you do this? How could you make such a big decision without even talking to me? We were always a team. How can you leave me with these fucking assholes?'

'It had to be done, Amanda. I had no choice.'

'And why the fuck are you interviewing with the Home Shopping Network?!? You're going to go from producing my show to hocking costume jewellery?'

'I don't want to work in news anymore. After all we've seen in this last year, after all that's happened, I've had enough. The lunatics have taken over the asylum, Amanda. So yeah, I'd rather hock costume jewellery than report daily on a Diamond administration.'

'Jesus, it sounds even scarier when you say it out loud like that.'

'Well, we could get lucky. Maybe Jessica can pull this off.'

ELECTION NIGHT (Two hours after polls have closed on the East Coast)

'So would you say that Krystal Diamond's rally in your district 48 hours ago was crucial to your victory, Congressman Herrera?'

Amanda has to be careful not to grimace on air as she hears Phil Rorshach's comments. She looks across the table at him and wonders if the saliva collecting at the corner of his mouth at the mention of Krystal Diamond is visible in high definition.

'Yes, absolutely Phil. In fact, I would go so far as to say I couldn't have won without Krystal and the support of the entire Diamond family. It was incredibly generous of Ron to have helped me out, despite our brief differences during the primaries.'

Jeez, Ryan, why don't you just open your mouth a little wider and meme-sucking Ron's dick off on national TV. 'Uh, Congressman, how do you account for the unexpectedly comprehensive victory for the Diamond campaign in Florida, when most polls were predicting a very close race in your state?'

'Well, Amanda, those were national polls that were predicting a close race. And most of those polls were run by liberal media organisations. Those of us who were here on the ground in Florida knew Ron was going to win easily. Let me say it unequivocally: Florida is Diamond country!'

'With Ron winning by a comfortable ten points, it certainly is.' Phil Rorschach looks so happy his expression is virtually orgasmic. Amanda sneaks a discreet look under the table and notes Phil's right hand resting on his crotch as he speaks. She retches and has to grab a glass of water to keep down her gag reflex.

'Thank you for speaking to us Congressman, and once again, congratulations on your victory. We're going to take a short break but we are expecting a couple of results when we get back, so stay tuned.'

'Off air!'

'Oh, Jesus! Oh Jesus this is bad!' Reading the message on his phone, Phil Rorshach goes from looking orgasmic to looking like someone just cut his dick off.

'What happened, Phil?' Amanda puts on her best faux concerned voice, pretending to care, even though she is repulsed by him.

'We're going to lose Ohio. And Georgia! Don't you pretend with me, Spano! I know you're thrilled about this. Christ, Georgia! How could we lose Georgia? Han said it was in the bag.'

'Well, if Han Diamond said it was in the bag, who are we lesser mortals to argue? Did Han account for the massive numbers of African-American voters who were incensed by Ron's comments about shooting the looters? Republicans were always going to lose Georgia this cycle. We'll be lucky if we hold on to North Carolina. Were you seriously relying on that fucking moron for your forecasts?'

'Han's my source into the inner Diamond campaign. And to Krystal, now that she isn't taking my calls anymore…'

'Maybe calling her twenty times a day like a stalker wasn't the brightest idea, Phil.'

'Oh fuck off, Amanda! What about you and that boob, Herrera? Your ex-boyfriend looked like he was really enjoying eating Ron's shit!'

Amanda bristles at the comment but doesn't respond. She sits silently through the resumption of the broadcast, as Phil and the third Wolfson anchor running the virtual map announce the Ohio and Georgia results, as well as a string of further Jessica May wins in New York, New Jersey and most of New England.

'…not looking good for the Diamond camp, Amanda? Amanda?'

'Sorry Phil, just checking up on some interesting contests in the midwest. I'm hearing that Jessica May will definitely lose Iowa, despite the President's last minute call to support her. My sources tell me that despite his public show of support, the President had privately signalled his supporters in his home state to stay home, and so a state that Lincoln King won twice, will now turn back from blue to red. The key battles remain in Pennsylvania, Michigan and surprisingly Illinois, where it seems that, unlike Georgia, African American voters are not turning out for Jessica May and Ron Diamond is being helped by his homeboy status. That race is going to get very, very close.'

Her assistant passes her a slip of paper as the commentary drones on. It's a message from Ryan Herrera, asking her to call him as soon as she's off air. A sense of alarm creeps into her. She recalls Leonard Wolfson's threat to her. But to her surprise, despite the Maranzano interview, it's a threat that Leonard has, till now, not acted upon. She had assumed that he had decided to get even with her by going after Gary instead, perhaps calculating that demolishing a future Republican party star would look too fratricidal, even for him. But Ryan's urgent message indicates that may have changed.

She waits another 30 minutes for the segment to end, and then walks off the set to her dressing room. She's a little taken back to see her hands shake as she punches in Ryan's number in her phone.

'Ryan?'

'Amanda! Thank God you called! I wasn't sure you were going to respond.'

'I had to wait till my segment ended. What's wrong? Everything ok at your end? You must be happy at your re-election.'

'Yes, everything's fine. It's all great... actually no... it isn't fine, it isn't great. It's horrible, actually. Why didn't you ever call me after Super Tuesday, Amanda?'

'What did you want me to say, Ryan? You lost due to circumstances beyond anyone's control.'

'You could have consoled me.'

'I'm not your girlfriend anymore, Ryan. That's not my job, that's why you have a wife, remember? I didn't call exactly because of this kind of thing. Too many people are already speculating about us and our past. Neither of us needs more drama in our lives.'

'I don't.'

'You don't what?'

'I don't have a wife anymore.'

'Jesus. What happened Ryan?'

'She's dumped me. We had agreed not to make any public announcement till after the election. But she's been gone for months.'

'Why?'

'When I decided to contest the nomination, she was totally on board. She felt, like you, that even if I lost, this would make me a national figure in the party. But neither of us realised what a huge deal Ron had become. After Super Tuesday, the Diamond supporters kept abusing me and trolling us online. My brand within the party became toxic because the Diamond zealots tagged me as a traitor for challenging the Great Ron. They even started up a campaign in my district to challenge my re-nomination. Alexis couldn't take the fact that everything we had built up over the past few years was coming apart. Then, to top it all off, the *Diamondistas* started spreading rumours about you and me, about how we were lovers and how you were using me in your personal vendetta against Ron.'

'But Ryan, nothing happened between us! You're not my goddamn lover…'

'Alexis wouldn't believe that. She's convinced herself that we've been fucking and that's why I suddenly decided to run. Aside from that, she wants a place in the party and I'm considered damaged goods, so she doesn't want to get dragged down with me. And she really hates you. They all do, because of your opposition to Ron.'

'I'm a big girl and I've been in this party a long time. If a bunch of South Florida kooks have a problem with me because I don't think Ron Diamond is Zeus descended from Olympus, they can kiss my ass. And that includes Alexis. The Republican party has always been a pretty big tent.'

'You're not getting it, Amanda. It's not just South Florida. The entire party is turning to Ron. You're too far away and isolated in Washington to understand, but he's tapped something deep in the party. I've seen his impact on the trail. They love him. The grass roots, the small towns, the guys who hammer in lawn signs. They believe he's the only real candidate up there. I'm a four-term congressman and I thought I had a mortal lock on my district, but I had to literally beg for forgiveness from my supporters for having stood against Ron. The only way I was able to ward off a primary challenge was to make a public sign of contrition with the Diamond family. And I've been told in no uncertain terms by my voters and by the party, that I'm on probation until I prove my loyalty to Ron. If I step out of line, I'm finished.'

'*Prove your loyalty to Ron?* What is this, the Mafia?'

'That's why I called, Amanda. You can't say this came from me, but I wanted to give you a heads-up, that they're coming for you. Han and Krystal have made it clear in influential circles that if Ron loses, you're the one who's responsible. They're saying it was in the bag until you had to dig up Maranzanogate. They're even going to make me denounce you.'

'And what if he wins?'

'If he wins, he's going to ask for your head, as a sign of loyalty to the new regime, and to bring the party together. But there's still time. Maybe. You need to kiss the ring immediately.'

'Hell will freeze over before I do that Ryan.'

* * *

ELECTION NIGHT (Eight hours after polls have closed on the East Coast)

Amanda awakens to the dulcet tones of Condoleeza Rice droning on in her ears. For some years now, she has found the former Secretary of State's audible autobiography a perfect tool to put her to sleep. As a book, it is unreadable. Amanda tried to finish it several times but could not get past the author's long-winded self-justifications about the Iraq war. But as a sleep aid, it is perfect. She plugs it in any time she needs to doze off but cannot do so naturally. It works better than counting sheep.

It's pitch dark in her office with the blinds all drawn, but she is surprised at the silence outside. Normally the newsroom is a hive of activity, buzzing constantly on a night like this. But this campaign has exhausted everybody. After hours of deadlock, even Wolfson News' crack team of professionals has run out of steam. She checks her watch. She's been sleeping for almost two hours, which means that the election remains undecided. When she went off air after a marathon seven-hour broadcast, she had told her PA to wake her the minute there was a result.

She scrolls through the newsfeed on her phone. Not much has changed. Jessica predictably took California and most of the West Coast, although one source from LA has reported dozens of sightings of adult actors at polling stations. And Pornhub is offering 24 hours of free subscriptions if Ron Diamond wins. If nothing else, Ron Diamond's candidacy has at least mobilised the adult entertainment industry.

She would laugh if it wasn't so tragic, or if it were another country. It's the sort of human interest story she occasionally covers from places like Burkina Faso. God, what she wouldn't give to wake up one morning and find out all this had happened in Burkina Faso, instead of in America.

But say what you will, Ron Diamond has shown a resilience and uncanny political understanding. He's hung on, despite the porn star background, despite the certifiably dysfunctional family, despite the allegations of incompetence, rape, and foreign interference. He's actually won in places no Republican since Reagan would have even dreamed of: New Hampshire, Maine, Michigan. And Pennsylvania and Illinois are still too close to call.

There's a gentle knocking on her door as she turns on her lights. She opens it to find Gary holding two cups of coffee.

'Fucking Illinois. Who would'a thought it?'

'He's won?'

'No. Still hasn't been called, but he's leading, by about a thousand votes.' He sits down on her couch and stares aimlessly through the blinds at the newsroom. 'I'm going to miss this place.'

'Gary, you don't have to do this. We can work something out with Leonard, I'll find a way…'

He snorts. 'Jeez Amanda, you really need to wake up. That ship has sailed. You of all people, are the last person who's in a position to work anything out with Leonard. They're coming for you. Saw a tweet going around, from Luke Diamond of all people, saying that if Ron wins, the Diamond campaign will call for all those media persons who were instrumental in spreading fake news about Ron, to resign or be fired, since they have been morally rejected by the American people. And Wolfson is apparently considering it. Can you believe that shit? We now live in a world where Luke fucking Diamond is a major influence within the Republican party.'

Amanda takes a sip of her coffee. 'You know, I've been a Republican since I was 14. Do you have any idea how tough it is to be a teenage Republican in South Boston?'

'I would wager that it was about as tough as living in New York City, speaking the way I speak and espousing my political views.'

'Yeah, probably. It was always taxes for me. I went to work at an early age, started supporting myself, and I could never get over how much of my hard-earned money was taken by the government. Then during the '96 campaign, I happened to watch one of the Republican debates on TV and there was this guy, Steve Forbes, one of the candidates, who called for a flat tax rate of twenty percent. I bet no one in the party even remembers who the fuck Steve Forbes was, but to me, he was a genius. I genuinely believed that a flat tax rate would solve all of this country's problems. Hilarious, isn't it? That my journey into this party started because of a guy who was a presidential candidate for about five minutes and whose best showing was sixth or seventh, probably, in one of the primaries.'

'Yeah, and now you're being forced out of the party because

of a date-raping porn star who decided to run for President. It's a fucking Ha ha joke.'

'I can't believe that I'm actually hoping Jessica pulls it off. Her politics is anathema to me, but right now, I want her to win so bad. I want her to beat this son of a bitch.'

'I don't think she can pull it off. You remember I predicted this when she first announced she was running? Before Ron had announced. I said her problem was she was a horrible candidate. She was great at high-brow policy, but she sucked at retail politics. Voters don't connect with her. They think she's fake. I mean, look at what's happened. There's evidence of multiple foreign countries trying to interfere in our election in favour of Ron, and people think Jessica is the self-serving one for bringing this stuff to light. She just can't make the sale.'

'Even against him?'

'He's a shark. I hate to say it, but he is. None of us saw him coming. We all thought his campaign was the clown car at the circus but he saw something in this country that we didn't see. He saw a resentment against all of us, bubbling under the surface, waiting to explode. He just pulled back the cover and waited for it to blow up.'

'You're the second person who's said that to me today about Ron. As if he was some latter day Nixon or Reagan, grasping the zeitgeist of the nation. As if doing porn somehow prepared him to become this cultural and political icon.'

'Who was the first?'

'Doesn't matter. You'll find out when he denounces me at the first show trial of the Diamond regime.'

'What will you do if Leonard fires you?'

'I don't know. Maybe I'll move to Mexico. Sure as shit don't want to live here in Ron's America. Heck, maybe I should take a job in porn and run for office in the next cycle.'

Gary can't help laughing. 'Well if you decide to do that, give me a call. I'll be your campaign manager. I would have had my fill of selling vacuum cleaners and hair straighteners by then.'

'I'm sorry, Gary.'

She hugs him, something she has never really done before, despite having worked together for so many years. Their moment is interrupted by a sudden outbreak of cheering from the newsroom and the simultaneous buzzing of her desk phone.

'It's Leonard. Do you think…'

'Yeah. Ron's won.'

20.
MORNING
IN AMERICA?

KARACHI, 15TH NOVEMBER (Ten days after Ron Diamond's election)

This time, instead of slippers, it's a cricket bat that greets the men who enter Shakaib's house in the middle of the night for the second time in three months. He is amazed not only by the presence of the bat, which he was unaware Umber had kept but also by her dexterity at wielding it. The officer who enters his bedroom, the same one who had kidnapped him three months ago, is even more surprised. As he winces in pain, clutching his groin with one hand and trying to protect his face with the other, he croaks out that he is not here to arrest him.

'Then why are you here?'

'To keep you safe…' His response triggers another blistering on-drive from Umber, directed at his buttocks.

'Sir, please!! Please control your wife! Madam, I am a police officer…'

'Yes, yes. Special police. I heard that rubbish last time. And this is my special bat to deal with special police.'

'Please hear me out!'

'Please explain to me, Inspector…were you an inspector? I couldn't quite get your details after you beat me up in the car! Please explain to me what you and your thugs are doing in my house, again, holding all of my staff hostage, again!'

'Sir, orders from Hamza sahib. He asked us to take you into protective custody before the Interior Minister tried to do anything funny.'

'Wait, you're not working *for* the Interior Minister?'

'No, sir. I mean, we were, sir. Last time we picked you up. And actually, until about four hours ago.'

'What happened four hours ago?'

'Not sure, sir. Something's happened in Islamabad. We're not getting any messages from our headquarters or from the ministry. Then sir Hamza called and said there had been a coup, and that I was to secure you, for your own safety, and that I was to do it before I received any contradictory instructions from the Minister. Sir Hamza is flying in from Islamabad. I am to take you to the airport to meet with him.'

'A coup? I haven't heard anything about a coup. There's nothing on the news.'

'Yes, sir. We haven't heard anything else either, sir. But it is curious that we've lost all contact with our HQ. Something's going on. And sir Hamza, well, he usually knows about these kinds of things.'

Umber leans on the bat like a cricketer contemplating her next run. 'What do you think, Shakaib? I don't think you should go anywhere. Even if there has been a coup, what does that have to do with you? You've only just got back from New York after getting Wajahat out, don't get into another mess.'

'Please, sir. Sir Hamza said it would be my neck if I wasn't able to bring you to the airport.'

The officer looks nervously towards Umber.

'Alright. I'll come with you to the airport.'

'The hell you will, Shakaib! If you step out of this house with this man, you see what I'll do!'

'Umber, there's no other way. He doesn't need to lie. He could have come in here and just taken me like last time, if Turhan Agha and Afridi had ordered him to. He could take you too, now that you've assaulted him. I have to figure out what's going on. We can't have these men just standing around in our house, without any resolution to the issue.'

'Fine. Then I'm going with you.'

'Umber…'

'And I'm bringing my bat with me, Mr. police man, so you better watch out.'

'Yes, Madam.'

Still nursing his aching back, the officer leads them outside. This time, Shakaib's abductors are far more solicitous, saluting him and Umber as they get into the same car in which he was taken months before. The journey is far shorter, with the motorcade speeding its way through empty streets to the old airport terminal. As they get out of the car to enter the VIP lounge, Umber still keeps her bat with her. A security man approaches her, but thinks better of it when he sees the officer with them, and allows her through to the lounge with her bat.

The lounge is huge, with sofa settings littered across a space the size of a large hall. One side looks out onto the tarmac. The officer informs them that Hamza's flight has just landed, and a waiter offers them tea. Just as they are taking their first sips, Hamza comes bursting through the door from the tarmac, looking completely harassed, his shalwar riding higher and higher on his legs, his neat hair out of place, and crumbs falling from his beard.

'Oh Shakaib bhai, thank God! Oh, and Bhabi too! How nice to see you! Have you taken up cricket, at your age? That's so heartening to see.'

For the first time, Umber looks down at her bat, somewhat sheepishly, and is struck by the absurdity of the situation. The waiter helpfully comes along and offers to keep the bat for her and she relents.

'Sir! The package has been delivered…with one additional parcel…' The officer discreetly points to Umber, not sure how Hamza will react to her presence, but Hamza brushes him off.

'Thank you, Inspector. I can see the additional "parcel". Please wait outside for us and do not let anyone else into this lounge. And please ask the waiter to get some hot food. I've only had half a dozen of those silly finger sandwiches on my flight. Coups make me very hungry.'

'I thought you had retired. What the hell is all this about?'

'Well, I've been rehired. As of today. It's a whole crisis type thing, all hands on dick kind of situation.'

'Excuse me?'

'Bhabi? Did I say something wrong?'

Shakaib slaps his forehead. 'All hands on deck.'

'Exactly. What did I say?'

'Never mind. Why have you brought us here like this?'

'I was so worried, Shakaib bhai. This whole operation was a real hit or miss thing. Coups always are, in my experience. This is my third one, so I know a bit about these things. Islamabad was a real mess tonight. They were able to secure the PM House and parliament and the TV and radio station, but there was traffic on the way to the interior ministry, so Turhan Agha got away. I was worried that he would start ordering the arrests of all the anti- Afridi elements. So as soon as we were done in the PM House, I rushed to call this fellow. He was the only one I knew here in Karachi, but I was desperate to get you to safety, because I knew that your name was on the top of Turhan's new list.'

'Turhan's new list?'

'After sacking my boss, Javed Afridi and Turhan had made a list of individuals who were opposed to them or who supported us. They wanted to purge all of them. They had figured out that the information to Ron Diamond had been passed through your son, so they wanted to have you locked up again. This time for a significantly longer period, under some fresh TSP-FETA clauses. Incidentally, I was on the list as well.'

'You stupid man! My husband has become a target because of you! Because you introduced him to this imbecile footballer! Because you convinced him that this pea brain was the saviour of the country! Because of the fool's errand that you had him perform, which resulted in my son being put in an American jail! Now every time your bloody Javed Afridi makes a list of people opposed to him, Shakaib will be on it, even though he hasn't done a damn thing!'

Umber's anger is very real and puts Hamza on the back foot. He thinks of saying something placatory and when nothing immediately comes to mind, he absurdly offers her the tray of fresh samosas that the waiter has just placed in front of him.

'You think giving me a bloody samosa will shut me up!'

Now Hamza's fear is genuine. 'No bhabi, but I thought your anger may have made you hungry. Please sit. Please. It was my fault, I admit it. There is nothing to fear anymore. We have taken care of the problem. Javed Afridi will never again be a threat to Shakaib bhai.'

'You've killed him?!?' Now Shakaib grows alarmed.

'Good riddance.'

'Umber! Hamza, what have you people done?'

'No, no Shakaib bhai, please relax. Javed Afridi is very much alive. But he is now in custody and will remain so until there is greater clarity to the situation.'

'What exactly has happened?'

'Our hand was forced when Afridi sacked my boss. Not only was he going to launch this purge against all of us, but he was also contemplating bringing in one of his loyalists to fill our boss's post. Can you imagine, he made a committee consisting of Turhan Agha, the YouTuber and that slut Seema/Saima, who was his SAPM, to decide on the next intelligence chief? I'm sorry for my language Bhabi, but can you imagine? Two cokeheads and one… well… one very naughty woman, choosing this country's intelligence chief. Tauba Tauba.'

'Are you serious? Why didn't Taimur speak to him? If he wasn't willing to listen, you should have spoken to the SPM.'

'Javed Afridi had gone mad, Shakaib bhai. He was really, really angry at our attempt to approach Ron Diamond directly. He insisted on all power and all decisions being centralised with him. Can you believe, he actually called the Russian President and told him that in future all such sensitive intelligence should be shared directly with the Prime Minister? Our good luck that the Russian is an old hand at these sorts of games and was fully aware that the Americans were probably snooping on the conversation, so he completely deflected the question by changing the topic and asking about some football statistics. Even then, we tried to make a go of it. We tried to counsel him, to tone him down. Our Big Boss went to him. But he was like a man possessed. He responded to our requests for caution by holding larger and larger public rallies, asking the people if those who stood against his crusade, should not be purged. He did the same on social media. Of course, people are stupid, they all responded that of course all enemies of the state should be punished. And in his own echo chamber, he used this as a justification for making longer and longer lists of people to be locked up under TSP-FETA. Oh Shakaib bhai, you were so right about that infernal law. I told Taimur, I told him "Duffer, Shakaib bhai was correct! You should never have gone to the lengths you did to get that law passed for Afridi!" What can he say now? It was too late. In the end, we had to act or he would have thrown all of us in a cell and driven the country up a mountain.'

'Off a cliff. He would have driven the country off a cliff.'

'That too. Off a cliff and up a mountain.'

'No…forget it. How come there is no media coverage of your coup?'

'To be honest Shakaib bhai, we are making it up as we go along. We are still in the process of rounding up all of his cohorts. We got the YouTuber and the girl…they were together, astaghfirullah…but like I said, Turhan Agha has escaped our clutches. We didn't want to make anything public until the situation was fully in our control and until we had figured out some kind of interim government arrangement. So we have asked the channel owners to keep silent for the time being. In fact, we have asked them not to run any news segments and play pop songs instead, but not those by Mash n' Bangers, or sports highlights…but not football, lest Afridi's supporters take this as some kind of subliminal messaging. Preferably cricket or tennis. Or golf. Golf is best. Very relaxing to see all that greenery.'

'And Javed?'

'He's in custody. Ironically, we are thinking of formally arresting him under TSP-FETA. Might as well use the stupid law while it is around.'

'How is he? I mean … is he ok?'

'Shakaib, how stupid are you?!? After all that man has tried to do to our family, you're concerned about his wellbeing?!? Maybe I should use my bat on you!'

'Look … I worked with the man … for many months. I believed in him. He wasn't some task that I was assigned, as he was to Hamza or Taimur. I believed …'

'And for that, I apologise, Shakaib bhai. It was my fault. I also believed that he was a genuinely good man who just needed some proper guidance. But God teaches us the error of our ways. He did say one thing to me when we went to arrest him at the PM House … he said … this wouldn't have happened if Shakaib had still been here. And we couldn't agree more. Which brings me to my other piece of business with you tonight.'

'What business?'

'We need someone to run this madhouse, Shakaib bhai. Afridi totally destroyed the political opposition …'

'He didn't. You did. When you took me to that damn judge.'

'No use to cry over the spilt orange juice, Shakaib bhai. The point is, it will take them a long time to put themselves together before an election can be called. And they're not much better. That's where this problem started in the first place. In the meantime, somebody needs to run the country. We need to build a strong team, a team of dedicated professionals. We need you to be part of that team. With your experience as a senior minister, with your credibility in having stood up for principle against Afridi, and with your international contacts, you would be a perfect selection for the new cabinet. How would you like to be Minister for Energy and Natural Resources?'

Shakaib and Umber stare at him incredulously. The pause becomes so elongated that the silence starts to unnerve Hamza.

'Uh…not Energy? OK…Finance? Afridi has left the economy in mess, but perhaps your chartered accountancy background would be helpful. Or Foreign Affairs? That could be a natural fit, with your contacts. I guess you could really take your pick.'

Shakaib lets out a cackle that startles even Umber. 'You know, you're priceless Hamza. You don't even realise it, do you? This little speech of yours, about a team of good, honest men working together to save the country, how many times have you given it? And to how many poor saps like me? You've been lying to people for so long, you probably don't even remember it yourself. This was the exact same speech you gave to me when we went to meet Javed Afridi for the first time.'

'Really? No, no, those were different circumstances, Shakaib bhai. Now we are going to actually save the country…'

'Why, because Javed Afridi was the practice run? Now it'll be the real deal? You made me believe in the myth of a man, whom you built up as a saviour. Like all myths, this one was built on lies. But being the fool I am, I threw myself into it wholeheartedly because I was driven by this obsession that I wanted to make this country good enough for my children to return to. And what did I receive for my troubles? I lost my integrity, I was thrown into a stinking cell like a common criminal and my son was arrested by the FBI. I endangered the very children for whom I purported to take on this cause. And now that your project has fallen apart, which was to be expected since the man you banked on was so flawed that instead of a messiah, he became a fascist dictator, you want me to come back and become a minister? You really are something, you know that?'

There is pin-drop silence in the room as Hamza looks genuinely dumbfounded. Absentmindedly, he picks up another samosa from the plate and takes a bite. 'So, you actually don't want to do it, Shakaib bhai?'

'Umber, please get your bat from the waiter. And please promise me that if I ever even mention…no, not even mention, if I ever even think of, taking up Hamza's offer, you will crack open my head with that bat. Please have your inspector drop us home, Hamza. Good luck to you in your new scheme. But please keep it far away from me and my family.'

* * *

RIDGEFIELD, CONNECTICUT (Two weeks after Ron Diamond's election)

The old house has a deserted look. The Secret Service checkpost at the end of the driveway has been dismantled, with only the odd fox occasionally emerging from the forest to guard the property. The endless fleet of vehicles that plied the path up to the house for the past 18 months have vanished, and only a single Prius remains parked, being slowly covered by the shedding autumnal leaves. The old barn, once a humming nerve centre of a national presidential campaign, lies empty, looking exactly like what it is: just an old barn.

The housekeeper opens the front door after Maury's third knock, and leads him into the kitchen, where he finds Shai sitting on the kitchen table, sorting mail.

'Christ, Shai, you look like death!' She stares up at him, shorn of all makeup, the dark circles under her eyes extending all the way to her cheeks, her hair tied into a messy bun, her nail polish chipped to the point of extinction.

'You should see the other guy.' She says this without a trace of mirth. Maury hugs her and kisses her on the head. 'How ya' feeling, Princess?'

Shai just shrugs her shoulders. 'Like someone who betrayed a man who meant a lot to me.'

'You didn't betray anybody. You just did what you thought was right. You didn't go to the authorities. That was Jessica, it was her call, for the campaign.'

'And what did it get us? I sacrificed Waj, and for all her schemes, Jessica still couldn't win the election.'

'What does it profit a man to gain the world, but lose his soul.'

'You going religious on me, Maury? Doesn't suit you. Besides, we didn't even gain the world. All we got left with for our troubles is this crappy house, this crappy mail that I'm still sorting, although I don't know why I'm doing that because it's not like Jessica is going to respond to any of it, and whatever crap statistics you've brought with you to rehash our historic defeat. God knows why you'd want to do that.'

'It haunts me. It was a damn close thing. Ten thousand more votes in Pennsylvania and Illinois and we would have been sitting in Blair House working out cabinet selections right now. How's she doing?'

'She starts drinking, early. Real early, like ten in the morning. Then she wanders around the woods, getting more and more drunk, pissing her pants as she walks and crying. And that's the best part of the day. When she gets home, she tends to get nasty, shouting and abusing anyone who comes in front of her, accusing all of us for having voted for Ron Diamond. Alda and I tend to steer clear of her as much as we can. We leave a bottle for her, and a plate of food. When she's done shouting, she takes it up to her room. Apart from these episodes, she's virtually catatonic.'

'Where's Tim? I read that he was interviewed by the FBI last week.'

'He moved out almost as soon as the Secret Service did. I think it was the third day after the election. I didn't even know he had been called by the FBI. I don't really watch or read the news anymore. It makes me physically sick. Besides, I'm tired of reading articles that portray me either as a calculating bitch who threw her boyfriend under the bus to fulfil her unscrupulous boss's ambition, or some ditzy slut who was willing to get it on with anyone on the campaign trail.'

'Is she divorcing him?'

'I haven't really felt the urge to discuss the state of her marriage with her. I would assume so, but frankly, I could give a rat's ass about Jessica's life anymore.'

'So what are you still doing here, if you resent her so much?'

'I don't know. I guess it's just habit. This is what I've been doing since I was nineteen. Plus, there's literally no one else. Tim's gone, the campaign team's been dismantled, and since Jessica had the amazing foresight to not contest her Senate seat because she was so sure she was going to the White House, everyone in the Senate office is also gone.'

'Have you spoken to her about how you feel?'

'Nope.'

'This ain't healthy, Princess. You need to get out of here.'

'If I leave, she has nobody. I actually think she might harm herself. Or worse.'

'What's worse than harming yourself?'

'If the world finds out what a mess she is. If the expertly crafted persona of Jessica May were to be exposed, and people were to find out the ugly truth, that would almost certainly kill her. I don't think I would ever forgive myself if that happened, irrespective of what she did.'

'You really haven't been watching or reading the news, have you? That's already started to happen.'

'What do you mean?'

'An article came out in Politico two days ago. It's about the last days of the campaign. It compares them to the last days in Hitler's bunker. The theme of the piece is about how Jessica became seriously unhinged in the last month of the campaign. It's got everything, all the details, about her refusing to allow any vetting of Tim or his business, her deliberate decision not to speak out against the Onitolo verdict, and how when that backfired, she decided to leak your revelations to the press, while simultaneously taking it to the FBI Director. The article makes clear that Jessica's primary concern was not the national security implications, but rather the political advantage she could gain. And that she undertook these actions against the recommendations of some senior campaign staff, who were opposed to politicising a national security issue. I don't know who these clandestine staffers were, because apart from you, I don't recall anybody else opposing Jessica's plan.'

'Inside job.'

'Yup. Someone trying to burnish their credentials to come up smelling like a rose from this train wreck. Also trying to do an absolute hatchet job on Jessica. Because the article goes on to describe in great detail, the entire election night debacle. How she started having a virtual meltdown when the results started going Ron's way, how she called the President a cocksucker on the phone after she lost Iowa, how she threatened to sic the FCC on the networks when they called Illinois and when she was dissuaded from actually picking up the phone and calling the network execs, how she then started accusing her own staff of undermining her campaign. It's got every ugly detail. I don't think there's much left for you to cover up anymore. Thanks to this article, the world has seen Jessica May, warts and all.'

'Fuck. Who do you think did it? I know Johnny was pissed off…'

'It wasn't Johnny. Johnny's still a kid in Democratic politics. This was the work of an experienced operator, one who wants a future in the party and who doesn't want to be permanently associated with the Jessica May disaster.'

'Mike? No way. He's been with Jessica since forever. He would never do it.'

'There are a lot of people in the party questioning why he ran such an inept campaign. Why we lost places like Michigan, Illinois and Florida to a candidate as flawed as Ron Diamond. He's got to put the blame on someone. Jessica may not be the deranged ghoul that the article makes her out to be, but we all know she made some huge errors in judgment, including putting you in that impossible position of having to choose between her and that boy. Mike's always been smart. He's passing the buck to the one individual from where it's not going to rebound back on him: the candidate.'

'Wow. Didn't see that one coming. She'll go loco when she finds out.'

'From what you're tellin' me, she's already started her journey down that path. This was never going to be an easy loss to take. It was a batshit crazy election. Batshit crazy. In 25 years, I've never seen anything like it. We all thought she would make it. Hell, I was stupid enough to think it would be a walkover. None of us saw the coming of Ron Diamond and the madness he brought with him. That's something that she'll have to learn to live with. But I'm more concerned about you. You need to move on with your life. What do you want to do?'

'I want to become Rip Van Winkle. I want to sleep for four years, or God forbid, eight, and I want to wake up in an America where Ron Diamond isn't President anymore, and no one remembers Jessica May or Shai Naqvi.'

'I think there's quite a few people out there who are having the same fantasy. I bet Amanda Spano wishes the same thing.'

'What happened with her?'

'Wolfson fired her on election night. The ink wasn't even dry on the Illinois result by the time he had her escorted out of the building. A mob boss carrying out a hit for the new Don to prove his loyalty.'

'So…what do you think I should do? I don't have much of a career left.'

'You'll find a career, Shai. You're an amazing, extremely talented person. But you need to move on from here. Go find that boy. I heard they let him out.'

'Really?'

'Yeah. I saw something about that, a couple of days after the election. He made bail. Go to him.'

'Why would he want to have anything to do with me?'

'I'm just spitballing here, but maybe because he's in love with you too. A lot of shit happens in relationships. If you think you love him, then you've got to try.'

'And Jessica?'

'It's time you stepped out of Jessica's shadow, Princess. Jessica's story is done, for better or worse. You've got to write your own story now.'

21.

EPILOGUE:
A DIVISION OF THE SPOILS

WASHINGTON DC, late March (Two months after President Diamond's inauguration)

When I was growing up, back in Saudi Arabia and Pakistan, my dad used to say that great things came out of adversity. I always brushed it off as one of his dad-like maxims, like him saying hard work solved all of life's problems or some other bullshit like that. It never really registered with me until now, but it was true. The last three months had been perhaps the most amazing of my life.

I had walked out of the Manhattan Metropolitan Correctional Centre on election day absolutely clueless about what I would do. The one thing I was determined to do was to stand and face whatever was thrown at me. My fifteen days in the MMCC had drained the fear out of me. Also, I had a sneaking suspicion, which was confirmed by my new hotshot lawyer, that the government didn't have much of a case. Of course, the charges sounded really serious on CNN, but other than my confused hypothetical notes from my laptop, there was no other corroborating evidence to prove that any information had ever been passed on. If I didn't turn state's evidence, the government didn't have jack shit. There was no mention of Harvey Calzone having possession of a USB, or of any meeting on the 69th floor of Ron's Erection. I had begun to see the beauty of Ron's reliance on family as his closest advisors. The Diamond family enforced a code of Omerta like the Mob.

It was also increasingly evident that the Justice Department had a kind of unofficial wait-and-see policy for the case. Perhaps a Jessica May victory would have injected the requisite urgency into the prosecution. As it was, the FBI seemed to believe, as had most of my wardens at the MCCC, that the entire case was something the May campaign had cooked up to help them in the polls at the last minute. I was amazed at how intensely people were convinced that Jessica had been lying throughout. I almost wanted to stand up and shout the truth. Almost.

All of this, coupled with my super-charged, Saudi-funded legal team, meant that a prosecution or a protracted court case held little fear for me anymore. I was therefore not too surprised when I received word that the government had decided to drop the charges against me. I had half expected it, although I hadn't expected it to happen so soon. But that wasn't what had made the last three months amazing.

I didn't think I would ever meet Shai again, leave alone have a chance with her. I didn't take her betrayal particularly personally. Now I know what you'll say. That I was so whipped that I couldn't even distinguish the fact that her blabbing on me had been a cold-hearted, calculating political move. But that's what political operatives did. I understood Shai's relationship with Jessica. I knew the almost mystical hold the Senator had over her. There may have been a time, earlier on during the campaign, when we were first getting to know each other, when her choosing Jessica over me would have hurt. But I guess the one thing that had happened to me over the course of an American presidential campaign was that I had grown up.

So when she called me, out of the blue, two weeks after the election result, I didn't feel any need for recrimination. I just missed her. I was lonely. Dad had flown back to Pakistan to sort out the Pandora's box that he had opened due to his association with

Javed Afridi. And moving to Palo Alto to be with my sister wasn't practical, since my trial was going to be on the East Coast. Besides, after having traipsed up and down this country for 18 months and met real Americans of every political shade, my sister and her boyfriend's bullshit, beancurd-and-tofu style, aimless political liberalism had started to grate on me. And that's when it struck me: the campaign had turned me into a real red-blooded Republican. It was like coming out of the closet.

I had met Shai at a Starbucks in the Village, just round the corner from a temporary place I had rented, thanks to dad, while I stayed on in New York for the trial. Sometimes, two people meet each other at that perfect confluence point in their lives, which convinces them that they were meant for each other. Shai was shattered by the campaign, and the collapse of what had been her entire world for almost a decade. Other than aspiring to stay out of federal prison, I had no idea what to do with my life. I had always chased fame. That's what had brought me to Ron Diamond's door that day in April, a lifetime ago.

But now having actually achieved fame (or infamy, depending on your point of view), I didn't know where to go from here. The same late-night talk show hosts whom I had been so desperate to work for, were now using me for their monologues. Who would have thought that would ever happen?

It was only natural that we would fall into each other's arms. We had decamped pretty quickly from the Starbucks to my apartment, and life had taken over from there. We both wanted to see where this could go, whether something wonderful could emerge from the wreckage of the past year. She spent the rest of the week with me in New York and at the end of the week, we decided that it made more sense for me to move in to her place in DC. Taking the Acela down to New York a couple of times a month would be infinitely cheaper than what my dad was paying for the wall closet I was staying in. Plus, I had never been to DC. Strangely enough, I had trudged across the length and breadth of this country but never been to the capital. As

Shai and I started discovering Washington together, she too found that, despite having lived here pretty much since her Senior year at Yale, she hadn't really gotten to know the city.

I'll say one thing for the nation's capital: if you ignore the overwhelming stench of politics that emanates from every alley, it can actually be one of the most romantic cities in the world. Shai and I were done with that world, and so for us, Washington was no longer the Beltway. It was afternoon picnics at the Reflecting Pool and free evening concerts at the Kennedy Centre, and walking hand in hand through the Smithsonian and making out under the cherry trees near the Jefferson Memorial.

The new year came and brought with it a wintry spell that held Washington in a vice-like grip while the city began preparations to welcome a new President. But none of that affected us. We decided to escape the inauguration madness by flying down to Boca for that weekend. For two people who had spent most of the past two years so focused on bringing about political change in this country, we were oddly detached when that change finally arrived. We would spend hours without obsessively scrolling on our phones, and we actually spent Sunday mornings at brunch rather than glued to the TV watching the news shows.

Our life together had developed a gentle rhythm. The only issue was that neither of us had a job. Or realistic prospects of one. Well, that wasn't true. Shai's prospects were just fine, she would have been snapped up as a top staffer by any of a dozen leading Democratic senators and congressmen. It was just that she didn't want to go back to work in politics. It would remind her of everything that had happened, the choices that had been forced upon her by Jessica and the national humiliation that had followed with the revelations about us.

Despite the fact that so many months had passed since the election, Shai still got anxious going to restaurants and bars that were known for their political or media clientele. For months she burned through her savings and I through my dad's, till finally, she got a part-time gig teaching a class in political communications at George Washington University.

As an icy winter turned into a cool spring, I viewed my incredible fortune with a degree of ambivalence. Of course it was great to not have the Justice Department wanting to throw me in jail as a spy, there was no doubt in that. But the withdrawal of the case also raised the prospect of my no longer being able to live and work in America. I was quite sure that while the US government may not have been able to build a prosecutable case against me, they were never going to be so generous as to turn a blind eye to my continuing to reside here. So essentially, I was stuck in the same dilemma that I had faced when I first showed up at Ron's doorstep that rainy April day.

Then one day when I got home from my weekly trip to see my lawyer in New York, Shai said something to me that would change my life forever. She suggested that we should get married. That way, I could stay on in America. I had heard stories about things like this from my mom. Some friend's relative, marrying a gori to get a green card. I never imagined that would be me. I guess no one ever dreams of staying on in America through the green card marriage route. Well, maybe some do. Actually, probably quite a few do. But it wasn't exactly like I was marrying some random white girl from Idaho. I would be marrying the woman I loved. In truth, I had also never imagined that I would get married so young, and neither had Shai, but fate deals you curious hands sometimes. The most amazing girl in the world proposed to me. So I said yes.

Since my lawyer informed me that the formal notification of the withdrawal of the government case was imminent, Shai and I wasted no time in working out the details about how to get married. Timing was everything and we had to get it done before Homeland Security came knocking on our door. There was a lot to do: marriage licences to be acquired, residency applications to be filed, and parents to be informed. The parental thing wasn't such a problem in Shai's case. She had drifted from them in the years when she was in Jessica's service, and they hadn't made an effort when things fell apart. There wasn't much of a relationship there. She simply had to inform them of our decision and give them a date, time and venue to show up at. My parents would be trickier. It didn't help that they wouldn't be able to fly in at such short notice, and I fully expected a double dose of fire and brimstone from both of them, my mom presuming I had knocked Shai up and my dad fulminating on how I was embarking on another fuck up, perhaps even more egregious than my year in the service of Ron Diamond. But I was shocked at their reaction. They were overjoyed. My mom was supremely relieved that Shai was of Pakistani origin. As she said to me much later, she had been mentally preparing herself for some time, for a Mexican or Korean daughter-in-law. So to get one who not only actually conversed with her in fluent Urdu, but who also culturally understood the value of the heirloom jewellery mom would give to her, it was as if God had granted all of her prayers in one go. And dad was just so happy that something good had come out of the traumas of the last year.

It was a lovely spring day late in March, bright and crisp, when I received my next surprise. It came in the shape of an embossed invitation card with the seal of the president on it. I was cordially invited to attend a White House reception in honour of the visiting Crown Prince of Saudi Arabia. This really piqued my curiosity. Why would the White House invite me to an event like this? Why would they even remember I existed or bother to track down my current address? Were they keeping tabs on me?

And then it briefly struck me that I may have been invited at the behest of the Saudis. I had developed a good rapport with their ambassador since he continued to monitor the progress of my case very regularly. After all, it was their money that was funding my lawyer and the ambassador took Mo's instructions to monitor the case very seriously. I called him to ask him about my invitation but he too was in the dark. Curiouser and curiouser.

When I told Shai, she told me to throw the invite in the trash and forget about it. But then these days, this was Shai's reaction to anything that was remotely political in nature. I almost did bin the invite. I took it as far as the edge of the trash can. But then my curiosity got to me. I knew I had to find out why I had been invited, even if that risked Shai's opprobrium.

The event was in the afternoon so I could sneak out and go while Shai was at university. Thus, on the allotted day, I put on my best suit (my only suit, really) and took a cab the short distance from our apartment in Capitol Hill to Pennsylvania Avenue. And then another funny thing happened. As soon as the Secret Service agent ran my details on his computer, he called his supervisor. The supervisor gave me a funny look. Well, funny is the wrong term because I don't think Secret Service agents have ever given anybody a funny look in the history of the service. Let's just say it was a look of mild curiosity. 'Would you step aside please sir?'

I figured this must have something to do with my being a suspected felon. But it pissed me off. If my recent troubles were going to ensure that I was denied access to the White House, what was the point of sending me a card in the first place? I started to remonstrate, as much as a brown-skinned, Pakistani-origin Muslim male of military age can do with a Secret Service agent on the doorstep of the White House, when another serious-looking aide came out to join us. He pointed wordlessly towards me and the Secret Service supervisor nodded.

'Mr. Wajahat Shakaib?'

'Yeah.'

'Good afternoon, sir. I'm Henry, administrative aide to White House Chief of Staff Harvey Calzone. I've been asked to escort you to the reception, sir. The President wanted to be informed of your arrival. Please accompany me, sir.'

'The President…wanted to be informed of my arrival? The President of…the United States?'

'Yes sir. POTUS.'

'So I wasn't stopped here because of the…because I spent time in…because of my *situation*?'

'I believe the Chief of Staff ordered the Secret Service to expunge your record so you won't have a problem coming in to the White House on your next visit.'

'My next…visit…to the White House…'

'Yes, sir. If you'll come with me now, sir, the President and Crown Prince are about to arrive.'

By now I was convinced that Henry and the Secret Service agents must have thought I was a babbling idiot. I followed him into the main foyer and towards the Diplomatic Reception Room. The event was meant to be a formal reception and I found myself to be literally the last guest walking in. The others were a smattering of the diplomatic corps, a gaggle of senators and congressmen and others, who looked like oil lobbyist types. I spied Han glad handing a couple of the lobbyists and tried to make myself as unobtrusive as possible in a corner close to the canapes.

'Hiding from me?'

'Krystal!'

She looked statuesque in a smart, matching blue jacket and dress, like a Hollywood version of a White House staffer. The hem of the skirt seemed a little higher and the heels a little taller than what I assumed was standard issue in Washington political circles, but the one thing Krystal Diamond undeniably brought with her was glamour.

'No, I was just…a little hungry. Thought maybe I could sneak in a couple of crackers…'

'Jail seems to have suited you. You look good.'

'Thank you. You look great too.'

'So I hear you moved in with Shai Naqvi.'

'How did you know that?'

'I work in the White House now, Waj. We can find out pretty much anything we want.'

'You're working…in the administration?'

'Either you're trying to be funny or you've actually been living under a rock the past three months, Waj. Of course, I work here. Why wouldn't I?'

'No, I don't… I'm not trying to be funny. I actually haven't been following politics… as closely as I used to… not at all, actually. I didn't realise you had…you know…'

'Did you pick up a drug problem when you were inside?' She looked at me as if trying to evaluate what narcotic I was addicted to.

'No, no, it's nothing like that. We've just been busy with some personal stuff.'

'We. Oh. Right. Of course. Looks like this thing with Shai Naqvi is quite serious?'

'Krystal, I don't think this is something that you and I should really be discussing.'

'Right. No, yeah, absolutely.' She gave me the most plastic of smiles.

'Krystal, what am I doing here? Why was I invited to this, today? And what's with the special treatment?'

'Special treatment?'

'Some aide of Harvey's came and picked me up at the door, told me that my arrest record had been expunged so I wouldn't have a problem coming back in to the White House. You guys made it pretty clear to the entire world that I was the villain of the piece. None more so than you. So what is this?'

'We weren't sure you would come. That's probably why Harvey assigned a guy to receive you. To be perfectly honest, I was against the idea. But it was Ron and Harvey's call.'

'What call? What idea?'

'You'll see. Here comes the President. Excuse me.'

As the band took up Hail to the Chief, she brushed past me and made a beeline for the President and First Lady. I was dumbstruck. I could barely believe the scene in front of my eyes. I cannot tell you how weird it was, actually seeing them in this setting. Ron's tan had a healthy, bronzed glow and he even seemed to have lost a couple of pounds. And Erika seemed transformed into an icon of elegant yet smouldering sensuality, Catherine Deneuve meets Jackie Kennedy meets Cindy Crawford.

I finally understood something Shai used to tell me during our trysts on the campaign trail. No matter whether you'd been a senator for decades, or even an extremely wealthy man who could afford to book out entire resorts in the Caymans like Ron, the trappings of the presidency were simply overwhelming. The military aides with their chests full of medals, the intimidating Secret Service detail speaking into their mics, the Seal of the President, the backdrop of the White House. Nothing prepared you for this level. And it leant a degree of gravitas to even the unlikeliest of individuals. Ron looked positively Reaganesque as he greeted Mo and gave a brief speech.

I still wasn't sure exactly why I was here. Watching all of this felt kind of like the culmination of the campaign, and I was happy to see it all unfold, especially since I had missed the euphoria of election night. But I also realised that the longer I stayed, the greater the risk of my detection. Krystal had already found me and it was only a matter of time before the other two siblings came sniffing in my direction. I was in no mood to have a confrontation with either Luke or Han in the White House. I was also painfully aware that my most likely responses could lead me straight back into a jail cell. I'm pretty sure there was a federal law against striking a President's son. Krystal's cryptic words had piqued my curiosity though and as I looked for the exit, I saw Harvey, standing unobtrusively on one side of the room, watching everything like a hawk. He saw me, clearly, but made no gesture of acknowledgment or recognition. It was only once Ron finished his speech and started circulating among the room for meet and greets, did Harvey take a circuitous route to come and stand next to me.

'You did good, kid.' That was Harvey, no pleasantries, no small talk, not even a hint of what he was referring to.

'I did good in what, Harvey?'

'You know what I'm talkin' about. You kept your mouth shut.'

'You guys didn't really help.'

'I sent you a lawyer, didn't I? And we're helping you now.'

'You sent me a law student who you fired from the campaign

for dropping coffee. You didn't exactly send me Johnny Cochrane.'

'You got out. The charges are all gone now. So what's the problem?'

'What do you want from me, Harvey? Why'd you call me here?'

'The boss wanted to see you.'

'Why? Does he want to humiliate me some more?'

'He's the President. I'm his Chief of Staff. If he tells me he wants to meet someone, I ensure that happens. That's why you're here, kid.'

As we spoke, the crowd seemed to part around us, and I realised that we were in the direct path of the President. I realised to my utter horror that Mo was walking alongside him, chatting with Han. Ron had seen me even before Harvey nudged me right in front of him, and there was a twinkle in his eye as we came face to face.

'Mr. President.' I limply hung my hand out to him and I'm sure the sheer terror that I had started to feel was visible in my expression.

The President (Even now it feels strange referring to Ron that way) didn't miss a beat. Without shaking my outstretched hand, he glared at me sternly and turned to put his hand on Mo's shoulder.

'Your Highness, you know this guy?'

'But of course, Mr. President. We grew up together in Riyadh. His father was my teacher. I began my love affair with Baskin Robbins in their house! Waj, how are you? I am so glad to see you here! I had asked my ambassador to arrange a meeting with you but this trip is such a rushed one. I'm flying out this evening.'

'This guy is a real jerk. But he's got the biggest balls of anyone I've ever known. And I come from the porn industry!'

Mo and Ron laughed uproariously, and everyone else kind of looked nervously at the floor.

'But seriously Your Highness, don't waste your time talking to Han. He's not going to be able to deliver on any of the crap that he's whispering in your ear. If you want a loyal, reliable guy who gets things done, Iowa State is your man. I trust him over everybody else in this room except Harvey.'

My jaw dropped to the floor. Literally. What…the…fuck?

'I'm not surprised, Mr. President. Knowing his father as I do, I wouldn't expect anything less from Waj. But I'm curious, why do you refer to him as Iowa State?'

'That's because just like your father is the King of Saudi Arabia, this guy is the King of Iowa. Iowa was the first race I entered and I won, thanks to this guy's strategy. He knew the state like the back of his hand.'

Blatantly not true, but it was nice of him to compliment me like that. I don't think Ron had ever in his life, complimented anyone like that, unless it was maybe a co-star who was particularly good at giving blow jobs.

'Waj, we must get together properly next time I'm in Washington. I will tell my people to ensure it happens. But you're ok, yes? Have my people been useful? Is there anything else I can help with?'

'Your Highness, His Excellency the ambassador has been extremely kind. Thank you for all that you've done for me.'

'You know Your Highness, I'm thinking, since you guys are so close, maybe I ought to appoint Iowa State as my ambassador to the Kingdom.'

'Mr. President, I think that would be an excellent choice. It will radically improve relations between our countries, to have someone as your ambassador, who is trusted by both of us so implicitly. I think you should give it serious consideration.'

'Stick around, Iowa, I want to talk to you after this shindig.'

And with that, Ron and his entourage swept forward, leaving me in its wake, shell-shocked and on the receiving end of deathly glares from both Han and Krystal. Harvey's aide appeared at my side again and escorted me wordlessly through a maze of rooms and corridors that had paintings of former presidents hanging from the walls, until we reached a waiting room that had a middle-aged secretary with a particularly stern demeanour and two seriously menacing looking Secret Service agents on guard. Henry the aide pointed me to a couch and told me to sit tight. I still wasn't sure what to sit tight for, but a glance towards my fellow occupants dissuaded me from any further conversation. I sat there silently for what seemed like hours, but was actually only about fifteen minutes. Then, imperceptibly, the atmosphere seemed to change. The earpieces of the Secret Service agents seemed to cackle and all of a sudden, one of them pointed to a door that I hadn't even noticed was there, and put his hand on the latch, indicating that I was supposed to go there. I got up wordlessly and as I approached the door, I noticed something weird about the wall. It was curved and the door seemed to curve with the wall. I thought I was seeing things. Probably low blood sugar since I hadn't gotten a chance to sample the canapes. But then the agent held the door ajar and I really started seeing stars. I found myself stepping into the Oval Office.

But this wasn't the sober version of the Oval Office that you see in movies and documentaries. This was as if the Oval Office had been teleported and dropped in the middle of the Vegas Strip. Pictures of Ron in various phases, from the campaign trail to his TV show to his time as a property developer, adorned virtually every free space on the walls. There was even one from his porn actor days, with him receiving some kind of industry award that looked suspiciously like a dildo. Even the massive portrait of him from the conference room in The Erection had been transported across and now stared down, larger than life, on all entrants into the room. The furniture was all gaudy faux Versailles, not really in sync with the traditional sobriety of the Oval Office. In fact, the only thing that seemed to have been untouched by the new occupant was the historic Resolute desk and there, in the middle of the room, sitting with his feet on it, sipping a Cherry Coke, was Ron.

'What do you think, Iowa? Did you actually think I'd actually make it here?'

'Uh…well sir…I wasn't sure. Congratulations, Mr. President.'

'That's what I like about you, Iowa. You've always been honest. All of these other shmucks can't shut up about how they always knew this was inevitable. I didn't think it was inevitable. I think it's a genuine fucking miracle, the kind that'll make you turn to religion.

I never thought a guy like me, from the South Side of Chicago, who made his money by getting his rocks off on camera, would end up here, with his feet on top of the Resolute desk!'

Yup. Ron did have a knack for finding the perfect words to sum up a situation.

'Mr. President, sir, what exactly am I doing here? I was a bit surprised that you called me here today.'

'Why are you surprised? I got the Justice Department to drop their case against you.'

'I…was under the impression that the DOJ didn't think it was worth it to prosecute me without sufficient evidence.'

'That's the conclusion they may have come to eventually, once they got their heads out of their asses, but that could have still taken them months. I decided to expedite the process.'

'Thank you sir, but why?'

'Because you did good.'

'Because I kept my mouth shut.'

'Well, that too. I value loyalty. But not just that. You did well throughout the campaign. You have a knack for politics. You were even right about that USB. If we had used it, the press would have crucified us like they did Jessica.'

'You fired me for giving you that advice. You threw me out onto the street! Your spokespersons, including your daughter, humiliated me on national television! And now you say it was the right advice??'

'Well, it wasn't exactly the brightest move on your part to be banging Jessica May's girl during the campaign. Literally sleeping with the enemy. I had to let you go at the time. But it worked out great, didn't it? It gave us deniability when this shit storm broke.'

'I went to jail! My father had to fly in from Pakistan to bail me out by borrowing money from the Crown Prince.'

'You went to jail for fifteen days. Big deal. And it's not like the Crown Prince is short of cash after giving a loan to your dad.'

'I was humiliated! I don't have a job, and I could get kicked out of the country!'

'And I'm giving you the chance to make that over. Join me here. Nothing gives prospective employers a bigger hard on than a White House CV. Nobody laughs anymore if you're working the West Wing. You told me that, the first time we met.'

'What? You want me to work with you? Here?'

'Yeah. I may have fired you to protect the campaign but it was always my intention to bring you back in. After all, who's gonna help me run this country? My idiot sons? I mean I have my hands full just coming up with new shit to keep those morons out of Washington. A bunch of stiffs from the party? The losers who I kept beating the crap out of last year? Can you believe, old General Pattycakes and Little Ryan Herrera both came to me, begging for a job? If I'd opened my zip they would have blown me right in here.'

I was stupefied. Never in a million years would I have deduced that the reason I was summoned here, was to get a job offer. 'Mr. President, I can't work for you. How can I do that, after all that happened? What would people say?'

'That's why I waited a few months. To let the heat cool off. You don't have to come in from Monday. We'll give it another couple of months, just to make everything kosher. I hear you're gettin' married. Great. Go ahead and do that, and go off on your honeymoon. We can bring you in after that. Harvey's got your record cleared, so that shouldn't be a problem. We'll have to be a little careful of the media, but we can bring you in on a lowly job. Assistant to the Assistant Chief of Staff, or something like that. I could even actually send you to Saudi as the ambassador. That might be an idea. You could get us a couple of billion in weapons sales. At any rate, you'd do a better job than the foreign service pricks that are there right now.'

'I can't be an ambassador. I'm not even an American citizen.'

'You can be a special envoy and I can place the ambassador under you. I can do whatever the fuck I like. The Republicans got control of Congress thanks to me. They're not going to question anything I do.'

'Your family hates me.'

'You don't work for my family. You work for me. Besides, Han and Luke are in New York running the business most of the time. And Krystal's a big girl. I'm sure she can work past whatever there was between you two.'

'You … know?'

'Kid, I used to fuck women for a living. You think I can't detect sexual tension between my daughter and my aide?'

'Ron … Mr. President … I don't think my … I mean … I'm getting married … to Shai … after all that happened in the campaign … the animosity between us and them … and then after everything that came out in the media about her and me … how could I then just turn up for work at the White House as if nothing ever happened?'

'See, that's not an issue about working in the White House. That's about you being able to square this with your wife-to-be. You wanted to be famous, right? That's what America meant to you? Fame and fortune? That's what you told me, right? Well, here's your chance. Hell, you two can be the new Washington power couple.'

'I don't think she'll ever be able to accept me working for you.'

'If she doesn't like it, divorce her. Trust me, I've been through three wives. Easy come, easy go.'

* * *

I walked out of my first-ever Oval Office meeting completely shell shocked. I don't even remember how I got out of the White House. I do know that I wandered the streets of DC for a couple of hours, just as I had once upon a time wandered the streets of New York, disconsolate at the prospect of going back to Pakistan. That seemed a lifetime ago. It was bitingly cold, but I barely felt it. I got several missed calls from Shai, but I kept cancelling them. I wasn't ready to talk. Ultimately, I found myself sitting on the freezing steps of the Lincoln Memorial, staring out on to the Reflecting Pool. I thought about my father and his struggles this past year and all he had done for me. I remembered our meeting in London, in the middle of the campaign, and how he'd told me he was proud of me for making it on my own. His words had made my heart swell. I wanted to feel that way again. Above all, I thought again and again, about my dream. I had wanted my name in the bright lights of America. The stage didn't get any bigger than the White House. But what the late show monologues never tell you is the cost you pay, for the life you choose to lead. I didn't know that I had it in me to be a Ron Diamond.

Finally, I got up and took my phone out of my coat pocket and called Shai.

'Where the fuck have you been, Waj? I've been worried sick. Why haven't you been answering your phone? Are you OK?'

'I'm fine, Shai. Listen, I wanted to ask you something.'

'What?'

'How would you feel about moving to Riyadh?'

'What…the…fuck?'

ACKNOWLEDGEMENTS

This book, like the five before it, could not have been possible without the support of my family; my wife Samar, my son Suleyman, my mother, and my mother-in-law. My agent Jessica, for being with me for so many years, and my new agent Charlie, for charting a bright and exciting new future; My publishers Liberty Books; And, as always, to the fans who keep reading. It's been a wonderful ride.

www.ingramcontent.com/pod-product-compliance
Lightning Source LLC
LaVergne TN
LVHW040006070726
842759LV00026B/350